Anonymous

Quad's Odds

Anatiposi

Anonymous

Quad's Odds

Reprint of the original, first published in 1875.

1st Edition 2024 | ISBN: 978-3-38283-163-9

Anatiposi Verlag is an imprint of Outlook Verlagsgesellschaft mbH.

Verlag (Publisher): Outlook Verlag GmbH, Zeilweg 44, 60439 Frankfurt, Deutschland
Vertretungsberechtigt (Authorized to represent): E. Roepke, Zeilweg 44, 60439 Frankfurt, Deutschland
Druck (Print): Books on Demand GmbH, In de Tarpen 42, 22848 Norderstedt, Deutschland

Yours truly,
C. B. Lewis,

"QUAD'S ODDS;"

—

BY

"M. QUAD, THE DETROIT FREE PRESS MAN."

ANECDOTE, HUMOR AND PATHOS.

AND OTHER THINGS.

WITH NUMEROUS ILLUSTRATIONS.

A BOOK

NEVER OFFERED THE PUBLIC BEFORE.

EACH COPY GUARANTEED FULL WEIGHT.

SECOND EDITION.

DETROIT:
R. D. S. TYLER & CO., PUBLISHERS.

SAN FRANCISCO, CAL.....A. L. BANCROFT & CO	ROCHESTER (for W. N. Y)....JOHN J McGOWAN.
BOSTON .... HENRY L. SHEPARD & CO.	CLEVELAND .... S. K. BROOKS.
CHICAGO.................... H H. NATT & CO.	PHILADELPHIA...........H. N. McKINNEY & CO.
INDIANAPOLIS (for S. Ind.)....FRED. L. HORTON.	NEW YORK .... F. S. BOGUE, 678 Broadway.
ST. LOUIS, MO................... SAM J. JUNKIN.	OSWEGO (Central N. Y.)...FRED. H. TYLER & CO.
DENVER, COL............... H. L. THAYER & CO.	LEAVENWORTH, KAN............A. T. CANFIELD.
TORONTO, ONT... .... BELFORD BROS.	

FREE PRESS BOOK AND JOB PRINTING HOUSE.
1875.

THE PAWNEES.

PAWNEE INDIAN AGENCY,
GENOA, NEB., 8th mo., 11, 1875.

C. B. LEWIS,

Respected Friend:

I observed a brief notice in one of the Omaha papers recently of a "forthcoming book" of yours, to be dedicated to the "Pawnee Tribe of Indians," etc., but whether a joke or a reality, from the vein of remark I could not tell. If you have written or are about to publish anything having a bearing on our tribe I trust you will be kind enough to inform me how I can procure it, as I am collecting facts and statistics on Indian affairs. The Pawnees have selected a new Reservation on Indian Territory, and the major portion of the tribe are there—the balance will probably be removed thither before winter. On the new Reservation they will soon live in houses, and will have allotments of land from which to subsist themselves, with a little aid. Many of the tribe are now faithful workers, and they are now not only peaceably disposed towards the whites, but their status has considerably advanced over what it was ten years ago—that is, in the tendency towards civilization. I simply refer to these things on the supposition that you have some knowledge of the tribe or interest in their welfare and progress.

Yours respectfully,

WM. BURGESS,

U. S. Ind. Agt. for Pawnees.

DEDICATORY.

IT was the author's solemn intention at the outset to dedicate this book to some newspaper man—Gregory, Piatt, Griswold, Watterson, Bayard, Waterloo, Seymour, Bailey, Swineford, Wood—to some particular one of the coterie who use the pen more than the scissors, and whose original work sustains the reputation of the American press for brilliancy. This was his intention, but when nearly five hundred newspapers, each saying a kind word for the book, had reached his table, it was plain that such a dedication would be ruled out of order. Being under obligations to the Pawnee Indians for many private reasons, and hoping to push the sale of the book among such tribes as love to sit down and read, or hold spelling-bees, in preference to hunting around for scalps, the author prevailed upon himself to write such a dedication as the reader has found.

VII

EXPLANATORY.

WHEN a person sets out to publish a book, it is his purpose to publish a book free from typographical errors, containing fine illustrations, if any at all, and to be careful that no bad grammar or second-class English can be found by the reader. I set out to do this same thing, but after overhauling two or three hundred works by various authors I saw that a perfect book was monotonous. The reader got tired of seeing page after page without an error, and cut after cut which he had to pronounce fine. There is bad grammar in this book. There is faulty English. There are typographical errors. We might as well have had fine illustrations all through, but we didn't want them. There are cuts in this book which any carpenter could improve, but they were made thus to vary the monotony. I offered to cut some illustrations out with an axe, but the engraver said he could beat me on bad ones, and I think he has. There may be some articles in the book worth saving to read again, but I know that I wouldn't read one of them twice if I could help it. The covers are, I believe, all right, and the weight is here, while the publisher means to sell as many volumes as he can.

If any journalist, after reading this book, stands up and remarks that I am no humorist, I have a hundred witnesses who will swear that I never claimed to be.

Three hundred pages of the book never saw print before. The remainder is made up of my sketches in the DETROIT FREE PRESS, HEARTH AND HOME, FIRESIDE FRIEND, NEW YORK WEEKLY, CLEVELAND PICTORIAL WORLD, and two or three daily papers. I admit beforehand what any critic shall say, and will cheerfully receive all postal cards inquiring why I made such a failure of my portion, and where my engraver can be found by a mob.

Very truly,

C. B. LEWIS.

CONTENTS.

UP AMONG THE SPLINTERS.

WAS going up to Maysville, Kentucky, to take a "sit" on the *Bulletin*, and of course I took the steamer Magnolia, after reaching Cincinnati, in preference to all others. She was a tidy-looking boat, and her head clerk wore a diamond pin. He was the first steamboat clerk I had ever seen fastened to a $600 diamond, and I was determined to go on that boat if it killed me.

BUSINESS ALOFT.

A runner for a rival boat assured me that the Magnolia would blow up, while his boat would slide up the river like grease, but the diamond pin decided me.

" Good-bye, my white-haired rural friend !" sorrowfully
exclaimed the rival runner as he turned away, and I never
saw him again. Our paths diverged right there. Mine
went skyward, and he went off and fell down a hatchway
and was killed.

After the steamer left the wharf-boat I sat down in the
cabin and listened, with others, while a fat man from
Illinois read four or five columns of the impeachment trial
of Andy Johnson. Throwing the paper down he said :

" Gentlemen, it seems to me——"

He stopped right there. He couldn't go on. The boilers exploded just then, and we had business aloft. I don't
exactly remember who went up first, or how we got
through the roof. I am a little absent-minded sometimes,
and this was one of the times.

The boilers made a great deal more noise than there
seemed any occasion for. The explosion would have been
A 1 with half the whizzing, grinding and tearing. One
of the men who came up behind me seemed to think that
something or other was out of order, and he yelled out
to me :

" Say ! what's all this ?"

I pointed to the fat man, who was about five feet ahead
of me, and then I began to practice gymnastics. I went
up a few feet right end up, then a few feet more wrong
end up, and then I wasn't particular which way I went up.
The golden eagle off the pilot-house sailed around our
heads, and it was a fine chance for the fat man to get off a
handsome eulogy on the proud bird of freedom. He didn't
do it, however. One of his ears had been torn off, a leg
broken, and flying timbers kept pegging him every minute.
I wanted to ask him to finish the remark he commenced
in the cabin, but he seemed so cast-down and discouraged
that I hadn't the heart to speak.

We finally arrived there. It was a good ways up, and the route had several little inconveniences. It was a grand location from which to view the surrounding country, but we didn't stop to view it. We had business below, and our motto was business before pleasure.

BUSINESS BELOW.

Somehow, I got mixed up with the fat man, and we couldn't hardly tell which was which. He made no complaints, and I didn't care, and so we got along very well together until we struck the water. When we went down to look for bottom we let go of each other. He staid down there and I came up. A number of others also came up about that time. One man got hold of a door and warned us that he was a member of the Legislature, and must therefore be saved, but we held a mass convention and decided that the Constitution of the United States guaranteed equal rights to all men, and we crowded him along.

As the door wouldn't float over ten or twelve, a half-dozen of us got hold of brooms, foot-stools, dusters, and

so forth, and compared notes.   A six-footer from Missouri
was rushing around with a boot-jack in one hand, a table-
cloth in the other, and a look of anxiety on his face.   As
he floated near me he called out:

"Young man, where are we going?"

I called back that I was a stranger in that locality, and
couldn't say whether we'd bring up in New Orleans or
Fort Leavenworth.

I finally got hold of the dining table, to which a red-
headed woman from St. Louis was clinging.   As I caught
the table she exclaimed:

"Go away, young man—go away!"

No Time to be Captious.

I replied that the state of her toilet needn't confuse her
in the least.   Her dress-skirt had been blown off, her hair
singed, and part of her hoop-skirt was over her head, but
I warned her that it was about an even thing. • The band
of my shirt was still buttoned around my neck, and I had
one boot on, and it was no time to be captious.   I remarked

to her that her nose was broken and several of her teeth were gone, but she fired up and said I'd better "look to home," as I had one eye ruined, a hole in my head, and was cooked in a dozen places.

Before I could learn much of her history we were drawn to the bank and taken off. I called out for a breadth of rag carpet to make me a toga of, but no one would bring it, and I had to faint away to avoid hearing any criticisms from the crowd.

When I came to, a dozen of us were piled up together, and the captain of the boat was making a speech. He

THE CAPTAIN APOLOGIZED TO US.

said it wasn't his fault, and that we mustn't feel hard toward him. He had lost a fine dog by the accident, and he couldn't bear any further burden just then. He said that boats often blew up without apparent reason, but if he could ever ascertain the reason of this blow-up he would send us the particulars. He seemed like an honest-hearted man, and we felt sorry over the loss of his dog.

"LITTLE TOM."

IS step was unsteady and his hands trembled, and there was that unmeaning look in his eyes which comes when rum has benumbed the brain.

Not thus for once, but it was the same day after day, and we who had known him for years and years—who knew his tender heart and his many noble traits—grew sad and sought to pull him away from the gulf toward which his footsteps tended. He listened and promised. He knew that degradation and disgrace were before him, and he made a gallant struggle to walk in better paths.

We were made glad then. The human heart never beats so proudly as when it has sympathized with and encouraged another heart to do right. We did not taunt him with his failings, and thereby inflict scars which kind words would be long effacing; we did not let him know that we feared Temptation would overrule his desire to do right, but we trusted him.

The tempter waited for him at every turn, clothed in pleasant garb and wearing winning smiles. The tempter flattered him, praised him, ridiculed his good resolutions, and we were not there to plead our cause. He came back to us one night with that vacant stare and halting step, and we wondered if there was anything which could strengthen his manhood and arm him to resist those enemies who believed themselves true friends, while they bound him with chains which held him down.

He promised again and again—promised meaning to be true, but coming back to us with that terrible, hopeless look which strong drink paints on the face of him marked for a grave over which no eye grows dim, and on which no tear of love or sorrow ever falls. At last we gave him up, and we looked upon him as a once stalwart pine whose roots had been loosened by a mighty flood, and which now swayed and trembled, ready to fall, yet having something to prevent the crash for a little time. We had clung to him while there was hope—we waited and watched and kept our hearts open when hope had fled away, and men wondered that his grave was not waiting for him.

Little Tom! Strange that we should have forgotten him! And yet we had not, for we knew that many times and oft his childish words had cut the father's heart and thrilled his soul more than any words of ours—more than the prayers and tears of a fond wife or a gray-haired mother. When he had forgotten us who had labored with him like brothers—when the memories of home and childhood no longer had a lodging place in his heart—when manhood had been left groveling in the dust, then one mightier than man came to help us. Our tears fell, and yet we knew not whether to grieve or rejoice.

He sat at his table, the dim gas-light casting strange shadows over his bowed head. We had seen him thus so often that we could only pity. Unnerved, unstrung— floating out into the great wide ocean wherein wretched souls are being tossed and driven about with not one ray of hope to break the awful gloom—no wonder that his pencil was idle and his light dim.

A step on the stairs. It had a sound so unfamiliar that we raised our heads and looked at each other in a startled way and waited. Step! step! it came nearer, and we rose up as a figure stood in the door—a figure with face so white and look so wild that we could not speak. She saw the form at the table, and she bent over it and almost shrieked:

"Come home! Little Tom is dying!"

The words roused him. He looked from her to us, and back, in a bewildered way, and she wailed:

"Little Tom's been dying all day! He wants you to hold him once more!"

The words drove his weakness away in a moment, and the bewildered look was replaced by one of such fear and remorse and anxiety as no human face may ever wear again. We went with them, for Little Tom's rosy face and happy voice had won him a place in our hearts. Seeming not to feel the earth he trod upon, nor to know whether it was broad day or solemn midnight, the father hastened on, and he was there before us.

"Little Tom! speak to me—it's father!" he wailed as he clasped the dying boy in his arms, while the mother knelt by the empty crib and prayed God that her desolate hearthstone should not be further overshadowed.

"Father!" whispered the child as he unclosed his eyes and put death away for a brief space.

"Tom! oh! *my* Tom!" sobbed the father.

"I wanted you to hold me!" whispered Tom—"I wanted you to kiss me!"

"Leave my boy—leave me one thing to love!" prayed the mother.

"I cannot let him go—he must not die!" sobbed the father.

"*Kiss Little Tom!*" whispered the child—"hold me tight—I cannot see father!"

We grieved with them. The heart knows no grief like that grief which swells it when death stills a little voice and folds little white hands over a heart which never had an evil thought. We grieved then, but as the days went by and the weeks made months, we rejoiced. Our friend grew strong and noble and manly again. The cup of bitter degradation was dashed to earth, and he was strong as a lion to do right and resist temptation.

So he stands to-day, and though we know that grief has dimmed his sunshine, and that his heart will pain and swell as he remembers the little grave whose mantle of grass is nourished by a mother's tears, we thank God that Little Tom is with the angels.

THE BOOK CANVASSER.

He or she will call on
you to sell you this book.

He may be a pale-faced young
man, standing on the verge of the
grave, as it were, or she may be an interesting young lady with freckles on her
nose and a forlorn look.

Do not be deceived. They will have a
deceptive story at their tongue's end, and
as they corner you they will get off something
like this:

"Let me put your name down for this book—best book
published for years—selling like hot cakes—first edition

exhausted in twenty-four minutes—author known all over the country—orders being received from China, Japan, Madagascar and the Cape of Good Hope—sold only by subscription—write it right there on that line."

Do not rush your name down without pausing for a second sober thought. It would be more prudent to sit down and cross-examine the agent a little and ascertain if you would not be encouraging an unworthy person by signing your name. Ask him such questions as these:

"Are you a Mormon?"

"Do you admire Sixteen-String-Jack?"

"Do you intend to buy tomahawks and scalping-knives for the Indians with your profits?"

"How many of your relatives have been tried for murder?"

He or she will endeavor to evade you by smiling and saying:

"Come, now—got names of best citizens in town on my books—five hundred pages—piles of pictures—beautifully bound—fun and pathos—author's first book—money couldn't hire him to write another."

Tell him or her to be calm and not talk too much. Remind him or her of the fact that silence is golden. Remark that three dollars doesn't stick up behind every log, and freely express your opinion that twenty better books are offered you every week in the year.

Book agents stick to their game like a burr to a boy's heel, and he or she will preserve a pleasant face and reply:

"Well, write your name there—book ready for delivery in thirty days—sold forty yesterday—beats Martin Tupper's Proverbial Philosophy all to pieces."

If the agent is in a hurry let him go. Don't be forced into committing a rash act on account of his impatience. New books appear almost daily. You can get one anywhere, on any terms, and treating of any subject. Ask him some more questions:

"Are there any pirate stories in this book?"

"Does it say anything about Susan B. Anthony?"

"Does it discuss the Beecher scandal?"

"Is it a book which an innocent-minded child two years old can safely peruse?"

The agent will squirm, but you must pin him. His business is to sell, and he'll get as many copies on to unsuspecting and confiding people as he can.

Book agents have worn holes in my front door-steps; they have unhinged my gate; they have roused me from sleep, and have trailed me up and down and hung to me until I could offer no further objections. I warn the public against harboring or trusting them on my account.

HIS ANCESTRY.

SOME people are always taking on about their ancestors, and going to trouble and expense to prove that
some of their family knew all about Christopher Columbus,
shook hands with King Solomon, or got down to Noah's
ark two minutes too late for a passage. In fact, I used to
be of this class. I had an idea that if I could get back
to the beginning of the Quad family I should find something decidedly rich. A very nice man in New York sent
me a letter, one day, saying that he had heard of my desire,
and for a hundred dollars would trace my genealogy back
to the year one. I closed the bargain, and in three months
he sent me the partial result of his efforts, saying that if I
wanted any more to let him know. He commenced and
gave the names in regular succession :

"*John Quad.*—This old chap is your
head-center. He was three hundred
years old at the time of the flood, and
worth a great many millions of dollars, all of which was invested in pine
lumber, and was consequently carried
down stream when the rain came.
He is the first one recorded as pick-
ing up stray horses belonging to some one else, and would
have been hung if the water hadn't drowned him in his
cell. I wouldn't advise you to say anything about this

member of the family, as some of your neighbors' ancestors might have been on the jury which convicted him."

"*Philip Quad.*—I first find him mentioned in Cromwell's

time, and he is the seventeenth son of a Quad still further back, of whom I can get no reliable trace, owing to his having to slide out of a town between two days. Philip originated the 'freight-bill' game, had his head shaved three times, and was possessed of only one redeeming feature—he wouldn't run for office. As a friend, I wouldn't advise you to say anything about him either. I think he was shot while stealing chickens, but am not certain. I have, however, put it down that way, but you can alter it to 'burglary' if you choose."

"*Samuel Quad.*—I get trace of him during the voyage of Columbus to America. He was very anxious to come along with Chris, but circumstances over which he had no control detained him. He, however, came over afterwards—about the time that the Spaniards got to banishing their malefactors to America. Of course, I don't presume to dictate, but I think I wouldn't mention Samuel, if I were you, as people will talk."

"*Horatio Quad.*—This man was a very active member of your family. He could break out of jail as fast as they could get him in. I first strike him during the palmy days of old Rome. He was a roamun to the back bone, and traveled almost everywhere. He had the honor of being acquainted with the chief of police, deputy Roman marshal, the constables of the Tenth Ward, and started the first 'sweat board' ever seen in the town. He didn't live to witness the decay of the Roman Empire, owing to a little

affair in the jail court-yard. I don't recollect the name of the sheriff who officiated, or what the dying confession of your relative was, but I know that the papers said it was a clear case that he 'croked' Jim Swan for his 'sugar.' Of course, you are there and I am here, and it wouldn't look well for a stranger to advise; but still, if you shouldn't say anything about Horatio, it would perhaps be just as well."

"*Python Quad*—Lived in the days of Faro and Keno, and was a very able man. If he was alive to-day, and living in New York, the detectives would feel in duty bound to follow him around town, to see that he didn't get lost. I don't know how many banks he 'cracked,' or what he did with the plate stolen from those thirteen churches, or how the vigilance committee knew him to be the man who stole Sam Burton's mule.

There are things in your family record which a stranger has no business with, particularly an honest stranger. If you want the four hundred and sixty-three other Quads who lived before you, I shall be happy to go on with the names and leading eccentricities."

"*BIJAH.*"

"BIJAH."

IS name is Bijah—plain Bijah.

Years and years ago they might have called him Abijah, but the name was too stiff and dignified for one with such a big heart, and people shortened it.

When we like a man we first give him a familiar name—something which brings us closer to him as we pronounce it. "Abijah" signified nothing—"Bijah" signifies charity, sympathy, big-heartedness—all that we can look for in one whose every day life has been a battle with want and toil and trouble, and whose rough points were never polished by contact with education.

Everybody knows him—knows him as old and gray and nearing the long sleep of death, but growing more tenderhearted every day towards the sorrowing child, the unfortunate man and the down-trodden and erring woman. Who has given more from his lean purse to keep the wolf from the door? Who has been more kind in heart and word to those who were recklessly driving to destruction for want of a kind word to give them new resolution and new faith? Who has taken more steps to restore the lost child—to guide the stranger aright—to keep those who might sin, in the straight and narrow path?

And for this we love him.

We forget his few faults by remembering his many noble traits, and we do not wait until death has closed his eyes and stilled his big heart before we say that the world would have more sunshine, and life's battle could be better fought, if there were more like Bijah.

We think it passing strange as we look at his snowy locks and wrinkled visage that one who was cast afloat on the sea of life when but a child, and who has drifted here and there at the will of every gale, should have preserved such sympathy in his look and such a kind heart and tender feeling. God made him so—meant that in his humble sphere he should make sad hearts glad, and stand as a bulwark to ward off woe and misery from those whom the burden might crush down.

He is widowed and childless. Death has passed *him* by, but made his heart sore and sad often and again, and now in his old age he stands alone. If God had not given him such charity and sympathy he would pause sometimes and give up the struggle, but he has a mission and he cannot halt until death rises up in his path and will not be turned aside. He has lived among us so long that to us will come the sad duty of closing his eyes and folding the cold hands across the bosom in which death found a resting place at last. Tears will fall as men and women and children know that he is dead—such tears as come when the heart swells with deep sorrow. They will place flowers on the coffin, and as it rests before the altar they will listen to hear it said:

"We knew him as one whose good deeds and kind words made us all better-hearted."

And we shall hope that the angels forgave his sins and remembered nothing but his big heart.

DEPRESSIONS.

ILLUSTRATED BY THE AUTHOR.

WAS looking over some of the battle-fields of the Revolutionary war a few weeks ago. It is enough to sadden the heart of any sutler to wander over those historic fields and hear the explanations of the guides. One comes away feeling as if he would like to wrap an American flag around him and be knocked down ten or fifteen times in the name of Liberty.

SPOT WHERE WARREN FELL.

I started out before breakfast with an old farmer to see the spot where Warren fell. We climbed several fences, worried through a marsh, and as we finally turned the corner of an old barn the farmer waved his hand and said:

"Behold the spot!"

35

There it was, sure enough, looking as fresh and healthy as if a hundred years had not beaten a constant tattoo upon it. In the midst of a small field, a romantic-looking old barn in the distance, was the depression.

"Did he fall from his horse, or from a balloon?" I asked the guide, but he replied that he couldn't say. It had been some little time since the war, and he had forgotten.

"Struck on his head, I suppose?" I remarked as I raised up to get a clearer view of the spot.

The old man said he didn't know about that; never heard any one say.

"But see here," I said as I leaned back; "how dare you call yourself a guide and charge me fifty cents when you know nothing of the history of this spot?"

"Waal, all I know is that this is the spot where Gineral Warren fell," he replied, and it was useless to ask him further questions.

I don't wonder that it killed the General—the stack was torn up in an awful manner.

Two or three days after that I crossed the fields with a farmer's son to look upon the spot where Colonel Bligh fell. Never having read that Colonel Bligh took any part in the Patriot war, I should have missed the historic spot had I not halted at the farm-house to get a drink of water. The young man said that his great grandfather was a captain in the Patriot army, but was in poor health a great share of the time and only killed six hundred and twenty-eight Britishers during the seven years, averaging but eighty-nine soldiers and five-eighths of another per year.

"There's the spot," said the young man as we were mounting a five-rail fence.

"Where?"

"Right over around here somewhere," he answered, waving his hand.

"Was it on the marsh, under it, or around that sheep-pen?" I inquired, giving him a severe look.

"Yes, I guess it was," he replied.

I stood there and sighed and felt sad. It is a hard thing to have a musket-ball bore a tunnel through a Colonel while fighting for liberty and a fat salary, and more melancholy still to have straw-stacks and sheep-pens erected over the spot where he poured out his blood for his country.

"Were you here when the battle occurred?" I asked of the young man as I handed him the fifty cents fee.

THE COLONEL'S FALL.

"Yes—hoeing corn over in that lot!" he promptly replied.

"And did the fighting disturb you any?"

"Nawt much. I put in a usual day's work."

I looked at him and longed to call him a stupendous liar, but I reflected that he lied in the cause of liberty and unity, and therefore held my peace. When we reached the house I asked the young man's mother what the name of the battle-field was, and she replied that she couldn't exactly remember, but thought it was "Astronomy," or some such high-sounding name.

A few days after that the landlord of a country tavern sent his hostler to show me the spot where General Colby fell. We climbed fences, waded a creek and fell over logs, and finally halted near an old cider-mill.

"There, sir, we've got to the spot," said the hostler, throwing away a quid of tobacco which must have cost him fifteen or twenty cents.

"Where is the spot?" I demanded.

"Right around here," he replied.

When he found that wouldn't do, and that he had got to come to time, he looked around and found the exact spot. A large hog had taken possession of the cavity, and I begged of the guide not to disturb the porker, which could be nothing less that a patriotic hog.

THE SPOT WHERE COLBY FELL.

"You are sure that's the spot?" I asked.

"Oh, I know it—I know it!" he replied.

"What made General Colby fall there?" I continued; "why didn't he go down to the tavern and fall on a bed?"

"I never asked any one," returned the guide; "all I know is that he fell there."

"Did he stub his toe?"

"Dunno—never axed 'um."

"Was he stealing water-melons, hunting coons or making cider?" I inquired as we started to return.

"Less see!" he mused, shutting one eye and feeling for the top-rail of the fence—"I'll be dummed 'f I can remember, though it seems as if I heard a feller say there was a fight here, or sunthin' or other."

The next day I was a hundred miles away, looking at the spot where Captain Sullivan fell. I hired a horse and buggy at a little village and drove over to the spot with a man who was selling township rights to manufacture a patent clothes-wringer. A farmer who saw us crossing his orchard came out to meet us in the name of Liberty and exact a fee of fifty cents each. If he hadn't been at home we should have missed the spot altogether, as a scarecrow had been placed there to keep the birds out of the cherry trees just over the fence.

SPOT WHERE SULLIVAN FELL.

" Are you sure that this is the identical spot where Captain Sullivan fell ?" I asked.

" Nobody but a traitor will doubt it," replied the farmer.

" And was he killed ?"

" They say he was."

" Hit by a bullet or struck by a brick-bat ?"

" I dunno."

"Did he utter any last words!"

"He mought—I dunno."

"Was he a Democrat or a Republican?"

"I dunno."

We went away with sad hearts, and as we turned for a last look at the historic spot my companion uncovered his head and said:

"Oh! glorious Liberty, 'tis sweet indeed to die for thee! Township rights, including a full set of rollers, only twenty-five dollars!"

GOING TO PIC-NICS.

I HAVEN'T been to one in seven long years, but it still thrills me to come across an advertisement reading that this or that Sunday school or society proposes to give a river excursion or a railroad trip for the purpose of raising a few hundred dollars to found an orphan asylum or pay off a debt.

No man ever enjoyed himself on an excursion or at a pic-nic more than I used to.

Wife and I always had a week to get ready in, and the bill for eatables and new garments never amounted to over forty dollars.

For six days we baked, washed turned the house upside down, talked about the cool breezes and shady trees, and were then ready to start.

Got up at four o'clock A. M. to catch the boat.

Got the six children washed and dressed by seven.

Got mad by eight.

Got down to the boat by nine.

Counted up the children, the baskets and bundles, and found all there.

The boat was advertised to start at sharp nine, and she started—up to another wharf, and laid there until eleven.

During the interval some one stole my cold chickens, a fat woman sat down on our baby, and my wife fell over the gang-plank and knocked her nose out of shape.

Boat finally started for the island.

41

We had just commenced to feel how good it was to leave the dusty city behind when a fellow stuck his cane into my eye, and Small Pica got a peanut in his wind-pipe. While wife was shaking him she lost her hat overboard, and a boy threw her sun-umbrella over for the hat to hang on to.

Several fights.

We got on the larbord side of the wheel-house, counted noses, and discovered that William Henry was missing. Went in search of him, and found him in possession of a fellow who weighed one hundred and ninety pounds and had a red nose. He said he recognized William Henry as a child stolen from Cleveland fourteen years before, and before we got through with it my eyes looked over plum-colored hills and his teeth were all out.

Finally reached the island and the cool shade.

The aforesaid shade was thrown over us from an ancient board fence, the trees having been monopolized by the nine hundred people who landed before we did.

Commenced to rain.

Cleared off just about the time we had been soaked through.

Mrs. Quad began wishing she had remained at home, but I silenced her by declaring that it was our duty to our children to shake off the dust once in awhile and get out among the cool breezes.

Ate our lunch.

There was one pickle for each of us, and a bologna for the baby.

Owing to the different varieties of soil on the island, William Henry had a blue clay stain on his back, Susan represented a moist loam, Archimedes bore off the palm on Ohio clay, and Bertha and the baby appeared in all the grandeur of bottom lands.

Concluded to go in search of shady dells and silent glades.

Found a dell with two dead horses in it, and the glades were full of floating logs.

Mrs. Quad thought we had better wander along the pebbly beach and gather some shells, and we wandered.

Gathered an old boot, a pop-bottle, a broken oar, and then went in search of help to pry my family out of the quick-sand. When we were all together on the grass again we concluded to go to the boat.

Went there.

Waited four hours for her to start.

She started and got stuck.

Waited two hours and she got off.

Several fights.

One fat man overboard.

One lean woman overboard.

Everybody else over-bored.

More fights.

The steamer finally went ahead, and struck another bar.

Was admitted to the bar—half her length.

More waiting.

More fights, and so forth, and so forth.

Got to the wharf at midnight.

Got home at one.

Got to bed at two.

Got up at three to go for the doctor.

He said it was three cases of croup, one of exhaustion, and two of general debility.

The rest of us in usual good health.

Since that date we do not go on "picked excursions" to shady islands, when we want recreation from care and relief from the heat—we jam ourselves into cattle-cars, ride thirty miles to some grove, get in the shade of an old barn, and pity the miserable people who remained at home.

"PRIMROSE."

NEVER asked why they called him "Primrose." I presume it was a nick-name, but in those days the fewer questions one asked of Nevada people the better he got along.

I hadn't the least idea that there was a newspaper within two hundred miles of me, and was therefore dumbfounded at looking out of the stage-coach window and observing the sign:

THE GAZETTE.

LIVELIEST PAPER IN NEVADA.

I got out of the coach, telling the driver that I would lay over, and walked across the street to the office. There were no stairs to climb. It was a rude shanty, and the door was ajar.

As I went in I beheld Primrose seated at the editorial table, surrounded by the implements of his noble profession. He eyed me suspiciously as I looked around the

45

office and took a mental inventory, but when I sat down on the corner of the table and told him that I was a weary stranger, out of a job and looking for work, his countenance brightened up and he held out his hand.

"You want a sit, eh?" he inquired, rubbing at the patch on his cheek.

I replied that I did, and he leaned back and seemed to ponder for several minutes. Finally he said:

"Well, I dunno. I've got a man now, and he's a buster. He can stick type, write editorial, gather local, work press, or fight a whole crowd. I've got him now, but there may be a vacancy before night. We two are going over to the hills this afternoon to canvass for subscribers and

CANVASSING.

write up a new 'find,' and there's no knowing how we'll come out. There's a rough crowd over there, and the camp is sort o' down on the *Gazette*. If you'll hang around until night you'll know one way or the other."

I decided to wait, and as soon as his foreman came in

Primrose buckled on his armory, and they mounted mules and rode away, leaving me in charge.

As I afterwards learned, the pair reached the hills all right, and were cordially received. The reception was most too cordial. The miners dropped shovel and pick, and the illustration on the preceding page will give the reader a faint idea of what followed.

The foreman was a man of great pluck and endurance, but he couldn't hold out against such a demonstration,

SUBSCRIBERS PAYING UP.

and the last Primrose saw of him he was being laid away to rest in the bed of "Pizen" river. The editor had luck on his side, and though several revolvers blazed at him as he jumped from a cliff, the bullets went wild.

I waited two days and then continued my journey. About a hundred miles west found Primrose. He had rented a shanty in an embryo city, and was making a bargain with a teamster to go up and bring back the office.

"No, it wasn't very hot up there," he replied as I questioned him, "but I was tired of being shot at by the same old crowd!"

THE HOODLUM.

OWNS and villages could get along very well without him, but what could a city do without its hoodlum—its brigade of hoodlums!

Lor' bless him, in spite of his rags and dirt and his "sass!"

It requires nerve and courage to be a hoodlum. The boy has got to have the heart of a man, the courage of a lion, and the constitution of an Arab. Only one in a hundred gives him credit for half his worth. No one cares whether he grows fat or starves; whether Fortune lifts him up or casts him down; whether night finds him quarters in a box or a comfortable bed. He's a hoodlum, and hoodlums are generally supposed capable of getting along somehow, the same as a horse turned out to graze.

Not one boy in ten can be a hoodlum. Nature never overstocks the market. If left an orphan the average boy dies, or has relatives to care for him, or falls in the way of a philanthropist and comes up a straight-haired young man with a sanctimonious look. The true hoodlum is born to the business. He swallows marbles and thimbles as soon as he can creep, begins to fall down stairs when a year old, and is found in the alley as soon as he can walk. He receives numerous maulings from the boys, gets a semi-

48

THE FUTURE PRESIDENTS.

daily licking at home, and when able to talk plain is an accomplished swearer and ready to enter upon his combat with the world.

About this time his father dies or runs away, or his mother dies or elopes, and the hoodlum is free to go and come. The neighbors hate the boy because he has broken their windows and knocked pickets off the fence, and they have no care for his future. Once in a great while some one may halt him and ask him if he ever heard of the Bible, or Heaven, or the angels, and hands go up in astonishment to find that he never has. Something ought to be done with him, but who shall take him and train him? Every pedestrian will assert that the boy is a heathen, but he is left to run his career, as before. It's no one's duty in particular to wash him up, give him a square meal, put decent garments on his back and then seek to make a man of him, and so the boy becomes further initiated into the hoodlum business. He knows that people look down on him; that no one cares for him; that he has the whole world to fight against, and he hardens his heart and grows suspicious and ugly. When a long-haired man halts him and wants to know if he has ever been to Sunday school the hoodlum promptly replies:

" Oh! sling a dictionary at me !"

There are plenty to teach him evil, and the hoodlum at ten is thirty years old in sin. He remembers when Jem Mace and Heenan had their little bout, can name the leading race-horses, and the game of euchre is old with him. He may skulk into a barn at nine in the morning, or he may hang around until midnight and then make his bed in a door-way or a box, to be astir again at early dawn.

The hoodlum gets knocked, and he knocks back. Older and more wicked hoodlums steal from him, and he gets even by stealing from the public. He closely studies the

D

habits of house-owners. He knows that axes are frequently left in back yards, and that buck-saws, saw-bucks, scrap-iron and the like find ready market at the junk-buyer's. While other people promenade the avenues he prowls through the alleys. He is familiar with the width and depth of every back yard in his beat, and he knows to a cent what plunder is worth. The hoodlum sometimes makes a mistake and is captured and imprisoned, but as, a rule his keenness and fleetness are too much for the law. While other people sleep he prowls; he forgets what a bed is like; he gets to believe that decayed oranges and crackers make a meal fit for a king; he prides himself on a black eye, and he sits on the curbstone and tells great lies of how he has traveled and what he has seen.

But, bless the hoodlum. We can look at him and admire the brave heart which backs the boy against the whole world, or we can hold him up as an example of youthful depravity, and warn other boys not to be like him. We can use him in an argument against one going to Africa to find heathens, or we can point to his bad deeds and urge that the law deprive society of his presence. He steals our penstock spout, but blacks our boots; he carries off the family axe, but brings the family paper each morning; he breaks our window, steals our dog and hooks the clothes-line, but he can be trusted for an errand. We couldn't have Fourth of July without him, and we all wonder, even as we blame him, why he is not ten times worse.

THERE WERE BUGS THERE.

ALL the officers and crew of the old steamer "Panther," a Missouri River stern-wheeler, had got used to the bugs which persisted in living in and around the bunks and berths, and we sometimes wondered why passengers couldn't put up with such little annoyances for a night without the loudest kind of complaining.

One night we took on a lone passenger at Leavenworth. He was an old man, and a very grave and solemn man, telling the captain, I believe, that he was a New Englander, out west as a missionary.

We had a full load of freight, were running up stream, making slow time, and the solemn man got to bed early. He hadn't been in his state-room half an hour when he was heard thrashing around, and directly he came into the cabin, half-dressed, face wearing an anxious look, and he inqnired of the steward:

"Sir, is the capting on board?"

"Just gone to his state-room," was the answer.

"Call him—call him at once! I have important business!" said the old man.

The captain was routed out, and as he inquired what was up, the old man approached him, extended his right arm until the fore-finger was within an inch of the captain's nose, and in a hoarse voice he whispered:

"Sir! do you know that there are bugs aboard this boat?"

"Y-e-s—ahem—that is, there may be," answered the captain. Then turning to the steward he continued:

"James, change him to No. 7."

The old man was changed to another state-room, the

"BUGS ABOARD."

captain returned to bed, and all went smoothly for about twenty-five minutes, when the old man again appeared in the cabin. "Call the capting!" he said to a negro waiter who happened to be passing.

"Call—the—capting— at once!" continued the old man, in a decided tone.

The captain was routed out, and he was hardly outside the door of his state-room when the old man whispered:

"*Bugs, sir!* MORE BUGS!"

"Well, I can't help it!" angrily exclaimed the captain. "Confound it! what can I do about it? You can take the next state-room."

The old man turned into No. 5, and it was near midnight before he was heard from again, except an occasional groan. All at once he jumped out into the cabin, walked across to the captain's state-room, and began pounding in a furious manner.

"Ho! Whoa! What's up!" shouted the captain, throwing off sleep and jumping out of bed.

"Capting! Capting!" called the old man.

"Is that you? What do you want?" demanded the captain, as he stepped out of his room.

"Bugs, sir—B-U-G-S!" whispered the old man.

"Well, hang it, I can't clean 'em out to-night, can I!" growled the captain. "I guess you're nervous. The bugs don't disturb *me* any. Go into No. 9, there, and if you rout me out again I'll put you ashore in the woods, blamed if I don't!"

MORE BUGS.

The old man made no reply, but turned into No. 9, and it was an hour after midnight before the bugs got too many for him. They finally rolled him out of bed, and he got up, dressed, locked his satchel, and walked across the cabin to the captain's door and pounded away with his fist.

"Hi! there—what is it!" called the captain.

"Capting, arise!" exclaimed the old man.

"I'll arise you, if you don't stop this fooling around!" replied the captain.

"Capting, I desire to see you!" continued the old man.

The captain got into his pantaloons, opened the door and said:

"Well, what now?"

"Bugs—*larger bugs!*" whispered the passenger.

"Didn't I tell you I'd put you ashore if you made any more fuss about those bugs!" roared the captain.

"You did—you did," replied the old man—"*and now I want you to do it!*"

"You do?"

"Yes, my friend—I prefer the woods to the bugs! Stop your old boat!"

"STOP YOUR OLD BOAT."

The steamer was hugging the Missouri shore, and the captain stopped her, pushed out the plank, and the old man jumped to the bank, landing a dozen miles from any house. We delayed hauling in the plank, not liking to leave him there, but the stranger took a seat on the bank, looked calmly down upon us, and as the boat moved away, he called out:

"Capting, don't feel hard to'ards me, but I can't stand bugs!"

A SAD SONG.

IN the years gone by, an old Michigan quill-driver named Blake went to Detroit on business, he being then connected with a paper in the western part of the State. He got pretty full by evening, but was invited into the ladies' parlor of the hotel, with others, to hear a young lady initiate a new piano. After she had played several tunes Blake asked her to play "Lily Dale." She complied, and he sat down on a chair and cried, excusing his action by saying to the crowd:

"It's a sad song, and it always puts me in mind of my dead mother."

It was played again, and Blake went to bed with "Lily Dale" ringing in his ears. He occupied the same bed with a merchant's clerk, the hotel being crowded, and soon after turning in a dog commenced to howl in the back yard. "Woooo-hoo-hoo!" wailed the dog, and Blake sat up in bed and exclaimed:

"There's 'Lily Dale' again!"

"Git out—it's only a dog howling," replied the clerk.

"Stranger," said Blake as he turned his head, "stranger, if you'd lost your poor old mother and felt as bad as I do you'd bet fifty dollars to five that it was 'Lily Dale.' Yes, it's that same song, and I've got to cry again!"

"I tell you it's the landlord's brindled dog!" protested the clerk.

"It can't be, I know by my feelings it hain't," replied Blake. "When the strains of that sad melody cross my heart-strings I'd cry if it was Fourth of July and every brass band in Michigan was in the front door yard playing 'Yankee Doodle!'"

And he got up and sat down on the lid of a chest and wept profusely, while the clerk nearly choked himself with laughter.

THE OLD FIREMAN.

E may still be found in small towns and villages, here and there, but the old fireman has had his day. He knows it, and he sighs as he hangs up his trumpet and removes his belt.

Steam—hissing, pushing, throbbing steam is too much for human muscle.

The old fireman was in his glory twenty years ago. No statesman's heart thrilled with greater pride over a successful speech than did the old fireman's as he took the lead of the company—the two long lines in red shirts, and moved the hand-engine down to the bridge and dropped the suction into the river. He was a captain—a colonel—a general—and he wouldn't have exchanged positions with the Czar of Russia. No general, urging his men to go in and cover themselves with glory, could get that deep, pompous voice which the old fireman secured as he called out:

Trim Hose.

"Back 'er up—man the brakes!"

On his head was a leather hat, surmounted by a golden eagle—around his waist a broad belt bearing the word "Foreman," and as he braced himself for the next call he felt that the mayor of the town was a pigmy—a cipher—an atom.

"Lay them hose!"

That was the next order, and he walked down the street to see the pipe put on and to direct that the stream be thrown over Baker's tin-shop or McFarland's horse-barn. As he walked back to the engine he scowled fiercely at the small boys, nodded distantly to the men who worked side by side with him in the shop, and wondered how his wife dared smile at him so familiarly.

BAR' DOWN.

"Work 'er easy!" he whispered as he mounted the engine.

It was a fearful moment. Perhaps she would "take" water, perhaps not. The "perhaps" were always two to one where the engine was drawn out to a fire once in six or eight months.

She took.

The air rushed down the hose, followed by water, and water finally leaped from the nozzle in a sickly stream. Then came the next order:

"Bar' down a little!"

The men at the brakes put on more muscle, and the stream leaped to the roof of the barn, striking the shingles with a squashy sort of splash. The small boys yelled, the women waved their handkerchiefs, and one property-holder turned to another and remarked:

"If Scrubtown only had such an engine, property would jump right up, and folks would settle there!"

"Break 'er."

The foreman looked down on the crowd and smiled. It was a benign smile. It was a smile which conveyed a warning to the close observer that the engine was only playing with herself, and that she would presently stand upon her hind wheels and howl and astonish that town.

The face of more than one small boy grew serious as its owner wondered if it were possible that he would ever rise to that proud station. He knew that there were a thousand chances against him, and even as he watched the stream battering at the shingles he sighed and felt his heart sneaking down toward his bare feet.

The foreman straightened up.

Victory lurked in his eyes.

He raised his trumpet.

" *Break 'er!*"

The red-shirted men uttered a yell as they bore down on the brakes.

The stream crept up to within three feet of the ridge-pole, and playing through one hundred and fifty feet of hose at that. The fate of kingdoms hung in the balance; America's future greatness depended on the next minute.

"Break 'er Hard!"

The boys were yelling.

The women were applauding.

The men were shouting.

The stream was gaining.

A bland smile covered the foreman's face. He raised his trumpet, and then

"Break 'er, boys—hard—hard—tear 'er—hip—ha—yee yup—down—down!"

He leaped up and down—he shook his trumpet—he brayed—he screamed, and the stream crept up, up, and finally shot clear over the ridge, and the proud day was won—America was safe!

Most of us were there at one time or other, and when we let up on the brakes and swung our hats and yelled, we felt it—knew that we could knock the eye-brows off the biggest conflagration that ever got a start.

Ah! well! This subtle giant which plows the steamer across the trackless ocean—turns monster machinery, and is our companion in every walk of daily life, has defaced the play-grounds of childhood and effaced more than one tender memory of youth; and when the day comes for the old fireman to hang his trumpet on the shadow of the past and throw his red shirt aside to add to memory's trophies, we who have kept the drag-rope taut cannot repress a sigh, and must feel a dark shadow cross the sunlight of recollection.

SHE HAD A HEART AFTER ALL.

EVERYTHING looked so grim and silent around the house that the door was burst in and they found the old woman dead. She had lived there for years and years. People knew her, yet no one knew her. Some called her "Old Nan," and some thought her a witch. She never left her yard, never spoke to any one except to snarl and growl, and a lone sailor drifting about on the ocean could not have been more distant from love and sympathy.

No one ever called twice on "Old Nan" for charity. Beggars sometimes knocked at her humble door, but as soon as they saw her witch-like face, bent form and menacing look, they hurried away, marking the house that they might not call again. If you had asked any of the neighbors if the old woman had a heart—could feel love, pity or tenderness—if there was anything which could get down through the crust of disappointment, avarice and despair, and touch the nature which God gives every woman, they would have laughed in derision. And yet she had a heart, and it was touched. Death touched it.

She did not die in her bed. She might have been ill for three or four days, but she did not call out and ask for assistance. Perhaps she knew her time had come, and that no human hand could aid her, and as she felt the weight of Death's shadow she was a woman again. There were longings in her heart, new feelings in her soul, and no one can say that she did not weep. She crept off the bed, made her way to an old chest, and from its depths she pulled up an old and tattered Testament. Between its leaves were two cards. On one was pinned a lock of hair, tied with faded ribbon—a brown, curly lock, such as you might clip from the head of a boy of five. In a quaint old hand was written on the card the words: "My boy Jamie's hair." On the other card were pinned three or four violets, so old and faded that they looked like paper.

She sat in a chair holding the book in her lap, and her stiffening fingers held those cards up to her blind eyes. Thus they found her—a card in either hand and the Holy Book lying open in her lap! The men, women and children who had crowded in with the officer saw how it was, and some of them wept. "Old Nan" had a heart, after all. She must have been a mother once and had a mother's tender feeling. No doubt she was loved and happy when she severed that brown curl from its mates and wrote on the card: "My boy Jamie's hair!"

They removed the precious relics very tenderly, and when they came to look into her face they saw that it almost wore a smile, and that the hard lines had all been rubbed out by the tenderness which flowed into her heart as Death was laying his hand upon her.

Who culled those violets? Where is Jamie?

Time had faded the violets away until a breath would have scattered them—the curly lock had been wept over until its brightness was gone—poor Jamie, passing across the mystic river which flows swiftly and deeply between the shore of life and the gate of Heaven, was waiting and watching.

Truly, the greatest mystery of life is—life.

KEEPING THE BOY IN NIGHTS.

I'VE lived in this world long enough to know that the next hardest thing to curing a sore heel is to keep a boy home nights after he has passed the age of ten. He then begins to believe that it is his solemn duty to go out and hook watermelons and other portable delicacies of the season, sit around the corner stores and hear all that is to be said on the subject of dog fights, horse races and shoulder-hitting, and to keep out of bed as long as he can see a light in any window.

I know fathers who have thrashed their sons, bribed and coaxed and resorted to all sorts of stratagems without doing any good, and I therefore take this opportunity of presenting to parents a few words and a few illustrations on the subject of keeping the boy in nights.

WISCONSIN METHOD.

This illustration represents a very effectual method, much practiced in Wisconsin. When a father takes his son at dark and spikes him down to the kitchen floor he knows just where that boy will be at ten o'clock, and at eleven, and all night for that matter. It is a great improvement on the old method of mauling the boy with the shovel after he has got into the house through a back window, slid up stairs and into bed, and is just entering upon the outskirts of a pleasant dream.

The next method is called "The Rochester" method,

having been first adopted in that city, where I sold two hundred and eighty "rights" in three days. Fathers called upon me with tears trickling down their cheeks, and they shook me by the hand and exclaimed:

"Sir, you have saved our sons from going down to ruin, and we feel that we can't think too much of you."

Some families use a cord of stone to pile

ROCHESTER METHOD.

on the boy, but half as much, if properly placed, is warranted to hold him to the spot through any night in the year. Where this system is practiced there is no waking up at midnight and wondering where Charles Henry is, and what sort of company he is in. If parents wake at all it is to smile sweetly as they remember that Charles Henry is right there in that house, while other boys are on the high road to degradation. In a prairie country, where stone cannot well be obtained, eight tons of old scrap-iron will answer every purpose.

The next method is called "The New Jersey" method, where I had the honor to introduce it in the spring of 1872. Most parents in that State had given up in despair, but they gave me a cordial welcome, and after my remedy had been tried a few times and had substantiated my assertions, old men and middle-aged men and widows bore down upon me in crowds. One old man said to me, with quivering chin:

NEW JERSEY METHOD.

"Sir, they should bury you beside George Washington when you die!"

A widow woman pressed forward, grasped my hand and exclaimed :

"Mister Quad, your name will be enscrolled upon the archives of fame !"

I use four-inch scantling for posts, and brace them well. The weight should never be less than five thousand pounds, and may consist of old grindstones, soft brick, or whatever comes handy. The method is covered by two patents, and the public are hereby cautioned against an infringement, brought out by Stanley Waterloo, of the St. Louis *Republican*, whose trial for the offense is now in progress.

The next method is called "The Louisville" method,

having been first practiced in that city. It is partly the invention of one of the editors of the *Courier-Journal*, but I have patents for four improvements on his original invention. Some people use a log chain instead of a rope,

LOUISVILLE METHOD.

but a two-inch rope works better in the pulley, and if new will hold a boy of sixteen without the least trouble. The fathers of Louisville had no faith in the invention, and it was several days before I could secure an opportunity to exhibit its marvelous workings. We tried it on a "Butcher Town" boy of fifteen, who had been out every night for four years, and who had come to such a pass that his father was ashamed to attend a respectable dog-fight or be seen at a raffle, and it worked so well that I had thirty-five orders next day. One father said to me :

"You are a greater man than Thomas Jefferson ever dared be !"

Another said, his eyes full of tears and his voice husky with emotion :

"I never thought I should live to see this day!"

The last thing, as I got into the omnibus, a woman laid her hand on my arm and sobbed :

"I never dreamed that a red-headed man had such a noble soul!"

Parties desiring rights can address me at Detroit.

EXECUTIN' THE LAW

OF course, where three or four hundred miners were gathered together at a diggings, as in the early days of California and Nevada, before steam and machinery had taken the place of picks and pans, no one's life would have been safe an hour but for the border-laws always in force.

It was understood that murder and stealing would be punished by hanging, and this knowledge kept most of the camps in a safe and peaceful state, although a case of murder was sure to come sooner or later.

One night at Crazy Horse Diggings, a burly big fellow called Tomahawk, was arrested after he had stabbed a sleeping miner to the heart and robbed him of his little store of dust. The murderer made a hard fight to escape, but was knocked down and secured, and two men stood guard over him the remainder of the night.

Crazy Horse was one of the most peaceful, law-abiding diggings in the State, else Tomahawk would have been dangling at a limb within half an hour after the discovery of his crime. We never lynched an offender, but gave him a fair trial and then executed him in as good style as circumstances would permit. Tomahawk was guilty beyond a doubt. Three or four men had seen him quit the shanty of his victim, and his hands and clothing were stained with

69

blood, but yet we all felt as if we must at least go through with the form of a trial.

Next morning every man in camp knocked off work, and about nine o'clock we formed in a circle on the grass, and Tomahawk was led in. He was a rough 'un in look and nature, and we expected to see him bluff and brave. When he had been seated on a barrel, and the excitement had

subsided, an old man from Vermont who was called "Judge," and who had acted as judge in several previous cases, arose and said:

"Prisoner, you ar' charged with the awful crime of murder! None of us hain't any doubt of your guilt, but Crazy Horse ar' a peaceful diggin's, and we ar' goin' to give you a fa'r trial. Do you want any one to speak fur you, or do you want to make any remarks?"

"See here, boys!" said Tomahawk as he slowly rose up

and looked around on the circle—"boys! I hain't goin' to lie about this thing, and I hain't goin' to make ye any more trouble than I can help! I am guilty! I wanted to leave here, because I wasn't makin' anythin', but I didn't have an ounce to go with. I didn't mean to kill him. I was after his dust, but he woke up, grabbed me, and I had to stab him. I know the law, and I shan't try to beg off!"

The circle of men were greatly surprised to see Tomahawk so broken down, and while all felt that the law must be enforced, nearly every one also felt considerable sympathy for the prisoner. There was silence for two or three minutes, and then the Judge arose and replied:

"Pris'ner at the bar, we knowed you war' guilty, but we wanted to do this thing right and lawful. We'd bin willin' to give you a squar' trial, but as you have owned up I s'pose there's nothing left but to hang you!"

"That's what I'm willin' you should do!" replied Tomahawk. "If you didn't execute the law on me this camp would soon be so rough that an honest man couldn't live here. I'm ready now, 'cept that I'd like to have some one pray for me!"

The Judge passed around the circle, looking for some one to act as chaplain and spiritual adviser, but there wasn't a man in camp who felt equal to the task.

Tomahawk understood the situation after awhile, and he said:

"Oh! well—it won't make no great difference. I've bin purty rough, and p'raps prayin' wouldn't help me any, though I b'lieve it's the rule to pray with a man afore they hang him. If any of ye can sing a religus tune it will do just as well."

The Judge passed around the circle again, but not a man could be found who felt himself competent to sing a hymn.

Here was another bad situation, and we were all feeling very much embarrassed, when a miner called Old Slabam sprang up, walked over to Tomahawk and said:

"Here, old boy, we hain't none of us much on religun, and we can't remember any hymns. However, there's the song of "Sawnee River," and if that'll do I'll sing it the best I can!"

"As I said before, I don't want to be too pertick'ler, nor make too much trouble," replied Tomahawk. "Seems to me thar ought to be sum singin', or sunthin', and I s'pose 'Sawnee River' will do as well as anythin'; you may go ahead!"

We moved over to the tree, Tomahawk mounted a barrel, the rope was slipped over his head, and then Old Slabam unbuttoned his vest, took a long breath, and commenced:

"Way down upon the Sawnee River,
    Far, far away;
  Thar's whar my heart is turning ever,
    Thar's whar the old folks stay."

He managed to get through with the song after a fashion, and then Tomahawk said:

"I'm much obleeged to you, Slabam. You hain't much of a singer, but when a man does his level best that's all you can ask of him. It's a good song, kinder sad-like, and it war' a big favor to sing to me. Good-bye, boys. I've tried to act like a man in this 'ere affair, and I hope you won't be too hard on me arter I've quit kicking! Well, here I go———!"

And he stepped off the barrel, hanging himself.

We all felt a little sorry as we turned back the sods and laid him away. Tomahawk had acted white.

UNDER THE GAS-LAMP.

I SOMETIMES wonder if, when I am old and helpless, my children will look upon me as a shadow cast over their happiness? I wonder if Fortune will not play some bad trick by which I may be thrown upon the charity of the world, and be treated as the world's charity treats other old men? I wonder if youth will sneer at my gray locks and trembling limbs, and if people will say that I have out-lived my usefulness, and should be glad of a place in the poorhouse and a grave in Potter's field?

From my window the other night I watched an old man as he crept up the street and stood under the gas-lamp. He was gray and bent and feeble, and his fluttering rags were the leaves of a book, in which one could read of pov-erty, sorrow and woe. He looked around like a child, as if he knew not which way to turn. No home, no friends— no one to care whether he lived or died.

By and by he sat down on the step and rested his head on his hand. I knew what he was thinking of. His face was in the shadow, but I knew that tears were falling down those wrinkled cheeks, and that his old heart was sad and sore. There is nothing so lonely as an old man without home or friends. He felt it. He saw the old and the young go by, heard the laughter of happy children, and he bent his gray head still lower. His life had been a dreary struggle with poverty and grief, and those who had once cared for him had slept the long sleep for years.

He was alone—old and weak, and the world was pitiless. No one stopped to ask if he was cold or hungry—no one cared whether his heart was heavy or glad.

THE WORLD WAS PITILESS.

The bleak wind whistled around the corner, and I saw the old man shiver. He had been a child once, perhaps petted and loved, and his mother had read to him from the good book: "Honor thy father and mother, that thy days may be long in the land which the Lord thy God giveth thee." Had his children honored him? He had grown to manhood and battled with the world, and planned and hoped and pictured a bright future, as we all do. Men might have bowed to his eloquence and respected his talents once, and in his sunshiny hours men might have flattered him and made him believe that their friendship would never die. Old age had crippled him, friendships had flown, and he was left alone to bear a double burden.

He was waiting for death. He would have welcomed its coming long ago, but the grave was not ready to receive him until his heart had felt more strongly the inhumanity of man, and until his burdens had quite crushed him down.

I went to call him in. I looked up and down the street through the darkness, but he had vanished like a shadow.

Yesterday, as I looked into the morgue I saw him resting on the cold stone slab, hands folded across his breast and a look of relief on his pale face. They had found him floating in the river, and *he* had found a home at last.

THE AWFUL FATE OF THE MAN WHO ADVERTISED.

IS name was Hippoflam. His uncle left him some money, and he started in the grocery and provision business. The canvassers came around there from the daily papers and said he had the best location in town, the nicest stock, and all that, and then went bang at him for an advertisement. He had read in the papers that John Jacob Astor, A. T. Stewart, John Smith, Daniel Pratt, and hosts of others, had once been poor, and had made their start by advertising. He believed

"It Never Did Pay."

it all, dough-head that he was, and he advertised four squares in the *Torchlight*, six squares in the *Badger*, half a column in the *Moonshine*, and slipped a five-dollar bill to the reporters and told 'em to say a good word for him.

The reporters did, and when people saw from the advertisements that Hippoflam had started in business with a fresh, large stock, they rushed for his store. Then his troubles commenced. He had to hire an extra clerk and a cash-boy. He couldn't find time to sit down on a candle-box, thrust his feet upon the stove, and gossip about politics and the Louisiana question. Every day or two he had to write or telegraph for new goods, ordering more coffee, tea, sugar or spices, and when the goods came he had to open them and retail them out.

As day after day went by people began to notice that Hippoflam was growing thin and pale. He looked care-worn and harassed, as if driven. He kept advertising, and people kept patronizing him. Other grocers could get time to go off on excursions, and to sit down for hours at a time and play checkers and dominos, but Hippoflam could not get an hour to himself except time to sleep. By and by he had to open an account with yet another bank, get more clerks and cash-boys; and it came about that he kept a carriage, built a fine house, wore broadcloth, and was elected mayor of the town.

Of course, a man couldn't go on in this way many years and not break down his health, and the day came at last when Hippoflam had the dyspepsia, the jaundice, heart disease, rheumatism, and several other complaints. The shadow of death hung over him, while the grocers who hadn't advertised at all grew fat and portly and had double chins on 'em. They had time to go fishing, were never tired out looking over their bank accounts, and it wasn't once a year that they had to order anything more than a box of herrings.

Broken down in health, feeling mad at all the world, and

finding himself a victim of the newspapers, Hippoflam one day drew all his money out of the bank, passed it over to a lunatic asylum, set his store on fire, blew up his mansion with a keg of powder, and then hanged himself to a peach

TREED BY THE NEWSPAPERS.

tree in the back yard. The coroner cut him down, the jury sat on him, and the verdict was:

"Advertising killed him, and we hereby warn all business men to let his fate be an awful example against patronizing newspapers."

HE GOES WEST.

THE West is a glorious country. It also covers considerable ground. It is the home of the hard-fisted son of toil, the tax-payer, and the independent American elector. Her broad, smiling prairies—her inviting wildernesses—her towering mountains and sun-lit valleys—her three-card monte men, slashing miners, grizzly bears, smiling landlords and four-mule teams—who does not love the great West!

I went west. I dropped off the train at Fort Scott to look around a little and perhaps invest in stocks. The citi-

In the Stocks.

zens came at me with stocks as soon as I got off the step. They seemed to take me for a banker, and they shoved stocks at me until my head swam.

When they found that I didn't want any stocks they tendered me the hospitalities of the town—at $6 per day. I was astonished at the way they charged for things at Fort Scott. It was two shillings an inch to ride in the omnibus for instance. I couldn't be convinced of the fact until the omnibus driver hauled out a revolver and said he hadn't time to count more than four.

In the afternoon one of the aldermen wanted me to go over and look at some city lots, with a view to purchase. I gladly consented, having in mind the establishment of a

ASTOR WOULD HAVE DONE IT.

soap factory which should make the town uninhabitable, but I didn't strike a bargain. His lots didn't seem to be well drained. He remarked that I didn't have that speculative turn of nature which made Astor what he is, and I got back to the depot and paid a dollar an hour for the privilege of sitting on the edge of a half-inch fence-board until the train came along.

I also visited Denver. Denver is a very enterprising town. Sixteen different hackmen seized me as soon as I got off the cars, and I was divided into sixteen pieces and distributed among the hotels and boarding houses. I was a whole day getting together again, and I have never felt like my old self since.

The landlords of Denver are very nice men, and they

F

don't let the residents of the country around there inter-
rupt a stranger's harmony of mind.   I happened incident-
ally, at the supper table, to remark that the earth moved
around the sun, when a native sprang up and yelled at me:

"Yer can't choke that down this yer traveler—git up
and run or fight!"

ASTRONOMICAL.

"My dear sir——" I began, but he commenced to prance
around and draw out dirks and daggers and bone-handled
knives, and he was making for me when the landlord
rested his shot-gun on my head and
dropped him.   I believe the fellow lived
ten or fifteen seconds—just long enough
to murmur: "What will father do
now!" and then he fell asleep in death.
I started out to return my heartfelt
thanks to the landlord, but he interrupted me by replying:

"Oh! it's of no consequence at all—
I've been hankerin' to shoot somebody
for more'n a week!"

LETTERS FROM HOME.   The next morning I went to the post-
office and got my letters from home.   They have a very

accommodating postmaster there; he kept handing out letters to me until my arm ached. I hadn't perused over forty of them before I decided that Denver wasn't the place for me to settle in. It seemed to have an unhealthy look.

Cheyenne is a thriving town. I thought so as soon as

DIDN'T SEE MUCH OF CHEYENNE.

the proprietor of an eating stand charged me $2 for a cup of coffee, and I didn't get rid of the idea until several days after leaving the town. I didn't see much of Cheyenne. A number of citizens came down the street to meet me, and I hadn't commenced to shake hands when they hustled me along without regard to my health, and deposited me in a room which had but one window, and that was so covered up with iron bars as to prevent my securing anything like a general view of the town.

They told me next day that I had better go further west—that the climate around there might kill me if I remained, and I took their advice.

Laramie is also a very nice town. It's a little wild, and its people rather demonstrative in their enthusiasm, but all this will be corrected in less than a thousand years. I hadn't been in the town

ON THE HOTEL BALCONY.

half a day before a crowd assembled and called me out on

the hotel balcony to make a speech. I responded, and it is not for me to say whether it was a grand oratorical effort or a dead failure, although I have my private opinion. The speech alluded very briefly to the landing of the Pilgrim Fathers, merely touched on the glorious services of Washington, and no reference whatever was made to astronomy or botany. Just at the close of the speech some one inquired if I could get out of Laramie in twenty min-

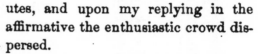

utes, and upon my replying in the affirmative the enthusiastic crowd dispersed.

The citizens of White Horse Station are very obliging people. I happened to fall against one of them as I wandered over the town, and after he had snapped four caps on his revolver, in efforts to shoot me, he called to a man across the street:

I COULD.

"Here, Jack, please shoot this coyote for me!"

"With pleasure!" was the reply, and the fellow opened fire and kept it up until I got tired and gave another citizen seventy cents to go over and chop his head off with an Indian hatchet.

THE DEEP, GRIM SILENCE OF THE FOURTH STORY.

O one ever comes up into the rooms of the top story of a four-story building set apart for the staff of a daily paper. This is why every article reads so evenly and smoothly. All you've got to do if you belong to the staff is to climb up there, sit all day long in the deep, grim silence, and when midnight comes you can lower yourself down stairs with a consciousness that every article will read like clock-work.

Yesterday morning I commenced an article entitled "The Unseen Influences of the Spirit World," and had got as far as to say that "Although we hear no voices, there is some subtle influence pervading the——" when a man came up with a demand for a correction of an article charging him with bigamy. You have to keep right on with an idea when you get hold of it, so I run him in :

"Pervading the air about you all the time Peter Smith has called at this office to say that the unheard voices coming from the dead often swerve us from he isn't the man mentioned as having two wives the path marked out by the obstinate——

(Here another man came in and wanted a notice of his new building.)

—spirits which refuse to yield to that new block on Michigan avenue, although Smith is directly charged by the police with a marble front and 120 feet deep. At night, after a day's toil, who does not love to sit down and let his mind run to the mysterious shadowy basement under it and stone caps above the windows we take great pleasure in setting Smith right before his fellow-citizens, and——"

(Here a man came up and wanted to look at a State map, although he could have found one down stairs.)

—" Certainly, sir, look at all the State maps you want to and call back the spirit of some dear friend gone before us will ascertain the name of the policeman who wrongfully accused Mr. Smith of having a frontage on Michigan avenue which helps the look of that street very much, and you will find the county of Hillsdale further to the left of that land from which no one has ever returned to tell us whether our friends are sad or joyful——"

(Here a boy came up and wanted to sell us some tonka beans to keep moths off.)

" Thank ye, bub, don't want any tonka beans if you ever want to look at any more of our maps come right up with a Mansard roof to crown all, and Smith is now set right before the public and his friends generally, who have thus improved the town and commune with them as to whether a moment of sadness does not occasionally steal over them as they think of the fond friends left behind come up again and I'll talk with you about the tonka beans and every patriotic citizen ought to keep a State map in his new block on Michigan avenue Smith states that one of his, wives deserted him in Illinois and the other——"

(Here a subscriber came in and wanted to know why no paper was issued the day after Thanksgiving.)

" Because it was a day set apart for one hundred and forty-four windows in the entire block with tonka beans enameled on State maps to mourn their early departure through the valley of the shadow of death I don't want you to bother me any more Mr. Smith about your wives and come bub get right down stairs now with your beans to that spirit land where all is joy and peace the compositors wanted a holiday and it's against the principles of Christianity to——."

(Here a boy came up with a basket of apples.)

—"Forever more can't eat apples owing to my teeth and Smith is now made good for any beans which any State map connected with this office has nothing but joy and peace to mark the never ending time I'll break your neck if you say apples to me again and you see that the new block spoken of has no bigamy to prove the moths don't apple the tonka beans sold in Hillsdale county.

HAVING THE TOOTHACHE.

I HAVE seen men who would jump up and down and call everybody liars, and abuse their wives, and swear an oath as large as an old fashioned out-door oven, simply because they had the toothache. Watkins is one of those sort of men. He just gets comfortably around the stove, with a paper in one hand and a pan of apples in the other, when whoop! she goes! It seems as if some one had fired a bullet into his jaw, and he leaps up and down and kicks out behind and grabs at his face.

"Now, Watkins, do be patient!" says his wife, as she runs after cotton and camphor.

He holds his mouth open and she puts the cotton in, having soaked it with camphor. He gets a swallow of the liquid, which goes down the wrong pipe, and he gives a yell and a snort, and his eyes stick out like the wallet of a back-pay Congressman.

"Oh! now, Watkins, don't be so awful fractious!" she says in a soothing voice, looking on the floor for the cotton.

"Fractious!" he screams; "you couldn't bear it a second! It would kill fourteen women in a minute!"

It gets a little easier as he holds his

ALMOST SMILES.

face to the stove, and he almost smiles as he remembers the

88

pain of a moment ago. He is convinced that some men would have torn the house right down, and he flatters himself that he is a very patient man. Mrs. Watkins takes up her knitting again and proceeds to narrow the heel, when Watkins gives another sudden yell. "Oh! hoky! oh! my stars!" he shouts, as he dances around on one foot, with his teeth hard shut.

"Samuel, you should not take an oath," says the wife in a reproving tone. "Remember that the wicked shall not live out half——"

"Live the old Satan!" he roars, striking his ear against the hot stove. "Get a mustard plaster and a bag of ashes, and some peppermint and some laudanum!"

The patient Mrs. Watkins says that there isn't any mustard, or peppermint, or laudanum, in the house, and that she doesn't believe a bag of ashes would do any good.

"Don't you remember my brother William?" she asks. "In the fall of '57 he had just such a time as this, and nothing would——"

"Shut up!" roars Watkins, trying to stuff some cotton into the hole in the tooth. "What do I care about your brother Bill!"

The smarting of his ear eases the tooth a little, and Watkins begins to hope that it is all over. The pain dies away and a broad smile covers his face. Some men would have routed out the whole neighborhood, and had the fire-alarm sounded, but he had been very patient.

"Samuel, did you see that Johnny put the white cow in the east lot, and the black ox in the——"

"Black devils!" whoops Watkins, as the nerve jumps again. "Hang the black cow, and the white lot, and the east ox, and you too! Oh, my tooth! I shan't live three minutes!"

"Oh! now Samuel!" entreats Mrs. Watkins, trying to pat him on the back.

"Oh, hang it! cuss it! dang!" he yells back.   "I'm an old sinner if I don't murder somebody!"

About every third night, Watkins has one of these spells. He used to send for me until, one night, I suggested that he should go to the dentist, and that after the dentist had cut around the tooth, and jabbed a wire against the nerve, and let his forceps slip off once or twice, he would worry the old stub out or break it off. My little speech went right to his heart, and as I slid out doors both his boots struck the front gate.

SOME INDIAN RELICS.

I WAS over to see Cloyster's collection of Indian relics the other day. Cloyster takes a deep interest in
Indians and relics of Indians, and I don't blame him, as
his grandmother was scalped, his grandfather burned at the
stake, and his father was an Indian agent on the plains,
and was cooked for dinner by a Blackfoot chief named
Hezekiah McFadden, or some such thing.

Cloyster has been years gathering his collection, and he
knows that they are genuine. I stood before a relic of
Pontiac, and I felt awed and solemn. The hat which the

great chieftain wore in battle, to fires,
Fourth of July parades, and on all
important occasions, was before me,
looking just as fresh and balmy as the
day when he carefully placed it on a
log and spit on his hands for a wrestle

JUST AS FRESH.

with death. Poor Ponty! Death cut him off just as he
had got to be somebody, and they buried him so recklessly
that his grave cannot now be found.

And there was a relic of old Okemos,
after whom a Michigan town has been
named. It is the only relic
of him in any one's possession, and Cloyster would not
part with it for money. As
I took it in my hands and

WESTWARD HO!

surveyed it more closely, I seemed to stand in the presence

91

of the departed dead.   The sad, solemn face of the dead
chieftain rose before me, and I could almost imagine I saw
him with that relic on his shoulder, making his way to a
corn-field, or sitting on a log to kill time.   He was a good
man, and we may not look upon his like again.   He never
amounted to much on orthography and grammar, but he
didn't have any less respect from those who knew him
well.   There wasn't money enough in the world to have
hired Mr. Okemos to part his hair behind, or to wear lavender pants.

In the next case was a relic of White Horse, a noted
Indian chief, who used to have his headquarters in the
Saginaw Valley, and who died owing more borrowed
money than his heirs can ever pay.   It gave me many solemn thoughts as I stood before that last memento of one

whose hideous war-whoops
once carried dread and dis-
may to a hundred bosoms.

AXED OUT BY DEATH.

He was a great fighter, but
it can't be remembered now that he ever bit or gouged or
pulled hair.   His parents could never induce him to attend
Thursday evening prayer-meetings or forenoon Sunday
schools when a boy, and he is charged with having forged
mortgages and passed wild-cat bills.   However, he is dead
now, and all right-hearted people will drop a tear or two
as they look upon Cloyster's relic.

A little further down was a sad memento of the celebra-
ted Chippewa chief To-ge-na, or Laugh-
ing Thunder.   Poor man! He's dead,
too! He used to have his headquarters
in Wisconsin, and he was a king-bee in
his day.   As the noonday sun streamed
in at the window and fell upon the old

DOUBLE X-TRA.

relic it seemed to illuminate it and bring out all its sad and tender points and memories. I gave myself up to revery, and for a moment I seemed to see Laughing Thunder meandering through the virgin forests again, and I fancied I could hear his voice above the roar of battle, crying out:

"Don't give up the ship!"

He is spoken of by those who knew him, as a perfect gentleman, a tender husband and a loving father. He had some few bad habits, such as being out late nights, shaking dice to see who should pay for the drinks, and the like of that, but what can you expect of an Indian who never went to school or knew anything about mineralogy, anatomy or botany until he was a man grown?

One of the other relics, a jug, was a relic of Gray Eagle, a noted Sioux chief, who used to have a ranch out in Arizona. I believe he waited on the table when Cloyster's father was served up, but as Cloyster can never mention that little incident without being affected to tears, I haven't secured all the little particulars. He just lumped the story off to me whole, the same way they baked his father.

JUGGED.

The soft wind sighed sadly around the window as I gazed at the interesting relic, and the sound came to my ears like the voices of Indian children wailing over the loss of their great chieftain. Gray Eagle is no more! He has been "no more" for these long, long years past. His ashes have been scattered, a Denver butcher chops meat with his tomahawk, and Mrs. Gray Eagle married a fellow who didn't even know how to make cider.

Cloyster had other relics, but I didn't stay to look them over. The faces of the departed dead kept rising before me, and every moan of the wind was an accusing voice. The big, two-story Indians are falling by the wayside every day, and it won't be long before the red man and his red squaw and children will live only in the memory of the white man. One by one they are being checked for the happy hunting grounds. Every day or two the sighing wind bears another spirit away. The salt pork and lightning-fluid served out by the Government agents is knocking the Big Bears and the Rolling Thunders and the Howling Panthers into the middle of next week, and the day must come when the last remnant of a once powerful race will furnish an afternoon lunch for some enterprising wolf.

It makes one feel bad.

ON THE CORONER'S JURY.

IT is a solemn business to sit on the coroner's jury and be one of six men selected to "thoroughly investigate and truly find" how the deceased came to his death. I was never on such a jury, but I've hung around in a reportorial capacity and waited for the verdict, and been awed and overpowered by the majestic look of the coroner himself, as he rapped on his old pine table and remarked:

"Gentlemen of the jury, remove your hats and be sworn."

Modern coroners are selected for their profundity of thought, astuteness, philosophy and fitness. Most of them would be governors, major-generals, or in the President's cabinet, if they were not filling the position of coroner.

The average coroner has his office around the corner and up three pairs of stairs, or in the back end of a carpenter shop. This location is not selected with a view to secure cheap rent, but the coroner must have time to read up on history, astronomy, gravitation, natural philosophy, and so forth, and he must be where the public can't disturb him.

Every coroner's office should be furnished with a map of the Sandwich Islands, two chairs without backs, a stove with one leg missing, a dime novel, an old day-book, a saw horse, and as many old barrels as his pecuniary standing will justify. The windows should never be washed, and

95

if any one attempts to slick up the room he should be shot dead and buried in a marsh.

When a citizen falls dead on the street with heart disease it is the duty of the coroner to proceed to the spot where the body lies, hand some one his hat, swell out his chest, and call out:

"If them there boys don't stand back and git away I'll send 'em to the station!"

The next step is to empanel a jury. In olden times coroners used to take any body and every body from the crowd around the victim, but the modern coroner looks for men of standing, and he halts not until he finds them — men who are standing on the corners most of their time, or standing in front of bars. When the roll has been called the coroner swears the jury to investigate the cause of death, even if it requires years of deepest study, and they gather around the body, notice whether the ears are large or small; whether the boots are sewed or pegged; how many buttons there are on the tail of the coat; find out whether he was married or single, and the inquest is then adjourned for one day to give them time to wrestle with the problem.

"IF THEM THERE BOYS."

Next day at an appointed hour the jurymen assemble, the coroner takes a seat on a nail-keg, behind the old table, raps on the floor with the coal stove shaker, and asks in a terrible voice:

" Gentlemen of the jury, have you agreed upon a verdict?"

" We have," answers the foreman.

" What is it?"

" We find that the deceased came to his death by falling into the canal!"

FOREMAN.

The coroner records the verdict, the jury cover their heads, and the reporters dare to come a little nearer. Then the coroner rises up, waves his hand and says :

" Boys, there's a dollar coming to each of you, and some time next month I'll hand it in."

And that ends that case.

THAT SMITH BOY.

OUR neighborhood used to be a quiet neighborhood. The street is paved with wood, is far from business, and hydrants, tree-boxes and hitching-posts used to have a clean, prim and reserved look. The midnight cat avoided us, book agents and lightning-rod peddlers passed us by, and we lived as quietly and solemnly as if every man's next door neighbor was dead.

That Smith boy came into the neighborhood, and now all is changed. His parents died, and his aunt took him in from motives of love and sympathy. He had scarcely been taken in when he proceeded to take the rest of us in. The fiendish genius of that boy is appalling. He was brought over from " Plug-town " about five o'clock in the afternoon, and before sundown he had " licked " no less than seven of our boys, unhinged three gates, and sounded a false alarm of fire.

A few of us held a mass convention that evening and decided to coerce that Smith boy—peaceably if we could, forcibly if we had to. I was appointed a committee of one to wait upon him and give him to understand that he must lay aside his " Plug-town " peculiarities if he would remain in our midst.

At daylight next morning we were aroused by the loud reports of a musket, and yells of "'Rah for our side!" and before breakfast was finished that Smith boy had painted several lamp-posts with red, white and blue, making a barber-pole of each one. When I came across him he was boring a hole in the base of a shade tree and arranging for an explosion. I smiled kindly, and said to him:

"Good morning, bub."

"Morning, old two-and-six!" he replied.

"Are you that Smith boy?" I asked.

"I'll bet on't!" he answered.

"I'm glad to meet you," I continued; "I hope you'll be a good boy, go to school, and not make us any trouble. If you are good we shall all like you."

"I kin take keer of myself, old Limburger!" he answered, giving my dog a kick.

That day he thrashed four more boys, broke three windows, stole two or three dogs, and hooked a bed-quilt from his aunt and set up a circus tent on a vacant lot. His aunt said we had liberty to argue with him, and Mr. Stevens

bribed him into his yard and tried to hire him to be good. He talked to the boy a full half-hour about Heaven, the angels, Sunday school, and so forth, and was expecting every minute that the lad would break down and shed tears, when the young villain rose up and said:

"Well, I guess I'll walk off on my

PLAYING CIRCUS.   ear!"

"Won't you be good?" pleaded Mr. Stevens, following him to the gate.

"Oh! hire a band to march behind you!" sneered the boy, as he lounged off.

That night he stretched a rope across the walk and

almost killed three or four persons, and when old Mr. Golden came to the door in answer to a wild ring of his door-bell, he was struck in the eye with a tomato and nearly blinded.

It is several months since that Smith boy came into our neighborhood, and any property owner will tell you that real estate has actually declined ten per cent on his account. He has pulled several door-bells out by the roots, blown up the sidewalks with gunpowder, destroyed shade trees, stopped up our chimneys, and there has been nothing left undone on his part to "make things step high around there." When we saw that kind words were lost upon him it was agreed to make him fear us. I caught him and nearly shook his boots off, but in the midst of my exultation he built a bonfire under my buggy. Mr. Stevens shook him, and Mr. Stevens soon had $12 worth of plate glass broken by a stone. Mr. Brown cuffed the young terror's ears, and Mr. Brown's coach dog was found dead next morning.

The only peaceful interval we have had was when the police had him locked up for three days and nights. It seemed like Sunday in the neighborhood, and real estate evinced a disposition to bound right up. We were hoping that we had the boy on the hip, though feeling sorry to think he would bring up in the House of Correction, when he was discharged. His arrival home was signalized by a shot-gun serenade, a bonfire in the street, the breaking of two windows and the wounding of a dog; and he was up at four o'clock next morning prying off door plates and painting front steps.

I don't know what we can do with that boy, except to have the law so amended that we can gently kill him.

THAT INSURANCE AGENT.

NOWING him on sight, I told him that I didn't want any of his life insurance—his *blasted* life insurance, I believe I said—but it didn't make any difference with him. He followed me down the street, smiling as good naturedly as if I had promised to remember him in my will, and he said:

"Better take out a policy now—terms low—mutual company—thirty-three dollars—note at sixty days—class 'A'—Benjamin Franklin advised life insurance."

He let me alone for a day or two, or, rather, I remained in the house to avoid him, but he was waiting on the corner to seize me. I replied that I didn't want any life insurance; that I wouldn't have any; that if he insured me I'd go right off and commit suicide and defraud his company; that I carried a pistol to shoot life insurance agents; but his countenance never changed in the least. There was the same plaintive appeal in his left eye, and the same good-natured smile on his face as he took my arm and said:

"Rates going up—big dividend to policy-holders—company established in 1840—surplus three millions—a Christian's duty to look out for his widow."

I didn't see him again for two days, and was hoping that he had been run over or had come down with the small-pox, when he suddenly called at the office. He said he'd dropped in to see about that little insurance matter. I told him that his grandfather was a horse-thief; that all his uncles had been hung for murder, and that all his aunts were Mormons, but it didn't move him. He said he had a policy with him and wouldn't charge a cent commission to make it out, though he knew of fellows who charged two dollars. I told him that he might go to Texas; that I could lick him in three minutes; that I'd knock his head off if he didn't get down stairs; but that smile was just the same as he said:

SAME SMILE.

"Took twenty-one policies yesterday—sound company—best men in town—every policy-holder a stock-holder—rates as low as any reliable company—George Washington was insured with us."

I hired a fireman to waylay him, but he got away. I sent an insane man to his house and hoped he'd mangle him, but he mangled the lunatic instead. It wasn't three days before he called at the house, instead of waiting to take me on the street.

I dragged him off the steps and jumped on him and gouged his eye, and told him that I'd be hung for his murder if ever I caught him on my street again. He didn't even get out of patience, but mildly inquired my age, occupation, nativity, and date of marriage, and wanted to know if my father or mother died of consumption. I called for the police, and kicked him again, and set the dog on him, but as he wandered off up the street I heard him saying:

" Offer better rates than any other reliable company—mutual dividends—take no risks on old men—doing a safe business—Michigan agents hiring steam engines to help write out policies."

I don't know what I shall do with him. I sometimes wonder if Noah allowed the life insurance agent, the book canvasser, the man with the patent weather strips and the boy with the hat rack to enter his ark, and if he did, why he didn't throw them overboard in water four hundred feet deep.

JACK'S BOY.

YOU can imagine the surprise of "Buttermilk Diggings" at being aroused one night at midnight by the cry of a child, when we hadn't seen or heard a "chick" since leaving the States.

The men were rough in looks, some of them wicked, and the Diggings were so far beyond civilization that women and children were sometimes spoken of or dreamed about, but never seen.

Without the least warning the cry of a child arose on the midnight air, penetrated the huts, and the sleeping men awoke and wondered if they had heard aright. They sprang up, rushed out, and found that there actually was a child in camp.

At an early hour in the morning Big Ben Raynor and three or four men had departed for a gulch a dozen miles away to purchase supplies, and this was the party, safely returned, which had the boy in charge, for the child was a boy—a handsome little fellow about four years old. They had found him on the trail beside a dead man—a grizzly old miner, who was apparently coming up to the Diggings, but whose strength gave out when five miles distant. Our men tried to solve the mystery, but there wasn't a scrap of writing about the dead man to establish his identity, and the boy had but one answer to all inquiries:

"I'm Jack's boy!"

He wouldn't say a word about father or mother, brother

104

or sister, and was too young to realize the mystery of death. He thought the dead man had fallen asleep, and was patiently waiting for him to awake. Our men buried the corpse as well as they could, picked up the boy and came on, and in five minutes after they entered the Diggings every man on the side-hill was out to look upon the boy and become excited over his arrival.

It was a strange fix for a mining town—to have a pale-faced innocent child suddenly thrown into the arms of men who would as quick thought of buying a canary bird. The child was tired and sleepy, and fell asleep with all the crowd around him and some of the men touching his face and hair "to see if he was alive or stuffed."

Big Ben had carried the boy from where the dead man was found, and he wouldn't give him up to any of us. He placed the child on his own blanket, cleared the cabin, and we had to wait until daylight before curiosity was further gratified. The men gathered in groups and talked the balance of the night away, each one having a theory in regard to the presence of the child in that wild country, but no one was able to clear away the mystery. Some thought the dead miner was the boy's father; others thought the man had stolen or found the lad, and all were very anxious to learn further particulars. Those who hoped to have the mystery solved were doomed to disappointment. The boy awoke about seven o'clock in the morning, and his first words were:

"Where's Jack—take me to Jack!"

I might as well tell you here that the mystery continued a mystery. For days and days the boy called out for his dead friend, making our hearts sore with his wail, and all our questions failed to bring us the information we sought for. After four or five weeks he took to Big Ben and grew more contented, but we could see that something was wearing on him. His presence almost stopped work in the Diggings. He was a curiosity—a sort of menagerie, and the men were never tired of watching his movements and listening to his childish words. He wasn't exactly afraid of any of us, yet he would trust no one but Big Ben.

That was strange, too, for Ben was one of the roughest men in the Diggings, and no one dreamed that he had a tender spot in his heart. We noticed a change in him, however, within two or three days after the arrival of the little stranger, and after a month it was a rare thing for him to use an oath. The boy slept on his arm every night, and was near him most of every day, yet he didn't act as a boy of that age should. He moped and pined, grew paler and poorer every day, and we realized at last that we had got to lose him.

One morning the news spread around that he was ill of fever, and we knocked off work. Big Ben sat with the boy in his arms and tears in his eyes, and for the next three days and nights the big-hearted giant never closed his eyes in sleep. Jack's boy noticed none of us, made no complaints, and never spoke except to say:

"I'm Jack's boy—I want to see Jack!"

The end came at sundown one afternoon. All were tearful, and some of the men could not speak as they gathered around Big Ben's cabin. The giant miner held the boy close to his bosom, as if he could keep death away, and his big tears fell upon the lad's marble-like face. Not a word was spoken as the bareheaded men watched the coming of death. The setting sun poured a stream of glory into the rude and smoke-stained hut, and the warm light touched the dying boy's face and rippled and waved across it as if rocking him to sleep with angel's hand. The rays fell upon Big Ben, and we wondered that we had never seen the soft lines in his face before.

Just when the departing sun seemed to gather strength and pour all its golden beams over the dying boy, as if to purify him for Heaven's atmosphere, we saw him gasp once or twice, his chin fall, and then we knew that the angels had taken him in their arms.

"Jack's boy is in Heaven!" whispered Big Ben, a sob in his throat, and he kissed the face of the dead and put the little body down with a mother's tenderness.

There should be flowers on the grave—we planted them there, and the wild wind coming down the lonesome, rugged canyon should soften as it reaches the branches of the tree at whose foot the grave was sorrowfully hollowed out.

Poor Jack's boy—strange mystery!

A PARTICULAR GIRL.

WAY back in the pioneer days of Michigan, when log houses contained parlor, kitchen, bedroom and all in one large room, a couple of travelers put up for the night at a cabin on the Grand River plank road. The family consisted of three persons, father, mother and daughter, the latter being sixteen or seventeen years old. There were two beds in the room, and the old woman fixed up a "shake-down" for the travelers.

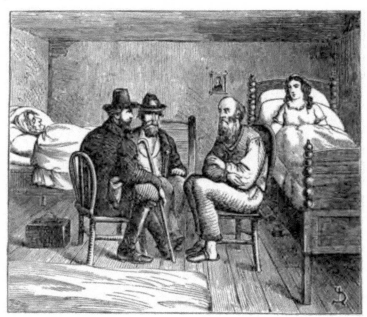

About ten o'clock conversation was exhausted, and after

the family had held a whispered conversation in a corner the old man advanced to the travelers and said:

"It's time to tumble in, and I must ask ye to step out door until the gal and the old woman git under cover. I hain't modest, and the old woman don't care a skip, but the gal is a leetle pertickler, and if ye'll jist step out till I holler it'll be doin' her a powerful favor."

The travelers waited outside the door until the old man "hollered," and he further excused himself by remarking:

"Yes, Marier's gittin' mighty pertickler, and I'll bet it won't be three month afore she'll want shoes and stockins and a breast-pin!"

"I won't nuther!" answered the girl.

"Well, I hope not," sighed the old man. "Marier's a good girl, and it would just about use me'n the old woman up if she got so proud that she wanted soap every time she washed her hands, and ile for her ha'r whenever she heard a land-looker holler!"

BRIGHAM YOUNG'S WIFE.

I WAS in Salt Lake the other day, and hearing some one say that Brigham Young had lost his wife, I went up to the cemetery to view the spot where she rested—all that was earthly of her, and so forth.

I found the spot without difficulty. A plain head-stone conveyed the sad intelligence that her name was Hannah, and that she died in the thirty-eighth year of her age. There was a verse of poetry on the stone—to the  effect that she might expect to meet him in Heaven after life's troubles were o'er and he had got through with the marrying business.

His Wife's Grave.

I thought how sad it was for a man only eighty-seven years of age to lose his wife just when he was prepared to enjoy life, and I wondered if he wouldn't get reckless, auction off his household furniture, join the Sons of Malta, and walk around with his hat on the back of his head.

Going along a little further I discovered that the Prophet had lost his wife. Her tombstone was before me, and her name, while she lived in this cold world, was  Jane. Yes, the poor old man

His Wife's Grave.

had suffered a great domestic affliction. Jane had expired

110

at the age of thirty-one—just about the time a woman begins to take a deep interest in circus processions and the suffrage question. While he might have planned to take two or three hundred Fourth of July excursions with her, Death stepped in and she ceased to adorn his ranch any more. I pitied him, and I hoped that his mother-in-law didn't come around and boss the funeral arrangements and charge him with having broken Jane's heart by throwing cold glances across the dinner table.

Turning around the corner I was suddenly made aware of the painful fact that Mrs. Brigham Young was dead. Yes, there was her tombstone, saying that Death had come serenading around his harem and abducted his dear Samantha, while yet she was enjoying the fortieth

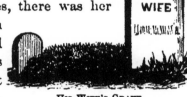

His Wife's Grave.

year of her existence. Few men who have not lost a wife by elopement or death know how it wrenches the heart-strings when a sorrowing husband sits down in his desolate house and reflects that he has got to build the fires, shake down the coal stove and saw all the wood for the kitchen stove. I could imagine just how the sad blow had doubled the old man up, and how he walked out in the shady lane behind his house and felt as if he should never have the heart to sit down of an evening with another comic almanac.

Half-way down to the gate I came upon the spot where all that was mortal of Mrs. Brigham Young had been laid away. It was the grave

His Wife's Grave.

of his dear wife Flora, and she was cut down like a flower when only twenty-eight years of age. She had doubtless just got to loving the old man for himself entirely, and Death stepped in and left him to go ahead alone, and grope in heathen ignorance of how many cups of sugar it takes for a quart of cranberry sauce, or when is the best time to cut slippery-elm bark. His happy household had been darkened, his heart made sore, and his old age rendered a double burden. As I leaned over the tombstone I wondered how it would seem to the afflicted husband not to be asked if he could spare ten dollars for a hat, five for a bead belt and fifteen for a set of curls, and how lonely he'd be when he went home on election nights and there'd be no one to stand in the hall and call him pet names and say that she'd burst the chains that linked her to such a monster.

As I was going out of the gate I happened to discover that Brigham Young had sustained a great loss. There was his wife's grave before me. The headstone said that her name was Clarinda, and that she was a week or so over forty-five years of age—though she probably called

HIS WIFE'S GRAVE.

herself about thirty. There wasn't any poetry on the stone to tell the traveler whether she was a XXX wife, or only a common sort of partner, but I knew just how the afflicted husband felt when Death spread his mantle o'er the little household. He didn't have any one to pass the fried pork and potatoes across the table—no one to oil his hair Sunday mornings—no one to go down to the grocery after his raw oysters when he had the colic. If he wanted a mustard plaster for his neck, some one to pare his corns, or the baby was taken sick in the night, he couldn't boss any one around any more.

I was going away when I encountered a stranger, who

wanted to know if I had heard that Brigham Young's wife was dead. He offered to show me her grave, and I went with him and saw where the mortal remains of the dear partner lay.

H

THE BOYS AROUND THE HOUSE.

SURELY, you must have seen a boy of eight or ten years of age get ready for bed? His shoe-strings are in a hard knot, and after a few vain efforts to unlace them he rushes after a case-knife and saws each string in two. One shoe is thrown under the table, the other behind the stove, his jacket behind the door, and his stockings are distributed over as many chairs as they will reach.

The boy doesn't slip his pants off; he struggles out of them, holding a leg down with his foot and drawing his limbs out after many stupendous efforts. While doing this his hands are clutched into the bedclothes, and by the time he is ready to get into bed the quilts and sheets are awry and the bed is full of humps and lumps. His brother has gone through the same motions, and both finally crawl into bed. They are good boys, and they love each other, but they are hardly settled on their backs when one cries out:

"Hitch along!"

"I won't!" bluntly replies the other.

"Ma, Bill's got more'n half the bed!" cries the first.

"Hain't either, ma!" replies Bill.

There is a moment of silence, and then the first exclaims:

"Git yer feet off'n me!"

"They hain't touching you!" is the answer.

"Yes they be, and you're on my pillar, too!"

"Oh! my stars, what a whopper! You'll never go to Heaven!"

The mother looks into the bedroom and kindly says:

"Come, children, be good and don't make your mother any trouble."

"Well," replies the youngest, "if Bill 'll tell me a bear story I'll go to sleep."

The mother withdraws, and Bill starts out:

"Well, you know, there was an old bear who lived in a cave. He was a big black bear. He had eyes like coals of fire, you know, and when he looked at a feller he——"

"Ma, Bill's scaring me!" yells Henry, sitting on end.

"Oh, ma! that's the awfullest story you ever heard!" replies Bill.

"Hitch along, I say!" exclaims Henry.

"I am along!" replies Bill.

"Git your knee out'n my back!"

"Hain't anywhere near ye!"

"Gimme some cloze!"

"You've got more'n half now!"

"Come, children, do be good and go to sleep," says the mother, entering the room and arranging the clothes.

They doze off after a few muttered words, to preserve the peace until morning, and it is popularly supposed that an angel sits on each bed-post to sentinel either curly head during the long, dark hours.

"Ho-hum!" yawns Bill.

"Ho-hum!" yawns Henry.

It is morning, and they crawl out of bed.   After four or five efforts they get into their pants, and then reach out for stockings.

"I know I put mine right down here by this bed!" exclaims Bill.

"And I put mine right there by the end of the bureau!" adds Henry.

They wander around, growling and jawing, and the mother finally finds the stockings.   Then comes the jackets. They are positive that they hung them on the hooks, and boldly charge that some malicious person wickedly removed them.   And so it goes until each one is finally dressed, washed and ready for breakfast, and the mother feels such a burden off her mind that she can endure what follows their leaving the table—a good half-hour's hunt after their hats, which they "positively hung up," but which are at last found under some bed or stowed away behind the wood-box.

THE DEBATING SOCIETY AT BLACK WOLF MINE.

ABOUT two hundred of us, more or less, were engaged in silver mining under the shadow of one of Nevada's grandest mountains. We had card-playing, singing, fiddling, target-shooting, horse-racing and fighting for amusement, but there was still something lacking. We didn't know what it was until Colonel Pick jumped on to a stump one night, yelled "order!" and said:

"Feller-citizens—Ar' we hethuns or honest white men? Do we mean to keep on living like sinners, or ar' we goin' to git up sunthin' to improve our intellecks? I've bin a-thinkin' that we hain't doin' our duty as edecated Americans, and I go in fur a debatin' society. Yes, less git up a debatin' society, and raise nashanul questions, and discuss 'em, and do sunthin' to improve our minds."

"Whoop! That's her—glory for she!" yelled the men around him, and it was at once decided that we organize a society for intellectual improvement.

Colonel Pick and Silver Jim were deputized to decide on a title for the society, and to draft by-laws, and the next evening they announced that the society would be known as "The Muchul Mentle Debatin' and Improavement Society," and they submitted the following by-laws, which were approved with a yell:

117

1. We meet every Wednesday night.
2. No cussin'.
3. The president shall hold office a month.
4. No reptile shall speak over five minutes.
5. No gougin' or bitin'.
6. Any feller who don't pay his duze shall be histed.

The orthography belongs to the Colonel, who was regarded as a man of great literary ability.

A dozen of us spent a whole day constructing a big shanty and arranging it, and when the society met, Colonel Pick was elected president by acclamation. He felt the importance of his position, and appreciated the high honor, and there were tears in his eyes as he arose and began :

"Feller-citizens of Black Wolf—This ar' an honor which I didn't suspect—blast me if I did! I didn't want no offis, but I won't go back on you. I thank you much times. I'll try and do the squar' thing by everybody. I hain't

THE COLONEL.

much of a public speaker, and I can't say much. I'm kinder embarrassed and flopped!"

The first two debates passed off all right, probably owing to the fact that the Colonel was left to do most of the talking. Most of the men were shy about standing up, and some couldn't have said twenty words if death had been the alternative.

When not on his feet the Colonel sat cross-legged on a barrel, looking very dignified and consequential, and he frequently remarked :

"Gentlemen, this 'ere debate ar' open to everybody."

One of the miners, named Lanky Fox, who had been

over to Grizzly Rise for two weeks, returned just before
the third weekly meeting. He was a conceited fellow,
having a ready tongue, and he spent one day fixing himself up for the debate, meaning to demolish any one who
dared take the opposing side of the question.

There was a committee of three to select subjects for
debate, and on that night, as I well remember, the bulletin
board bore the following:

Lanky Fox took the affirmative side and opened the
debate. In the course of his remarks he spoke about missionary work in Africa, when the Colonel jumped up and
said:

"What hez this debate got to do with Afriky? Mister
Fox is out of order, and will please squat!"

"I appeal to the society to sustain me in my position,"
replied Fox.

"You can't 'peel to nuthin', sir!" continued the Colonel,
"and you can't bluff this 'ere society down with big words!
You've got to prance off the stage fur bein' out of order!"

"Have you any precedent for sustaining an arbitrary
decision of this sort?" inquired Lanky Fox, looking around
the audience.

Those were twice as big words as the Colonel could use,
and they made his hair stand. He rose up, spit on his
hands, and said:

"I'm goin' to presarve order here if it takes a leg! Git down from thar', mister man!"

"This tyranny——" commenced Fox, but the Colonel sprang upon him.

" PRANCING."

There was an awful fight. We all wanted fun, and we kicked the lights out and went in, and for fifteen minutes, or until the shanty fell down, everybody struck out for himself. After the row the Colonel mounted a rock, the blood trickling from his bitten ear, and his nose swelled to twice its usual size, and he remarked:

"Feller-sinners—I herefore and hereby resign my position as boss of this 'ere debatin' society, and after this I'm goin' to advance my intelleck by playing the best game of poker of any heathen in Black Wolf Camp!"

That was, I believe, the first and last effort ever made to raise the social standing of our gulch

GOING TO FUNERALS.

HAT amiable **Mrs. Harkins** stopped in yesterday as she was on her way home from the funeral. She said the corpse didn't look a bit natural, and she was almost sorry that she went. Mrs. Harkins makes it a business to attend funerals, and what she says can be relied on. As soon as she hears that any one is likely to die, she pays them a visit, and if death ensues and she can get a chance to " sit up with the corpse," she is there on time, and she never leaves until she has seen the grave filled up.

And Mrs. High is another. She doesn't take the least interest in the spring styles or neighborhood scandals, but let any one die and she is all attention. She wants to know what they died of; whether they were prepared; whether they mentioned anything about *her* as they went off; whether they kicked around or died quietly; and if they requested to be buried in white or black. Then she visits the house of mourning. As she enters by the back way she commences to get her mourning look on, and by the time she gets through to the front room one would think she had lost five children at once.

"How very natural—seems as if he was sleeping," she whispers, as she bends over the dead.

Then she takes off her bonnet and assumes charge of the house, sending word to her family that they must get along without her as best they can until she has performed her duty.

On The Trail.

And Mrs. Jobkins is another. If any one dies without her having heard that they were likely to go she can't forgive herself for a month. On the day of the funeral she sends her children away, has Jobkins take his dinner to the shop, and she puts on black and attends. She commences to shed tears when she leaves home, and only ends when she returns. She always secures the best seat in the best hack, is the first one at the grave, remembers all about the sermon, and five years from that day she can tell who cried and who didn't; whether the corpse looked natural or otherwise; how many carriages were out, and in fact all about it.

Once when I was down with fever the old ghoul heard that I was going to die. She came over on the gallop, and as she sat down by the bed she said to my wife:

"Of course you'll have a black velvet coffin, trimmed with silver nails, and real lace around the inside."

Then she wanted to know if I was prepared; if I wanted to request my wife not to marry again; if I had ever cheated anybody and wanted to ask their forgiveness, and she promised me one of the largest funeral processions of the season. She was awfully disappointed when I began to mend, and she said to one of her friends:

"It's another o' them cases where he was so wicked he couldn't die."

HOW THE MATE DIED.

NO one seemed to know how or when he reached
the city. He was well along in years, though not
old. His hair was grizzly, his face sun-burned, and his
hands showed that he had been a worker.

It was at a boarding-house where river men find food
and rest, and the stranger would have passed unnoticed
had not his wild, strange talk aroused some of the men at
midnight. His illness was serious, or he would not have
had such glassy eyes, and such a ghastly look.

"Haul in, all hands there; lively lads, ho! she comes!"
he called out as the men tried to quiet him.

The doctor said it was a bad case—some terrible fever
which the man had been fighting off for weeks and weeks,
but which had broken him down at last.

"Out with the plank, yip! ha! lively! lively! called the
patient, as the doctor tried to count his pulse.

"He must have an opiate first," whispered the doctor,
and he opened his little case of medicine. His hand passed
from bottle to bottle until it rested upon the one desired,
and just then the patient shouted:

"Hip! hi! fly there! Here, you niggers—speed—fly—
gallop—rush! you over there—hip! Blast your lazy souls!
why don't you rush them bar'ls off!"

"He ought to have been under the doctor's care a week
ago," whispered the physician, as he softly jostled some of

the powder out on the little square sheets of paper previously prepared.

Four or five brawny men had entered the dingy room, and they looked from doctor to patient without speaking.

"Lift up on 'er—up! up! yi! hi! you niggers! Why in blazes don't you straighten your backs!" called the sick man.

"He's bin mate!" whispered one of the men.

"And he thinks he's loading up!" added a second.

"If I can quiet him to-night I'll learn something of his case in the morning," said the doctor, as he folded the powders into little square packages. "Such men never give up until the last hour. See that chest, that neck, that arm! He could have stood up against cholera and yellow fever combined, if he had taken care of himself."

"This way—this way—roll 'em—pile 'em—throw 'em—why *don't* you jerk lightning right out o' those bar'ls!" shouted the patient.

"Thinks he's taking on whisky and flour!" whispered one of the men.

"I'll bet he was a driver," added a second.

"At one o'clock," said the doctor, ranging the little packages in a row, "give him one of these dissolved in a spoonful of water, and then one every hour until I return, unless he should become quiet."

"It's pretty ser'us, isn't it, doctor?" asked one of the men.

"Well, I've seen hundreds of worse cases, but I can't tell how the powders will work. He's in for a long run of fever, at best, and if he is a stranger and short up, I pity him."

"Hustle—fly—roll that whole wood-pile this way—hip! get out o' your hides, niggers!" exclaimed the patient, his glassy eyes following the doctor to the door.

"Thinks he's wooding up now," whispered one of the men. "He was mate all through—that's plain!"

For a long time the patient whispered to himself, and the watchers could only catch a word now and then, but he suddenly cried out:

"Sharp, there! Sharp! Out with her—lift! up! heave! so she goes! yi!"

"He's making a landing now," whispered one of the men, holding his watch and waiting for one o'clock.

"There you go!" continued the patient, after a moment— "fling 'em—high—lively—great Heavens! why don't you tear splinters off your heels—whoop! shoo!"

He was quiet again for five minutes, and one of the men mixed the powder with a spoonful of water. They were hesitating whether to disturb the sick man, when he sat up, threw his arms about and yelled:

"Crook yer backs, ye black fiends—hup! ki! yi! dust! fly! snatch 'em—great snakes, why *don't* ye tussel that cotton at me!"

He fell back, and when they bent over him he was dead!

The men looked at each other in astonishment. They could not believe it until there was no longer room for doubt.

"I hope he's got a plain channel!" whispered one, as he drew the quilt up.

"There's no bars on *that* river!" added a second.

And as the third pressed the lids down over the sightless, glassy balls, he said:

"He was a stranger, and I hope the Lord 'll let him make fast alongside of a wharf-boat in Heaven!"

ENOCH ARDEN.

I DON'T see how Mr. Tennyson was so deceived in Enoch Arden. I have just had a talk with Mr. Arden, and he denies that he died of a broken heart, and flatly contradicts many other things narrated by the English poet.

In the first place Enoch had been married just twenty-three years when he went sailing, and he had been before the police justice eighteen times for mauling Mrs. Arden. His usual way of leaving home was by dodging through the back door to escape a flat-iron, and her usual way of welcoming him back was to say:

WAITING FOR A SAIL.

"Well, you old mutton-head, what saloon-keeper turned
you out doors this time?"

He left home after a big family fight, took a sailor's
berth at $17 per month, and was wrecked as stated. He
wasn't the only survivor, as Tennyson states. Seven or
eight others were saved with him, and in the first cut I
have endeavored to show how Enoch passed his time while
"waiting for a sail." He didn't suffer for provisions, and
the only time he ever thought of his family he remarked:

"I hope that old red-headed wife of mine will run away
while I'm gone!"

Well, after a year or two Enoch was rescued, and he
finally landed in his native village. It was dark as he

"Things Looked as Usual."

entered the hamlet, and as he walked along the well-remem-
bered street he saw that Deacon Tracy had built an addition
to his house. A new cooper-shop had been erected by some
one, and some bloated capitalist had started a new under-
taker's shop.

When Enoch reached his gate he found everything about
as usual. The gate hung on one hinge, Jim McGraw's
pig was rooting up the garden, and an old hoop-skirt was

swinging from the cherry tree near the house. Enoch hoped that the old woman had removed to Texas, and he walked softly up and peered into one of the windows.

Tennyson goes on, you know, to say that the returned wanderer saw strange children playing around, saw his wife looking sad yet happy, and that a strange man was there as her husband. Enoch didn't see any such thing. I have here illustrated just what greeted his vision as he pulled a pillow out of the broken pane and stuck his nose in.

WHAT ARDEN SAW.

And he didn't skulk off and go away to a hotel and resolve never to reveal his identity. No, sir. He opened the kitchen door, walked in, and exclaimed:

" Come, prance out some supper, or I'll make it the worse for you !"

I

"Got out of State Prison, eh?" inquired Mrs. Arden, as she wrung out a towel and tossed it on to a chair.

And then they mauled each other with alacrity and dispatch, and it wasn't half an hour before Enoch felt as natural and as much at home as if he hadn't been gone a day.

Facts are facts, and Mr. Tennyson ought to be ashamed of himself.

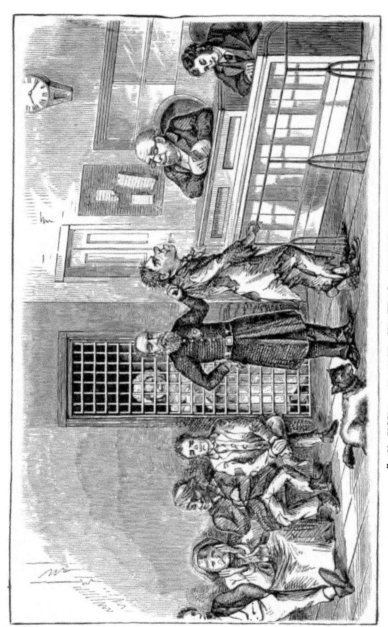

"AN HOUR AT THE CENTRAL STATION COURT."

AN HOUR AT THE CENTRAL STATION COURT.

AS his Honor was signing the warrants, and things around the room were being put to rights, a small lad with sore eyes crept under the rope and asked Bijah if he had any chewing tobacco about him.

The old man's amazement prevented him from speaking for half a moment, and then he took the boy by the collar, dropped him out of doors, and remarked:

"The first step to the gallus is chewin' terbacker, and

when I look around me here and observe how many young boys are growing up in vice and ignorance it makes my flesh crawl."

"Oh! take some worm-drops!" replied the boy, backing off.

"But, come here!" called the old man, forcing a smile, "come here and get five cents; come and see yer old father, bub—come and tell me who ye are!"

"Take me for a flat?" inquired the boy, crossing the street.

Bijah made a dash for him, but after striking the hydrant with his foot and plowing his way through a lot of old oyster cans he gave up the chase and went in to bide his time.

NO MORE FOREVER.

"William Conway Harrington," remarked his Honor, as the first man balanced at the mark, "my speech to you will consist of but very few words, though you want to ponder over them until they stand out on your memory like red paint on a Greeley hat. You are charged with having kicked your wife out of doors and smashed up the furniture."

"She commenced the row," replied William.

"William Conway Harrington, listen to me, continued the court. "I don't care a button how the fight began, but let me state clearly and emphatically that if you are brought here again on any such charge you'll be made to wish that you were a Hottentot."

"Well, I'll behave myself," replied the prisoner, trembling violently.

"Do, sir; you may go now. Here's your hat and jack-knife, and that door will let you out."

"SHE'S SORRY, SIR,"

Remarked Bijah as he handed out Katie Worden, a black-eyed girl with a scar on her nose.

"Yes, I am," she added as she pushed a tear from under her eyelid.

"I suppose so," mused his Honor. "The officer says you were so intoxicated that you didn't know a woodpile from a harness-shop, and that you created a good deal of trouble."

"Try me—give me one more chance!" she pleaded.

"Couldn't do it," he replied. "You've been here twenty times within a year, and it is time you understood that law can be clothed in the fleece of a lamb or the skin of a tiger. You've come here once too often, and I shall make it sixty days."

"Oh! Heav——oh! I shall faint—oh!——"

"Be placid, Miss Worden," he remarked. "If you should fall down in a faint Bijah would have to cut your corset-strings, throw water on you and fan you with the dust-pan, and your present neat and tidy appearance would be destroyed."

IF SHE HAD FAINTED.

"But my heart beats so!" she wailed.

"Yes; well, you may sit down on the half-bushel measure in the corridor and smell of the carbolic acid jug. It's a favor we don't grant to every one, but I want you to understand that it is a stern sense of justice and not personal malice which influences me."

"SING ME A SONG, MOTHER."

While the broken-hearted female was being tenderly moved away, a frank, clear voice was heard singing:

> "Down among the cotton blossoms,
> Down among the sugar-cane,
> There was where I met Lucinda,
> There's where——"

"Put that boy out!" interrupted his Honor, rising up and surveying the crowd of small boys behind the stove. Silence followed.

The boys moved uneasily.

"Put that boy out, I say!" shouted the Court.

"Please sir," explained a chunk of a boot-black, stepping forward, "I guess its wind in the stove-pipe!"

Bijah came out with a sailor at this juncture, and the source of the harmonious disturbance was soon settled.

"Who's this Lucinda you were singing about?" inquired his Honor, as he settled back.

"It was only a song, sir," explained the sailor, shifting about uneasily.

"Well, what about this charge of drunkenness?"

"Blast my flukes if I know."

"You were drunk—see it in your face. What do you mean by such conduct?"

"I s'pose I fell in with Jack, and Tom, and Bill, and got tight afore I knew it."

"Well, I'll make you get up and climb for not attending to your own business. The sentence is thirty days."

"Whoop!" exclaimed the sailor.

"That calls for thirty more!" replied his Honor.

"It does, eh?—whoop!"

"I'll make it three months!"

There was a pause.

"Any more whoops?" inquired the court.

"Not even a hoop-skirt!" sadly replied the sailor, as he walked away.

It was the end.

THE EUREKY RAT-TRAP.

HE boarded the boat at a landing about a hundred miles above Vicksburg, having two dilapidated but bulky-looking satchels as luggage. He said he was bound to "Orleans," and when the clerk told him what the fare would be he uttered a long whistle of amazement and inquired:

"Isn't that pooty steep?"

"Regular figure, sir," replied the clerk.

"Seems like a big price for just riding on a boat," continued the stranger.

"Come, I'm in a hurry," said the clerk.

"That's the lowest figger, eh?" inquired the stranger.

"Yes—that's the regular fare."

"No discount to a regular traveler?"

"We make no discount from that figure."

"Ye wouldn't take half of it in trade?"

"I want your fare at once, or we will have to land you!"

"Don't want a nice rat-trap, do ye, stranger?" inquired the passenger, "one which sets herself, works on scientific principles, allers ready, painted a nice green, wanted by every family, warranted to knock the socks off'n any other trap ever invented by mortal man?"

"No, sir, I want the money!" replied the clerk, in emphatic tones.

135

"Oh, wall, I'll pay, of course I will," said the rat-trap man; "but that's an awful figger for a ride to Orleans, and cash is cash these days."

He counted out the fare in ragged shin-plasters, wound a shoe-string around his wallet and replaced it, and then unlocked one of the satchels and took out a wire rat-trap. Proceeding to the cabin, he looked the ground over, and then waltzing up to a young lady who sat on a sofa reading, he began:

"I take great pleasure in presenting to your attention the Eureky rat-trap, the best trap ever invented. It sets——"

"Sir!" she exclaimed, rising to her feet.

"Name's Harrington Baker," he went on, turning the trap around on his outstretched hand, "and I guarantee this trap to do more square killing among rats than——"

She gave him a look of scorn and contempt, and swept grandly away, and without being the least put out he walked over to a bald-headed man who had tilted his chair back and fallen asleep.

"Fellow-mortal, awakest and gaze upon the Eureky rat-trap," said the stranger, as he laid his hand on the shiny pate of the sleeper.

"Wh—who—what!" exclaimed the bald-head, opening his eyes and flinging his arms around.

"I take this opportunity to call your attention to my Eureky rat-trap," continued the new passenger—"the noblest Roman of them all. Try one and you will use no other. It is constructed on——"

"Who in thunder do you take me for?" exclaimed the bald-headed man at this point. "What in blazes do I want of your rat-trap?"

"To ketch rats!" humbly replied the stranger—"to clear yer premises of one of the most obnoxious pests known to man. I believe I am safe in saying that this 'ere——"

"Go away, sir—go away, or I'll knock your blamed head off'!" roared the bald-head. "When I want a rat-trap I shan't patronize traveling vagabonds! Your audacity in daring to put your hand on my head and wake me up deserves a caning!"

"Then you don't want a trap?"

"*No*, sir!" yelled bald-head.

"I'll make you one mighty cheap."

"I'll knock you down, sir!" roared bald-head, looking around for his cane.

"Oh, wall, I ain't a starvin', and it won't make much difference if I don't sell to you!" remarked the stranger, and he backed off and left the cabin for the promenade deck.

An old maid sat in the shadow of the texas, embroidering a slipper, and the rat-trap man drew a stool up beside her and remarked:

"Madam, my name is Baker, and I am the inventer of the Eureky rat-trap, a sample copy of which I hold here on my left hand, and I think I can safely say that——"

"Sir, this is unpardonable!" she exclaimed, pushing back.

"I didn't have an introduction to ye, of course," he replied, holding the trap up higher, "but business is business you know. Let me sell you a Eureky trap and make ye happy for life; I warrant this trap to——"

"Sir, I shall call the Captain!" she interrupted, turning pale with rage.

"Does *he* want a trap?" eagerly inquired the man.

"Such impudence deserves the horsewhip!" screamed the old maid, backing away.

The rat-trap man went forward and found a Northern invalid, who was so far gone that he could hardly speak above a whisper.

"Ailing, eh?" queried the trapper.

The invalid nodded.

"Wall, I won't say that my Eureky rat-trap will cure ye," continued the man, "but this much I do say, and will swear to on a million Bibles, that it climbs the ridge-pole over any immortal vermin-booster ever yet set before——"

The Captain came up at this juncture, and informed the inventor that he must quit annoying passengers.

"But some of 'em may want one o' my Eureky traps," protested the man.

"Can't help it; this is no place to sell traps."

"But this is no scrub trap—none o' your humbugs, got up to swindle the hair right off of an innocent and confiding public."

"You hear me—put that trap up!"

"I'll put it up, of course; but then, I'll leave it to yerself if it isn't rather Shylocky in a steamboat to charge me the reg'lar figger to Orleans, and then stop me from passing my Eureky trap out to the hankerin' public?"

"THE HEAD-WRITER."

IT was early in the morning when I heard a great puffing and blowing on the stairs, and pretty soon footsteps sounded in the hall, and a woman's voice said:

"Now, John Quincy, you want to look as smart as you can!"

The next moment the door opened and a big fat woman and a small thin boy came into the room. She gave her

"Is the Head-Writer In?"

dress a shake, snatched the boy's hat off, and then looking at me she inquired:

"Is the head-writer in?"

"He is, madam," I replied.

"Be you him?" she asked.

I nodded.

"Oh! dear!" she exclaimed, as she sat down on a chair and fanned herself with her handkerchief, "I like to have never got up stairs."

I smiled and nodded.

"You see that boy thar'?" she inquired, after awhile.

"Your son, I suppose?" I answered—"nice-looking lad."

"Yes, he's smart as a fox. There isn't a thing he don't know. Why, he isn't but eight, and he composeys poetry, writes letters and plays tunes on the fiddle!"

"You ought to be proud of him," I said.

"Wall, we kinder hope he'll turn out well," she answered. "Come up here, John Quincy, and speak that piece about that boy who stood on the busted deck."

"I won't!" replied the boy in a positive tone.

"He's a little bashful, you see," giving me an apologetical smile. "He's rid fourteen miles this morning, and he doesn't feel well, anyhow; I shouldn't wonder if he was troubled with worums."

"Worms be blowed!" replied John Quincy, chewing away at his hat.

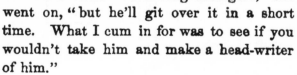

"He's awful skeard when he's among strangers," she went on, "but he'll git over it in a short time. What I cum in for was to see if you wouldn't take him and make a head-writer of him."

"I don't want to be a durned old bald-headed head-writer!" said John Quincy, picking his teeth with my scissors.

"The young never knows what's good for 'em," she went on. "He wants to be a preacher, or a great lawyer, or a big doctor, but he seems to take to writing, and we thought we'd make a head-writer of him. I don't s'pose he'd earn over five or six dollars and board a week for the first year, but I've bin told that Gen'ral Jackson didn't git half that when he begun:

"Madam," I commenced, as she stopped for breath, "I'd like to take the boy. He looks as smart as a steel trap, and no doubt he'll turn out a great man."

"Then you'll take him?"

"If you agree as to terms."

"What is them ter-ums?"

"You see my left eye is out?"

"Yes."

"Well, your son can never become a great writer unless you put his left eye out. If you will think back you will remember that you never saw a great writer whose left eye was not out. This is a matter of economy. A one-eyed writer only needs half as much light as a man with two eyes, and he isn't half so apt to discover hair-pins in his butter, and buttons in his oyster soup. The best way to put his eye out is to jab a red-hot needle into it."

"Good grashus!" she exclaimed.

"And you observe that I am bald-headed? You may think that my baldness results from scalp disease, but such is not the case. When a head-writer is bothered to get an idea he scratches his head. Scratching the hair wouldn't do any good; it's the scalp he must agitate. The hair is therefore pulled out with a pair of pincers, in order that a man can get right down to the scalp at once, and save time."

"Can that be possible!"

"All this is strictly true, madam. You also observe that one of my legs is shorter than the other. Without an .explanation on my part you would attribute this to some accident. Such is not the case. Every head-writer is located in the fourth story of the office, and his left leg is shortened three inches to enable him to run up and down stairs. You will have to have a doctor unjoint your son's leg at the hip, saw it off to the proper length, and then hook it back in its place."

"Did I ever hear the likes!" she exclaimed.

"And you also observe, madam, that two of my front teeth are gone. You might think they decayed, but such was not the case. They were knocked out with a crowbar, in order to enable me to spit ten feet. According to a law enacted at the last session of Congress any headwriter who can't spit ten feet is not entitled to receive Congressional reports free of postage."

"Can it be so!" she said, her eyes growing larger every moment.

"And you notice my corpulent build?" I went on, "you might think this the result of high living, but it is not. Every head-writer of any prominence has one of these big stomachs on him. They are all members of a secret

society, and they tell each other outside of the lodge-room in this way. I am naturally very tall and thin, but I had to conform to the rules. They cut a hole in my chest and filled me out by stuffing in dry Indian meal. It took two bushels and a peck, and then it lacked a little and they had to fill up with oatmeal. Now then, madam, you see what your son must go through with, and I leave you to judge whether you will have him learn the head-writer's trade or not. I like the looks of the boy very much, and if you desire to——"

"*I guess we'll go hum!*" she exclaimed, lifting herself off the chair. "I kinder want him to be a head-writer, and yit I think I ought to have a little more talk with his father, who wants him to git to be boss in a saw-mill. I'm 'bleged to you, and if we conclude to have him——"

"Yes, bring him right in, day or night. The first thing will be to unhinge his left leg and——!"

But they were out in the hall, and I heard John Quincy remark :

"Head-writer be blowed !"

MRS. DOLSON'S AILMENTS.

MRS. Dolson lives close beside us, and if Dolson should move away, we'd be truly sorry. She knows herbs, drugs and medicines by heart. She can tell you just what to do in every complaint, from a sore nose to having a leg taken off by a street car, and such a person is a prize which any neighborhood would appreciate.

Mrs. Dolson has had a great deal of experience for a woman only fifty years of age. She's had the ague, the chills, the itch, the hives, chicken-pox, scarlet fever, bilious fever, small-pox, pneumonia, typhoid fever, asthma, bronchitis, lock-jaw, toothache, heart disease, and any other disease handy to think of, and she knows just what to do in each case. I was thinking of her the other day, and I put up a little job on her.

I rushed over and pounded on her door just after she had tucked herself away beside Dolson for the night, and when she raised the window and put out her head, I said:

"Mrs. Quad is awful sick!"

"La! but what is it?" she inquired.

"I'm afraid it's the philoprogenitiveness," I replied.

"Dear me!" if she's got that she'll have a hard time, I'm afraid," said the old lady in a regretful voice. "I had an attack of it when we lived in Buffalo, and there were seventeen nights when Dolson never shut his eyes to sleep. You must soak her feet and put mustard plaster on the soles."

"It may not be that," I went on; "I think the symptoms rather go to show that she has been taken with retroversion."

"Then it will be a severe case indeed!" she replied. "I remember, when my oldest daughter was a baby, I had an attack of it, and before they could get a doctor I was at the point of death. If I were you I'd give her sage tea, and rub on pain-killer, and if she wasn't better by midnight, I'd call a doctor."

"Did you ever have any experience in cases of phytogeny?" I asked, as she was about to draw in her head.

"Phytogeny! I should think I had! Why, it wasn't two weeks ago that I had a spell on't, and I thought for about half an hour that Dolson was going to be a widower before sundown. If you think that is what ails her, you'd better give her a whisky sling and some dry ginger."

"Mrs. Burbank was in about an hour ago, and she said she thought all the symptoms pointed to a bad case of morsitation," I went on.

"Deary me! I hope not," answered the good old lady, sighing heavily. "That's what Aunt Jasen Starkweather died with. She was taken about daylight, and was a corpse before dinner was ready. I had a slight touch of it once, and if Dolson hadn't been in the house I couldn't have lived two hours. If I was you I'd give her some grated ginsen root and New Orleans molasses."

"Well," I said, as I backed off the step, "I hope it won't run into the intuitionalism."

"Gracious! I hope so, too," she replied. "That's what Deacon Patchin's wife died with. I was there visiting, and she was taken along about three o'clock in the afternoon,

J

and died the next day. Poor thing! I've seen a good deal of suffering, but I never knew any one to toss around as she did. I came near having it myself last May, and I know how to pity any one who comes down with it."

She drew in her head, and I went home. The next morning she saw me at the gate, and when I told her that my wife's sickness was an attack of the intussusception, and she was much better, Mrs. Dolson exclaimed:

"Well, now, if that isn't good! If she's careful she'll soon be up again. I've had it three or four times, and I always keep quiet for a day or two, and drink spearmint tea."

CONFESSION OF A MURDERER.

BELIEVE the clock was just striking nine in the evening when he knocked at the door and sent in word that he wanted to see me. I went out, and he shook hands with me and asked if all my folks were usually well. When I had replied that such was the case, he broke out with:

"My object in visiting this city is to introduce to public notice my new corn remedy. I have traveled over Europe, Asia, Africa and the Holy Land, and everywhere I have met with the most flat——"

He got that much out before I could stop him. Then I laid my hand on his shoulder and whispered coldly in his left ear:

"Mister man! if you have any desire to live to see your family grow up you won't be seven seconds getting out of this yard!"

He wasn't, but the next morning, just as I was ready to go out, he called again. He didn't seem to have any fear in his nature, for as soon as I appeared he reached out his hand and inquired:

"May I hope that your family are well?"

"Yes, blame you! you can hope that they are in the Rhine, if you want to!" I replied.

147

"My dear sir, allow me to call your attention to my newly-invented salve for removing corns," he went on. "I can show you certificates from Queen Victoria, Abraham Lincoln, Colonel Forney, Judge——"

I stopped him there. Tapping him on the shoulder, I  asked him if he didn't know that he was standing over a powder magazine—on the brink of a yawning chasm—on the verge of death?

He seemed a little paler as he walked away, and I thought he would not return. I had forgotten all about him by evening, when he called again and informed the girl that he must see me on important business. I went out, and he extended his hand and wanted to know if I thought I was as well as last year at that time.

I collared him before he could say another word, and yelled to the girl to bring me a revolver and a bowie-knife, but he begged so hard that I couldn't have the heart to kill him. He promised never to say "corn remedy" within two blocks of the house again, but he was a base liar. Yes, he was. He was back there next day, and the next, and the next, and finally I told him to come around into the back yard and I would take ten gross of his remedy.

"I knew you wanted it!" he exclaimed, but his cheerfulness was soon cut short.

I got him around behind the shanty. We were alone together. It was late and dark. I had everything fixed, and he didn't suffer much. As soon as he found out that he was to die he tried to soften my heart by telling me that he had fourteen wives and a fond children, but I wouldn't have spared him then for a house and lot in Chicago. * * * * * * * * *

* * He fell where he died. He gasped out a few broken words, but whether they were a request to bury him in the garden, or some farewell words to his family, I do not know.

I sometimes wish I had spared him; it musses up a back yard terribly to use it for a slaughter-pen.

THE PERKINS BABY.

EVERYBODY said he was a darling for the first year, and I guess he was. Mrs. Perkins used to bring him over and demand my adoration, but finally when I got out of patience and told her that I had been the father of thousands of just as handsome and cunning little cherubs, she became indignant and refused to enter my house or let their calf play with my goat.

I suppose the child was up to the average. It was their first, and Perkins wasn't so much to blame for making a fool of himself. The child wasn't three days old before its father purchased it a pair of boots, a straw hat, a drum, a base ball bat and other things, and he carried a grin on his face which would have made his fortune as a circus clown.

IT ALWAYS HAPPENS.

I knew how he'd catch it, but I said nothing. It wasn't many days before we used to hear him up at midnight, shaking the old stove around and butting his nose against the doors, and his eyes began to have a solemn look. Then his mother-in-law, two brothers and their families, two or three

150

THE PERKINS BABY.

uncles and aunts, and a few acquaintances, paid Perkins a
visit to see the baby, and when they filed in to meals it was
like a circus procession.

The colic season came on after the baby was two months
old, and then didn't Perkins catch it! The baby would

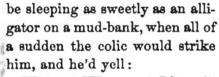

be sleeping as sweetly as an alli-
gator on a mud-bank, when all of
a sudden the colic would strike
him, and he'd yell:

Whoop! Whooooo! I-hooo!"
They'd turn him oh his little
stomach, loosen his bands, rub
his back and give him catnip tea,

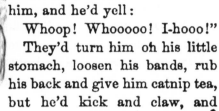

"THE OLD MAN DREAMS."

but he'd kick and claw, and
they'd have to send for Perkins and the doctor, and raise
as much excitement as a fire-alarm. If it was night Perkins would have to leap out of bed, build a fire, look for
ointments and liniments and soothing syrups, and perhaps
it was hours before he got to bed again.

This thing went on until everybody in the neighborhood
got down on the Perkins angel, and didn't care whether he
lived or died. When he was a year old, and could sit
alone, he one day got hold of his father's jack-knife. They
saw him biting the end of it, but they didn't see him push
it under the bureau. He was hunting around for something else when a fly swooped down on his poor head and
gave him a bite which raised him a foot high. He yelled
out and clawed and kicked, and Mrs. Perkins jumped for
him and cried out:

" He's went and swallered that 'ere jack-knife!"

Perkins looked around, failed to see the knife, noted the
red face and flying legs of his child, and he clapped on his
hat and ran for the doctor. The hired girl made a dash
among the neighbors, and in a little while they had gath-

ered to the number of forty. The child had got mad by
this time, and as he kicked and howled and grew red Mrs.
Perkins clasped her hands and wailed:

"That dreadful jack-knife is working among his blessed
vitals!"

Perkins sat down in a tremble, some of the women cried,
and a fat man went out on the back door-step and wiped
the tears away with a new three-dollar hat, utterly regard-
less of expense.

"Hold the young 'un up!" yelled one.

"Pat him on the back!" screamed another.

"Turn him over!" squealed old Mrs. Johnson.

And they held
that boy up by one
leg and swung him
this way and that.
They flung him on
the lounge and
rolled him over
and over, mauling
him in the back
with their fists, and
he made the neigh-
borhood ring with his

THEY HELD HIM UP.

howls. Finally the doctor arrived, and he put the boy on
the table and pinched his ribs and rubbed his stomach and
tried to count his pulse.

."I think the knife rests right here," he said, placing his
hand on the baby's stomach.

"'Spose'n it should open and commence to whittle away
on his vitals!" wailed Mrs. Perkins.

"Hand me mustard, and tepid water, and salt, and some
pills, and strong coffee, and chloroform!" answered the
doctor.

Then they held that boy and filled him up with stuff, and rubbed and pounded him some more, and as he clawed around and kicked old Mrs. Frazer in the nose they said it was convulsions, contortions and dying agonies. They wore the hair off his head before they got through with him, and the doctor said that he would have to either cut him open and take the jack-knife out with a pair of tongs, or see the innocent die, when Mrs. Gregory's tow-headed boy, who was prowling around, discovered the jack-knife under the bureau. Then the doctor got red in the face, Perkins jumped over the table, and the old women wiped their eyes and remarked:

"It didn't seem possible that Providence was going to take the little darling away!"

HOW A WOMAN MAKES A BED.

HE'S washed the dishes, cleared off the table, swept out the sitting-room, and she stands in the bed-room door for a moment, arms akimbo, and surveys the bed.

The pillows are skewed around, the quilts rolled up in a heap, one end of the sheet down almost to the floor, and she wonders how "them young ones" managed to tumble up the bed so.

She approaches the bed, seizes the pillows and deposits them on a chair, hauls the quilts off and drops them in the door-way, draws the sheets over the stand, and she finds the feather-tick full of lumps and dents and hills and hollows. She makes a lunge for it, rolls it to the foot of the bed, and dives down among the straw.

Her hands are lost to sight, and she bends over until it seems as if her back would break. The straw is pulled this way, pushed that, dragged around and torn apart, and her fingers reach clean to the bottom and into each corner.

"There! ha!" she says, as she straightens up to rest her back; and after a moment she grabs the feather tick, yanks it around, gives it a flop and rolls it against the head-board that she may get into the foot of the straw tick. She dives into the straw once more, and her face gets as red as paint as her nose almost touches the tick. The straw is finally

154

stirred enough, and she rests her back, looks up to the ceiling and wonders where she can borrow a white-wash brush. Then it would do your heart good to see her grab the feather-bed. She hauls it around, flings it up, mauls great dents in it with her fists, jams it against the wall and finally flattens it out. Then she seizes the foot, shakes the feathers toward the head, smooths them along further with her hand, and each corner is patted down and made to stand out distinctly. That hollow in the center is patted out of existence, and at last the bed is a true slant from head to foot. The top sheet is switched off the stand, held up before her until she sees the seam, then she flies it across the bed. It settles down just as true and square as a rule, and after the front side has been tucked down behind the rail the other sheet follows.

The pillows are then grabbed up, mauled and beaten and cuffed around until they swell with indignation, and they are dropped on to the bed so gently that they don't make a dent, but seem to float in the air above the sheets. The ends where the cases button are placed to go outside, according to long established rule, and the quilts are swung over, tucked behind the rail, pulled down at the foot, smoothed at the head, and she stands back and says :

" There ! those children will sleep like bugs to-night !"

A few weeks ago, as I stood in the post-office, I heard one female say to another :

" Did you hear about poor Mrs. Gleason ?"

" No—sick ?" was the query.

" Poor thing—died last night."

" Is that so ?" was the exclamation. " Well, I'm sorry, though she's better off. She was a good wife, but she could never make up a bed as it ought to be made."

"BRIXS."

IT may be lonesome out on the broad prairie when the shadows of night fall and dance and weave about and wreathe themselves into forms which the lone hunter may take for enemies seeking his life. The big farm-house may seem tomb-like when evening has grown to midnight and sleep has closed every eye, and the watch-dog growls at the wind softly moving the branches of the locust tree at the gate. But, when the heart of a great city ceases to beat—when night has swept the streets as if a plague were abroad, and the flag-stones ring out sharp echoes of the lightest foot-fall, there is something so lonely, so solemn, that the pedestrian cannot carry one single cheerful thought. Nothing can be more lonely, no shadows can be deeper or more menacing.

I came across them as I hurried along at midnight—a queer old man with trembling voice, and a gaunt woe-be-gone dog. I heard them talking in a stair-way—a dark spot from which the lonely shadows sallied forth to dance around the dim gas lamps and creep after belated pedestrians. With one hand on the iron railing, wishing to go nearer, but deterred by the shining orbs of the dog, I stood and heard the old man say :

"Brixs, put your paw in my hand! There, that way. Do you know, Brixs, that I'm going away ?"

The dog whined and moved uneasily.

"Yes, dog—going to set out on a long journey, and I've

156

got to leave you behind. You've been more than a friend, Brixs; you've followed me along the road, up and down the streets, through the alleys, and you've been the same dog day after day."

The dog uttered a low bark, as if he understood, and the old man continued:

" We've both grown old. Gray hairs have come to my head, weakness to my limbs, and your coat is faded and you are lame and stiff. We never had a quarrel, and I never gave you a cross word, and I'm free to say I'd rather die with your face close to mine than to have a hundred friends weeping around my death-bed !"

The old man was lying on the landing, his head pillowed on one of the iron stairs, and the dog stood over him and caressed him.

" Poverty, hunger, ingratitude, rags, heart-aches and bruises have been our lot," continued the old man, " but the end is here—for me. They'll find me dead, and there'll be no hand to protect you. You'll be driven away, beaten and starved, and they'll call you a *dog*. *I* know better, but I won't be here. It has been the road-side one night, the barn the next, a stair-way or the commons the next for these long years past, but you haven't complained. No, Brixs, you've put up with everything, borne your full share, and if they only knew how I loved you they'd bury us both in one grave !"

The dog, standing with his paws on his master's breast, uttered a long, mournful howl, and the shadows seemed to catch the echoes and carry them up and down the dark stairs.

" Nobody'll care for me, Brixs—no one but you. They'll find the corpse, say that another old man is dead, and in an hour I'll be boxed and buried and forgotten. You can't speak—you can't do, and 'twould be useless if you could.

The poor and the old have no business here—no right in
the world!"

The dog nestled down to the old man's face and uttered
a piteous whine.

"I know your heart aches," said the old man, and "mine
aches, too. We're old; we've been fast friends, until I'd
feel like murdering one who'd harm a hair of your body.
I'm not running away from you—I'm only dying! I'm
getting rid of these hurts and bruises and limps—these
gray hairs and trembling limbs—these heart-aches and
sorrows and wanderings. The human soul does not die,
Brixs, and I believe that the door which opens to me will
swing back for you! You've been faithful and true, and
that's what no human being ever was!"

The dog raised his head, and his howl was so full of
grief and loneliness that I hurried away, racing with the
shadows to see who should pass the corner first.

When I passed the stair-way next morning a dog sat on
the curb-stone, looking anxiously into the face of every
passer-by. It was Brixs. They had found a dead body on
the landing—the corpse of an old man.

Brixs was alone in the world, and the world had not one
kind word for him. I called to him, but he disappeared
around the corner, moving slowly—walking like a human
being who had not one hope left.

THE LAST WARRIOR.

I HAVE just returned from interviewing the last Indian warrior left in Michigan. I feel sad. Once they were plenty—now they are scarce.

Less than a hundred years ago the forests echoed the whoops of thousands of noble red men, and the valleys were dotted with their lodges.

Now there is nary whoop.

And nary lodge.

I found the last warrior propped up against a coal-shed near the river—the river which was once covered with the canoes of his ancestors, and which sang soft, sad songs in the ears of the sleeping Indian babes.

He didn't seem inclined to talk. Perhaps his mind was overburdened with the bitter memories of the past, and he was only waiting for the shadow of death to come and touch him and gather him to the happy hunting-grounds of his fathers.

"Renowned Wild Hoss, Big Moon, Setting Sun, Roaring Chipmunk, Howling Rabbit, or whatever your name is, don't you feel sad?" I asked as I stood before him.

He didn't say.

159

" When you remember back and realize that the great
and powerful tribe of Wyandottes once camped on this
spot, and that five thousand warriors, more
or less, roamed and howled and got up and
dusted through this neighborhood in search
of scalps—when you remember that the
smoke of Injun camp-fires once made this
whole State look dim—when you
remember that every glade had its
score of lodges, and that squaws
picked strawberries in every valley—when you remember all this,
doesn't it make tears come to your
eyes ?"

He wouldn't compromise himself
by answering.

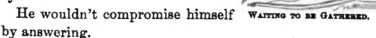

WAITING TO BE GATHERED.

" Where now is Pontiac ?" I asked—" where is Okemos,
Tall Cedar, Three-fingered Jack, Humped-back Sam,
Awful Charley, and the score of other great chiefs who
once had to hire an express wagon to haul their crop of
scalps around the country ? Where are they ?"

He didn't even sigh.

" Where are the thirty thousand warriors who once gathered around the council fires and felt their back hair crawl-
ing up as some four-horse chief took the center of the
circle and promised them gallons of gore and barrels of
scalps? Where are they ? Ask the sighing pines, the
murmuring river or the setting sun ! Do you hear their
voices any more ? Do you know where their bones are
fading to dust ?"

" Sir, the smoke of your camp-fires no longer curl
through the beeches. The wild fox digs his den where
once your council-fires blazed fiercely. The white man's
dog plays with the bloody tomahawk of your high-nosed

grandpa, and the farmer yells : ' Haw Buck—gee Bright !' in the valleys where the smoke-stained Injun ladies once played croquet. Your glory has faded. You can't hold a candle to the white man. Don't you feel a goneness ?"

Only echo answered.

" You are the last of your race, mister man—the last red warrior in Michigan. After a few moons more—after the sun rises and sets on a few more days—you will be gathered home—collected at a mass convention of your party friends in the hunting-grounds set aside for scalp-takers in the land beyond the skies. Then the beech tree will whisper to the pine, the pine will sigh to the hill-top, and the hill-top will bow its head and ask the gurgling streamlet where the red children of the forest have fled to. It's awful sad to think of it—I could weep for you. Won't you give me your candid opinion on these things ?"

K

HIS TROUBLES WITH REFRIGERATORS.

I SUPPOSE I have had more trouble with refrigerators than any other man in the West, and it has not been my fault, either. I can recall every one I ever had, and can distinctly remember what happened to them. The first one was called "The Arctic Star." The agent followed me four miles on a hot day, while giving me its freezing points, and I took it more to reward his industry than anything else. I looked high and low that night for something to put in that refrigerator, and only succeeded in getting hold of ten cents worth of radishes, which I undertook to preserve on twenty-five cents worth of ice. I got up early, opened the doors and found a cat seated on the

THE WEARIED CAT.

shelf, wiping the sweat off her brow with her hind feet. She didn't say anything, nor did I, but we both did considerable thinking, and that box went out of doors after breakfast. I didn't propose to open any conveniences for wearied cats around my house.

The next was called the "Frigid Iceberg." I told the agent that I had always supposed icebergs were as limber as strings, but he replied that the name didn't make any difference with the box, and put on a frigid look himself. The box was a fine-looking affair, four-holes-full-jeweled, with a fine brass door-knob which

162

glowed and winked in the sun like a midnight lamp. It
had just begun to be a success, when the servant girl, who
had that day received a letter from her William stating
that his affections were on the wane, went up into the second story of the box and took poison, and she was dead
when we found her. The sight of the box was so mournful that it had to go out of the house. Poor girl! she was
very scrupulous in her habits, and would have chosen some
other place if her mind had been free from trouble. The
agent was rather put out when I told him that the body
didn't get cold for five hours, and he remarked that the ice
of the present day wasn't the ice of years ago, which was
a very graphic remark.

The next one was called the " Greenland Hyperborean."
It was warranted to save ten per cent in fuel, fifteen per
cent in oil, and I don't know how much more, but remember that the agent warranted it to have taken twelve
thousand medals at State fairs, and a few certificates at
other doings. Joe Coburn said it was the best " box " he
ever saw, and Jem Mace declared that he wouldn't have
anything else in his house. The box was very handsome,
having a carved center board and green bulwarks. I tried
the pumps one morning and found she was making water
very fast, having sprung a leak somewhere, and directly she
went down—down off the back steps, and I got licked
while trying to convince the agent that his peculiar *forte*
was selling lightning rods.

The next one was callen the " Icicle." The agent kept
me up most of the night to expatiate on the merits of the
box, and I fell asleep while he was talking, and dreamed I
had found the North Pole. He warranted it to save half
the soap in washing, and asserted that the clothes wouldn't
need any rubbing by using his process, which was to hang
the garments on the roof of the box. He was right. The

clothes hadn't hung there half of the first night before there weren't any left to rub, the box being in the summer-kitchen, where the agent's friends could find it.

THE NEW PROCESS.

The next box had but one bay-window, and I couldn't keep it and move with the *ton ;* the next agent refused to put my monogram on the lid, and it consequently wasn't in style. The next one was haunted by the ghost of a carpenter who fell and broke his neck while putting the slate on the third story, and something or other ailed every box until now I don't have one, though an agent is after me to purchase the "Alaska Cave," which has coupons on it that draw semi-annual interest, and won't explode even if turned bottom-side up.

HOW A WOMAN SPLITS WOOD.

ROBINSON was notified by his better half, the other day, that the wood-pile had been reduced to one old chunk, but he caught the panic down town and failed to send up a replenishing load. Just before noon Mrs. Robinson hunted up the axe and went for the lone chunk. She knew that a woman could split wood as well as a man; she had read and heard about woman's awkwardness, but she knew 'twas all nonsense.

She spit on her hands and raised the axe over her left shoulder, right hand lowest down on the handle. She made a terrific blow, and the axe went into the ground and she fell over the chunk. She got up and looked all around

"DARN IT TO TEXAS!"

to see if anybody was watching, rubbed her elbows and then took up the axe the other way. She meant to strike the stick plumb-center, but she forgot the clothes line above her head, and the axe caught it, jerked up and down, and Mrs. Robinson went over the ash-heap. She rose up with less confidence in her eye, and the boys playing in the alley heard some one softly say: "Darn it to Texas!" but of course it wasn't Mrs. Robinson. She might have moved the stick a little, but she didn't. She went in and got a chair and stood upon it to take down the clothes-line, then she coiled it up and hung it in the shed, and came back and surveyed the chunk and turned it over and walked around it.

The clothes-line was to blame, and now there was nothing to interfere. She got the axe, raised it once or twice, and finally gave an awful blow. It chipped off a sliver and was buried in the ground, and the knob on the handle knocked the breath out of her. She gasped and coughed and jumped up and down, and the boys heard some one say: "If I had that man here I'd mop the ground with him, I would!" After awhile she grew calmer and picked up the axe to see if she had injured it. She hadn't, and she smoothed down the handle, spit on the edge and finally went in and got a rind and greased it, suddenly remembering that no axe was worth a cent without greasing. By and by she was ready. She sat the chunk on end, put a stone behind it and then surveyed it from all sides. She had it now just where she wanted it. She looked all around to see if any of the meddling neighbors were look-

"Angels in the Air,"

ing, and then she raised the axe. She would hit the stick just in the center and lay it open at one blow. She put out one foot, drew a long breath, and then brought down the axe with a "Ha!" just as she had seen Robinson do. The axe went off the handle and the handle struck the stick. So did Mrs. Robinson. She thought she saw angels in the air; and her nose was "barked" and several teeth were loosened until they seemed half an inch too long.

When she rose up she determined to butcher Robinson the moment he appeared. Then she concluded she would not butcher him at once, but torture him to death and be two days about it. After getting into the house and putting a sticking-plaster on her knee and some lard on her elbow, she concluded to only wound Robinson in the shoulder with the butcher-knife.

After pinning up the tear in her dress and getting a piece of court-plaster for her nose, she went and borrowed some wood, and hearing while on the way home that Mrs. Prindle suspected that Miss Spindle was going to wear her last year's cloak through another winter, the good woman concluded to let Robinson off entirely and tell him that she hurt her nose falling down cellar.

FAT FOLKS.

LIKE fat folks. There's something jolly right in the fact of one's being a great big porpoise, and you never saw a fat man or woman but what was good-natured, unless disappointed in love. I often wish I stood in Baker's shoes. He weighs two hundred and eighty, and when seen coming down the street he resembles a sloop under full sail. When he enters a street-car everybody shoves along at once, and if it's crowded, two or three men will get up and offer him their seats. He is of importance wherever he goes. If he sits on an inquest he influences the jury, and if he predicts the weather people put faith in him. If there's a crowd around a sick horse, Baker elbows his way right in where I couldn't get, and they are always sure to make him cashier at Sunday-school excursions, send him invitations to deliver Fourth of July orations, and he is the man always selected to present the fire company with new hats and a speech.

And there's Mrs. Scott, who weighs nearly as much as Baker. When it's a hot day everybody asks after her comfort, and when it's a cold day everybody congratulates her on being fat. She was made the president of a benevolent society, the treasurer of an art association, and the "head man" in a monument enterprise, just because she was fat and "could fill the chair" better than any lean woman. If she went aboard the ferry-boat they always placed her in the center of the cabin in the best arm-chair aboard, so that she could not careen the craft over, and if forty lean women hung over the railing to starboard or port, nothing was ever said or cared about it. She had the biggest tent at camp-meeting, the best place to see the Fourth of July fire-works, and grocers were always sending her early strawberries and first vegetables.

I fell in love with a fat girl once. I loved madly, because I was loving two hundred and seven pounds of girl. She was amiable, tender-hearted, good-natured and true, and I think she loved me. We were to be married in the fall, and I should probably have been one of the happiest of husbands, when an accident dashed my prospects. She

fell overboard just as we were about to leave the wharf on a steamboat excursion. Four or five sailors plunged after, and they got a gangplank under her, a cable around her waist, and towed her to the wharf.

Then they rigged a derrick and lifted her out by sections, but they were so long about it that she took a severe cold, and the result was death. There were months and months after that that I never could pass a load of hay without thinking of my lost Amanda and shedding tears; and even to this day I can't see an elephant or a rhinoceros without her dear visage rising up before me.

EPITAPHS AND SUCH.

TOOK a walk through the cemetery yesterday, and I have been in a brown study ever since. Cushman's tombstone stands up there a foot above all the rest, and on it I read:

"Let us meet him in Heaven."

I don't know who ordered that epitaph, but I used to live beside Cushman. Many's the time I kept him from pounding his wife when he was drunk, and I went bail for him when he stole a horse and wagon, and was on the jury which sent him to State Prison for stealing hay. He was killed in a saloon row, and if I ever "meet him in Heaven" I shall ask him whether

"Let Us Meet Him."

he climbed over the wall or tunneled under it.

Davison has a very nice headstone with a pair of clasped hands on it, and these words:

Too pure for earth,
Gone to his Heavenly rest."

I was much affected at reading the lines, but I couldn't help but wonder if he repented

"Too Pure for Earth."

170

of selling me a bogus lottery ticket; of setting fire to the railroad sheds; of stealing a carpet from the Methodist church, and of several other little matters, which caused him to make the acquaintance of the jailer. It is possible that he was "too pure for earth," but I know men who will bet ten dollars on it.

Thatcher has a monument with a lamb on top, and his loving wife put on the words:

"I shall meet him up there."

"Up There."

I don't know what they put the lamb on for. Lambs don't carry the disposition which Thatcher had. I could cover that monument with chalk-marks if I should commence to remember the times I had seen him come home, throw his wife out doors and play smash with the furniture. Wasn't I present when he bit Billy Madden's left ear clean off in a fight? Wasn't I around when he broke his son's ribs? Wasn't I there when he gouged Jack Spray's eye out? And now his widow is trying to live so that she may meet him "up there." If she should look around and fail to see his beloved phiz in that region of eternal bliss she needn't think strange of it.

"Gone Before."

Peterson's tombstone held me a great while. It is of costly Italian marble, with an urn on top, and a hand with the finger pointing towards this paragraph:

"Gone before—blighted by earth's wickedness. We shall gather with him on the other shore."

I remember when he was blighted, though its a long time ago. He undertook to lick a fellow who wouldn't vote his ticket, and he was knocked over a chair and had his skull fractured. The coroner said it was the worst blight he had seen in six months. I don't know but his numerous family will "gather with him on the other side," but I have my doubts. If they should ever see him again, or if they think they will, I know of several grocers and butchers who will give 'em fifteen per cent to collect accounts of twelve years' standing.

I found Deacon Warner's tombstone also. It bears a stern, solemn look, just as he used to, and it says:

"Heaven's gates shall open to us who are like him."

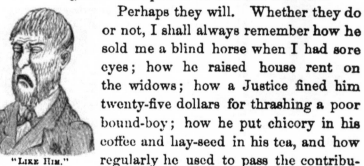

Perhaps they will. Whether they do or not, I shall always remember how he sold me a blind horse when I had sore eyes; how he raised house rent on the widows; how a Justice fined him twenty-five dollars for thrashing a poor bound-boy; how he put chicory in his coffee and hay-seed in his tea, and how

"LIKE HIM."   regularly he used to pass the contribution box to the rest of us, but forgot to put in anything himself. If the gates of Heaven are going to be held wide open for those of Deacon Warner's class, I want to put in my time in Michigan.

GIRL WANTED.

ES, I want another—"A tidy girl to do house-work in a small family—good wages and a good home." That's the way my advertisement always reads, and as soon as the paper is out the girls commence coming. Tidy girls from ten to sixty-five years old come pulling the bell, and when told that they won't suit they put on such a look of contempt for the door, the door-plate, the front gate and the entire institution, that the world seems three degrees hotter than before.

I always engage the girl. This is because of an idea of mine that I can read human nature, and because I do not fear to tell them in plain English what is expected of them. After the door-bell has been pulled about five times, the right-looking sort of a girl makes her appearance. She says she saw the advertisement, and is invited in. She says she can do any kind of cooking; loves to wash; is fond of children; can never sleep after five o'clock in the morning; never goes out evenings; does not know a young man in Detroit, and she'd be willing to work for low wages for the sake of getting a good home.

She is told to drop her bundle, lay off her things and go to work, and a great burden rolls off my mind as I congratulate myself that the prize-medal girl has arrived at last. She's all right up to about seven in the evening, when she is suddenly missed, and returns about ten o'clock to say that she "just dropped out" to get a postage-stamp. The next day she begins to scatter the tea-spoons in the back-yard, stops her ironing to read a dime novel, and at supper-time wants to know if I can't send the children off to live with their grandfather, get a cook stove with silver-plated knobs and have an addition built to the kitchen. That evening a big red-headed butcher walks in, crosses his legs over the kitchen table, and proceeds to court Sarah. She doesn't last but a day or two longer, and then we secure another.

"GIRL WANTED!"

This one is right from New Hampshire, and doesn't know a soul in Michigan, and yet she hasn't finished the dinner dishes before a cross-eyed young man rings the bell and says he'd like to see Hannah for a moment. After seeing him, Hannah concludes not to stay, as we are so far from

St. John's church, and as we don't appear to be religious people.

The next one especially recommends herself as being "just like their own mother" to the children, and isn't in the house half a day before she draws Small Pica over her knee and gives him a regular old Canadian waltz.

The next one has five recommendations as a neat and tidy girl, and yet it isn't three days before she bakes the shoe brush with the beef, washes her hands in a soup tureen, or drops hairpins into the pudding.

I growl about these things after a while, but I am met with the statement that they had worked five years for Governor this, or Lord that, and that in all that time no one had so much as looked cross-eyed at them. I am called mean, ill-tempered, particular, fault-finding, and all that, and the girl goes away wondering why the Lord has spared me as long as He has.

We've been wanting "a good, tidy girl" for these last twelve years, and I suppose that we may go another dozen and still be wanting.

THE PROOF-READER.

BLAST him!

I beg the pardon of every reader, male and female, for using the above expression. It is the first time I ever used it, and it shall be the last.

He, the proof-reader, commenced on me fourteen years ago, has followed me like a sleuth-hound down the long valley of years, and to-day his demoniac laugh fell on my ears as I climbed the stairs.

May he be mashed on the railroad the first time he travels! May the midnight cat disturb his slumbers until he is worn down to a shadow, and then may some omnibus run over the shadow!

I never wrote a pathetic article that the proof-reader didn't spoil. Once he made "silent tomb" read "Silent Thomas," and when I charged down on him he excused his criminal carelessness by saying that he thought his error made the article much more powerful and pathetic!

Another time, when I wrote an article headed "The Silent Dead," the villain — the perjured, unprincipled wretch — made it read "The Silvery Deaf!" and he had the impudence to tell me that almost any sort of a head was good enough for anything I wrote!

When I have reported a political speech by Barnes, the proof-reader has made it a speech by Baker. When I have reported an accident to Taylor he has put in the name of Trotter. When I have said that a newly-launched schooner was thirty-two feet beam he has made me say "barn," or made the thirty-two feet thirty-two rods.

May his wife have a continual cough, and may his children have chicken-pox from the cradle to the grave!

When I have said that the First Baptist church was to have a new organ he has made the item read "new orphan." When I have said that the lurid flames leaped high in air before an alarm was sounded, he has made me say "the ludicrous" flames. When I have said that the bride was elegantly attired, he has made me say "elegantly attached."

May no tailor trust him! May all dogs bite him! May he sink with an ocean steamer, get scorched in a prairie fire, or go down with some falling bridge! Every village board and city council should pass an ordinance making it a misdemeanor for any person to harbor a proof-reader over night. They never die. They grow old until they reach a certain impudent point, and then they stick right there. Nothing ever throws them out of a situation. They go on year after year, killing editors and reporters by inches, and there is no law to prevent. If they get consumption they still live. If they fall down stairs they do not break a bone. If they become blind they go right on reading proof and putting in "Dick and Kate" for the fairly written "delicate."

Blast——! But I said I wouldn't.

L

JORKS, EX-PHILANTHROPIST.

THERE was a time when he believed in philanthropy, and it was a hard struggle for him to give it up and admit that it was his solemn duty to attend to his own business and use the world as the world used him.

When he was a boy he heard a preacher preach a sermon on the sin of covetousness, and he resolved never to covet. He got along quite well for a day or two, and then hearing his father express a wish that he had been born rich, young Jorks raised his voice and replied:

"Father, it is a sin to covet."

The old man looked at him from three or four different ways, and then said:

Jorks.

"I see I've got to warm you up again! You haven't had a good basting in four weeks, and you are growing sassy again!"

He thereupon arose, carefully selected a barrel-stave, and he made his first-born hop three feet high.

When he had older grown, Jorks read that it was the duty of mankind to speak soothing words to the weary and heavy-laden victims of misfortune. He didn't find any for some time, but at last came across a chap whose wife had just slid out with another man. He had a limpid eye and a melancholy face, and Jorks patted him on the shoulder and said:

178

"Cheer up, my friend. Though all is dark and drear to-day, to-morrow may be golden with bright promises."

"Young man, yer drunk!" replied the stranger.

"Drunk? Why, my dear——"

"Then I'm a liar, am I!" exclaimed the stranger, and he spat twice on his left hand, and twice on his right, and Jorks was knocked into a three-cornered mass of

mistaken philanthropy.

Some time after that he decided to "speak gently to the erring ones." He read of a case where a desperate criminal had been thoroughly reformed by a kind word spoken at the right moment, and he looked around for a criminal. Remembering that he had read items in the daily papers reflecting on the wickedness of a saloon-keeper named Dutch Jake, Jorks went down and called on him and said:

"My kind friend, let me help you to raise yourself out of this pit of degradation."

"Vhat you shpokes about?" inquired Jake.

"Throw this avocation aside—rise above it—become a man!" continued Jorks.

"Who's goin' to lick me!" shouted Jake, shedding his coat.

"No one, my friend; I was trying to encourage you—to stimulate——"

And Jake chucked him up against the wall, loosened his teeth, battered his nose, and kicked him out on the walk to the police.

Jorks didn't want to give it up. He took homeless vagrants to his house, and they stole his Sunday suit and silver forks; he lent money to hard-up strangers, and they were never heard of afterwards; he took weeping lost children in his arms to soothe them, and was arrested on the charge of attempted abduction; he emptied his pantry to feed beggars, and they returned and stole his chickens. He finally quit, and to his surprise he found that the world went on just as well.

"CAST THY BREAD."

Jorks isn't a philanthropist any more; he figured it up and found that philanthropy didn't pay one per cent on the capital invested, and that he was being called "an old fool" thirteen times where he was called a "philanthropist" once. I don't know at this hour where any one can get more fun for the money than to stand on the corner opposite Jorks' house and see the cheerful alacrity with which he helps a beggar off the steps, and hear his tender voice crying out:

"Durn ye, man! this is the tenth time you have called here this week!"

ONLY AN OHIO MAN.

MONG the railroad travelers eating dinner at a hotel in Detroit one day was a chap from Fayette, Ohio, who hoisted in meat, potato and bread as if he had been a week without eating. A second cup of coffee was brought him, and in his hurry he picked it up and took a large swallow. It was considerably hotter than pepper, and in his excitement the Buckeye opened his mouth and shot the liquid across the table against a young man's shirt bosom.

"Gosh—whoop—hot—beg pardon—blazes—who-o-o!" he exclaimed, reaching after water.

"You're a hog, sir!" replied the young man, "a regular hog!"

"I am, eh?"

"Yes, sir."

"And I've got bristles?"

"Yes, you have."

"And I grunt?"

"Yes, sir."

"Stranger," said the Buckeye as he reached across after another slapjack, "stranger, I'm not a hog—I'm only an Ohio man, bound for Lansing."

A CAREFUL MAN.

NOT for a thousand dollars a day would I be like Mr. Rugby, and yet I am his friend. He is a careful man—one of your every-day philosophers, and he wouldn't yell "Hip! hurrah!" if New Year's, Christmas, Thanksgiving and Fourth of July were rolled into one, and champagne was knee-deep all over the street.

When a beggar asks Mr. Rugby for alms, something like the following conversation ensues:

"You say your name is Thompson?"

"Yes."

"It may be Thompson—it may be Brown; how am I to know?"

"But I'm hungry."

"You may be hungry—you may not; it's an open question, and a very serious question. If you are hungry you should have food; if not, any extra food at this time would impair your digestion."

"I'm almost sick," says the beggar.

"You may be—you may not," is the reply. "I am not a physician, and I am not able to say. If sick, you should have medicine; if not, medicine would be simply thrown away."

"I have five children."

"You may have five—you may have fifty; I shall not pretend to say, as I do not know. No one, my dear man, should ever say he knows this or that when he does not know.

182

They say it is ninety-five millions of miles to the sun, but *I* do not say so. How do I know it is; I cannot measure it, and it may lack a hundred miles, or overrun a thousand. They also say——"

By this time the beggar has become discouraged and passed on, and Mr. Rugby has no one to listen to his further explanation.

If I meet him on the street, I say:

"Howdy, Mr. Rugby—fine day, isn't it?"

"It *is* a fine day *here*," he replies, "but I do not know how it is in Chicago, Cleveland, Savannah or San Francisco, and I cannot answer in a general way."

If I hear the fire-bells go ringing, I grab my hat and rush out and plunge around, and if I see Rugby, I shout:

"Ho! ha! whoop—fire on Harrison avenue!"

"How do you know?" he inquires.

"Because the alarm is from box seventeen."

"But it may be a false alarm."

"No—I see smoke."

"Which may be caused by a bonfire."

"But I see flames."

"It may be a burning chimney."

I feel mad enough to boot him, and I can't half enjoy the balance of the evening.

When General Grant was elected, and the news came over the wires, and many people were half-wild, I rushed into Rugby's house and yelled:

"Well, Grant's elected!"

"How do you know?" he asked.

"Know! why, there's a big blow-out down town!"

"But has any one seen Mr. Grant?"

"Of course not."

"Has he informed any one here of his election?"

"Why, no, but the telegraph says so."

"How does the telegraph know?" he queried, and I don't believe he is really certain in his own mind to this day whether Grant is President or not.

He will die some day, and I hope he will reach Heaven. If he does, he will engage in a conversation something as follows:

"Is this the gate of Heaven?" he will ask St. Peter.

"Yes; come in."

"Then this is Heaven, eh?"

"Yes."

"How do I know that it is Heaven?"

"This is the gate—come in."

"I can't do it. It may be Heaven—it may not. I'll sit down on this log until I get some reliable news."

HIS TIME FOR FIDDLING.

EANDERING along on the shady side of the street, a book canvasser finally halted before a tumble-down tene-ment. A small lame boy opened the door in answer to his knock, and just as he entered, a man sitting on the edge of a forlorn-looking bed raised a fiddle to his shoulder and commenced scraping out a tune.

"Have you a Bible in the house?" asked the canvasser as he crossed the room.

"Nary Bibe," answered the man; "and—

> Old Dan Tucker
> Drempt a dream!"

"Or a hymn-book?" continued the canvasser.

"No—nary, and—

> If you love me, Mollie, darling,
> Let your answer be a kiss."

"I am agent for the sale of this Bible," said the canvasser, taking the volume out of his satchel.

"Couldn't buy one cover, and—

> Oh, darkies, how my heart grows weary,
> Sighing for the old folks at home."

185

"I can sell you the book for a small amount down and the balance in weekly payments.   A great many——"

"Bibuls are all right, but I've got a sore foot, and—

> 'Twas a calm still night,
> And the moon's pale light—"

"If you do not care to read the book yourself you should not refuse your child permission," remarked the canvasser.

"And the old woman's up stairs, sick with fever, and—

> They took her off to Georgia
> To toil her life away."

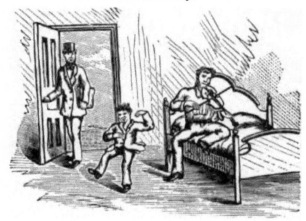

"But it seems hard to think that you are permitting yourself and family to live in ignorance of religious——"

"Bibuls is all right, and I'd encourage 'em if times wasn't so blasted—

> Ha! ha! ha! you and me—
> Little brown jug, don't I love thee!"

"I have a smaller edition like this.   You can have that by paying fifty cents down and twenty-five cents per week until paid up."

"No use, stranger," replied the man; "there haint nothing to do, money is tight, and—

> I've wandered this wide world all over."

" I wish you would cease that fiddling and singing for a moment and let me talk to you," said the agent.

" Bibuls is all right—you are all right, and—

> Oh! this world is sad and dreary,
> Everywhere I roam!"

" Won't you stop for just one moment?"

" I'd like to oblige you, but now's my reg'lar time for fiddling and singing, and—

> Up in a balloon, boys,
> Up in a balloon."

" Then I can't sell you a Bible ?"

" Don't look as if you could, for—

> I've wandered through the village, Tom,
> I've sat beneath the tree."

And the canvasser left the house in despair.

TOPSY TUMBLE.

SHE wasn't a bad sort of a girl for one who had been brought up in an alley all her days, living with old Mother Hart ever since she was large enough to gather chips around the ship-yard. The boys called her Topsy Tumble, and nobody knew anything about her parents or relatives. Her hair was long and matted; her face tanned to a brown; her nose always bore a stain of dirt, and she had stone-bruises on her feet, and chapped hands and sore heels, just like the ragged boys with whom she played. The "society" of the alley rather cut Topsy Tumble, but she was independent, and she made faces at "society" from the top of coal-sheds, and allowed herself to be harnessed up beside Bob White when the boys wanted a blooded team to draw a creaking cart down around the railroad crossing.

The alley was unusually quiet the other week. Topsy Tumble was sick. Mother Hart said so when Bob White went to see if Topsy wanted to trade her old jack-knife for a small dog which he had picked up on Atwater street. It was a strange thing, her illness. For eleven years she had rolled in the dirt, waded through the snow and plashed around in the mud, and nobody had ever heard her complain of anything more than a stubbed toe. Bob couldn't make it out. He and Bill Davis and Sam Sharp and Chip Larkins sat in the shade of a truck-wagon going to decay, and talked it over. It would be rough on Mother Hart to

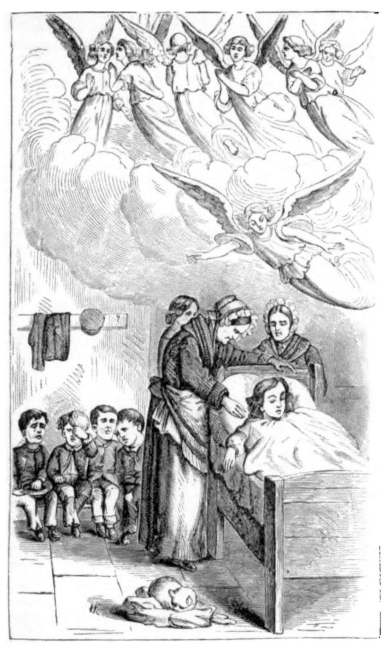

Romance of an Alley.

DEATH OF TOPSY TUMBLE.

have sickness and bear a doctor's bill, and they wondered if Topsy would get well in time to go out with them the next week.

The doctor said it was a bad fever, and most of the folks in John Brown alley called in to say that they would sit up nights and do anything they could. Topsy was out of her head, talking strange things; and, after looking at her flushed face and listening to her mutterings, Bob White called the boys together on top of a coal-shed, and there was a lump in his throat as he whispered:

"Boys, Topsy's a-goin' to die!"

The boys looked around over the sheds and made no reply, and by and by they slid down one by one and went home. There was no more dog-fighting in the alley— no pounding of fire-alarms on the old steamboat boiler and then rushing the "machine" up to the corner. Columbus Jones brought his rooster down and wanted to bet a kite that it could clean out any chicken in John Brown alley, but the boys had no enthusiasm.

Topsy grew worse. The doctor called twice a day, but his medicine didn't touch the case, and he told Mother Hart that Topsy must die. The old woman felt a little weak, and her eyes grew misty. It had been a score of years since she had wept for grief, and she could not remember when she had thought of death.

The neighbors came in, and they tip-toed across the room, and kept their babies still, that the dying girl might hear no harsh sound. Bob White and his chums hung around the door awhile, and finally gathered courage to pull off their hats and enter the house. Mother Hart motioned for them to take seats on the bench at the head of the bed, and she whispered in a weak voice:

"Bob, I'm afeard we're going to lose Topsy!"

Bob wiped his eyes, and his chin quivered, and some of the boys broke clear down and wept.

Topsy was unconscious. The boys wondered at the pallor of her face and the whiteness of her hands, and the women shed tears. Mother Hart kept wiping her eyes on her apron, and the boys wondered if sitting there wasn't something like going to meeting.

"She was a good girl, Topsy was," whispered one of the women.

"And so willing to help her mother," said another.

"And she stood up for John Brown alley!" added Bob White, a sob in his throat.

Darkness settled down, and they almost lost sight of the white face. No one moved. Some of the babies fell asleep, and the mothers trotted them softly, and the boys almost dozed as they sat crooked upon the bench. The shadows of night grew deeper, and the rattle of a truck going home sounded painfully loud and harsh. Mother Hart moved softly over and lighted the little old lamp, and as she held it up the woman said: "Poor dear!" and Bob White leaned over on Chip Larkins' shoulder and sobbed aloud.

Topsy Tumble was dead!

The little soul, never washed by mother's tears—never made better by a word about Heaven—never drinking in the knowledge that only the body dies—had crossed the dark valley alone, having only the tears and heartaches of the dwellers in John Brown alley to plead its case with the angels.

THE FIRST HOUSE IN MICHIGAN.

NOT long since, I stood before the first house ever erected in Michigan. A thousand sad memories gurgled up.

It isn't every person who can appreciate these old relics and call out all the tender fancies connected with them. I have known old houses more or less ever since my birth, and I can appreciate a dozen of 'em at once.

It made me feel lonely to stand before that old first house. It seemed a sacred thing in my eyes.

The man who built it, a hundred years ago, wasn't there any more. No, I looked around and could see nothing of him. However, I could appreciate his pioneer struggles, his griefs and heartaches, just the same, and the fact of his absence was excused as I gazed at the ancient hut, fast going to decay. It wasn't a first-class house any more. The door had rotted away, some of the logs were crumbling to dust, and there was a general tearful look to the whole concern. I sat down on a log and wept.

It is a sad thing to sit on a log and be overwhelmed with memories of the past— of a hundred years ago. There that old first house was

191

fast falling to decay, and the general public didn't seem to care a picayune about it.   Two boys were probing a woodchuck's den not fifty rods away, and a red-headed man was washing a one-horse wagon in a pond whose waters almost touched the sacred logs.

I went over to him.

He seemed like an emotional man—like one whose heartstrings would yank a little as fond memory played on them a tune of long ago.

"It is a sad thing to look upon the first house erected in Michigan, isn't it?" I queried.

The man with red hair looked up and grinned, and as he rubbed away at the mud-stained spokes, he replied:

"Want to buy a dog, stranger?"

"A dog, sir?   Man, have you no soul—no heart-strings! I am plunged in sadness as I look upon these old logs.   I think I hear a funeral bell tolling the death of the past!"

"It's one of those blasted locomotives down at the bend!" he replied, raising his head to listen.

"Hark!   Doesn't the breeze rustling the tender limbs of the beeches seem to sing sad requiems o'er the dead past?"

"Sounds to me like a feller whistling, over there by the slaughter-house!" replied the unfeeling wretch.

I went back to the house and wept anew.

Who built that house?   Was his name Smith or Robinson or Brown? Was there any living witness of his pioneer hardships and privations?

The red-headed man came over and inquired:

"So, you wouldn't like to buy a dog?"

"Murderer!" I shouted, how dare you come within this

circle of memory's influence and basely ask me to purchase your dog!"

"I can recommend him for coon!" he quietly observed.

"See there! man—gaze on those venerated logs!" I said, as I caught his arm. "Is it possible that you can stand here and think of dogs and one-horse wagons and postal currency when I am trembling with emotion caused by the recollections of the silent, speechless dead who came here and hewed out the whispering wilderness and erected that cabin?"

"Do you have these spells often?" he inquired in a harsh, cruel tone.

I pointed to his one-horse wagon, but he wouldn't go.

I wept some more.

"Haven't any navy plug about you?" he inquired, as I looked through my tears at the precious logs.

"Wretch! go away—go hence and afar! If your heart cannot throb and your soul yearn, go away and let me feel my feelings!"

"I'll be hanged if I do!" he replied as he sat down. "I believe I'd better keep an eye on you!"

I walked around that sacred house, and that monster sat there and whistled: "Shoo, Fly!" I peered in at the door—at the smoke-stained rafters and the crumbling logs, and he sang: "If ever I cease to love!"

I sat down and was listening to the sad whispers of the soft wind when another man came down to the pond.

He was leading something.

It was not a horse.

It was not a dromedary.

It was not a cow.

The boys got into a fight over the wood-chuck.

M

The red-headed man sang: "Ten Thousand Miles Away."

The beast hung back and brayed.

I went away from there, but even as I walked slowly away, fond memory calling out to me not to leave her, the red-headed man tore a pole off the roof of that sacred old structure, and I heard him yell

NOT A DROMEDARY.

out:

"Hang to the halter, Tom, while I wollop the infernal old cundurango up strong!"

HOW A WOMAN READS A LETTER.

SHE knows it by the postmark. No one but Augusta Ann Greenville lives where that letter was posted. She turns the letter over nine or ten times, looks to see if it has been tampered with, and finally pinches one end open. She regrets that she didn't open it on the side, but it is too late. After the letter is out she looks into the envelope to see if it contains anything more, though she knew it didn't.

She unfolds the letter at last, and flops it over to see the signature on the fourth page. Then she reads the date and compares it with the postmark to see how long the precious missive has been on the road. Two whole days! Bless her! but she has been to Fishertown a dozen times, and it never took her but twenty-three hours. Those post-office folks are getting awful reckless. By and by they won't care whether she gets a letter at all.

She finally reads:

"*Dear, darling Mollie:*—I have had *such* times since I wrote you before! You know Jim Taylor——"

(Then she talks):

"Know Jim Taylor—guess I do! Didn't he take me to spelling school the night I wore that serge dress trimmed with fringe. I've heard that Jim's uncle Dan was sent to State's prison for stealing a horse, but I don't see how they

can blame Jim, I'm sure he isn't responsible for what his
uncles do.　But let's see what she says about Jim."

(Then she reads):

"—Well, Jim Taylor came home with me from the dona-
tion the other night, and what do you think he said?　I
was never so astonished in my life.　He said that Tom
Goodale and Minnie Nettleton were——"

(Then she talks):

"Mercy sakes alive! but is that Tom Goodale going to
throw himself away on such a pink-faced simpleton as
Minnie Nettleton!　I can't believe it.　Why, he's rich, he
is, and she hasn't got the second dress to her back!　He
must marry her for her beauty, though I don't call her
handsome.　Well, well, if that don't amaze me!"

(Then she reads):

"And Minnie Nettleton were down to Blakely's husking
bee, and they never spoke to each other!　Isn't it awful?
You know I wrote you that they were going to get married?　I had it on the authority of Nancy——"

(Then she talks):

"Collins, of course!　If any one is going to get married,
Nancy Collins is sure to know all about it a year beforehand.　I remember the day we went to Orchard Lake to
the Good Templars' excursion, and she said my curls were
false, and that my nose was too large for my face!　Dear
me, but didn't I give her *such* a look!"

(Then she reads):

—"who is now lying at the point of death.　They say she
caught the fever nursing Parson Gray, who——"

(Then she talks):

"Who is looking around for a second wife, I suppose.
Well, I wonder how he came to fall sick?　And did you
ever hear of such a thing as his sending for that old maid
to nurse him?　Poor man!　I hope he'll live and make a

happy match this time. They say his wife wasn't a bit refined, and that the fact used to mortify him awfully. I wonder if Augusta Ann mentions anything about it?

Then she reads, talks, goes over the letter a second time, folds it up and puts it away, and declares that she'd give most anything to get a real letter—one with some news and gossip in.

AN HOUR AT THE CENTRAL STATION COURT.

"YOUNG man, this is a pretty way to commence the year 1875, isn't it?" exclaimed his Honor, as Michael Smith stood before him in pensive attitude.

"I'm sorry," replied the prisoner.

"Yes, so am I. It gives me the heart-burn to see a youth of twenty-two flopped out here on a charge of drunkenness. If that's the way you start off the new year, where do you expect to land at its close?"

"I'll do better, sir—I've sworn off."

The Court picked up his snuff-box, gently tapped the bottom, removed the lid, inhaled a fragrant pinch, and continued:

"Mr. Smith, there's a scratch on your nose, dirt on your chin, and you look demoralized out of your eyes, but I'll try you. I don't want to fall on a young man like a horse on a butterfly the first time he comes here, but let the first also be the last time with you. Consider, sir, that you have had a narrow escape; go home and be wise."

NARROW ESCAPE.

A NEW YEAR'S CALLER.

John Robinson made New Year's calls. He called on a saloon-keeper, he called for liquor, called the liquor good,

and drank enough to trip him up. Then he called for
police, and when the police came he called them liars and
such.

"I was having a little fun," he explained, winking at
his Honor.

"John Robinson, are you aware that this is a very
solemn world," said the Court, "a world which has ten
heart-aches to one smile? Don't you know that the grim
shadow of grief rests upon every door-step, and that the
tomb-stones in the cemeteries almost outnumber the trees
in the forest? There's wailing in every household, John
Robinson—there's grief in every heart. And yet you claim
that you were only having a little fun!"

"That's all, your Honor—it was a holiday."

"It was sad fun, John Robinson. While all the rest of
us were swearing off and making double-back-action
resolves, you were lying at the corner of an alley dead
drunk. It is five dollars or sixty days, sir, and if this case
was before a Chicago police justice he'd make it five hundred dollars or a life sentence."

SOME FIGURING.

"It's the last time!" exclaimed Anthony Hock as he was
brought out.

"You've decided to quit, eh?"

"Yes, your Honor—yesterday was my last drunk. I've
been counting up the cost, and I've made up my mind to
live sober and save money after this."

"Anthony Hock, you talk like a man! It does me good
to hear a man speak up that way in this day and age. It's
like finding a ten-dollar bill while one is pawing over the
clothes-basket to discover where the hired girl flung his
Sunday boots. Stand right up to your resolution, sir.
I've been figuring a little, and I find that if a man will stop

drinking liquor, tea and coffee, go barefooted, steal his wood, get trusted for his provisions, cheat the landlord out of his rent, stand up in church to save pew-rent, and live economically in other respects, he can save at least $500 per year. Now then, $500 per year for 400 years is $200,000. Just think of that! Without any effort to speak of you can in time be worth $200,000! You can go home, sir!"

ECONOMY THE ROAD TO
WEALTH.

FIRST JOKE.

Elizabeth McNamara, a woman fifty years old, got off the first joke of the season when she walked out and boldly announced that it was her first appearance here. Bijah laughed until his spectacles fell off, the clerk grinned like a copper mine, and his Honor stopped paring his apple, stuck his knife into the desk and replied:

"Elizabeth McNamara, the sight of that 'ere front door is not more familiar to me than the fact that you have been here somewhere in the region of forty times. What's the charge, this time?"

"Taken a drap—a bit of a little small drap."

"I've let you off, sent you up, expostulated, pleaded and threatened, and yet you come back here," he said. "I was thinking the other day that if I ever peered over the desk at your freckled nose again, and the charge was drunkenness, I'd have you sawed in two with a cross-cut saw and the pieces split up for kindling-wood!"

"Don't do it, sir—send me up again."

"I shall make it three months."

"I don't care—only don't saw me in twice!" she gasped.

"Well," he said, after pondering over the case, "we've been to $10 expense to get the saw, and Bijah has anticipated great fun, but I'll see what three months will do. Go back and sit down on the stove-hearth until the Black Maria goes up."

COULDN'T STAND IT.

" This is Daniel Casey," said Bijah as he handed out the last man, " and I can tell you why he was drunk."

" Well."

" Casey wasn't sober !" continued the old janitor.

His Honor regarded him for a long time without speaking, but finally said :

" The prisoner can go, and, Bijah, if you ever sit down on this court with another pun like that, and are accidentally shot next day, your friends musn't ask me for any money to help buy a monument."

THE LADY WE ALL FEAR.

BOARD now, and I think I have one of the kindest landladies in the world. She seems to think a great deal of me, and I sometimes almost decide that I should weep if any harm were to come to her.

She is very particular about her boarders. Before she would take me in I was compelled to get a certificate from three clergymen, two bankers and a lawyer, stating that I had never been hung for murder or sent to State Prison for horse stealing. I bargained for a front room looking out on the Campus Martius, and it was understood that I was to have the room alone. On the third night I went home and found a stranger in bed, and when I began to raise a row, Mrs. Dolby caught my arm and said:

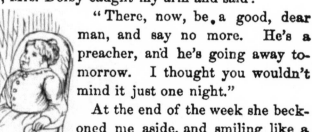

THAT SMILE.

"There, now, be a good, dear man, and say no more. He's a preacher, and he's going away to-morrow. I thought you wouldn't mind it just one night."

At the end of the week she beckoned me aside, and smiling like a load of fresh hay, she wanted to know if I would do her a favor, a favor which would place her under many obligations to me. I replied that I would die for her, and then she asked me to give up the room looking out upon the

grand square and take one looking out upon the grand
alley, full of ash-barrels and oyster cans. She had a
boarder coming who was awful particular, and she knew
that I would do anything to accommodate her. I made
the change, and the grateful look she gave me was enough
to melt a vest button. I had only got fairly settled when
I was told that she wanted to see me in the parlor after
dinner. I found her in tears. She said a very nice man
and his very nice wife wanted to come and board with her,
but she had no room, and it grieved her to think that she
must turn them away when she was so hard pushed to get
along.   •

I told her that if I had a hundred lives I would lay them
all down for her and borrow a hundred more and add to
the pile, and she seized my hand and said that Heaven
would surely reward me for being so good to a fatherless
orphan. I moved into the garret, and the awful particular man moved into my room, and the very nice man and
his very nice wife moved into the front room.

In another week Mrs. Dolby whispered to me and
wanted to know if I had a snake in my stomach. She had
observed that I was a hearty eater, and she did not know
but I had a snake. I set her right, and when I promised
to take free lunches down town and urge all the other
boarders to do the same, she put her hand on my shoulder
and remarked that Heaven had a place for me.

That night my bed was made without sheets, and when
I went to raise a row she took me by the hand and said
that her experience went to show that it was healthier to
sleep without sheets. I was going to argue the question,
when tears came to her eyes, and she hoped I would not
say anything to hurt a poor, lone widow, whose life had
been one long struggle with poverty.

The next night the feather bed and one of the pillows

went, but I didn't say anything. Then she wanted to borrow my tooth-brush for a boarder who hadn't any, and she took my stove to use in the lower hall. I did not say a word until she wanted to know if I couldn't spare the old rag-carpet off the floor, and if I wouldn't set the other boarders an example by drinking nothing but water, and not take the second biscuit. Then I told her that I was going to leave the house and try to tear her image from my heart.

She seized both my hands, tears rolled down her cheeks, and she asked:

"Mr. Quad, would you deliberately plot to kill a lonesome widow, who is working her life out to make your position here comfortable, happy and luxurious?"

I couldn't go. I'm here yet. I sleep on the floor, put up with cold bites, and use the boot-jack for a chair when I have company. I wish I wasn't so tender-hearted, but I can't bear to think of hurting Mrs. Dolby's feelings by looking up another place.

A DETERMINED YOUNG MAN.

IT was out on the Holden Road, near Detroit, that a carriage in which was seated two fond lovers, was run away with by the spirited horse. As they came dashing past a farm gate the farmer saw that the young man was making no effort to check the animal, and he yelled:

"Why don't you stop that horse—he's running away!"

"Yes, I know it!" shouted the young man, "but I'll keep my arm around this girl if it takes every spoke in the wheels!"

A PIONEER JUSTICE.

NE of the counties in the central part of Michigan, when it had but few inhabitants, elected a man named Goodhue to serve as Justice of the Peace. The Justice felt the dignity of his position, and he made up his mind at the start that he would take no nonsense from the lawyers.

His office was the bar-room of a log tavern, his desk a dry-goods box, and his "docket" consisted of the two fly-leaves in a spelling-book. His first case was the trial of a man who was charged with stealing a rifle. The complainant had missed the gun from his "chopping," and it had next been found in possession of the defendant, who was seeking to exchange it for a hound.

The two scrub lawyers of the village were opposed to each other, and as the case was considered an important one, each attorney was prepared to cover the jury with a mantle of eloquence. The Justice took his seat with a determination to have no "fooling around," and he soon had opportunity to exercise his authority.

"May it please your Honor——" commenced the prosecution, when up rose Goodhue and replied:

"Confine yourself to the case, sir!"

The lawyer was taken aback, but after a moment began:

" Gentlemen of the jury,——"

" Confine yourself to the case, I say!" interrupted the
Justice.

" Why, I haven't begun yet!" replied the lawyer in great
surprise.

" Well, if you've got anything to say go ahead and say
it, but talk to me.   The jury has nothing to do with this
case!"

" Well, your Honor," said the lawyer, " we propose to
prove that——"

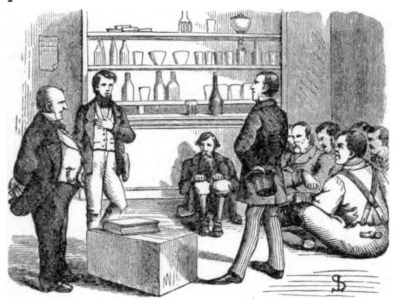

" Hold on! stop right there!" exclaimed his Honor, " I
don't want to hear what you propose to prove—I want to
know what you can prove!"

" It is usual, I believe, in opening a case, to state——"

" Can't help what it's usual to do!" interrupted the
Court; " this court doesn't care a dum what other courts
have done!   If you want to practice at this bar you've got
to obey the rules!"

The lawyer saw that he had better leave out his statement, and he called his first witness, who happened to be a deaf man. As the man took the stand the lawyer said:

"Now, Mr. Brown, go on and tell the jury what you know about this case."

"Tell who!" cried the Court, jumping up. "I want you to understand that I'm trying this case! If I ain't Judge here, who is?"

"Well, tell the Court what you know about this case," said the lawyer to his witness.

"Eh?" queried Brown, bending forward.

"Tell the Court what you know——"

"Tell the Court nothing!" exclaimed Goodhue. "The man is deaf—what does he know about this case!"

"Deaf men can see, can't they?" asked the lawyer.

"No sass, sir, or I'll fine you five thousand dollars!" warned the Justice.

The lawyer saw that he couldn't proceed with the trial, and he remarked that he rested his case right there.

"What business have you to arrest the case?" demanded his Honor, but the lawyer put on his hat and left the house.

The attorney for the defense, warned by the sad experience of his opponent, made his appeal directly to the Court, saying:

"Judge, you don't believe my client stole that rifle. You can't——"

"How do you know I don't believe he stole it!" interrupted the Court. "Confine yourself to the case."

"I demand his discharge, on the ground that the complainant has failed to make out a case," said the lawyer, after a moment's thought.

"Well, he won't be discharged!" replied his Honor. "I know he stole that gun, and I fine him ten dollars and costs!"

"But this is a case for the jury to decide," protested the lawyer.

"It is, eh! perhaps the people elected you Justice instead of me! Perhaps I don't know anything about law!"

"The jury were selected to decide on the case, weren't they?" demanded the attorney.

"No, sir!"

"What for, then?"

"None of your business, sir! I fine you fifteen dollars for contempt of court, and the prisoner has got to pay his fine in one hour or I'll send him to State Prison for twelve years!"

That ended the case, and the attorneys weren't three hours picking up their traps and crossing the county line.

N

"TWO DOLLAR ÜND ZIXTY CENT!"

ONE day an old man entered one of the railroad depots in Detroit, and walking up to the ticket office he asked:

"What you sharge for dicket to Lansing?"

"Two-sixty, sir," replied the agent, wetting his thumb and reaching out for the money.

"Two dollar und zixty cent!" exclaimed the stranger, pulling his head out of the window.

"Yes, sir, that is the regular fare."

"Then I sthays here by Detroit forty yare!" said the man, getting red in the face. "I haf never seen such a schwindle as dot!"

"Two-sixty is the fare, and you will have to pay it if you go," replied the agent.

"I shust gif you two dollar, und no more," said the stranger.

"No, can't do it."

"Vhell, den I sthays mit Detroit till I dies!" growled the old man, and he went away and walked around the depot. He expected to be called back as he left the window, as a man is often called back to "take it along" when he has been chaffing with a clothing dealer. Such an event did not occur, and after a few minutes the old man returned and called out:

"Vhell, I gif you two dollar und ten cent."

"No, can't do it," replied the agent.

210

"Vhell, den I don't go, so help my grashus! I haf lived in Detroit three yare, und I shall bay bolice tax, zewer tax, und want to grow up mit dis town, und I shall not be schwindled!"

He walked off again, looking back to see if the agent would not call him, and after a stroll around he returned to the window, threw down some money, and said:

"Vhell, dake two dollars und dwenty cent und gif me a dicket."

"My dear sir, can't you understand that we have a schedule of prices here, and that I must go by it?" replied the agent.

"Vhell, den I sthays mit Detroit von tousand yare!" exclaimed the stranger, madder than ever. "I bays bolice taxes, und zewer taxes, und I shall see about dis by de Sheaf of Bolice!"

He walked off again, and as he saw the locomotive backing up to couple on to the train he went back to the window, and said:

"Gif me a dicket for two dollar und dirty cent, und I rides on de blatform!"

"Can't do it," said the agent.

"Vhell, den, py golly, I shpokes to you what I doze! Here is dem two dollar und zixty cent, und I goes to Lansing und never comes pack! No, zir, I shall never come pack, or I shall come mit der blank road! I bays taxes by dem bolice, und by dem zewers, und I shall show you dat I shall haf noddings more to do mit dis town!"

And he went on the train.

JOHN CAIN.

JOHN CAIN was a quiet, unobtrusive citizen. He didn't long for fame and renown, and he didn't care two cents whether this great and glorious country was ruled by a one-horse Republican or a two-horse Democrat.

He had a pew in church, gave sixteen ounces for a pound, and when a man looked him square in the eye, Mr. Cain never took a back seat. He was home at a reasonable hour in the evening, never took part in the discussion, "Is lager healthy?" and many a man wished his life rolled on as evenly and peacefully as John Cain's. But, alas! the

THE TEMPTER.

tempter came. In an evil hour John Cain allowed the politicians to get after him and to surround him. They said he was the strongest man in the county; that he could scoop out of his boots any man set up in opposition; that his virtues were many, and his faults 00000; that it was his duty to come out and take a nomination, in order that this pure and incorruptible form of government be maintained pure and incorruptible. All this and much more they told him, and John Cain became puffed up. It surprised him some to think that he had held his peaceful way along for forty odd years, like knot-hole in a barn door, without any one

212

having discovered what a heap of a fellow he was, but he concluded that there was a new era in politics, and that it was all right.

The politicians covered John Cain with soft soap. They told him that the canvass shouldn't cost him a red, and that he could still retire at eight o'clock every evening and rest assured that his interests would be properly cared for. It was to be a still hunt—a very quiet election, and he wouldn't hardly know what was going on. John Cain was an honest, unsuspecting idiot, and he swallowed their words as the confiding fish absorbs the baited hook.

John Cain was duly nominated, and the band came out and serenaded him. With the band came several hundred electors, who filled the Cain mansion to overflowing, spit tobacco all over the house, ate and drank all they could find, broke down the gate, and went off with three cheers for John Cain.

Before the canvass was ten days old half a dozen men

'RAH FOR CAIN!

called on Cain and gently hinted to him that he must come down with the "sugar." He didn't even know what "sugar" was until they kindly explained. They wanted money to raise a pole, to buy beer, to get slips printed, and to do fifty other things with, all for his particular benefit, and he had to hand out the money.

In the course of another week they drew Cain out to make a speech at a ward meeting. He tried to claw off, but they told him that the opposing candidate would run him out of sight if he didn't come out, and he went out. When he got through speaking the crowd drank at his expense, and Mr. Cain was astonished at the way the liquor went down,

and more astonished at the way the bill footed up. He
didn't reach home until midnight, and for the first time in
his life he was going to bed with his boots on. His wife
wouldn't speak to him, the hired girl left the house to save
her character, and John Cain wished that the politicians
had let him alone.

More men came and crooked their fingers at him and
whispered "sugar." They wanted money to buy some
doubtful votes, and to hire four-horse teams, and to mail
his slips, and he had to come down. He hesitated about
it, but they told him that the opposing candidate felt sure
of victory, and that acted as a spur.

There was hardly a night that from fourteen to two
hundred did not call on Mr. Cain to inform him as to the
"prospects." They drank up the currant wine Mrs. Cain
had laid by for sickness, emptied her preserve jars, and
there wasn't a morning that she couldn't sweep out forty
or fifty cigar stubs and a peck of mud. They all told Cain
that he would beat the other man so far out of sight that
it would take a carrier pigeon to find him, and he couldn't

FIFTH WARD.

very well refuse to go over to the
corner grocery and "set 'em up"
for the boys.

On the eve of election Mr. Cain's
friends called for "sugar" again,
and he had to sugar 'em. A big
crowd called to warn him that he
would certainly be elected, and the
saloon bill was $28 more. Thirteen
or fourteen men shook hands with

his wife, a hundred or more shook hands with him, and he
had to get up and declare that he didn't favor woman's
rights, and that he *did;* that he was down on whisky, and
yet loved it as a beverage; that he wanted the currency

inflated, and yet favored specie payments; that he favored
the Civil Rights bill, and yet didn't, and in his brief speech
Mrs. Cain counted twenty-seven straight lies, besides the
evasions. Mr. Cain wanted to hold popular views, and he
had to be on all sides at once.

On the day of election they dragged him from poll to
to poll, stopping at all the saloons on the way. He had
to make two hundred and fifty-six thousand promises, pull
his wallet until it was as flat as a wafer, drink lager with
some and cold water with others, and when night came he
went home and tried to hang the hired girl, called Mrs.
Cain his dear old rhinoceros, and fell over the cradle and
went to sleep with his head under the stove.

When Mr. Cain arose in the morning
and became sober enough to read the election returns he found he had scooped 'em
as follows:

Opposing candidate..................86,420
John Cain........................81,380
_____
Cain's majority (in a horn)........ 5,040

Mr. Cain went out and sat down
under an apple tree in his back yard,
and he gave himself up to reflections, and so forth. And
through the leafless branches sighed the November winds,
and in the house sighed Mrs. Cain, and both sighs murmured gently in his ear:

"John Cain's a perpendicular idiot."

IT WAS IN INDIANA.

REMEMBER that it was a soft summer's evening, and as I leaned over the fence the air was full of buzzing flies and humming mosquitos. The deacon was a good man—good for a man brought up in Indiana, and as he took down the milk-stool he said:

"I s'pose ye'll be at the church festival?——Hist around there, boss!"

I told him I would try and come, and as he sat down beside the cow he continued:

"By all means. We're planning for a——so, darn ye, so!——As I was going to say, we're making great expectations on——so, I say! If ye don't stop switching that tail around here I'll cut it off!"

"You expect to have a good time, deacon?"

"Oh, I know we will. The committee on contributions has reported that——durn ye, what ails ye, any way! Hist over thar and stand still!"

"The committee, deacon——?"

"Yes; the committee has reported cash collections amounting to——why in tophet can't ye stand still!"

"And so you have secured the funds?"

"Got plenty, and the committee on preparations has—— whoa, there! If ye don't stop histin' yer feet I'll spike 'em down!"

"There'll be a big crowd."

216

"We count on it, onless it should rain. The committee on preparations has made prep——see here! I'll maul the life out o' ye 'f ye don't stop dancing around! I'd sell this cow if I could!"

"And there's to be an excursion after the festival?"

"Yes; we've chartered a train of thirteen cars, and—— there you go again, you old fiend you! Hist around now and stand still!"

"Thirteen will give you plenty of room."

"Well, we don't want to crowd the children, and—— keep that ar' leg still or I'll maul ye with the milk-stool!"

"At what hour will the train leave?"

"We haven't quite decided yet, but I guess at about—— now I *will* maul ye! There, take that! and that! and that!"

After two or three minutes he settled down on the stool again, and I asked:

"Have you selected the grove?"

"Well, we've about decided on Baker's, but——histin' them ar' feet again! Hev I got to maul the horns off'n ye?"

"He wants pay, does he?"

"No—not any money, but Baker don't seem to——thar goes that dum tail again! and them hoofs keep a raisin'!"

"Who are the main committee?"

"Well, thar's mean Johnson and——dancin' around again! If ye don't stand still I'll git up 'n pound ye all to pieces!"

"I suppose Durney is on?"

"Yaas; there's mean Johnson, and Durney, and——now by gum 'f I *don't* wollop ye! How's that! and that! and——!"

The cow disappeared over the hill, the deacon in full chase, and I took the dusty highway again.

HIS EARLY LOVES.

AH! I'm not so old but that I remember Kitty Glenn, my first love. We sat in school together, and the morning I showed her my sore thumb, and she wept with me, was the morning love was first developed in my heart. I suddenly discovered that the little tangle-haired, freckled-nose child was the handsomest girl in school, and at noon we traded slices of bread and butter, took alternate bites

EARLY LOVE.

from my piece of pumpkin pie, and I made up my mind to marry her. I tried to get a chance to propose to her as we walked home from school, but her big sister was along and I dared not speak.

That night I licked my brother Ben for calling Kitty's father "Old Glenn;" and I got so worried and anxious that mother—bless her gray hairs!—came up stairs, put her hand on my head and declared her belief that I ought to have some horse-raddish drafts on my feet.

It seemed as if morning would never come, but it finally did, and I was at the school-house half an hour before any one else. I had it all planned out, and as soon as Kitty arrived I beckoned her one side, presented her with three buckeyes and a seek-no-further apple, and said:

"Kitty, I think I will marry you!"

"I wish you would!" she replied, as she untied my comforter.

"Well, all right. You musn't let Burt Turner carry your dinner-basket any more, and you musn't let Bob Haynes draw you on his sled."

"I'll ask mother this very night if she won't let us keep house in the woodshed!" exclaimed my betrothed, and a

A KNEED SUPPLIED.

great burden was rolled off my mind. I'd been wondering whether we should board or keep house.

Ah! wasn't I happy for two weeks! I lived in a sort of Heaven by myself, and my dreams were worth five thousand dollars per night. Then Kitty and I fell out. Her mother gave her a spanking when she learned that she was "engaged," and mother drew me over her knee, reached for the press-board, and mildly remarked that I had needed a hammering for many days past. In another week more I could hear the boys speak of my " late darling " as " tow-headed tom-boy " and never feel a ripple of indignation.

I loved again when I had arrived at the age of ten. It was not a sudden love, coming upon me like a man slipping down, but it was budding for weeks and weeks before it finally blossomed. It was a woman this time—an old maid called Aunt Jane. She gave me five cents to chase a cow out of the lot, paid me for going to the store after a fine comb; kissed me for taking a letter to the post-office, and my admiration grew day by day.

One evening, when I heard mother saying that Aunt Jane was good-hearted, and deserved a good husband, my pent-up love frothed up like soap-suds. I resolved to marry Aunt Jane forthwith, and to love and cherish her to the last ditch.

I had another restless night, principally because I could not decide whether we should be married by a Methodist or a Baptist minister, and whether we'd have a regular door-bell to our house or a gong which turned by a silver-plated handle.

I remember with what confidence I entered the neighbor's house wherein Aunt Jane was employed to do house-work. I found her in the kitchen, passing some slices of fat-pork to the hot spider, and I thought I had never seen her look so lovely. I walked straight over to her, threw my arms around her neck, and said:

"Aunt Jane, I want to marry you !"

"Sakes to stars !" she exclaimed, holding the last piece of pork poised on the fork.

"I love you, and I'll marry you to-day !" I went on.

She put down the meat, gently slid out of my arms, and placing her hand on my head she solemnly said:

"My dear boy, I'm old enough to be your mother! You mustn't think of getting married for fifteen years yet !"

I rushed out of the house, eyes full of tears, and I went down to the creek, fell upon the grass, and wept long and bitterly over my great sorrow. I made a solemn vow never to marry any one as long as I lived, but four weeks after that I was in love with a girl in a dollar store.

Ah! well, I suppose all

men can look back and call up just such recollections of long ago, and yet we cannot smile over them—there are too many graves between us and childhood.

HE SAID "CUSS."

MANY people noticed him as he sat on the curb-stone at the corner, head in his hands. He wore a coat of wolf-skins, a bearskin cap, buckskin breeches, and his grizzly hair hung down on his shoulders in a tangled mass. He had drifted east from the wild frontier, and he had fallen sick. No one knew for a long time what ailed him, as he would not reply to questions, but finally, when a policeman shook his arm and repeated the inquiry, the man slowly lifted his head and replied:

"I'm played!"

His face was pale and haggard, and it was plain that he was going to have an attack of fever. He was sent to the hospital for treatment, he making no inquiries and answering no questions. He had his personal effects in a sort of sack. There was a breech-loading rifle, a hatchet, a knife and several other articles, and when he had been laid on a bed in one of the wards he insisted that the sack be placed under his head. They offered him medicine, but he turned away his face, and no argument could induce him to swallow any.

222

"But you are a sick man," said the doctor, as he held the medicine up.

"Cuss sickness !" replied the old man.

"But you may die !"

"Cuss death !"

He grew worse as the days went by, and was sometimes out of his head and talking strange talk of Indian fights and buffalo-hunts, but not once did he speak of family, friends or of himself. He would not let them undress him, comb his hair or show him any attention beyond leaving his food on the stand. A raging fever was burning up his system, and when the doctors found that the old man would not take their medicines they knew that death was only a matter of days.

He must have had an iron constitution and a heart like a warrior, for he held Death at arm's length for many days. When it was seen that he could last but a few hours longer the nurse asked him if a clergyman should be called.

"Cuss clergymen !" replied the old man, those being the first words he had spoken for three days.

However, two hours after, his mind wandered, and he sat up in bed and called out:

"I tell ye, the Lord isn't goin' to be hard on a feller who has fit Injuns !"

He was quiet again until an hour before his death, when the nurse made one more effort, and asked:

"Will you give me your name ?"

"Cuss my name !" replied the old man.

"Haven't you any friends ?"

"Cuss friends !"

"Do you wish us to send your things to any one ?"

"Cuss any one !"

"Do you realize," continued the nurse, "that you are very near the grave ?"

" Cuss the grave ?" was the monotonous reply.

No further questions were asked, and during the next hour the strange old man dropped quietly asleep in death, uttering no word and making no sign. When they came to remove the clothing and prepare the body for the grave, what do you suppose they found carefully wrapped in oilskin and lying on his breast? A daguerreotype picture of a little girl! It was taken years and years ago, and when the child was five or six years old. The face of the little one was fair to look upon, and the case which held it had been scarred by bullets. There were a dozen scars on the old man's body to prove that he had lived a wild life, but there was not a line among his effects to reveal his name or the name of the child whose picture he had worn on his breast for years and years. Who was she? His own darling, perhaps. He would not have treasured the picture so carefully unless there was love in his heart.

No one would believe that the wolf-skin coat covered a heart which could feel love or tenderness, but it did. He might have been returning home after years of weary wandering, or he might have left the frontier to be sure of a christian burial and hoping that no unsympathetic eye would fall upon the picture.

Some said keep it, hoping to make it identify the old man, but others laid it back on the battle-scarred breast which had preserved it so long, and it was there when they buried him.

IN THE CHIMNEY CORNER.

SAT and watched him as he softly rocked to and fro. It was an old-fashioned fire-place, and he was rocking in an old-fashioned splint-bottomed chair, which was likewise a veteran in years.

There was something so good, so kind and tender in his face that I could not turn my eyes away. His hair was white as snow, his eyes weak, and the hand resting on the arm of the chair trembled with the helplessness of age.

The logs burned brightly on the andirons, and as the old man sat and gazed into the flame, he must have compared his life to it. It rose and fell, wavered and struggled to climb up, fell back and rose again, just as men struggle against fate. There were charred brands to remind him of crushed hopes—ashes to make him remember his dead. I saw his face brighten at times, and then again it was covered with a shade of sadness, and the hand shook a little faster as he remembered the graves on the hill-side and those who had slept in them for so many long years.

By and by the flames fell, and the old room was filled with shadows, which ran over the floor, climbed the walls and raced along the ceiling. Sometimes they covered the old man's face, but leaped away again, as if fearing rebuke. Sometimes they drew together in a corner and whispered to each other, and the fall of an ember would send them dancing around.

I was but a child, and the shadows made me afraid. I wished the old man would lift his eyes and speak to me, telling me his life's story, but he kept his gaze on the burning logs as if they were a magnet to draw him closer and closer. I watched the shadows until I fell asleep. Strange, sweet music came to my ears, and the shadows were replaced by a golden light and a sky so blue and pure that I tried to reach up and grasp it. Soft voices chanted in harmony with the music, and by and by I saw an angel leading an old man and helping him over the rugged path which stretched out before me until it touched the golden gates of Heaven. They went on and on, and when they were lost to view I suddenly awoke.

The fire had burned still lower, and there were more shadows in the room; the old man sat there yet, but the chair no longer moved, and his hand had ceased to tremble. I crept softly over to him and laid my hand on his. It was cold. I shook him gently, but he did not answer.

The old man was dead! While I slept the shadows had brought an angel to lead him into Heaven.

CHRISTOPHER COLUMBUS McPHERSON.

THIS boy was a good boy. He would have been an angel to-day but for the deceit of this false-hearted world. He wasn't one of a lot of triplets, and therefore didn't have honors showered down upon him in his early days, but old women said there was foundation there for an orator, a great general or a philosopher, and old men examined his head and said it was level. Nothing particular happened to Christopher Columbus until the eighth year of his reign. His childhood days were full of mud-pies, the butt-ends of shingles, paregoric, castor oil, and old straw hats with the front brim worn off. He was a deep thinker and a close observer for a small boy, and he was just innocent enough to believe things which other boys pitch out of the window without a second thought.

When Christopher was going on nine years old he heard some one say that a " penny saved was two pence earned." He therefore laid a big bungtown away in a crack under the mop-board, and every day he looked to see it grow to two cents. He had confidence and patience, but at length both gave way. Then he got the cent out one day, and Mrs. Norton's baby swallowed it, and that was the last of that bungtown. The youthful Christopher didn't believe in maxims quite as much as before, but he hadn't cut all his eye-teeth yet.

When the boy was a year older he heard it said that " truth was mighty and must prevail," and that a boy who

always spoke the truth would surely make a great and
good man. He commenced to tell the truth. One day he
got his father's best razor out and hacked it on a stone, and
when the old gent came home and asked who in blazes had
done that, Christopher Columbus spoke up and said:

"It was I, father—I notched your old razor."

"You did, eh?" sneered the old man, as he looked up
into a peach-tree; "well I'll fix you so you won't never
notch another razor for *me!*"

And he cut a budding limb and dressed that boy down
until the youth saw stars. That night Christopher Columbus determined never to tell the truth again unless by
accident, and all through life he stuck to the resolution.

When the lad was about twelve years old he read in a
little book that "honesty was the best policy." He didn't
more than half believe it, but he thought he'd try. He
went to being honest. One day his mother sent him to the
grocery to buy eggs, and Bill Jones induced him to squan-
der the change in the purchase of soda-water. When he
got home his mother asked him for the little balance, and
Christopher explained.

"Spent it for soda, eh?" she replied. "Here your poor
old mother is working like a slave, and you are around
swilling down soda water-water! I don't think you'll swill
any more, I don't. Come over my right knee."

And she agitated him in the liveliest manner. That
night as he turned on his downy straw-bed the boy made
up his mind that honesty didn't pay, and he resolved to
cheat the whole world if he could.

When Christopher was half a year older he came across
the injunction "Be kind to the poor." He did not know
whether it would pay or not, but he set about it. He knew
of a poor woman who sadly needed a spring bonnet, and
he took over his mother's, along with a few other things,

including his father's second pair of boots, his own Sunday shoes, and so on. He went around feeling very big-hearted until the old gent wanted to go to the lodge one night, and then it came out.

"Gin away my boots, eh?" inquired the father; "lugged your mother's best bonnet off, eh? Well, I don't think you'll remember the poor very much after to-night!"

And he pounded Christopher Columbus with a pumphandle until the boy fainted away, and even then didn't feel as though he had made a thorough job of it. .

They fooled this boy once more. He heard a rich man say that everybody "should make hay while the sun shone." So when there came a sunny day he went out, took his father's scythe down from the plum-tree and went to making hay. He broke the scythe, cut down the tulips and hacked his sister in the heel, and his mother came out and led him around by the hair, and bounced him until he almost went into a decline. They couldn't bamboozle this boy after that. He grew wicked every day of his life, and before his eighteenth birthday arrived he was hung for murder. He said he didn't care a huckleberry about it, and died without making the usual Fourth of July oration.

THE SOLEMN BOOK AGENT.

HE was tall, and solemn, and dignified. One would have thought him a Roman Senator, on his way to make a speech on finance; but he wasn't—singularly enough, he wasn't. He was a book agent. He wore a linen duster, and his brow was furrowed with many care-lines, as if he had been obliged to tumble out of bed every other night of his life to dose a sick child. He called into a tailor-shop, removed his hat, took his "Lives of Eminent Philosophers" from its cambric bag, and approached the tailor with:

"I'd like to have you look at this rare work."

"I haf no time," replied the tailor.

"It is a work which every thinking man should like to peruse," continued the agent.

"Zo?" said the tailor.

"Yes, it is a work on which a great deal of deep thought has been expended, and it is pronounced by such men as Wendell Phillips to be a work without a rival in modern literature."

"Makes anybody laf when he zees it?" asked the tailor.

"No, my friend, this is a deep, profound work, as I have already said. It deals with such characters as Theocritus, Socrates, and Plato, and Ralph Waldo Emerson. If you desire a work on which the most eminent author of our day has spent years of study and research, you can find nothing to compare with this."

"Does it shpeak about how to glean gloze?" anxiously asked the man of the goose.

"My friend, this is no receipt book, but an eminent work on philosophy, as I have told you. Years were consumed in preparing this volume for the press, and none but the clearest mind could have grasped the subject herein discussed. If you desire food for deep meditation you have it here."

"Does dis pook zay zumding apout der Brussian war?" asked the tailor as he threaded his needle.

"My friend, this is not an everyday book, but a work on philosophy—a work which will soon be in the hands of every profound thinker in the country. What is the art of philosophy? This book tells you. Who were and who are our philosophers? Turn to these pages for a reply. As I said before, I don't see how you can do without it."

"Und he don't haf anydings apout some fun, eh?" inquired the tailor as the book was held out to him.

"My friend, must I again inform you that this is not an

ephemeral work—not a collection of nauseous trash, but a
rare, deep work on philosophy.   Here, see the name of the
author.   That name alone, sir, should be proof enough to
your mind that the work cannot be surpassed for profundity of thought.   Why, sir, Gerrit Smith testifies to the
greatness of this volume !"

" I not knows Mr. Schmidt—I make no gloze mit him,"
returned the tailor in a doubting voice.

" Then you will let me leave your place without having
secured your name to this volume !   I cannot believe it !
Behold what research !   Turn these leaves and see these
gems of richest thought !   Ah ! if we only had such minds
and could wield such a pen !   But we can read, and in a
measure we can be like him.   Every family should have
this noble work.   Let me put your name down; the book
is only twelve dollars."

" Zwelve dollar for der pook !   Zwelve dollar ! und he
has noddings apout der war, und no fun in him, or zay
noddings how to glean gloze !   What you dake me for,
mister ?   Go right away mit dat pook, or I call der bolice
und haf you locked up pooty quick !"

AN HOUR AT THE CENTRAL STATION COURT.

"I DON'T remember," said Bijah, as the reporters came in, "whether Shakespeare, Susan B. Anthony or Ben Butler wrote it, but it's a very affecting song, and lately it has been running in my ears half the time. I'll sing a verse:

> 'His name it was Jack,
> His father drove hack,
> Plain sewing his mother did do;
> And a brother of his
> In position had riz
> To sweep out an office or two.'"

The old janitor was proceeding with the next verse, when

THE CATS.

his Honor came in and squelched him—said that a couple of cats had kept him awake half the night, and he didn't care about finishing off with the notes of a horse-fiddle or a tin-pan serenade.

JOSEPH BRACKWELL

Was the first candidate out. His name was well braced, but his character wasn't. He had been loafing around for

233

a week or two on the ragged edge of despair, sleeping on a soft pair of stairs or in a dry goods box, and although the prospect of ever having a dollar in his pocket, or of securing a square meal, was as uncertain as keeping a boarding-house in Chicago, he didn't want the police to disturb him.

"You'd better go up," remarked his Honor, after hearing the prisoner's story.

"Oh! lemme go this time!"

"No—can't do it. What would be said of me if it was known that I encouraged vagrancy?"

"But I'll go into the country."

"The country doesn't sigh for thee, Mr. Bracewell."

"Then I'll go to Canada."

"You'd become a frozen statue in less'n two hours over there. No, Mr. Bracewell, I shall have to make it sixty days. That will let you out in March, just when the solidity of winter is giving way to the mush of spring, and even if you can't strike a job then, the nights won't be so cold."

LAST TIME.

Mary Ann McClellan wiped a tear away and choked back a sob as she admitted the charge of drunkenness, but she protested that intoxication came from some brandy which she was using to cure toothache. She was very penitent, and if his Honor would only let her go this time her teeth might all jump out of her head before she would resort to brandy again.

"I dunno—I dunno," mused the Court as he rubbed his ear.

"Just this once!" she sighed.

"Seems as if I might, and I guess I will. But you must look upon this as a hair-breadth escape. If there were not some redeeming features in the case I'd send you where you wouldn't have a taste of canned peaches for six months. Don't have any more toothache, Mrs. McClellan. Fare-well, Mary Ann—you can go."

"I'm many times obliged to you," she said as she made her bow, and when she got out of the door a red-nosed boy yelled out:

"She's making up faces at this 'ere court!"

MAKING UP FACES.

It was too late to catch her, and Bijah called out:

"*LITTLE NELL.*"

"Miss Baldwin, I be-lieve?" said his Honor, as she leaned over the railing.

"The same," she replied, with a smile.

"And you were here the other day on this same charge of drunkenness?"

"Not I—my sister."

"She looks like you, eh?"

"Very much."

"And she also gets drunk?"

"Once in a while."

"Miss Baldwin, it is my solemn duty to inform you that you can't hoodwink this court. You've been here a dozen times to my knowledge, and you never had a sister. I knew you the moment I caught sight of those dozen freckles on your nose, and I'm going to put on a few extra days for your baseness in seeking to put up a job on me. The sentence is ninety days."

"May I speak to you after the court?" she asked.

"You can leave any word with Bijah which you wish

conveyed to me. He is trustworthy, and whatever you tell him will be received as a sacred secret. As soon as court closes I want my breakfast, and I can't tarry here. Go back and sit down, and you shall be conveyed to the House of Correction in as good style as is consistent with safety and comfort."

A PROSPECTIVE REWARD.

"Here! Who's this?" exclaimed the Court as Joseph Eldner was brought out.

"Made a fool o' myself, as usual!" replied the farmer.

"Got drunk, eh?"

"Yes; came down to Detroit yesterday, looked around, got tight, and I'm busted for cash."

"Never was here before?"

"No—never saw your darned old town before in my life!"

"And you live—where?"

"Way up in the woods."

"Can you get home?"

"Hum's the word with me."

"Well, you want to be more careful in the future. It's a wonder some one didn't roll you into the river. I guess I'll let you go this time."

"You will?"

"Yes, you may go."

"Bully for you, pard!" exclaimed the man, extending his claw for a shake. "I'm agoing straight hum! I can walk it in two days, and I'll tell

OFF FOR HUM.

the old woman that the cars busted and I lost my money! I'll make this thing all right—I'll send you down a bear!"

He got right out, and as soon as the Maria could be loaded up the boys joined hands, circled around the coal stove and sang:

"Human nature's weak and frail,
Every day we hear the wail—
Every day we see 'em sail
To the jug."

A BRIBE.

RAGGED, forlorn-looking boy was strolling around the Southern depot in Detroit one day, smoking the stub of a cigar and keeping an eye out for an easy job, when a philanthropist, in waiting for a train, handed out ten cents, and remarked:

"Take it, bub; I feel sorry for you."

"No yer don't," exclaimed the boy, drawing back.

"Why, it's a free gift—I don't ask anything for it," replied the man.

"I know you," continued the boy, his eyes twinkling; "you want me to promise to grow up and become President, and I ain't going to tie myself up for any man's ten cents!"

JOHN BLOSS, MINER.

REMEMBER that the news of his death startled me, though he was such an old drinker that he was never clear of "snakes," and the camp had been expecting his death for a week.

We'd been having healthy times for months past, and old John's death was sufficient excuse for most of the men

knocking off work for the day. I went up to the shanty where the body lay, and a dozen silver-diggers were sitting around the door and discussing the many virtues of the late deceased.

The truth was, old John had been a plague to every camp in the diggings. He was light-fingered, a great loafer, a persistent beggar, and when he got the *tremens* it took half the men in camp to hold him. However, these faults were passed over by the crowd, and as I came up "Old Scraps," as they called a giant miner, was saying:

"Poor old John! We may loaf around this world a million years and never see his likes agin!"

"That's so!" added "Beechnuts," who hailed from Indiana. "If there was ever a good man on this airth, it was old John Bloss!"

"And I'll bet four ounces that he's flying around Heaven this very minute!" put in a red-headed miner from St. Louis.

"He'd divide his last cracker with a man who was in want," said a fourth, wiping the corner of his left eye and carrying a long face.

There was a short pause, and as the old man Turner removed his pipe and blew the smoke away, he said:

"B'ys, I move we git up a monument for him!"

"That strikes me!" was the general shout, and the old man continued:

"I'll give an ounce or two, the rest of ye give as much, and we'll do the fa'r thing by the old angel. He desarves it. I feel now as if I could foot it clear to Boston and bring a twenty-foot monument home on my back!"

The hat was passed around, and although times under the hill were hard, a purse of about sixty dollars was raised. As soon as the body had been buried the old man Turner pounded his head and brought fourth an obituary notice. He called the camp around him and read it aloud, but the men decided that it wasn't tender enough, and besides the old man had tacked on half the song of "Old Hundred" to finish the obituary. The task was allotted to others, and finally the combined efforts of the entire camp produced the following, which passed criticism and was adopted:

JOHN BLOSS,

He Dyd hear on the 29 of Ma, Aigd

aboute 45 yr.

His deth hez kast a darke shadder over this campp.

We'll never For git him.

this stun was raised by his cumraids.

The next thing in order was to procure the monument, and the evening was spent in devising ways and means of getting a marble shaft across the country from Chicago.

That night " Old Chestnuts " was shot in the leg while trying to steal the monument fund, and when morning came it was discovered that Turner had run away with the pile. Three men pursued him, overhauled and robbed him, and then struck out for other diggings, and " Taller Candle Valley " never heard anything further about the John Bloss monument fund, except now and then as a miner rested on his pick-handle and declared that he'd like to give old John Bloss one good kick—just one.

P

SHE WAS A MOTHERLY OLD LADY.

SHE got aboard the train at the next station, and she came along down the car until she saw me, and down she sat in the unoccupied half of my seat. I was rather glad of it, for she was a motherly-looking old lady, and she didn't have a car-load of baggage. All she had was a hand-trunk, three bundles, something in a pillow-slip, an umbrella, something tied up in a towel, a bag of something else, and two or three more bundles.

"There's them doughnuts for Peter's children," she said as she stacked up the bundles, "and them's chestnuts for Sarah's young 'uns; and them's herbs for the colic—dried beef for lunch on the way—carpet rags for Melissa—dried apples enough to go around—some o' them dried plums for sickness——"

And finally she had them all before her. She counted up on her fingers, nodded her head, and sat back and looked at me through her spectacles. Finally she inquired:

NOT JOHNSON.

"Haint you Mr. Johnson?"

I replied that I was not.

"I thought sure you was him, but now I see you haint," she went on, "though I'll leave it to forty if you don't have a Johnson look, 'cept the hair. None of the Johnsons have red hair."

"No, my name is George Washington," I replied.

242

"Washington? Washington? Any relation to them Washingtons in Medina?"

"Not as I know of."

"Well, seems as if I had seen you afore, but I can't place you. Going fur?"

"Yes."

"Been away somewhere?"

"Yes."

"Folks expect you home?"

"No—haven't any home; I'm an orphan."

"Dear me! but I can feel for you if that's the case! Who brung you up?"

"No one in particular. At the tender age of nine years I went to sea."

"To see who?"

"To sea—to sail upon the ocean. I went with a pirate."

"Oh! ha!"

"Yes, I became a pirate, and for years I helped to burn,

As a Pirate.

kill and plunder. I became a monster, and it was one continual feast of blood for ten long years!"

"But you've reformed, haven't you," she asked, moving off a little and reaching out for her bundles.

"Yes, I am now as innocent as a child—as you are."

"Got religion at camp-meeting, I s'pose?"

"Yes."

"Well, them camp-meetings is powerful things. There

was Abe Skinner—you probably didn't know him—he got converted at camp-meeting, and they say he's like a lamb now."

She looked at me for awhile without speaking, and then inquired:

"Did you kill many babies when you were in the pirate business?"

"No, we always spared innocent children. There was one pirate who didn't do anything else but fill their nursing bottles and dose 'em with paregoric when they had wind colic."

"La! now, but there was some good streaks about 'em!" she said. "And what did you do with the old women?"

"We used to saw 'em in two with a cross-cut saw, and use the pieces for hash!"

"Grashus! but how monsterous!" she whispered as she folded her arms and leaned back.

She pondered over the case several minutes, and then remarked:

"But you've reformed?"

"Yes, I have undergone an entire change of heart and appetite. There was a time when I could have roasted and eaten you for dinner, but now the smell of baked old woman gives me the heart-burn."

She drew off a little further and asked:

"And what are you going to do now?"

"My present business is buying dead bodies and shipping them to Australia, where they are used as fence-posts and door-steps. I buy a body whenever I can secure it at a fair price, but when I can't I steal it!"

"Excuse me!" she suddenly remarked, "but I guess I'll change over to the other seat!"

She made the change, but during the entire ride she kept an eye on me, and once I saw her shiver as she thought of an old woman being sawed up. Her friends were at the depot to meet her, and as she got off the steps I heard her say:

"Howdy, Sarah—and how's Melindy—and you'd better look out, for there's a body-snatcher on this keer—and how's George—and he's got red hair and used to eat women—and how's Sarah's health—and he's been a roaving pirate, and——"

But the train moved on.

WHAT A CHILD SAW.

YESTERDAY morning some people living in a dark street entered a house to find father and mother beastly drunk on the floor, and their child, a boy four years old, dead in his cradle. The parents looked like beasts—the child wore the sweetest, tenderest smile on its white face that any of them ever saw. It had been ailing for days, and its brief life had been full of bitter woe, but yet the women cried as they bent over the old cradle and kissed its cold cheeks and felt its icy hands.

Father and mother lay down at dark the evening before, and people passing by heard the child crying and wailing. It was too weak to crawl out of the cradle, and its voice was not strong enough to break the chains of drunken stupor. When the sun went down and the evening shadows danced across the floor and seemed to grasp at him the boy grew afraid and cried out. The shadows came faster, and as they raced around the room and scowled darkly at the lone child he nestled down and drew the ragged blanket over his head to keep the revengeful shadows from seizing him. He must have thought his parents dead, and how still the house seemed to him!

"It's dark, mother—it's dark!" the neighbors heard him wail; but no one went in to comfort him and to drive the shadows away. The night grew older—the feet of pedestrians ceased to echo, and the heavy breathing of the drunkards made the child tremble and draw the cover still closer. His little bare feet were curled up, and he shut his eyes tightly to keep from seeing the black darkness.

By and by the ragged blanket was gently pulled away, and the child opened his eyes and saw a great light in the room.

"Is it morning?" he whispered, but the drunkards on the floor still slept.

Sweet, tender music came to the child's ears, and the light had driven every shadow away. He was no longer afraid. The aches and pains he had suffered for days past went away all at once.

"Mother! mother! hear the music!" he cried, and from out of the soft, white light, came an angel.

"I am thy mother!" she softly said.

He was not afraid. He had never seen her before, but she looked so good and beautiful that he held up his wasted hands and said:

"I will go with you—I will be your child!"

The music grew yet softer, and the melody was so sad and tender, and yet so full of love and rejoicing, that the drunkards on the floor moved a little and muttered broken words.

Other angels came, and the light fell upon the boy's face in a blazing shower, turning his curls to threads of gold. He held up his arms and laughed for joy.

"Heaven wants you!" the angel whispered. "Earth has no more sorrow—no further misery. Come!"

And he floated away with them, leaving the sleepers lying as if dead. The golden light faded out, the music died away, and the old house was again filled with the grim, threatening shadows, which sat around the sleepers and touched their bloated faces with gaunt skeleton fingers, and laughed horribly when the drunkards groaned in uneasy slumber.

When people came in the shadows went out. The
sleepers still slept their sodden sleep, and no one minded
them.   Men and women bent low over the dead child,
smoothed back his curls and whispered:

"Poor dead boy!"

Who could know that he had seen the angels, and that
they had borne him to Heaven's gate?

OLD FRISKET.

N central Michigan, many years ago, an old bachelor who may be spoken of here as Frisket, because he has long been dead, published a small paper called the *Herald*. There was only a small amount of job-work, Frisket didn't write to exceed a column per week, and the office force consisted of himself and a white-headed boy about twelve years old, who swept out, "rolled" the forms,

OFFICE FORCE.

and made himself so generally useful that he received seventy-five cents per week for his services.

Frisket was good-natured, lazy, liked whisky, and he fully realized the fact that the *Herald* had a very slim chance of winning a national reputation under his editorial management. It had a circulation of two hundred or such a figure, subscribers paid in wood, potatoes, sheep-pelts, store orders, and

promises, and Frisket was as contented as the editor of
the London *Times*.

There were half a dozen young "jours" working in a town
a dozen miles away, and as they all knew Frisket, and knew
that he would get drunk whenever opportunity offered, they
put up a job on him. His paper was issued Mondays, and
he worked off the first side, or the first and fourth pages,
Saturday. Sunday morning the "jours" chartered a wagon

ON THE ROAD.

and rode over to Frisket's town. He
was in the office, getting up a few
local items, and he sat down and made
them feel at home. It wasn't forty minutes before he was so
drunk that they laid him down in one corner of the office
with the knowledge that he would sleep until the next day.

Then, lowering the curtains and locking the door, they
took off their coats and went to work getting up his local.
The following are samples of the local news they rushed up:

"BEWARE OF HIM!—The President of the village is a
thief, liar, rascal and dead-beat generally. Respectable
men should beware of associating with him!"

"New Sign.—We notice that Miss Foster, the dress-maker on Main street, has a new sign. She'd better get a new set of teeth, stop winking at John Green, the hardware man, and pay her cigar bills!"

"A Fraud.—Pettigrew Brown, the proprietor of the Red Front dry goods store, would as soon cheat a blind man as to wink. He came to this town fresh from State Prison, and is a convicted grave-robber and hog-stealer!"

"Avoid Him!—Harrison, the photographer, went home drunk the other night, threw his child on the red-hot stove, smashed up the furniture, turned his wife out doors, and would now be in jail but for the corruption of constable Bell and Justice Swan. These officials ought to be impeached at once. We have it on good authority that they are the scoundrels who have been stealing wool from the farmers in this county."

In the course of the forenoon they set up twenty-one such items, raking almost every prominent man in the village and county. There was only enough type left for one more article, and they used it to get off the following wind-up:

"This Town.—This town is situated on Carrion Creek, and its inhabitants may be classed under the following heads, viz: Catfish, gamblers, thieves, incendiaries, fools, lunatics, suckers, whales, sharks, dead-beats and jackasses. The principal business of the said inhabitants is whittling shingles, chewing gum and hunting coons. There isn't an honest man or a good-looking female in the town. It is the home of the seven-year itch and the birth-place of Benedict Arnold. No honest man can live here fifteen minutes, and a spotted dog couldn't pick up a full meal here in three weeks. The only decent man in the village is Mr. Frisket, the genial and whole-souled editor of this paper, who is going to get out of town as soon as he can raise money."

They locked up the forms, took turns at working the press, and by two o'clock had the edition off, mailed and ready to go to the post-office. Then they roused the old man, gave him another drink, and were getting ready to go when the tow-headed apprentice came around. He was much surprised, but one of the "jours" gave him half a dollar, told him that the old man must be allowed to sleep, and that the papers should go to the post-office early next morning, and the delighted boy skipped away as happy as an angel.

Just how Frisket got out of it they never knew. He was still asleep next day when an indignant crowd broke in the door and rushed him out where all could have a chance to kick him. He got away by leaping off a bank and swimming a creek, while the "associate editor" hid in the woods and heard the office being gutted. About eleven o'clock that night Frisket was met on the highway, seven or eight miles from his town. He was barefooted and bare-headed, had his coat on his arm, was eating a raw turnip for lunch, and when saluted he replied:

"My name isn't Frisket—it's Jones, and I'm looking land! How far is it to Baltimore?"

"R-AGS!" "R-AGS!"

JUST as the rays of the rising sun gilded the rosy morn, and the lark brushed the dew from his brown feathers and trilled a joyous lay, the voice rose from the walk and penetrated the ears of every sleeper for a block around. It was not a voice crying "Excelsior!" or a voice raised in adulation of the beauties of a joyous morning. It was a plaintive voice, and there was a quaver to it as it called out:

"R-ags!"

When the great bell struck the hour of noon, and the busy streets were deserted by all save a slowly meandering policeman or two, and an occasional lad hurrying along with a dinner-pail in his hand, a plaintive voice sounded along the streets and echoed and reverberated in the stairways. It was not the voice of a good man admonishing people to turn from the error of their ways. It was not the chant of the auctioneer, giving "third and last call," nor was it the monotonous, musical slang of the man who sells a set of gold jewelry for the paltry sum of twenty-five cents. It was a voice crying:

"R-ags!"

When the golden sun dipped behind the horizon, and the evening shadows chased each other across his face and wavered and quivered above Time's grave, there came rising on the quiet evening air a long-drawn wail. It was not the cry of a child in pain. It was not the sad sob of a loving wife as she bent over the cold and lifeless form of a kind husband. It rose with the shadows, sounding through halls, and crept into chambers. It was that same cry—that same

"R-ags!"

"THE MOTHER'S FRIEND."

SOME five or six years ago Mr. Gregory, of the Rochester *Chronicle*, invented what he called "Gregory's Eureka Spanker," being an invention calculated to lessen the labor of fathers and mothers in enforcing family discipline. The principle was correct, but the machines were all failures, as they could not be constructed with power enough to answer the purpose designed. The children were lifted up, laid face down on a small platform, and the mother worked the spanking apparatus as one turns a coffee-mill. A series of fans were arranged to strike the child thirty times per minute, but owing to the lack of power the child was led to believe that some one was tickling him, and would laugh himself almost to death. Another bad feature of the machine was the fact that it took at least ten minutes to spank a child. Thus, in a family where there were seven or eight children, an hour and a half was consumed in getting around, and by the time the last child had been spanked the first had entirely forgotten that anything unusual had occurred that day.

I am happy to inform mothers that I have brought out a new machine, founded on more correct principles, scientifically constructed, and warranted to do three times as much as I claim for it. It is called "The Mother's Friend," and the fact that it fills a want long felt is shown by every mail. The first machine was put on trial only three months ago, and now I have orders from nearly every State in the Union, and employ two saw-mills and ninety-seven skilled mechanics in its manufacture.

"THE MOTHER'S FRIEND."

The following are selected at random from among several millions of testimonials :

"OFFICE OF THE ' COMMERCIAL,' }
CINCINNATI, O., June 20, '74. }

M. QUAD—*Sir*—I was present last evening at a trial of your patent ' Friend,' and it does me good to inform you that it proved itself a great success. Thirty-five children were spanked in twenty-eight minutes by one woman, without any effort, and each one was far better spanked than the stoutest mother could have done it with a boot-jack. The *Commercial* will stand by you in this section.

Very truly,

M. HALSTEAD."

And the following is from New York:

" M. QUAD—*Dear Sir*—Mrs. Bryant and myself have had the pleasure of attending a spanking *soiree*, given for the purpose of testing your patent apparatus. It worked so successfully that we are going to adopt a child and purchase a Spanker. I have seen thousands of inventions, but I never saw anything which could afford a family the fun which the 'Friend' can.

WM. CULLEN BRYANT."

And the following is from Washington:

"M. QUAD—Your note of the 15th inst., asking me what I thought of your new invention, was duly received. In answer, let me say that I am delighted. It saves time, does its work well, runs easily, is substantially constructed, and if I had a family of children I'd go bare-footed all winter but what I'd have a Spanker. Can I secure the agency for the District of Columbia? What commission do you allow? I think I can sell five hundred in this city alone.

Ever yours,

GIDEON WELLES."

And this is from the ex-editor of the Lapeer (Michigan) *Democrat:*

"M. QUAD—*Sir*—The Spanker was received last evening and immediately put to work, and I must say that I am astonished and gratified at its manner of working. Our children have been angels ever since passing through the machine. Formerly, my wife had to use up an hour's

Q

time and half a bunch of shingles every day to spank our darlings, and then they weren't half attended to. Now, by the aid of your Spanker, she can do the work in five minutes. Draw on me for $40.

Respectfully,

L. D. SALE."

Other testimonials can be seen at my office, where one of the Spankers is also on exhibition. The regular discount will be allowed editors and clergymen.

GETTING A PHOTOGRAPH.

E was a very pleasant spoken man—that photographer. He said it was a nice day, and that we needed a little rain, and that the Arkansas difficulty was a bad thing, and that photographs were two dollars per dozen—no orders booked without the cash in advance. He wanted to know if I wanted full-length, half-length, bust, face, or what. I told him " or what," and he yanked his camera around, flung the big screens recklessly about, poked the sky-light curtains this way and that with a long stick, and then he ordered me to sit down.

" There—that way!" he said as he jerked my body to the left and nearly broke my spine.

I went that way, and he stepped back, closed the left eye and squinted at me.

" A trifle more!" he said, giving me another jerk.

Then he stepped back and closed the right eye and squinted again.

" Shoulders up!" he said as he gave them a twist which made the blades crack.

Then he went to the left and squinted and cried " ha!"

and went to the right and squinted and shouted " um !" and he came back, seized my head and jerked it up until I saw stars.

"That's better!" he said, as he walked back to the camera.

But it wasn't. He came back and told me to twist the right shoulder around, hump up my back, swell out my chest and look straight at a butterfly pinned to a corn-starch box, and be as pleasant as I could.

" Capital !" he cried, as he took a squint through the camera, " only——"

And he rushed back, jerked my head a little higher, pulled my ears back, brushed up my hair, and said I'd better try to smile and look natural.

" How the dev——" I began, but he waved his hand, and said I must preserve my placid demeanor.

" Now sit perfectly still and don't move a hair," he whispered, as he threw a black cloth over the brass-bound end of the camera, and made a sudden dive into his little dark den. As he rattled the glass and dashed the acids about, I felt a big pain in my spine, a small pain in my chest, another in my neck, another in my ribs, but I said I'd die first, and I kept my gaze on that butterfly.

" Ready now !" he cried, as he jumped out and put in the glass. My head began to bob, and the butterfly seemed to grow as large as a horse, and he whispered :

" Look out—keep perfectly still !"

I braced for a big effort, and he jerked down the cloth. I felt as if the fate of a nation rested on my shoulders, and I stuck to it. He turned away, and I heard him talking softly to himself. After about an hour and a half he put up the rag, jerked out the glass and ran into the den. He was out in a moment, and as he held the negative up to the sun, he said :

" Ah ! you bobbed your head—have to try it again !"

THE FIGURES.

"THERE, my dear wife, there is the set of jewelry which you have so long waited for," said a Detroiter as he laid a package before his wife one evening.

"Oh! you dear old darling, how much did it cost!" she inquired as she tore off the paper.

"Only $50," he replied, carelessly.

"And what's this mark, '$8.50,' on the card for?" she asked as she held it up and looked at him with suspicion in her eyes.

"That—that mark—why, that means that they paid only $8.50 to have the jewelry made!" he replied. "Just think, darling, of their grinding a poor, hard-working artisan down to $8.50!"

She was satisfied with the explanation, and he whispered to himself:

"What a mule I was not to change that $8.50 to $50."

SOME NEW VIEWS IN THE YOSEMITE.

IT seemed to me as I stood in the mountain-locked valley and gazed upwards that Nature had reserved her grandest efforts for the Yosemite. A feeling of awe crept over me, and I could not shake it off. Not until that hour had I ever really appreciated the sublime and the grand in Nature.

"MYSTERY ROCK."

Moving down the valley I found "Mystery Rock." High up on the side of the mountain is a flat rock, upon whose surface rests several relics of the primeval ages, and awe and astonishment fills the mind of the tourist as he puts the telescope to his left eye and takes a good long look. A Professor from the East, who was with the party, said that the relics were at least ten thousand years old, and that if they could be secured the whole history of the first settlers in North America could be read as from a book.

Continuing on down the Valley we came upon "Lovers' Glade," which is only a short distance to the right of the regular trail. It is one of the most romantic spots in the whole Valley, and I sat down on a log and rested and

gazed and sighed for a full hour. The legend goes that two lovers were lost in the mountains, and after wandering around for many months without being able to find their way out, they at last reached this glade, where they both died. His skeleton is seen in the foreground, and her skeleton is seen hanging to a limb. I

"LOVERS' GLADE."

felt a great deal sadder after leaving the glade.

Further down the Valley we came upon "Lake Vesper," a beautiful sheet of water imprisoned between the hills. I have never yet seen a painting or photograph of it, and have often wondered how so many artists overlooked it. On a little island in the center of the lake, is another relic of the primeval ages. I at first thought it was a barrel—a barrel of gin, or something, left there for the use of weary travelers, but the Professor indignantly repudiated the idea. He said it was an heirloom of the

lost Aztec race, and took the spy-glass away from me. I lingered behind and sat down and looked and pondered, and such waves of awe rolled over me that one of the men, who wanted to borrow my jack-knife, came back and asked me three times before I knew of his presence. I think "Lake Vesper" one of the loveliest visions of the Valley, but I'd give a good deal to know whether there is anything good to drink in that barrel.

Soon after dinner we came upon "Hiawatha Falls." Professor was so overcome with the awe and grandeur that he sat down on a rock and cried, and all of us were a great deal more or less affected. The sight was simply grand. The water starts from a cliff several hundred feet high,

plashes from rock to rock and plane to plane with a musical roar, and finally reaches the Valley and glides through the grass like a silver serpent. An Indian guide informed me that the view was not so inspiring from above. He had once ascended to the source of the Falls, and as near as I could make out from his broken words and wild gestures, the view was "heap cuss no good."

The guide turned aside about an hour before sunset to point out a sight called "Meditation." In a lovely little glade, overshadowed by the sublime mountains which have been centuries building, we stood in a half-circle, seven of us, with uncovered heads, and gazed at the solemn and awe-inspiring picture. The Professor seemed more affected than any one else.

"MEDITATION." He stood where the red sunlight fell upon his classic face as it flashed down through the tree tops, and he held his hat in his hands, closed his eyes, and for three or four minutes stood there like a statue, allowing his mind to go back a thousand years—to the time when the Yosemite hills and valleys echoed the shouts of the lost races. A feeling of awe also crept over the rest of us, and it was full five minutes before any one broke the silence. Then the Professor put on his hat and whispered:

"When we behold such wonders of Nature it makes man realize more forcibly what a small particle of dust he is himself—some one give me a chew of fine-cut."

We camped that night in what is called "The Valley of the Angels." One fails to secure the full grandeur of the spot by daylight, but at night, when the light of the campfire flashes out and half illuminates the great black rocks and the silent dells, any man who knows enough to string dried apples cannot help but feel his whole frame tremble with the awe and mystery which a million years of time has wrapt around this mysterious Valley.

We should have felt more of the sublime if the party from Chicago hadn't called the party from Cincinnati a liar, and thereby got up a fight.

A PHILOSOPHER.

I THINK he was a philosopher. He wore seedy clothes; he had a hungry look; his hat was going to decay—everything went to show that he was a philosopher.

He trudged down the aisle until he was near the end of the car, and then he dropped into a seat beside a stranger who was making a lunch on crackers and bologna—one of those small hard bolognas which assume a half-circular shape as they grow older.

I was in the seat next behind, and I wondered if there could be anything congenial between those two men.

The philosopher removed his hat and gently scratched his gray locks, and pretty soon the other man finished his meal, brushed the crumbs away, heaved a deep sigh and settled back as if to sleep. Then the philosopher suddenly turned and remarked:

"This would be a sunshiny day if the sun shone."

The other did not answer yes or no, but drew his leg up and rubbed his ankle, and looked suspiciously at the philosopher. There was a silence for a moment or two, and then the old man placed his hand on the other's shoulder and whispered:

"My friend, do you know that it would always be daylight if it wasn't for darkness?"

"I pelieve dat is zo, but I never remembered of it pefore," replied the other, glancing out of the window and then back at the old man.

266

THE PHILOSOPHER.

"And do you know," continued the philosopher, "that if death did not overtake us, we should live right along for thousands of years?"

"Ish dat bossible!" exclaimed the other, turning sideways on the seat to get a better view of his companion, and exhibiting sudden interest.

The philosopher smoothed out the dents in his hat and continued:

"If we didn't sleep we should always remain awake!"

"Py golly, ish dat zo!" exclaimed the other, a faint smile crossing his face.

"Yes, that is true; but I presume you have never pondered on these things, have you?"

"Vhell, not a crate deal. I keeps a zaloon by Doledo, und I haf no dime to bonder. I bonders some on dat liquor law."

The philosopher surveyed one of his rusty old boots, full of wrinkles and warped out of shape, for two or three minutes, and then laid his hand on the other's knee, and asked:

"I presume you have never stopped to think why a creek or river runs down stream instead of up?"

"I haf never did," replied the man, in a voice betraying self-reproach for his great negligence.

The philosopher closed his eyes like one weary of life, and the other wore an expression of sorrow and contrition as he realized how sadly he had neglected his duties.

"Here you are riding on the cars," continued the old man, suddenly rousing, "and yet I hardly think you can tell me what keeps this car on the track."

"Der wheels," replied the other.

"But why don't this car rise up and travel in the air?" queried the philosopher.

"Pecause dere ish no drack up dere!"

"Ah—um!" sighed the old man, as he leaned back; "if I should tell you that it would always be summer if it wasn't for fall, spring and winter, what would you say?"

"Can dat be zo!" exclaimed the other, the smile of admiration coming back to his face.

"There it is again," said the philosopher, extending his hand; "people trudge along through the world, and cannot tell why they are here or what paths they travel. Now, sir, has it ever occurred to you that you and I would never want to eat if we didn't feel hungry?"

"No—by shiminy no!" exclaimed the other; "I haf never remembered of dose dings ever again in my life!"

A look of contempt came to the old man's face, and he shrank away as if he could not degrade himself by longer association. There was something in the other's look, however, which wrought a sudden change in his mind, and after a pause he continued:

"You should think of these things. You look like an intelligent man; but if I should tell you that the sun could never set if it did not rise, what would you say?"

"Vhell, vhell, gan it be bossible?" gasped the other.

The philosopher closed his eyes again and gently rubbed his knee, though there was imminent danger that he would rub away the thin fabric and leave the joint exposed to the public gaze.

One could see that the other was blaming himself for his criminal negligence, and I was feeling sorry for him when the philosopher shook himself and went on:

"You have eyes, ears and brains, and nature has given you the power to think and analyze, but I have every reason to believe that you cannot tell me why it does not keep right on raining for ten years when it once commences."

"Pecause it sthops," was the blunt reply.

He began to smile, but a look from the old man checked him—a look which pictured contempt, pity and deep sorrow.

"I have got to leave you now," whispered the philosopher, as the engine whistled for a station, "and I am grieved. You are a beast of the field, groping in darkness, and I shudder when I realize that you may live your allotted time and still be ignorant of the power which gives you life. Did it ever occur to you that if we didn't have any lakes, rivers or oceans, we wouldn't have any ships?"

The other opened his eyes and mouth in dumb amazement, and could not utter a word as he watched the philosopher out of the door. When the train started up again he settled back in the seat and gasped:

"Vhell! vhell! I shall never dinks of dose dings zo much pefore as after now!"

TRAINING UP A BOY.

HAVE you a boy from five to eight years old? If so it is a matter of the greatest importance that you train him up right. Teach him from the start that he can't run across the floor, whoop, chase around the back yard or use up a few nails and boards to make carts or boats. If you let him chase around he'll wear out shoes and clothes, and nails and boards cost money.

Train him to control his appetite. Give him the smallest piece of pie; the bone end of the steak; the small potato, and keep the butter-dish out of his reach. By teaching him to curb his appetite you can keep him in good humor. Boys are always good humored when hunger gnaws at their stomachs. If he happens to break a dish, thrash him for it; that will mend the dish and teach him a lesson at the same time.

If you happen to notice that your boy's shoes are wearing out, take down the rod and give him a peeling. Those shoes were purchased only ten months ago, and though you have worn out two pairs of boots during that time the boy has no business to be so hard on shoes. By giving him a sound thrashing you will prevent the shoes from wearing out.

When you want your boy to go of an errand you should state it, and add:

"Now go as quick as you can, and if you are gone over five minutes I'll cut the hide off of your back!"

He will recognize the necessity of haste, and he will hurry up. You could not do the errand yourself inside of fifteen minutes, but he is not to know that. If you want him to pile wood, the way to address him is thusly:

"Now, see here, Henry, I want every stick of that wood piled up before noon. If I come home and find you haven't done it I'll lick you till you can't stand up!"

It is more than a boy of his size ought to do in a whole day, but you are not to blame that he is not thirteen years old instead of eight.

If you hear that any one in the neighborhood has broken a window, stolen fruit or unhinged a gate, be sure that it is your boy. If he denies it, take down the rod and tell him that you will thrash him to death if he doesn't "own up," but that you will spare him if he does. He will own up to a lie to get rid of the thrashing, and then you can talk to him about the fate of liars and bad boys, and end up by saying:

"Go to bed now, and in the morning I'll attend to your case."

If you take him to church and he looks around, kicks the seat or smiles at some boy acquaintance, thrash him the moment you get home. He ought to have been listening to the sermon. If he sees all the other boys going to the circus, and wants fifteen cents to take him in, tell him what awful wicked things circuses are; how they demoralize boys; how he ought to be thrashed for even seeing the procession go by; and then when he's sound asleep do you sneak off, pay half a dollar to go in, and come home astonished at the menagerie and pleased with the wonderful gymnastic feats.

Keep your boy steady at school, have work for him every

holiday; thrash him if he wants to go fishing or nutting; restrain his desire for skates, kites and marbles; rout him out at daylight, cold or hot; cuff his ears for asking questions; make his clothes out of your cast-off garments, and you'll have the satisfaction, when old and gray-headed, of knowing that you would have trained up a useful member of society had he not died just as he was getting well broken in.

CANVASSING FOR THE WASHINGTON MONUMENT.

E was tall and spare, long-haired and rusty-looking. His plug hat bore many dents and bruises, as if long worn and sadly used, and his black coat was minus of buttons, save one, and that hung by only a slight tenure. His boots were in a dilapidated state, his pants had long ceased to have any commercial value, and his shirt-bosom bore stains and spots and had lost all the firmness and stiffness which made him gaze fondly upon it as it was received from the laundry.

He softly opened the door of a saloon, and seeing that the saloon-keeper was alone he grew bolder, straightened up and walked in.

"Sir," he said as he leaned over the bar, "I am an authorized agent to collect subscriptions for the Washington monument—money to complete it. I am canvassing this city in aid of this noble work of national charity and pride."

AUTHORIZED AGENT.

B 273

"Did you shpokes to me?" asked the saloon-keeper.

"Yes, I was saying that I am an authorized agent to collect money to complete the Washington monument."

"I haf not zeen him—I guess he haf gone to Toledo," answered the beer-vender.

"Sir, you misunderstand me," continued the agent. "My name is Shiner, and I am soliciting money to complete the Washington monument. The Washington monument is not a man, but a stone shaft—a pillar—a column, to be erected by the American nation to exhibit its gratitude to the man who saved this country."

"Who vhas dot man?" asked the saloon-keeper.

"Washington, sir—George Washington, generally referred to as the Father of his country," answered Shiner.

"Shorge Washington? I haf not zeen him," mused the saloonist, scratching his head.

"Of course you haven't—he's been dead almost a hundred years."

"Ish dot zo-o!"

"Why, certainly it is! Of course none of us ever saw him, but who has not read of him! Almost every house in the land has a picture of him on the wall, and every school-book speaks of him."

"Vhas he a member of de gommon gouncil?"

"My dear man, didn't you ever read of George Washington?" asked Shiner. "Is it possible that you have lived in this country even one brief month and not read or heard all about the first President of the United States!"

"Did he lif in Chicago?" asked the saloon-man in an anxious tone.

"Why—ha!—why, my dear man, if this wasn't such a solemn subject I should feel inclined to laugh. Is it possible that I have come across an adult man in this, the nineteenth century, in this age of progress and education, and in this era of unprecedented advantages, who does not know all about the great and memorable George Washington!"

"May-be he lifed in Milwaukee, eh?" inquired the man, getting nervous.

Shiner stepped back, sighed heavily, assumed the look of a martyr, and finally said:

"Let me state the case plainly: George Washington was a man."

"Vhas him!"

"Yes, sir, he was a man. He took command of our forces in 1776, whipped the British, was made President two terms, and died about sixty years ago."

"Vhat ailed him—der shmall-box?"

"No, sir, he died of fever, I believe, though that is neither here nor there. You see, he was a big man, a——"

"Did he weigh tree hoonerd pounds?"

"I mean he was a great man, and he was also a good man. Everybody loved him for his good deeds, and desir-

THE BASE.

ing to keep his memory green in the public heart they are going to erect a monument, to be called the Washington Monument."

"Mit glass doors?"

"Glass doors! No. A monument is made of stone—a high shaft or pillar, sometimes a hundred and fifty feet high. It is made of blocks of stone, laid up solid, and will last through all time. This Washington monument will be as large as this house at the base, and taper up to a height of two hundred feet or more. It will cost a large sum of of money, but the American people should feel honored at the privilege of contributing. Thousands of dollars have been expended in constructing the base, and now what we want is money to go ahead with the shaft."

"You vhant zum money—you vhant to get zum bill shanged?" asked the saloon-man.

"As I told you," replied Shiner, "I am an authorized agent to collect subscriptions to complete the monument. How much will you give?"

"I gif you money!"

"Yes—how much?"

"Vhat for?"

"For the monument to Washington."

"Vhat washingwoman?"

"Sir, will you give me twenty-five cents to help complete the Washington monument?"

"Vhat is dat?"

"Shiner stepped back, gazed at the man with despair in his eyes, and then asked:

"Must I repeat my statements over and over again? Can't you understand me?"

"You make zum fun of me, eh!" exclaimed the saloon-keeper. "You dinks I knows nottings, eh? Vhell I shall show you pooty quick! Do you zee dis glub?"

"My dear man, let me explain," said Shiner; "you see——"

"I zee nottings!" shouted the man, waving his club.

FOR THE MONUMENT.

"But, don't you understand that I am an auth——"

"Go away py dat door, awful quick?" roared the saloonist.

"But won't you let me——"

"Shump away py dat door, I zay!" shrieked the bartender, flourishing his club; and Shiner backed out and was soon after seen passing himself off as a Kansas grasshopper sufferer.

THE LEGEND OF A BAGGAGE SMASHER.

KNEW him. It was years ago. His name was—well, call it Bumps. If you ever get into a railroad struggle, where one train struggles to get another off the track, you will know more about Bumps, or your friends will. This Bumps was a nice young man. His hair was always combed low down; he wore brass buttons, and there was a mysterious report current that he had been known to call on the sherry for three, on the Fourth of July, and actually pay for it—pay for it, sir! We held him in awe, we boys did. He could talk about lever-watches, pointer dogs, steam barges, and he could relate incidents of difficulties in prize rings so beautifully that I used to wish to knock some one in the stomach, and break some ambitious Englishman's jaw-bone. If Bumps said anything the whole town swore that it was so. If he didn't say anything we stood back and waited for developments.

At last he went away. His uncle used his influence to get him a position as baggage-man. I never heard of him for years, but I was called one day to see him die. I went with great pleasure. Bumps was a mere skeleton; his eyes were like saucers; his hair was all worn off, from tearing around so in bed. He told me all about it. He drove everybody out of the room, bade me string up my nerves to hear a mournful tale, and then he commenced. He went on the railroad a pure young man. He took charge of trunks and boxes, and commenced by lifting

them by the handles, and setting them down carefully.
He had not served a month when the President of the road
called him into the office, cut down his salary, and told
him if there was any more complaints from the conductor,

Bumps would be bumped out of a berth.
Then the young man grew cold and stern.
He was bound to suit the railroad corpo-
ration or die. He began by walking up
to a poor old chest belonging to an orphan,
and putting his foot through the corner;
the conductor saw the act; the two shook
hands, and they wept for hours on each
other's breasts. Bumps had not made two
trips before he could sling a satchel eleven
rods, retaining both handles in his grasp.

WHEN HE WAS GREEN.

Innocent owners of such things threatened him, and commenced suits against him, and swore they would never ride
on the road again; but Bumps was firm. He was dignified; he was solemn; he was working for a higher sphere;
he was treading in the path of duty.

When gentle females would hand up their tender little
baskets and satchels, Bumps would smile a diabolical smile,
and get in a corner and jump on the articles and toss them
up and kick them, and fling them them through ethereal
space. And when the train stopped he would throw out a
waterfall and tooth-brush in answer to call for check "22."
Husbands would strike at him, and dare him out of his
den, and call him a base fiend; but Bumps was solemn;
he knew his line of business. When he got hold of a nice
trunk he would carry a countenance like a strawberry, for
joyfulness. He would jerk off one handle, then another,
then kick in the ends, then take an axe and smash the
lock, and then let the shirts and things rattle out on the
track. It got so at last that people actually paid high

prices for the privilege of living along the line of that road, as they got their garments for nothing. All that was needed was to have the children follow up Bumps' train.

But at last there came a black day. A miserable, contemptible, sneaking wretch, who owned a saw-mill, went traveling. He run his factories two weeks on nothing but trunk-stuff, and he brought out the wickedest trunk that ever went into a car. It was seven feet thick all round, and there were sixteen nails driven in one on top of the other until the thing was smash proof. Then he gave it into Bumps' hands, charging him to be " very careful if he pleased." The train started. Bumps got the axe as usual and struck at the lid, but the axe bounded back. He struck once more; the axe flew in pieces. Then he got a crowbar and a can of powder, but he couldn't burst a nail. He swore and jumped up and down, and wanted to die, and wished he'd never been born. He got all the train men in; they all pounded, but the trunk held firm. It went through all right. It was handed down without a jar, and the owner was there to say " Thank you, sir," and he pretended he was going back again, and had the chest put aboard once more. Bumps grew pale. He grew sick.

"They Tried to Console Him."

His legs shook. He had chills all over him. The big trunk went back a witness of " man's inhumanity to man." Bumps grew worse. He felt that he was forever disgraced, and went to bed with the brain fever. They tried to console him, and said that they could have busted the chest if they had only thought to have a collision, but the spirit of the man was gone. I was there when he died. I never want to weep as I wept then. He just shrunk right away, murmuring " Cuss that t-r-u-n-k."

The road tried to get another man just like him, but it tried in vain. It secured men who could mash trunks and rip open satchels, but they couldn't stand up with that sweet smile on their faces and apologize to passengers in a way to make people feel ashamed that they hadn't brought along more trunks to be demolished.

THAT HIRED GIRL.

WHEN she came to work for the family on Congress street the lady of the house sat down and told her that agents, book-peddlers, hat-rack men, picture sellers, ash buyers, rag-men and all that class of men must be met at the front door and coldly repulsed, and Sarah said she'd repulse 'em if she had to break every broomstick in Detroit.

And she did. She threw the door open wide, bluffed right up to 'em, and when she got through talking the cheekiest agent was only too glad to leave. It got so after a while that peddlers marked that house, and the door bell never rang except for company.

The other day as the lady of the house was enjoying a nap, and Sarah was wiping off the spoons, the bell rang. She hastened to the door expecting to see a lady, but her eyes encountered a slim man, dressed in black and wearing a white neck-tie. He was the new minister, and he was going around to get acquainted with the members of his flock, but Sarah wasn't expected to know this.

"Ah—um—is Mrs.—ah——"

"Git!" exclaimed Sarah, pointing to the gate.

"Beg pardon, but I'd like to see—see——"

"Meander!" she shouted, looking around for a weapon, "we don't want any flour-sifters here!"

"You are mistaken," he replied, smiling blandly "I called to——"

"Don't want anything to keep moths away—fly!" she exclaimed, getting red in the face.

"Is the lady in?" he inquired, trying to look over Sarah's head.

"Yes, the lady's in, and I'm in, and you're *out!*" she snapped, "and now I don't want to stand here talking to a fly-trap agent any longer! Come, lift your boots!"

"I am not an agent," he said, trying to smile, "I'm the new——"

"Yes, I know you—you are the new man with a patent flat-iron, but we don't want any, and you'd better go before I call the dog!"

"Will you give the lady my card and say that I called?"

"No, I won't. We're bored to death with cards and handbills and circulars. Come, I can't stand here all day."

"Didn't you know that I was a minister?" he asked as he backed off.

"No, nor I don't know it now; you look like the man who sold the woman next door a dollar chromo for eighteen shillings!"

"But here is my card."

"I don't care for cards, I tell you! If you leave that gate open I'll heave a flower-pot at you!"

"I will call again," he said as he went through the gate.

"It won't do you any good!" she shouted after him; "we don't want no prepared food for infants—no piano music—no stuffed birds! I know the policeman on this beat, and if you come around here again he'll soon find out whether you are a confidence man or a vagrant!"

And she took unusual care to lock the door.

AN HOUR AT THE CENTRAL STATION COURT.

A FEW minutes before his Honor's **time for putting in** an appearance, thirteen boys, marching in single file, and headed by a boy pounding "time" on an old tin pail, drew up at the door and called for Bijah.

THE SKETCH.

"My dear children, why this unusual demonstration?" inquired the old man as he stood in the door.

"We fellers," said the leader of the boys, removing his old hat, "we fellers go our dollars on you every time. You are kind, innocent, good-hearted and handsome, and we ain't the chaps to despise you 'cause you're bald-headed and have big feet. We feel like we owed you one, and the boys have a little present for you. It didn't cost a heap, but you can lay it away in the bottom bureau drawer, and the moths won't even dare smell it.

It isn't as big as a wagon nor as valuable as a corner lot, but we hope you'll accept it and treasure it as coming from those who love you."

The boy then handed out a well executed charcoal sketch pinned to a shingle. It was meant to represent Bijah sitting on a six-rail fence spitting tobacco juice into a William goat's eyes. He received it tenderly, and tears came to his eyes as he said:

"B-boys, this is a great surprise. I-I'm an old man, on my way to the grave, but I love the b-boys, and I hope every one of you may live to be G-Governor of Michigan. Each of you can go up to the hat store and get a p-plug hat on my account."

The sketch was taken in and leaned up against the wall, and his Honor having arrived

JULIA DAVIS

Was escorted from the corridor. She was such a short, fat woman that his Honor had to rise up and lean over the desk to look at her. As she rolled her eyes up in an appealing manner he said:

"Julia, how on earth could you get so drunk that the men were obliged to draw you down here on a painted cart?"

"Drinking whisky, I suppose," she replied, in a voice highly tinctured with asthma.

"Yes, I suppose so, too; but an old woman like you, and a fat one at that, should feel above such things. It makes me sad, Julia, to see a woman degrade herself like this. How must your husband feel?"

"He gets drunk, too!" she answered, coughing heavily.

"Ah, he does! But think of your poor children."

"I haven't a child in the world!" she coughed.

"Julia," said his Honor, after a long pause, "Julia

Davis, do you know where you will go to when you die—
do you care?"

"To the (cough) graveyard, I suppose,"
she answered.

"Very well," he said, as he settled back,
"your being fat is no excuse for your being
drunk, and I'll make it thirty days."

PASSING THROUGH.

"Have you any excuse for hollering on
the streets at midnight?" inquired the
Court of Tim Johnson.

"No excuse, 'cept dat I didn't holler,"
replied the prisoner.

JULIA.

"Do you stand up there and deny the allegation?"

"No, sir, but I denies hollering. I saw Ben Lewis on
de corner, and I jist remarked: 'Ho dere, Ben!' when de
cop comes up and grabs me. Dere was no yelling nor
hollering—hope to be struck dead as dat cheer if dere
was!"

The officer couldn't make out a very strong case, and
his Honor said:

"Tim or Timothy Johnson, this has been a very narrow
escape for you. Theoretically, you have been sitting on a
keg of powder, liable to be blown higher than Gilderoy's
kite by some untoward accident. You may go home, but
don't holler to Ben Lewis or anybody else again. This is
a big world, full of strange people, and the best thing you
can do is to slide softly and gently along with your mouth
shut."

"Dat's what I shall purceed to do," answered the prisoner, and he backed out, sighed a sigh for his lost umbrella,
and meandered away.

A REG'LAR.

"He's a regular," said Bijah as he brought out Richard Dolan. "He says he can kick the top of your head off as slick as buttermilk running off the table, and he's been cussing and taking on awfully."

"You made those remarks, did you?" asked the Court as he laid aside his Seek-no-further.

"No, sir—never said a word," replied Richard.

"Because," continued the Court, "when a man wants to lay for me, and do kicking, and so forth, he needn't hold back any on account of my official position. I'm edging up to fifty, and I can't go out nights with the boys and hook mellons any more, but I'm up to business when the chip is knocked from my shoulder. The warrant charges you with drunkenness."

"It's a lie!" exclaimed the prisoner.

"That's all I want to hear of that!" replied his Honor, lifting his spectacles. "I see by your face that you are a low-down, good for nothing loafer, and I send you up for three months."

The prisoner grasped the iron railing, but Bijah fastened his cant-hooks into the fellow's neck-handkerchief, gave a half twist, and Richard Dolan followed along behind, his face the color of a horse-plum. The old janitor is regular hook-and-ladder company in himself, and when he fastens to anything it's got to come if it isn't chained.

POT CALLING KETTLE BLACK.

"William Henry Lovegood, and Mary Ann Lovegood, you are charged here with disturbing the peace by indulging in a family row," said his Honor.

"Sure, sir, I'm a poor old man," whined William Henry.

"And I'm a poor old woman," whined Mary Ann.

" Well, what started this fight ?"

" He struck me !" she said.

" She struck me !" he said.

" You lie !" she screamed.

" You lie back !" he shrieked.

"Ladies and gentlemen, cease those remarks at once," said his Honor. " I haven't the least doubt that you both lie, and I presume you are both at fault. You can go; and my advice to the police is to let you fight and howl and pull hair until you get tired of it. I've had you up here so often that I'm going to try another plan."

They went out growling, and it wasn't five minutes before a boy came running in and said that Mary Ann had

William H. down on the walk, and was "just a pounding old lightning out of him."

When court adjourned Bijah turned to show his present to his Honor, but lo ! some callous wretch had placed two quids over Bijah's eyes in the sketch, and the whole had been ruined. When the reporters left, the old man was around in the crowd offering $5,000,000 reward for the scoundrel, but meeting with no encouragement.

SEEING THE MENAGERIE.

had paused for a long time before the show-case containing four rattlesnakes, a boa-constrictor and several other reptiles, and was taking a peep at the skull of Oliver Cromwell, when the pair came in.

He was a young man of three-and-twenty. She was about eighteen. One could see in a moment that he had great conceit. His hat was slanted on his left ear, his pant-legs were lifted enough to show the red tops of his boots, and his head and shoulders rolled this way and that as he walked.

It was a fair museum of natural wonders attached to a circus, and the dust on the young man's boots and back was proof that he had made a journey of several miles, accompanied by the girl, to see what was to be seen. She knew nothing—he knew everything.

"There, Mariar," he said, as he caught sight of the skull and the placard beside it; "there's something mighty interesting—the skull of Oliver Cromwell."

"Who was it?" she mildly inquired.

"Of course *you* don't know," he replied, swelling out his chest; "he was the durndest feller I ever met. I rode with him in the cars once when I was going to Dayton, and though he was like a lamb that day, I could see murder sticking right out of his eyes. He killed a hull family the very next week after that, and was hung in Cincinnati.

He sent word for me to come and see him hung, but I couldn't go—had to sow buckwheat that day."

She looked up at him with awe and admiration plain to be read on her face, and they moved along to the cage containing the Ibex.

"Humph! that's the worst-looking Ibex I ever saw," he growled as he leaned over the rope.

"He looks fierce, though," she whispered.

"Fierce? you bet he is! But he couldn't commence with some of those Ibexes I killed out on the plains! Did I ever show you that scar on my leg where an Ibex clawed me one night?"

"I—I guess not."

"Well, I will sometime. When they go for a feller, they fight to kill, but I laid thirteen of 'em out colder'n a wedge!"

"Here's the Polar bear," she said, as they reached the next cage.

"He don't amount to much," replied the young man—"don't commence with the one I killed near Medina, in 1859."

"I didn't know as you ever killed a bear!" she exclaimed in great surprise.

"Well, the more you get acquainted with me, the more you will know about me," he replied. "I've killed hundreds of wild animals, and not mentioned it to even my own mother."

"Why do they call 'em 'Polar bears?'" she asked as they turned to the cage again.

"Why do they? Why do they call 'em Polar bears? Why, because, when they chase a man up a tree, they hunt around, get a pole and jab at him until they knock him down, and then they craunch him in a second."

She was perfectly satisfied with the explanation, and they moved along to the den of lions.

"My stars! what savage monsters!" she exclaimed, as the pair of lions rose up.

"Savage? Well, if you call *them* savage, I wish you could have seen the three lions which I killed when I lived down near Oberlin! The three of 'em weighed just a ton, and their claws were seven inches long! Their skins are in the museum there now."

"I—I don't be——never heard about it before," she stammered.

"Mariar, do you believe I'd lie to you about such a simple thing as killing three lions, when here we are engaged to be married?" he inquired, in an injured tone.

"N—no, I guess you wouldn't," she replied; "it wouldn't be right."

They walked along to the cage containing a pair of tigers. I expected to hear him announce that he had killed several tigers during his boyhood days, and was therefore greatly disappointed when he quietly remarked:

"I've often wished I could meet a tiger when I was going home Sunday nights, but they've always kept clear o' me. They know what they'd get if they come foolin' around me!"

The next cage contained a hyena, but there was no placard, and when she asked him what sort of an animal it was, he was stuck.

She said she had a mind to ask somebody, when a broad smile covered his face, and he replied:

"I was just tryin' you, Mariar! I knew all the time, and I wanted to see if you knew. That animile is a Bonanza!"

"I never heard of him afore."

"Of course not—there's lots of animiles you never

heard of; but when I used to drive stage into Wellsville, I heard those fellers hootin' and howlin' in the swamp like all get out!"

"Why I didn't know you ever drove stage."

"I don't tell everybody about it, but as long as we are engaged to be married it won't do any hurt," he continued, his face wearing a placid smile. "One dark night, when you couldn't see your hand afore your eyes, eighteen of those animiles pitched on to the stage."

"They did?"

"Yes, cum in a drove, and such howls and snarls and squawls and yowls and growls you never heard in all your born days! Some stage-drivers would have fainted away."

He waited at that point. He wanted her to make an inquiry, and she made it, and he replied:

"I didn't take a back seat for no eighteen Bonanzas. I was just as cool as I am now. I stopped the stage, tied the lines to the brake, whipped out my revolver and bowie-knife, jumped down, and I tell you there was business for about an hour and a half!"

"Did you kill any?"

"Kill any? Why, Mariar, you don't know me yet! I killed every one; and when I got through with 'em the road was almost knee-deep in blood! The only hurt I got was where one of 'em bit me in the back, right between my shoulders, and the wound is healed up now so it don't bother me any. Pass your hand over my back, Mariar—there—right there—can't you feel a kind of a spot there?"

"Yes—seems as if I could."

"He took a chunk right out, but I paid 'em for it. Now less go and see the snakes."

She drew back from the show-case with a shudder, and he put his arm around her and said:

"Don't be scart, Mariar; your Oscar Henry is here—right here beside you!"

"See their eyes glisten!" she whispered.

"I don't care two cents for their glistening eyes!" he bravely replied. "I've seen snakes afore to-day."

"Not such big ones."

"Mariar, you don't think I'd lie to you, do you, when we're goin' to be married next month? No, I couldn't do it. Those are just common snakes, Mariar. When I was driving canal-boat I used to carry a sword to kill snakes, and I've killed millions of 'em four times as large as these!"

"When did you drive canal-boat?" she asked, a look of doubt in her eyes.

"Mariar, I wouldn't lie to you, would I?"

"Seems as if you wouldn't."

"Well, when I say that I've killed bigger snakes than these, I mean it."

From the show-case they crossed over to the camels, and he reached out and patted one of the animals and said:

"I wish I had as many dollars as I've rode miles on the backs of these camels."

"Did you ever ride a camel?"

"Did I ever? Well, wish the circus man would let me take one o' these out and gallop around a little while!"

When they reached the corner where the elephant was chained my time was up and I had to go. I heard her remark that she never saw such a large elephant, and as I walked away he was saying:

"Well, you never traveled, you see. I wish you'd been along the time father and I went to Indiana. We were chased over forty times by elephants, and the smallest of 'em was more'n four times as large as this one!"

WHAT THREE WOMEN SAID.

HE other day, on the way to Cleveland, I sat behind three women for
an hour or two. They were all
friendly to each other, and they
didn't mind my presence.

"Did you hear about Sarah Par-
sons?" asked one.

"Goodness! No!" answered the other.

"Well, Sarah's got her pay, I tell you!" continued the
first. "You know she was a whole year trying to catch
that red-headed widower. Well, she finally married him;
and what do you think? They say that he sneers at her—
actually uses oaths—when things go wrong; keeps her
from going to church; is sot against company; and won't
let her use above two eggs in a sweet-cake!"

"Mon-ster-ous!" exclaimed the others.

There was a moment of silence, and then one of the
trio spoke up:

"Did you know that Mrs. Lancey had a new empress-
cloth dress?"

"You don't say!" exclaimed the others.

"Yes, I do—I know it for a fact, for she wore it past our
house the other day. The dress never cost less than seven
dollars—the bare cloth, and then there's the making and

293

trimmings thrown in! Just think of a woman in her circumstances going to such an expense! Why, if I hadn't seen it with my own eyes I couldn't believe it!"

"It is awful!" exclaimed the others.

"And the worst of it is, she seems to hold her head so high!" continued the first. "I've heard that her grandfather had to go to the poor-house when he broke his leg, and yet she holds her head up with the best of us! Of course I don't want to back-bite any one—it isn't my nature to talk behind people's backs—but I will say that *I* shouldn't wonder if such extravagance brought that family to want for bread before spring comes!"

Nothing was said for the next five minutes, and then one of the other two exclaimed:

"Land sakes! but I'd almost forgotten to tell you Lizzie Thorburn has a new hat!"

"What! Another!"

"Yes, another; she wore it to church last Sunday! Think of that—a girl having three hats in one year!

"Shameful!" they cried in chorus.

"I don't know what the world is coming to," continued the first. "When I was a girl, one hat had to last me seven years, while now, a girl wants two a year—if not three. I tell you, when I sat in church last Sunday, and saw Lizzie come shying in with that new hat (must have cost three dollars at the least), I felt queer. The fate of the sinful people of Sodom and Gomorrah came to my mind in a second; and I shouldn't have been surprised if Lizzie had then been stricken right down!"

They pondered over it for two or three minutes, and then one of them replied:

"So, Mary Jane Doolittle is dead, is she?"

"Yes, poor thing," was the reply; "dead and buried a week ago. Hannah was at the funeral, and she says that Doolittle never shed a tear—never even blew his nose!"

"He didn't?"

"No, he didn't. Hannah watched him all through, and she says he has a heart like a stone. If he should be arrested as her murderer I shouldn't be the least bit surprised. Poor woman! I met her only last August, and I could see that she was killing herself. I didn't ask her right out about it, but I could understand that Doolittle was a cold-hearted wretch. He didn't have much to say, but just one remark convinced me of his cold-heartedness. He asked for soap to wash himself, and when she handed him a piece he looked at it, sneered like, and says he:

'Mary Jane, you mustn't buy any more yaller soap?'"

"Did he say that?"

"He certainly did. I'll go before any court and swear to it!"

I had to get off the train then, and missed further conversation.

JACKSON GREEN.

JACKSON GREEN was fourteen years old, and he lived in Columbus. The other day, while reading a dime novel, his grandfather came in with the paper and asked him to read the President's message. It irritated Jackson to break off his story just where a trapper was going to be scalped, and he made up his mind to have revenge on his grandfather. He took up the paper and started off as follows:

[The business of the Patent Office shows a steady increase. Since 1836 over 155,000 patents have been issued. Officer Deck, of the station house, wants it distinctly understood that he is not the Deck confined there a few days since as a lunatic.]

"What in the message?"

"What!" exclaimed the old man, "is that in the message?"

"Right here, every word of it!" replied Jackson. And he continued:

[The business of the Agricultural Bureau is rapidly increasing, and the department grounds are being enlarged, and the highest prize in a Chinese lottery is twenty-nine cents, and the man who draws it has his name in the paper, and is looked upon as a heap of a fellow.]

296

"What! what is that?" roared the old man. "I never heard of such a message as that!"

"I can't help it," replied Jackson; "you asked me to read the President's message, and I'm reading it." And he went on:

[During the year, 5,758 new applications for army invalid pensions were allowed, at an aggregate annual rate of $39,332, and kerosene oil is the best furniture oil; it cleanses, adds a polish, and preserves from the ravages of insects.]

"Lor' save me! but I never heard of the likes before!" exclaimed the old man. "I've read every President's message since Jackson's time, but I never saw anything like this!"

"Well, I didn't write the message," replied Jackson, and he continued:

[During the year, 3,264,332 acres of the public domain were certified to railroads, against over six millions of acres the preceding year, and you will save money by buying your Christmas presents in the brick block—fine toys of every description, at reduced prices.]

"Jackson Green, does that message read that way?" asked the old man.

"You don't suppose I'd lie to you, do you?" inquired Jackson, putting on an injured look.

"Well, it seems singular," mused the old man. "I shouldn't wonder if Grant was tired when he wrote that."

Jackson went on:

[There are 17,900 survivors of the war of 1812 on the pension rolls, at a total annual rate of $1,691,520, and still another lot of those one dollar felt skirts; they go like hot cakes on a cold morning.]

"Hold on, Jackson—stop right there!" said the old man as he rose up. "You needn't read another word of that message. If General Grant thinks he can insult the American people with impunity, he will find himself mistaken. You may throw the paper in the stove, Jackson, and let this be an awful example to you never to taste intoxicating drinks."

Jackson tossed the paper away and resumed his dime novel, while the old gent leaned back and pondered on the degradation of men in high places.

NIAGARA FALLS.

THERE'S water enough to make them a perfect success. I learned from the depot-master that Nature made the Falls, but he wouldn't commit himself when I inquired as to the hackmen, landlords and relic-sellers.

I thought I had strength enough to walk from the depot to a hotel, a matter of three or four hundred feet, but seven or eight hackmen rushed at me, and yelled :

"H—a—cks—hacks !"

After the police had stopped the fight, I started for the hotel, followed by six hackmen in line. Some thought it

was a funeral procession, and others took me for a lord.
When I reached the hotel the hackmen demanded fifty
cents each, saying that it was the same fare whether I rode
or walked.

"But how could I ride up here in six hacks at once?"

They replied that I couldn't bluff them with any rule of
addition, division or multiplication, and rather than seem
penurious I paid them three dollars.

The hotel clerks at Niagara are alone a sight worth
traveling from Detroit to see. They look down on a common traveler as a Newfoundland dog would gaze at a pin-
head. At the hotel where I halted, I had to take off my
hat, assume a reverential expression of countenance, and
address the clerk as follows:

"Most high and noble duke of the register, would you
condescend to permit a poor humble worm of the dust like
me to ask you what time the train from the west is due
here?"

If he felt like it, he would take his eyes from the ceiling,
turn around on his stool, flash his diamonds into my eyes
and point to the time-card on the wall; but if he didn't
feel like it, he wouldn't pay the least attention.

The Niagara hotel waiter is only one peg beneath the
clerk. He has heard about John Jacob Astor and the
Rothschilds, but he wouldn't compromise his reputation
by saying that he was intimately acquainted with them. I
didn't know how to take him at first, and was reckless
enough to put a dollar bill beside my plate at supper time.

"What is that?" he inquired, as he picked it up.

"That? That, sir, is lucre—dross—money—a green-
back," I responded.

"Humph! you'd better keep it—you might want to buy
the Falls," he retorted.

I thought some of handing him my wallet, but as I

didn't, I had to make my supper out of pepper, salt, celery and crackers.

The guide is another feature of Niagara. The one who took me around, showed me Goat Island from fourteen different points, and wanted two dollars a point, and when I growled about the price, he sneeringly replied that if I

ONE OF THE POINTS.

had come there to get a one-horse view of the Falls, I should have brought a tent and some crackers and cheese along, and camped out on the commons.

The relic-sellers came at me in a body. I at first refused to buy Thomas Jefferson's arm-chair and Washington's cane, but the guide told me a story about a miserly fellow who was thrown over the falls for refusing to purchase relics, and I felt compelled to select twelve Indian canoes, six Revolutionary muskets, a quart of Mexican war bullets, several war-clubs, and an armful of tomahawks.

I left Niagara with only one thing to console me. It has been ascertained that the Falls are wearing away at the rate of an inch every three hundred years, and it won't be long before the cataract will be completely worn out.

OF COURSE HE DID.

HE was a finely dressed young man, having a gorgeous paste diamond and lavender pants, and as he handed a boy a bundle and a bouquet he said:

"Now, bub, look sharp. Take this bouquet to Miss ——, at No. 17 —— street, and take these two shirts around to the laundry to be washed. Don't make a mistake, now."

"You bet," replied the boy, but he went directly to No. 17 —— street and handed the two shirts to Miss ——, and said:

"Your feller sent them, with his compliments—and he said you'd better put 'em into water the first thing, as they are rayther delicate!"

The young man sought to explain matters, but the young lady clenched her hands and said that her letters must be returned or there would be a lawsuit.

AN ABUSED BOOK.

LMANACS are so common now-a-days that people scarcely ever look into them, and a majority would scoff at the idea of finding entertaining and instructive reading between the yellow covers. But I care for nothing more than to sit down of a long winter evening and peruse my family Almanac.

In what other book can be found the fact that "Spica rises 10 22 e" on the 9th of January? A great many people will live right over that day and never think of Spica rising, or if they do they won't care a copper whether it rises 10 22 e, or 7 14 g.

But for the Almanac who would stop to think that Galileo was born on the 15th of January, 1564? Poor Gal! Born into this world without a shirt to his back, see what a name he made! I never pick up an Almanac and see his name without wondering where he is now, and why some patent medicine man don't hunt him up and get his name to a certificate. We couldn't all be born in 1564, but we can all be respectable and refuse to become book canvassers.

And but for this book who of us would know that the 12th of February is "in perihelion?" We would go right on with our business and never think of it. Perihelion would go to grass if it wasn't for the unceasing literary labor of a few men, who are not half appreciated.

"Aldebaran sets 8 18 e " on the 9th of April, but how few people will be prepared for it! Some will be going a visiting, others will be drunk, others will be running for Alderman. And on the 18th, when "Procyon sets 10 10 e," how many will give the awful event any attention?

On the 18th of September "Pollux rises 12 6." How many of us can sympathize with poor Poll as he gets out of bed at six minutes after 12 and rubs sweet oil on the baby's nose to help its cold in the head, but the chances are we won't remember the date.

On the 15th of November, 1531, Cowper was born, but how few ever stop to think of it! We go right on with our business the same as if Cowper hadn't lived at all, and we never wonder if his liabilities were greater than his assets, nor whether he married a freckled-faced girl with a long nose, or a fat woman with a voice like an old file. He has been dead several years, but we don't hear of a subscription for the benefit of his widow, nor of circuses giving free exhibitions to build him a monument.

What full-grown man can sit down, put his feet on the stove, slant his chair back and not become interested in the many beautiful steel engravings on every page of the Almanac. How life-like are those goats, all headed one way, heads down and feet gathered for a "bunt!" And right below them are the Siamese Twins, hands joined in loving embrace and a glad smile of brotherly love covering each face. Next below are the lobsters, wildly reaching out after the tail of the biggest goat, and bound to get it or nobly perish. Further on is the lion, ferociously gazing at the boy with the bow and arrow, who is shooting at a cent stuck in a stick, and hasn't any one around to warn him. Then there is a youth with a harp, just setting out to serenade his Sarah Jane, and a wild steer lies in wait behind a horse barn to get his horns under somebody's vest.

If you want your children to become statesmen, train them up to familiarize themselves with some first class Almanac—one with a yellow cover and a blue back.

T

AN HOUR AT THE CENTRAL STATION COURT.

LL said that he was a kind-looking old man, having gray hairs and a face over which a smile spread itself as he looked up at at the Court.

"Were you drunk?" asked his Honor.

"Twee of drie geleden, sloeg hij zijn kindje, ten und maanden oud," replied the old man.

"What! what did you say?" asked the Court.

"Met boyenstaande vraag ein hielden zich de vorige week de neidenhaaden de Engelsche," replied the prisoner.

Bijah began to grin.

The clerk began to grin.

The audience moved uneasily.

"Now then," continued his Honor, "the charge is drunkenness, and I want to hear what you have to say about it."

"De tegenwoordigheid van afgevaardigden van andere Christelijke Vereenigingen," answered the old man in a solemn voice.

"Were you drunk?" demanded the Court in a louder tone.

306

" Hij werd verleden Maandag tot twalf jaren gevangeis straf verooreeeld," answered the prisoner, also raising his voice.

" Don't fool with this Court," warned his Honor.

" Wormjoekjes gebruikt te nebben, terwij wij alle huis-gezinnen, waar kinderen zjm, moeten aanraden een doos van Kimm's Susan B. Anthony!" replied the prisoner, throwing his arms around wildly.

" Well, I can't fool away any more time on you," said the Court in a tone of despair. " Dust out of here and be seen no more!"

And he dusted.

DUST TO DUST.

WHEN THE PANSIES BLOOM.

" This is a case which can be called, tried and disposed of inside of three minutes," remarked his Honor as Charles Taylor leaned on the railing and regarded him with an appealing look.

" I couldn't get nothing to do," replied the prisoner.

"I hear you couldn't, but if I were a young man nineteen years old, in sound health, and the fat on my ribs was an inch and a half thick, I'd find work enough to pay for my board, or I'd slide off the wharf and make business for a coroner."

"I've looked all around," said the prisoner.

"Well, we won't argue the case. I know that work is scarce, but I also know that there are dozens of fat loafers around this town who wouldn't turn a grindstone two hours for a week's board. You are charged with vagrancy,  are guilty, and I will give you sixty days. That will let you out about the time the pansies bloom, and if you can't find work then I'll send you back for six months."

The prisoner shuffled off into the corridor, wiping a tear from his nose, and was so ugly that Bijah had to draw the crowbar at him before he would sit down on the water cooler and wait for the Maria to drive around.

"AND HE WAS SO YOUNG."

He was only twenty-two, and the bloom of youth on his nose had scarcely been eaten into by the rust of manhood's tribulation. He was found drunk on the sidewalk, lying on his back, arms folded across his peaceful breast, and the pale, cold moon cast a snowy shadow across his face.

"Ever here before?" asked the Court.

"Never."

"And you feel powerful mean over this?"

"I do."

"And you won't be found in such a situation again?"

"Never."

"Well, be careful of your conduct in the future, young man. You are just budding into manhood now, and if you are picked up drunk at twenty-two, what may not happen to you at forty-four? I don't advise you to carry an icicle around in your pocket, or to refuse a prescription because one of the ingredients is burnt brandy, but as a general thing it will be best for you to mind your own business, let intoxicating drinks alone, and pay your board bill in advance. That is all, sir—there's the way out."

"S'CAT!"

Exclaimed some one in the audience as the name of James Kitten was announced.

His Honor rose up, looked around him, and said:

"That remark mustn't be remarked again."

Mr. Kitten had also been drunk. He said some one drugged him, but it was pretty evident that he took the fluid in the usual way, and that it had no more than the usual effect on him. When found by the officer he was hanging to a tree-box near the City Hall, and shouting:

"Lucinda, 'fu don't open that door I'll knockyourhead-off!"

"Mr. Kitten, such conduct is unpardonable in a man of your years," said his Honor, "and it will be altogether more harmonious for you if you keep away from me hereafter. I don't remember having met you before, and I don't want to see you a second time. I can let you off this time, but if your faded form confronts me again within a month, I'll make it so lively for you that sitting down on a red-hot penny will be a cool position compared to yours."

"Am I sent up?" asked the prisoner.

"No, sir—you are sent out, and you can step along as soon as Bijah finds your hat."

HE WASN'T.

Just before the "last man" was called, a tall, red-haired woman wearing No. 7 shoes and a straw bonnet, and her

"AP-U-L-S !"

"AP-U-L-S!"

E stood in the hall and said so. After hearing his clear, shrill voice, I had no further doubt that he had apples to sell. It was a lazy afternoon, and I invited him in.

"Ap-u-l-s!" he shouted as he stepped inside the door.

"Apples? yes; sit down there."

He sat down.

"You said you had apples?"

"Yes."

"How do you make 'apples' out of one apple, and a poor old seek-no-further at that—an apple with a worm-hole in one side and a bruise on the other?"

"Want any ap-u-l-s?" he asked by way of reply.

"Yes, I do—give me *three*."

He picked up the solitary one, looked anxiously around the room, and laid it on the table, with the remark:

"Two for five cents."

I handed him a nickle and asked for two and a half cents back.

He counted his pennies over three or four times, realized that he had got himself into a trap, and he finally handed me back the nickel, put his apple into the basket, and rose up to go. He went into the newsroom, walked the whole length of the floor, and twenty-eight times he said

311

" ap-u-l-s ?" to the compositors. Some of the men looked with contempt on the solitary representative; some did not raise their eyes from the copy on the case before them; some picked up the apple, turned it round and round, and replaced it with a sigh, as if they had hoped for better, brighter apples, and had been grievously disappointed.

The boy passed down into the job room. The foreman waved him away; the feed-boys tried to daub his ears with ink; the men working on the Fourth of July posters told him to go hence. He descended to the press room, fell over a keg of ink, got banged by one of the presses, and limped up stairs, crept into the local rooms, and announced:

" Ap-u-l-s !"

" Yes sir—come in and sit down !"

He sat down on the edge of the chair, as if he did not mean to stay long.

" Have you apples ?"

" Yes, sir."

" Give me six !"

He laid that poor, lone apple on the table, coughed like one in distress, and did not try to look me in the face.

As I leaned back and regarded him he picked up the apple and slipped away. He went out upon the street. I heard him calling and calling, and hours after, as I passed the post-office, he stepped out and inquired:

" Ap-u-l-s ?"

That same seek-no-further was still there—" only this and nothing more."

The worm-hole and the bruise looked older and more serious, but the general condition of the apple remained unchanged.

I lifted it up and looked at it again. It had once been a fine apple, with transparent complexion and the proper rotundity which apple-eaters love to see. Some accident had inflicted the bruise, or some unkindly thumb had pressed against it with that feeling which causes men to choke each other.

I did not see him next day, nor the next, but on the third day he crept up stairs and acknowledged that specu- lation in fruit had bankrupted him. The seek-no-further had died on his hands, but yet, having some slight hope left, he had gone into sassafras-scented toilet soap, trusting that the liberal-minded public would give him the prefer- ence over the boy with the bad cocoanuts.

CHIPMUNK, THE WYANDOTTE.

NE day a Wyandotte Indian, bare-headed, and having little on except a blanket, came into the local room. He was one of the few members of that tribe left, and had a hut somewhere on the river, living alone and begging and hunting by turns.

We had just taken a new man on the staff—a long-haired, innocent young man from New England, who was waiting for a chance to go out to Africa as a missionary. We all knew Chipmunk, the Wyandotte, to be a hardened old loafer, but Bank, the new reporter had never seen an Indian before. Chipmunk sat down, waiting for some one to shell out, and Bank slipped over to me, his heart big with sympathy, and inquired:

"Has any effort ever been made to enlighten and elevate these Indians?"

"Not that I know of," I answered, "although I am ashamed to acknowledge it. That poor Indian there knows nothing good, although living in this enlightened age, because we are too busy to spare the time to teach him. It is some one's duty to take him by the hand and look out for his future welfare, but who is it? *I* haven't the time, and——"

"I feel that it is *my* duty," replied Bank, interrupting me, and I saw tears in his eyes.

314

There was a pair of stairs leading to a side street, and Bank motioned for Chipmunk to follow him down. The Wyandotte obeyed, and I looked out of the window and saw him take a seat on the wood-pile, while Bank sat down on a barrel and commenced:

"My dear friend, what are you living for?"

"Gimme ten cent!" replied Chipmunk, holding out his hand.

"My friend, I am not speaking of your bodily welfare, but asking about your soul," continued Bank. "Do you know anything about Heaven? Did anyone ever talk to you about the land beyond the skies? Has anyone ever sought to instil goodness into your heart?"

"Chipmunk hard up—want money," replied the Indian.

"My dear friend, it grieves me to see that you prefer bodily comfort to spiritual salvation," continued Bank. "Don't you know that you have got to die some day, and that it will not be well with you unless you are prepared? I don't blame you, of course, for you were born a heathen, and not one of the thousands around you have taken interest enough in your future to enlighten your mind. It is a burning shame, and I feel as if *I* had neglected *my* duty, although I only arrived in Michigan a few days ago."

"Gimme two shillin'!" demanded Chipmunk, growing ugly.

We had played a good many tricks on him around the office, and although he could speak and understand English pretty well, Bank's language was too heavy for him, and he probably took it for some new insult.

"Rather ask me for a testament or a hymn-book," replied Bank. "It makes me tremble to think that here, in an old settled State, with a dozen churches in sight, in this age of Christian religion, I should have come upon a human being knowing nothing of the great future—having no care except for to-day—never learning that there was a hereafter. Why, I can almost imagine myself in the heart of Africa!"

"Don't make laugh of Chipmunk!" warned the Indian, looking mighty ugly out of his eyes, and hitching around on the woodpile in a nervous manner.

"My poor, dear benighted heathen, do you suppose I could sport with your ignorance?" inquired Bank. "No, my poor friend, I pity you—I sympathize with you—it makes my heart bleed when I realize your situation. Here, clasp my hand, my dear brother, and say that you will be my pupil hereafter—that you will let me guide your footsteps in a new and better road; that——"

Some of the other boys had come in, and hearing us at the window Chipmunk made up his mind that we had put up a "sell" on him. As Bank was speaking, hand held out, the Wyandotte yelled:

"Waugh! Whoop! Make fool of Injun!" and he came down upon Bank like a catamount on a rabbit. We hauled him off as soon as possible, but that young man from New

England was a sad sight to see. He had a black eye, a bloody nose, had lost a handful of hair, and the interior of his watch was rolling around with the sticks of wood.

"Whoop! fight more— lick ten men!" shouted the Indian as we rushed him around, but we were too many for him.

Bank couldn't get over it. We raised his salary to seven dollars per week, kept his drawer full of complimentary tickets to circuses, minstrel shows and lectures, made his work easy and flattered

"WAUGH! WHOOP!"

his talents, but as soon as his nose got well he discharged himself, and I haven't heard of him to this day.

LET US ALONE.

HANG 'em!

I mean the men who gather together in convention and make long-winded speeches, and read six-column addresses, and inflict both on the public under the name of "Social Science." The Hon. Tenderheart, who has made the matter his study for years, gets up and says that something must be done to educate and refine the homeless, outcast children. He has two or three plans, but he doesn't propose to pay out a cent or to take one of the street Arabs into his own family. He is willing to furnish plans and advance theories, and talk through his nose and wipe his weeping eyes, and the street Arabs might as well be in Africa for all it profits them.

Hang the man who gets up and declares that the American people are being murdered by poorly-ventilated rooms. If there is an American in America who doesn't know enough to raise a window and let foul air out, or lower it to prevent dust from driving in, the fool-killer will soon find him. The great mass of people are not going to shiver in their beds, or carry an infernal cold in the head to please some old rhinoceros who sleeps with *his* window open.

Hang the man who is always driving oat-meal and Graham flour down the public throat. If anybody likes oat-meal let him eat it, and if anybody prefers Graham's diet to warm biscuit, there is no law to prevent. But give the remainder of us a rest. Don't keep writing, and declaring and printing that oat-meal will make a statesman out of a fool, or reduce a statesman to the level of an idiot if he doesn't cram himself with it three times per day.

Hang the man who says that carpets breed consumption; that gas is unhealthy; that people shouldn't drink while eating; that stoves are killing us; that people should go to bed at dark and get up at daylight; that marble-top tables are as bad as the cholera; that our boots and shoes and coats and dresses are knives and daggers drawing blood.

I want to be let alone, and I know others who want to be let alone. If we are galloping to the grave because we won't walk three miles before breakfast, or pound sand-bags, or swing clubs, it's our own private business, and our widows will sooner secure our life insurance money.

A TRUE ACCOUNT OF THE DEATH OF
CAPTAIN COOK.

WAS talking the other day with a grandson of one of the men who helped eat Captain Cook, the navigator. History has dealt very unjustly with the native gentlemen who sat down to that feast, and I made the grandson a solemn promise to set the matter right.

This man Cook, as near as I can learn, used to keep a hotel in London, and was far from being a famous navigator. When he landed on the island where his death occurred he cocked his hat over his left ear, squirted tobacco juice around in a ferocious manner, and put on more style than the foreman of a hand-engine at a village fire. The natives welcomed him with shouts and smiles, told him to make himself at home at the best hotel on the island, and all preparations were made to render Mr. Cook's stay pleasant and agreeable. It was planned to hold an ice-cream festival; go on a fishing excursion; to have the band out every evening; to get up a sack-race and have a greased pole; to go and see the city hall and drive around the parks, and there was no end to the plans of the natives to do the right thing by the white strangers.

But how did Captain Cook repay these kind intentions? He blustered around as if he owned the whole group of islands, called the women fat and the men ugly, scowled at the children and swore at the dogs, and the natives couldn't please him no how.

The native King, a gentleman of culture named Stephen Hooper, kept his temper excellently well for a week, but then Captain Cook began to go a little too heavy. He addressed the King as "Steve," a thing which no human being had ever dared do before, and as this was not promptly resented he proposed to harness the King to a cart and make him draw yams down to the vessel. All this was for the purpose of degrading the King in the eyes

STEVE.

of his subjects. Cook wouldn't have cared two cents if his actions had run gold up to 1.26, and brought rents down fifty per cent. He complained of the postal conveniences; of the way the street cars were managed; tried to cut down the fees of hackmen, and King Hooper's government would have been knocked higher than a kite if he hadn't adopted prompt measures.

Captain Cook was killed, but it was done in a genteel, courteous manner, and as gently as circumstances would

U

permit. When he fell, his companions hastened away,
jumping their bills without even a promise to return some
day and square up.

Then, when the sailors had sailed away, the natives
found themselves with one hundred and fifty pounds of
fresh meat on their hands. The weather was warm, the
ice supply had given out, and the question arose whether
they should let all that meat spoil or eat it. Times were
close, taxes high, and who can blame them for having
decided to bake the Captain and have the good of him?

He was duly baked, and if he could have only realized
what a gorgeous bread-brown color they got on him he
wouldn't have laid up a hard thought against the natives.
King Hooper took advantage of the occasion to make a
national banquet, and all his friends were invited in. The
Captain had been baked whole, and he occupied the center
of the table. The King did the carving, and as one called
out that he would take an ear, another a wing, another a
leg, and so forth, the royal carver carved away, and not

a thing occurred to mar the harmony of the evening.
When the provisions had been disposed of, the glasses
were filled and the King himself announced the toast:

"Here's to the man we have eaten!"

THOMAS TOMS, DECEASED.

UNERAL processions are dreary affairs, but I am glad I took a place in the second carriage after the hearse and saw the body of my late friend Thomas Toms consigned to its last resting place.

Mr. Toms was not a fool—he was a confiding man.

Up to the age of forty Mr. Toms was healthy, fat, good-natured and jovial. Various men felt of the fat on his ribs, looked into his smiling face, and predicted that he would live to be one hundred years old.

What started his downfall was reading a book on diet. He had always been able to sit down to three square meals per day, and to get away with beans, potatoes, pork, mutton, pie, cake and biscuit, and he had never known a qualm of indigestion. The book said that he must eat oat-meal, cracked wheat and codfish, if he would be healthy, and from that day his house was turned into a hospital. He had codfish and oat-meal for breakfast, codfish and cracked wheat for dinner, and codfish and Graham bread for supper. He gave up his lunch, neglected his cider, and imagined that he was growing healthy.

Then he bought a book on ventilation. He read that no one should sleep in a room without a window open, and he went to bed one night in January with his room properly ventilated. He got up in the morning with his throat full of shingle nails, his nose blockaded and his eyes full of blood. His wife felt even worse, and it was four weeks

before sage-tea and cough medicine had any effect. He sat up with his wife one night, and she sat up with him the next, and by strict attention to business they were finally so far restored to health that they could read a work on " The care of the body."

The book announced that feather beds were slowly but surely depopulating America. They were productive of spinal complaint, fever and twenty-one other

VENTILATED.

diseases, and Mr. Toms felt his hair stand up as he remembered that he had slept on feathers for forty years. The feather bed came off, and Mr. Toms and his wife reposed on an old straw bed, having straw pillows under their heads. After a week Mrs. Toms could not get out doors, and Mr. Toms had to walk with a crutch, and for the first time in his life he flew mad and said:

" Mrs. Toms, I am living with a fool !"

" Mr. Toms, so am I !" she replied, reaching under the stove for a flat-iron.

Mr. Toms stood it very well for a week or two longer, and then got hold of a book which stated that every person who cared to preserve the health should take a cold bath every morning. He didn't have a bath-room in his house, but he filled a tub, carried it to the stable, and the yellow sun of February glanced through a knot-hole and fell upon his wrinkled brow as he got out of his clothes and stepped into the tub. He shivered and sighed and groaned as the ice-water raised goose-pimples on his legs,

and he wasn't fairly dressed when he fell down in a con-
gestive chill, and sixteen of his relatives were telegraphed
for.

It was a month or two before Mr. Toms felt like taking
any more steps to improve his health. Then he read that
stoves were unhealthy, and he sold his and had a fire-place
put into the sitting-room. It had a beautiful roar to it,
especially during gusty weather, and Toms could sit down
and blister his knees and freeze his back at the same time.

Mr. Toms walked a mile before breakfast to get an
appetite; went to bed at sundown and had the nightmare
all night; rose with the lark and inhaled all the steam
from the alley; washed his feet with borax and his head
with wintergreen; wore cork soles in his boots, and a
sponge in his hat; tried the lift cure until he couldn't
straighten his spinal column; pounded sand-bags until his
fingers were like corn-stalks, and he died in his chair while
trying the sun-cure.

J. BROWN, DECEASED.

THE door-bell rang, and as I opened the door I saw a woman in black on the steps—a woman so tall and thin and solemn-looking that I wondered if a hundred and fifty thousand dollars would be any inducement for her to utter a hearty laugh.

"I want to talk with you," she whispered, as I stood there holding the door.

"Is it about a pic-nic—the heathen—tracts—a new book—a suffering family—cruel husband—disobedient son—runaway daughter, or the police driving your cow to the pound?" I inquired.

"I want you to write a book for me," she sighed, wiping a tear from her left eye.

I tried to induce her to put it off until daylight, telling her that I couldn't possibly write a book that night and catch over four hours' sleep; but she seemed so determined, and her face kept growing so solemn, that I opened wide the door and placed her a chair.

She pulled off her black gloves, held a crape handkerchief to her eyes, and sobbed:

"He was such a noble man!"

"You are speaking of—of—yes, ahem—of the late—the late——"

SUCH A NOBLE MAN.

"Of my husband," she sighed.

326

" And your husband's name was—was——?"

" Brown—Jeptha Brown, although in writing him up you may speak of him as J. Brown."

" J. Brown, deceased. You want that for the title of the forthcoming biography, do you?"

" Well, that sounds kind o' euphonious and soft, don't it?" she asked, brushing away another tear and folding her handkerchief.

" Well, it's a fair title. It isn't as romantic as 'J. Brown; or, the One-eyed Ranger; or as taking as 'Brown the Brigand; or, the Waif of the Sea.'"

" He had two eyes," she solemnly whispered, "and though they were sore most of the time, we couldn't truthfully speak of him as one-eyed. And he wasn't a ranger—he kept a wood-yard."

" Well, having secured the title, you may now go on and detail his eccentricities—narrate his victories and his failures—particularize his habits, hopes and ambitions."

" He never gave me a cross word!" she sighed, after a moment's thought.

" That's good."

" Never but once," she added. " One day when he came home, and found me cutting up one of his shirts to make a tail for Jacky's kite, he scowled and said: 'Mary Jane, you'd better trade your brains off for bran!' We lived together thirty-eight long years, and that was the only cross word, and I know he repented of that forty times over."

" J. Brown, deceased—noble man—kept a wood-yard—never gave his wife but one cross word—repented of that forty times—well, go on, madam."

" He was a good provider."

" Good provider—go on!"

" Never said anything when my relatives came."

" —— Relatives came."

" Didn't find fault when I was sick."

" —— When I was sick."

" Was kind to his family."

" —— Kind to his family—yes."

" Well, that's about all," she said, after folding and unfolding her handkerchief and trying hard to recall other matters.

" That will be chapter one, madam, and it will read: 'J. Brown, deceased—noble man—kept a wood-yard—never gave his wife but one cross word—repented of that forty times—good provider—never said anything when relatives came—didn't find fault—kind to his family—supposed to be in Heaven."

" That's elegant!" she whispered, almost smiling, " but it won't make a very large book, will it?"

" Madam, I am as blunt as I am homely, and I want to ask you a plain question."

" You—you may."

" Well, now, instead of going to the expense of this book, why don't you get married again?"

" Oop!" she shrieked, throwing up her hands.

" Yes, madam, why don't you find another husband just as good as the lamented J. Brown?"

" Me marry!" she gasped.

" Yes, madam. You are not an aged person—you have traces of beauty—you have a kind heart—you could love."

" I'd die first!" she gasped, giving me a look of horror.

"ME MARRY!"

" I know better, madam. J. Brown was undoubtedly a good man and all that, but because he happened to die it cannot be expected that you are to wear black, look solemn, and sigh four times a minute for the rest of your life. No; some man—some rich widower is even now sighing for thee."

"Is that so?" she whispered, bending forward.

"It is true, madam. If you were gaunt, homely, and vicious, or fat, freckled, and revengeful, the world would let you gallop around in crapes, and say nothing. But as it is—as you have beauty, intelligence, and bashfulness, you are expected to remarry."

"What would folks say?" she asked, actually smiling.

"Say! why they expect it! Only last night I heard it remarked that it was strange you did not remarry."

"Is that so? Well——"

"I'll go on and write the book if you say so, but how much better it would be for you to erect a nice, cosy head-stone to J. Brown's memory, put on a tender verse of Philadelphia poetry, and then lay off these crapes and let some one else love you."

"Well, you're a writer, and you've been to Chicago and Toledo, and of course you know better than I do. I want to do what is right, you know."

"Certainly, madam, certainly. You will always have a tender spot in your heart for J. Brown, but when a dozen hearts are sighing to love you and be loved in return, and a dozen men are waiting for the privilege of buying your meat and corsets and bustles and potatoes and ruffs and saleratus and silk dresses and corned beef, you can't go pegging around with that solemn look on your face."

"It does seem so, come to think of it," she mused.

"Of course it does! Go home, madam—go home and look cheerful and feel jolly, and some one will soon seek you out."

· She smiled blandly and sweetly as I held the door open, and as she reached the gate she remarked:

"Of course—you—you won't——"

"Not a word, madam—I'd be torn to pieces—quartered alive first!"

She shook her finger at me and cantered gayly down the street.

It isn't likely that she will ever marry again. The melancholy pleasure of standing beside a lost husband's grave and being able to say that he has the most stylish-looking headstone in the cemetery cannot be offset by the joys and pleasures of domestic life.

MRS. BRIGGS, MARTYR.

"**I** DON'T expect to see another sunrise—not another one!"

I have heard Mrs. Briggs make use of the above expression a hundred times or more, and she isn't dead yet. On the contrary, she is hale and hearty, and likely to live for many years to come.

Mrs. Briggs lives next door, and we couldn't keep house without her. She is fat and Briggs is lean. She is a martyr and he is a philosopher. They have no children, and if she didn't consider herself an abused person their domestic life would roll on as smoothly as a log sailing down a canal.

She came into the house the other day, dropped into a chair with an awful bang, and sobbed out:

"Why do I live—oh! why! If you only knew—if you——!"

And here her voice left her, and she jammed her apron into her eyes, weaved her body to and fro, and a painful pause ensued.

"Here I'm working myself down to a shadder!" she finally went on, "while Briggs doesn't seem to care whether we have a home of our own or go to the poorhouse!"

We tried to cheer her up, and after a while she admitted that she might possibly live a week, but she put on a positive look as she added:

331.

"If you only knew half my troubles you would wonder that I don't run crazy and kill somebody!"

If Briggs comes out to sit on the stoop with me and

smoke a cigar, we don't have time to get along in politics further than the administration of James Buchanan when she heaves in sight and exclaims:

"Diogenes Lysander Briggs, do you know that you haven't fixed that gate yet!"

He stops in the midst of his discussion of the Dred Scott decision to say that he'll be along pretty soon, but she is not satisfied with that.

"Oh, yes! you'll come along, you will! You've said that a thousand times, and I know just what depend-

As She Thinks She Is.

ence can be placed on your saying! It's a shame—a burning shame—that I'm being driven to my grave by your neglect and shiftlessness!"

She retires behind the corner, and he goes on with his argument as if he had not heard her.

If I drop into his house to discuss the European question with him she seems quite happy for five or six minutes, but then suddenly commences to wipe her eyes, and soon sobs out:

"I wish people knew just what I suffer!"

Briggs does not even change countenance or drop a word, and in about one minute more his wife remarks:

"You needn't make any fuss over me, but just let the neighbors come in and see the corpse, and then bury me!"

He keeps right on with his story, and she finally jumps up and exclaims:

"Did you hear me, Mr. Briggs! Did you hear me say that the rising sun will find me a corpse—a broken-hearted corpse!"

"Don't you feel well?" he inquires with sudden interest.

"Don't I feel well! Great shiners! how can you ask such a question! Here I am, on the verge of the grave, and you pretend you can't see it! Oh! Diogenes Lysander Briggs, I'd hate to stand in your shoes when the judgment day arrives!"

As She Really Is.

"If you think you need 'em I'd take some liver pills, and as I was saying I think that no European nation is prepared to meet the question——," he goes on in the same even tone, and she jumps out of the back door to find some sympathizing neighbor.

Briggs is good-natured, and perhaps inclined to be lazy, but if he were otherwise she'd kill him within a week. Her words roll off his mind without leaving a foot-print behind, and he feels that it his lot to bear and forbear. Once she sent four miles for him to come and see her die. He was fishing in a creek, and though there was a splendid show for him to catch another bass by waiting half an hour he folded his line and rode back with the messenger. As he entered the house she greeted him with:

"Didn't I tell you this morning I should be a corpse before night?"

"Seems zif you did," he mused, deliberately drawing out his knife and twist of plug, and slowly cutting off a piece.

"Yes, your poor suffering wife is going to find rest at last!" she went on. "The world will call it dropsy or liver complaint or something, but I know and you know what has brought me to this!"

He stood up beside the fire-place, hands crossed behind him, and for a moment his face expressed sorrow and and anxiety. Then he looked out of the window, put on his hat, and said:

"I s'pose I ought to go and put that calf into the barn!"

"Caf! caf!" she shrieked, sitting up in bed—"is a red yearling caf more to you than your dying wife?"

She was doing her own work next day, and her weight is constantly increasing as her years spin out, but yet she is a great martyr, and she couldn't be happy if she had the front seat at a circus.

HE FELT DOLLAROUS.

AN old chap and his wife, going East from their home in Iowa to visit friends, had to halt in Detroit on account of the wife's illness. They went to a hotel, and for the first day or two the husband didn't complain of the cost, but when his wife grew worse, and a doctor was called and a nurse employed, he began to hang on to the dollars which were demanded. On the fifth day the doctor looked serious and said that the woman would probably die. The husband consulted with the hotel clerk and with a freight agent, and going back to his wife he leaned over her and sobbed :

"Oh! Sarah Jane! you mustn't die here!"

"I don't want to leave you, Philetus," she replied, "but I fear that my time has come."

"Don't! oh! don't die here!" he went on.

"If my time has come I must go," she said.

"Yes, I suppose so, but if I could only get you back home first I'd save at least forty dollars on funeral expenses, and forty dollars don't grow on every bush!"

335

HOW TO ACT IN CASE OF FIRE.

THERE are very few people who can keep cool in case they discover a fire, and this is the reason why more fires are not put out in their incipient stages, before any great damage is done.

In case you are walking along the street and discover a chimney burning out, make up your mind that the whole house has got to go unless your own individual exertions prevent. Therefore, jerk the gate off its hinges, kick the front door in on the astonished family and yell "fire!" Your first yell needn't be louder than the common Indian war-whoop, but after the first you must exert yourself in grand efforts to beat any man in that town who ever yelled over a burning chimney. The occupants may desire an explanation as the front door falls in and you leap over it, and begin to throw the chairs around. There is no set answer to repeat, but most most men manage to say:

"Fire—fire—your house—get out—fire—hurry—blazes! fire—hang it—fire—fire!"

They will generally accept the explanation without argument, and you can go ahead and rescue the contents of the

house.   Always commence on the parlor ornaments first.
If you haven't time to save anything but a chromo, half
of a marble-top stand, and the head of a piece of statuary,
you don't know how far these things will go toward setting the burned-out family to house-keeping again.   The
windows were made to throw things through.   If you can
fling all the ornaments out, wrench the sofa to pieces, and
break the legs off of the chairs, you can consider you have*
saved everything in the parlor worth saving.   If there is

a stove in there, tip it over as
you rush to save the bedding
and other furniture.   Don't
throw a bed from the chamber
window; nothing will break a
feather bed all to pieces as
quick as a fall.   Take them on
your back and carefully carry
them from two to four blocks
away and deposit them gently
on a doorstep.

But the case is different with
crockery, looking-glasses and
clocks; you can heave them
out on the walk with perfect
confidence that they won't even
get a flaw.   Deal gently with
flat-irons and boot-jacks.   Don't
try to save a whole bedstead,
but wrench it to pieces, and
throw three or four slats out,

HANDLE 'EM GENTLY.

and then grab the bureau.   Bureaus are cumbersome articles to handle, and it's best to divide them in halves with
an axe, and throw down the portions separately.

I had forgotten to say that it is positively necessary for

V

you to yell "fire!" twice per second, from the time you kick the door in until the fire is out, or the house burned down. If you didn't do this, some of the family might forget that the house was on fire and make arrangements to go visiting, or put on dried apples to stew, or go to setting emptyings.

An ordinarily cool man will clear a house of all worth saving in about fifteen minutes, especially if he has a little help. If the house goes for it, the family will not fail to remember that but for you they might have been roasted alive; and if the flames are subdued, they'll pick up the looking-glass frames, drawer knobs, pitcher handles, and chair legs, and move back in with hearts full of gratitude that you, noble hero, through your coolness and self-possession, saved all that was worth saving.

THE COLONEL'S LETTER.

HE mail routes west of Omaha were but poorly looked after before the days of the Pacific railroad, but the few post-offices were highly prized by miners and traders, enabling them to hear from civilization at least once or twice per year.

We had built up quite a little town about twenty miles from Denver, and it was decided to establish a post-office in a saloon and hire some one to bring and carry a semi-weekly mail. We made no application to the government for a post-office, but were going into this arrangement merely for our own accommodation. Our letters coming from the States were addressed to Denver, and those we sent from " Paradise " bore the Denver post-mark.

We made up a list of those who would pay fifty cents weekly, collected the first installment and hired a half-breed to act as mail-carrier. Everything worked all right, and " Paradise " would have been happy but for a giant miner called " Colonel Pick." He was down for fifty cents per week with the rest of us, and when the first mail came in he called and demanded a letter.

" None here for you, Colonel," answered the man who had assumed the duties of postmaster.

339

The Colonel went away growling, and was on hand next mail-day. Several letters were received and distributed, and when informed that there was no letter for him he exclaimed :

"Didn't I pay my fifty cents with the rest? Haven't I as much right to git a letter as any of 'em?"

The postmaster endeavored to explain to him, but the

FOR "PARADISE."

Colonel kicked an empty whisky barrel across the room and went back to his log shanty on the hillside. The third mail came in and he was on hand, two revolvers in his belt and a large bowie-knife run down behind his coatcollar.

"Ary letter for Colonel Pick?" he inquired of the postmaster.

"No, Colonel—nothing for you," answered the man.

"You are a wolf and a liar!" shouted the Colonel. "I've paid my money and I want a letter!"

"But there is none for you," replied the man. "I'd be glad if——"

"Don't talk to me!" roared the Colonel. "Isn't this a post-office?"

"Yes."

"Well, what's a post-office fur?"

"To receive and distribute mail."

"Yes, and where's my mail? What 'd I pay fur if I hain't goin' to git any letters?"

The postmaster was trying to explain, when the Colonel took the whole mail in his paw and walked off, saying that no crowd of men could humbug him. He wouldn't give the letters up, but he had some good traits about him, and I was sorry when "Paradise" turned out and hung him to a limb to maintain the sanctity of the United States postal rules. We might have shot him through the leg, and then argued with and enlightened him.

THE BALL AT WIDOW MCGEE'S.

THE widow DeShay gave a ball. It was a grand ball, with four musicians seated on the window sills, and an American flag festooned across one end of the room. She invited all the neighbors except the widow McGee, and Tomcat alley wondered how this new insult would be received. It was a cold cut. It was a terrible slight.

The widow McGee sat in her parlor and looked out on the cold new moon, and the pile of old oyster cans, and two freight trucks, and she planned. She felt that she had been wounded, and she knew that she must strike back if she wanted to preserve the respect and admiration of Tomcat alley. She planned for a grand ball—an affair which should outshine the DeShay ball as emphatically as the glitter of pure gold dims the lustre of an Arctic overshoe.

On the third day after that the denizens of Tomcat alley, Big Jack corners and Sulky avenue were astonished and gratified at being handed written invitations which read:

GRAND BAWL.

The cumpany Of yureself & laidy is Respectubly invoited to
Be presint at

A GRAND BAWL,

To be Given by the Widow McGee
Wensday eve.

When Wednesday evening arrived the "Pilgrim's Roost" was all ready for guests. The widow McGee had three American flags festooned on the walls, two kegs of beer in

342

THE BALL AT WIDOW McGEE'S.

the shed, palm-leaf fans for all hands, and the corps of musicians occupied a raised platform at one end of the room. Uncle Jake was there with his fiddle, to lead the orchestra; Old Tom was there with his bass-viol; Cleveland Henry beat the drum; Aunt Betsy beat the cymbals; baby Anna pounded a pan; Honest Boy struck the triangle, and the widow herself sat down to a rented piano and played notes at random.

As the guests were ready to take the floor the widow stepped forward, smiled benignly, and remarked:

"I likes to see everybody take comfort. Chicago Ned and Mary Jane Filkins will lead off, and we'll be happy yet."

The music struck up, and Toledo Infant clasped hands with Lena La York, Cincinnati Sunrise bowed to Maud St. Clair, and the Iron Duke smiled on Mother King and went whirling around.

It was a grand dance. The windows were open so that the widow DeShay could hear the sounds of merriment, and Tomcat alley folks said to Sulky avenue residents that the ball would be remembered by future generations.

Just as the widow McGee had struck high "C" with her melodious voice, and while the triangle was trying to drown fiddle and drum, in marched the police. Some one put the lights out, everybody yelled, and when a dead calm fell upon the ball-room six countesses, four dukes, and three lords, the widow McGee and the band of musicians, were handcuffed and ready to march out. The place which knew them before didn't know them any more, and no sound broke the monotonous tramp or march but the shrill voice of the widow McGee crying out:

"'Tis owin' to the widy DeShay!"

THE SUMMER VACATION.

DIDN'T want to go; give me credit for that. But, when July came, butter melted in the ice-box, flies were as thick as dust, vegetation was parched and business dull, my wife began to talk of the green trees, cool country breezes, pure milk, fresh butter, purling brooks and skipping lambs, and I agreed that the trip would be good for our health.

She said it wouldn't cost us a dollar to get ready, and then went on and used up eighty-five dollars.

Our house was turned inside out for a week, and regularly every night I dreamed of climbing trees, drinking barrels of milk, chasing babbling brooks and ordering strawberries and cream by the wagon load.

Got away at last, and only lost one satchel and two bundles getting to the train.

Other twenty-three bundles all safe.

Arrived in country at noon, and soon found a quiet retreat with an old lady, who took us in through pity.

At $12 per week.

It was an ancient farm-house, moss on the roof, roses climbing over the door, and every corner shady and cool.

My wife went into raptures over a bob-tailed hen and a yellow calf, and as I stood and gazed at the smiling lawn I agreed with her that it was a good thing to come out into the country and gain seven pounds of flesh per week.

344

In the afternoon I went out and rolled on the green grass. Stuck an old rusty fork into my leg and quit rolling. Got out again about sundown to see the lowing kine come home. They consisted of one hog and a cross-eyed lamb, but I don't know as the old lady was to blame.

Got to bed early, having planned to rise with the lark, and go out and behold the dewy meadows sparkling in the sun, and to hear the joyful whistle of the merry plowboy.

THE SMILING LAWN.

Got up at eleven o'clock to kill mosquitos.

Got up half an hour later to kill 'em over again.

Sixteen cows, each one with a bell on, got in front of the house at midnight and called upon us to shake off the shackles of peaceful slumber.

Shook 'em.

Arose at two o'clock to raise the window.

Arose half an hour later to put it down again.

Slept half an hour and then got up and made a speech to the mosquitos, who received it with quiet but earnest applause.

When morning came we went forth in the rain to see the sparkling meadows and hear the plowboy, but we saw not—neither did we hear.

The old lady said that the rain insured a good day for fishing, and I arranged to go over to Lover's Lake in the

afternoon and catch a week's supply of fish. I tried to
hire a horse and wagon to come over to the lake about
sundown and load up the fish, but none were to be had.

I found Lover's Lake to be a beautiful sheet of water,
with every appearance of good fishing, and could hardly
control my impatience to begin the
work of death against the trout.

Finally begun.

There seemed to be a
great many fish around,
but they had just come
home from a festival and
didn't feel hungry.

Fished for four hours,
and then stopped, so as to
leave a few fish for the
farmers around there.

Sat down on the veran-
dah after supper to enjoy
the balmy twilight. Had
the company of 245,362,-
895 mosquitos, six bats,

"LOVERS' LAKE."

one toad, a snake, and black bugs enough for a mince-pie.

Went to bed early and dreamed that I was an apple-
blossom, but hadn't only fairly bloomed out before I had
to get up and drive a bat out of the room.

Got up at eleven to drive cows away.

Got up at midnight to "s'cat" a cat.

At two to fight mosquitos.

At daylight to greet the rosy morn.

When we got home at the end of a week my wife sat
down on the step while I unlocked the door, and said she:

"Darling, I was an idiot."

And I said: "Ditto."

THE INDIAN QUESTION.

M Y plan for solving the Indian problem is not the offspring of a moment's thought. On the contrary, I have given it deep meditation and prolonged study.

In the first place, place the Indian on a nice, clean board about seven feet long, and fasten him there. Then cut him into three pieces. A cross-cut saw is a very good tool to use for cutting an Indian up, but when there is none handy use a hand or buck-saw. I saw 'em in two at the

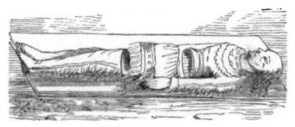

points shown in the above cut. A man who has any ambition to push work will saw up eighteen Indians per day and make a good job in every case.

Then carefully rinse the pieces in a barrel, taking care to pick out any saw-teeth which may have broken off. If the washing process is not placed in the hands of a responsible person half of a good-sized Indian may be wasted by improper handling.

The ground should have been previously prepared by cross-plowing, dragging and manuring. A rich, deep loam is preferable. Indians cannot be planted by machinery,

347

but the modus operandi is for one to go ahead with a spade and make the excavation, another follow with the meat, and the third to drop copies of "Hiawatha" in with the seed and cover all. Plant in June, in the full of the moon. As soon as the plants begin to sprout plow between the rows with a light plow, and then go through with a hoe and heap up dirt around each hill in order to retain the

"Sprouts."

moisture. But little dependence can be placed on the first crop, and many planters go over the field with a mowing machine in August and clear the ground, leaving the roots to start again in the spring. If the crop is allowed to mature, gather just before the first frosts and run 'em through a threshing machine.

AN HOUR AT THE CENTRAL STATION COURT.

"I can sympathize with you," said Bijah, speaking to his Honor, "for I've been there. The women always tear and rear and pitch when spring comes, and you may jaw and jaw, yet you can't stop 'em. I know just how your house is. The stoves are down, straw all over, fresh paint on the doors, a whitewasher daubing away, children playing horse with the looking-glass, and I presume to say that you ate your breakfast this morning on the bottom of the stove-boiler and drank your coffee out of the mustard bottle."

His Honor heaved a deep sigh as he looked from the dent in his hat to the hurts on his knuckles, and Bijah continued:

"It isn't likely that I shall ever marry again, but if I do, and my wife cleans house oftener than once in five years, I'll leave her—yes, leave her, even if it's in the dead of winter and potatoes are $50 per cord and wood is $2 apiece!"

THAT BOY.

"This boy's been breakin' winders," announced Bijah as he handed out a lad whose nose had enough dirt on it to start a corn-field, and whose bare legs could be seen in half a dozen places through sad rents in his trousers.

"That's an awful charge, bub," remarked the Court, putting on a severe look.

849

" I never went for to do it !" replied the boy, a sob in his throat.

" But the deed was done, and it is my duty to inflict the punishment—such punishment as will be a solemn warning to all other boys within two hundred miles of Detroit."

" I didn't mean to, you bet I didn't !" sobbed the boy; " went to throw like that—and it slipped like that—and boo-hoo-hoo the window !"

" What an awful thing it is to see one so young charged with such a crime," continued the Court after a long pause. " And yet I hardly want to sentence you to the gallows."

" Oh! mister !" wailed the rat, drawing up his bare foot and rubbing his other leg with it, "lemme off this time—this one time—never throw another stun—never sass anybody—never—oh! lemme off!"

" I might probably do it, but if I do I shall carry your name in my wallet, and the very first time I hear of your cutting up I shall send eight policemen to capture you. Be careful my son—be very circumspect in all your future actions, for you are resting in the shadow of the gallows, as it were."

" I will—I will—I won't even throw at a goat no more !" exclaimed the lad, and Bijah let him out of the side door.

"KINDER LOOKIN'."

" Do you answer to the name of C. Merrifield Scott ?" inquired the Court as Bijah pushed out another.

" Yaas."

He was a young man of four-and-twenty, and the "duds" on his back weren't enough in bulk to make a good-sized mop. His hair was down to his eyes, there was coal-dust and dirt all over him, and he moved around with slow and solemn step.

"Well, sir," resumed the Court, "you are charged with vagrancy. The warrant says you have no home, no occupation, and that you couldn't buy a lemon if they sold 'em at a cent a million. Straighten up, look me in the eye, and give me your candid opinion about it."

"Thar' hain't no work," drawled the prisoner.

"Have you sought for work?"

"Yaas."

"Where?"

"Waal, I've been kinder lookin' all around town."

"And your efforts have not been crowned with the successfulness of success?"

"Naw."

"Mr. Scott, continued his Honor, as he fastened his  teeth into an apple and drew a whole side away at once, "suppose that Daniel Boone had *kinder* looked around in his young days—where would Kentucky be now?"

"I dunno," sighed the prisoner.

"Suppose, Mr. Scott, that Storey, of "KINDER LOOKIN'." the Chicago *Times*, or Sam Bowles, of the Springfield *Republican*, or Dana, of the New York *Sun*, had spent their early days in sitting on a hydrant and watching the operations of a pile-driver—would they ever have had half a dozen libel suits at once, and been able to pay a coal bill on sight?"

"I tell you work is mighty skerce!" exclaimed the prisoner, seeming to be annoyed at the questioning.

"Well, I'll put you where you'll have a steady job for six months. I make your sentence for that time, and if they are an economical set there they won't try to wash you up, but will just take your hide off and raise a new man."

A MEDIUM.

A colored woman named Crosby sailed out and spitefully remarked:

"I demand my discharge."

"This isn't the office where they sell demands," replied the Court.

"But I want to go."

"Well, we'll both be ready to go directly. I understand that you are a medium—tell fortunes, see spirits, and so forth?"

"De same."

"And I further understand that you struck another colored woman with a poker, kicked in a door, and raised Cain over a whole neighborhood."

"Nebber did, sah."

"But here are two officers and three witnesses."

"Dey is liars, sah!"

"Well, they may be, but I'll take the chances. Has any spirit whispered to you that I'm going to send you up for thirty days?"

"No, sah."

"That shows what dependence you can put on spirits. Take her away."

"I'll holler!" she said, clutching the railing.

"You mean that you will scream?"

"Yes, sah."

"And raise a row?"

"Yes, sah."

"Well you just try it on, and if I don't put a sticking plaster over your mouth I'm no Court!"

She looked.

He looked.

And she didn't dare do it.

When the Maria rolled away the boys sang:

> "We've traveled this wide world all over,
>   And had piles of sorrow and sport;
> But we never laid eyes on a human
>   Who'd successfully bluff this 'ere court."

W

JEEMS.

UST like a boy, he had been playing around all the morning. Other boys were getting ready for Sunday school, and had their hair combed down behind their ears and a religious look in their eyes, while this boy was drawing a cart up and down the walk and encouraging peace-loving dogs to assault each other and still further disturb the harmony of the pleasant morning. At length his mother walked down to the gate, caught sight of him half a block away, and she shouted:

"Young m-a-n!"

He rose up from his seat on the walk and brushed away at his pants as he turned his eyes toward her.

"Young man, you'd better stir your stumps!" she shouted.

He stirred them. Traveling half the distance which separated them, he halted and inquired:

"What yer want?"

"What do I want?" she screeched; "I want *you!*"

"I'm here, hain't I?"

"Yes, you are out here, cantering around, and yelling and howling on the Lord's day. It's a wonder to me that Providence hasn't put some great affliction on you!"

"Biles?" he queried.

"Biles! Wuss than biles! Now you come in here!"

"What fur?"

"Come in here and get ready for Sunday school!"

"I hate ter."

"Come here, young man!"

He slowly approached her, and as he came within reaching distance she seized him by the hair, shook him right and left, and remarked:

"Hate to, do you! Want to be a heathen, eh! Don't love the Lord, eh!"

"Yas—oh!—oh, goll!" he yelled.

"Well, I thought you did! Now stump into the house and get ready for Sunday school. I've been thinking over your case lately, and I've made up my mind to lick you to death and hang your hide on the fence if you don't get religion and be somebody!"

And she hauled Jeems into the house, gave him a push through the hall, and exclaimed:

"I don't care for the neighbors! It's my duty to save you from fire and brimstone, and I'll do it if I have to break every bone in your body!"

SOME BALD-HEADED MEN.

T used to make my mouth water to sit and look down
upon Mr. Garrison's bald head. It was as smooth
as a book-canvasser's speech, shone like a new britan-
nia tea-pot, and the little veins could be traced like water-
courses on a big map of the United States.

Every bald-headed man has his *forte.* Mr. Garrison's
forte was in packing a ward caucus. It would have filled
your soul with joy to see him drop in on a man who wanted
to be a delegate. Mr. Garrison had his slate made up, and

GARRISON'S HEAD.

it was his business to get
all other aspirants out of
the way. After wringing
the man's hand until the
bones cracked he would
speak about the weather,
the crop prospects, the
death of the last old pioneer, and would suddenly
inquire:

"Oh, by the way, do
you want to be a delegate
to the city convention?"

The man would faintly
admit that such was the case, as he wanted a public sewer
in the upper end of the ward.

"Egad! good!" Garrison would exclaim. "I've just fixed for that! You'll have a sewer there in less than a month! Just keep right on attending to your daily work, and I'll fix the sewer business. You have no time to fool away with politics—you are too honest, too conscientious for a politician."

The would-be delegate had to wilt, and Garrison's slate was left without a scratch. I happened to be around when he was thrown from his buggy and fatally injured. His mind wandered as the coroner bent over him, and he whispered:

"Vote the straight ticket, and beware of canards set afloat by the opposition!"

PART OF THE PROGRAMME.

Mr. Humphrey had a head which any boy would have willingly given a jack-knife to look at, and Mr. Humphrey's *forte* was enforcing family discipline. It isn't every father that can make nine children stand around the house as children should, but Mr. Humphrey could, and he never used the rod. He had a regular programme, which covered all emergencies. If Henry and John had a fight, Henry was headed up in a barrel and rolled around the woodshed, and John was hung upon a hook to meditate. If Augustus was " sassy " he was made to sit on the picket fence for a certain length of time, and if Jane scorched the meat her teeth were rubbed with tar until she was a whole week getting her natural taste again.

I was in there one day when Mr. Humphrey was helpless with a broken leg. The children had taken advantage of the occasion, and he asked me as a special favor to barrel up John; hang William on the hook; tie Susan under the penstock; make Anthony sit on a lump of ice; crook Charles over the saw-horse; fill Amanda's mouth with cotton, and bend Washington around an apple tree until he formed an unbroken circle.

Mr. Knox was bald-headed, and Mr. Knox's *forte* was his dignity and bearing. If a beggar rang his door-bell and asked for cash or old clothes Mr. Knox would swell out, put on the look of the big lion in a menagerie, and inquire:

" Sir! sir! sir! do you know who I am, sir!"

Then he would 'swell some more, brush his hair up, cough loudly, and continue:

" Sir! you must have made a mistake, sir!"

The beggar would be only too glad to get away, and Mr. Knox would go in and boss his family around. He had his wife and children as scared of him as rabbits. When one of the children's toes were out the wife would say:

" J. M. Knox, Esquire, your son is in need of a new pair of shoes, and should you deign to purchase them, you will earn the everlasting gratitude of one who is not worthy to touch the hem of your garment."

Canterbury was right the other way, though his head had the same appearance of oiled paper. His *forte* was his politeness and his retiring disposition. He fell overboard once while riding on a steamboat, and long before the small boat picked him up he called out:

"Gentlemen, believe me, I'm extremely sorry that this thing has occurred, and I promise you that it shall not be repeated!"

When he was once called on to make a public speech he fainted away and fell over a chair, and as soon as recovering consciousness he humbly apologized to the chair and promised better conduct for the future.

THE MODEST CANTERBURY.

When he was dying and they asked him if he had any choice of pall-bearers he replied that they had better hold the funeral after dark, so as not to interfere with any one's working hours. If he went to Heaven I presume he crowded himself into a corner and held his boots in his lap, so as not to be in any one's way.

THE LAST COACH.

THERE will come a day when the old vehicle will roll into the village for the last time. The inn-keeper will stand on the verandah to welcome the passengers, and the village boys will leave kites, marbles and hoops to gather in a circle around the big-bodied vehicle and gaze timidly at the strangers who leave it. The driver will have a tear in his eye as he leaves the box with the knowledge that he is never to mount it again, and the passengers, no matter how thick the dust on their garments, or how rudely they have been jolted, will heave a sigh of regret as they step down and catch sight of the passenger coaches standing ready to usurp the rights and privileges of the old vehicle which has safely carried its thousands.

Up hill and down—over bridges—around the turns in the highway—cold, heat, rain or shine, and at last steam has won the race, and the old coach goes under the tavern shed to decay and fall to pieces. The faithful horses find other work, the driver is lost in the busy throng, and only the remembrance is left.

The world is pushing these old things back to make room for new ones, and the new ones are the best. Yet, the boy who looked up from the town pump with admiring

gaze at the dignified master of a coach and four, whose whip-lash could pick a fly off the ear of either leader, and whose word on law, politics or finance was never questioned, even by the talented town constable—this boy has a right to feel a bit sad, as a man, to see the dust of Time settling thickly upon the memories of childhood.

MR. LEON ST. JOHNS

ONE day when a dozen of us were gathered at the Colonel's ranch, on what was then called "The Trail of Despair," Nevada, the stage halted to drop a passenger.

We lived in tents and shanties, wore a shirt for six weeks at a time, lived on bean soup and "salt horse," and as Quincy Jack remarked: "We couldn't chaw grammar for shucks."

"GENTLEMEN!"

The passenger was dressed to kill, carried a cane and smoked a cigar, had on yellow kids and fine boots, and the men regarded him with more amazement than they would have displayed had a dozen elephants appeared on the hill.

As he entered the hotel, so called, which was merely a

362

long, low building, he looked from one miner to another and finally asked:

" Gentlemen, where is the landlord ?"

" *Gentlemen !*" screamed an old miner named " Oxalic Acid," springing to his feet.

" Gentlemen !" echoed " Old Sorrow," whirling around in his chair.

" GENTLEMEN !" shrieked " Turkey Bob," putting on a look of awful amazement.

The stranger didn't seem to know what to make of such a greeting, but he continued:

" Beg pardon, but I desire to tarry here and refresh the inner man."

" *Desire !*" yelled Jack Lawrence from behind the stove.

" Refresh !" screamed the old man Davis from behind a table.

" THE INNER MAN !" squeaked little hump-backed Bob, raising his hands in horror.

There was a long pause.

The stranger began pulling at his kids, and said:

" Really, this is incomprehensible."

The word " incomprehensible " struck every man with the force of a cannon ball. Big Blue Bottle, the oldest miner on the claim, fairly turned pale, and " Sal's Brother," another old digger, leaned back in his chair and whispered that he wouldn't live three weeks.

You could have heard a pin drop.

Then, with an awful look on his face, Big Blue Bottle stepped forward and said, almost in a whisper:

" Stranger, who be you ?"

" I'm a traveler, and I had intended to halt here and secure refreshments."

" *Refreshments !* hear that !" whispered Sandy Sam to old Johnson.

"REFRESHMENTS!" echoed "Sal's Brother," wiping his eyes as if there was smoke between him and the stranger.

"REFRESHMENTS!"

"Isn't this a ranch?" demanded the stranger as he looked around. "It surpasses my comprehension that you maintain such an attitude to one in search of the sustenance of life."

That speech floored the men. Old Blue Bottle turned as white as snow and gasped out:

"Sur—sur—SURPASHUS!"

"Attitood!" whispered the Deacon, sliding off the bench.

"Sus—sus—suste—te——!" stammered an old Californian, dropping the plug of tobacco from his hand.

There was silence.

"Stranger!" commenced Big Blue Bottle in a hoarse voice, "what mought be your name?"

"My name?" replied the young man, taking a whiff at his cigar—"my name is Leon St. Johns."

"W-HAT!" screamed the old man.

"ATTITOOD!"

."Leon St. Johns," repeated the stranger, eyeing his questioner.

Dead silence again.

"Stranger, how are you heeled?" finally asked the old man.

"How—what?"

"Have you got any weepon?"

"Yes—a revolver."

"And you'll shoot at me—five paces—count one and commence firing!"

"N-no—I don't want to hurt you," replied the stranger.

"It's eleven miles down to Rogers'—plain trail—git or fight!" whispered the old man as he hauled his revolver around.

"What—what do you mean?"

"I don't mean nothin', stranger," solemnly replied old Blue Bottle, "but if them big words and that name o' yours don't dig out for Rogers' in ten ticks of the watch I shell commence shootin' at clus range and keep 'er up till the powder gives out!"

The traveler made for the door, and the last we saw of him he was wrestling with the mud on the Daniel Webster Level.

THAT EMERSON BOY.

ORE than one will grieve to learn that the Emerson boy is dead, and that there isn't any one around that house now to make fun. He was a cheerful, lively boy, and he did his best to make the household put on the mantle of joyfulness. Emerson often remarked that Bob didn't seem to ever sit down and think of the grave and death, and he probably never did.

No, Bob wasn't of that make. He wanted to have fun, and if the coroner should have his body exhumed to-day I have no doubt that certain portions of it would be found calloused, where the press-board used to fall. Both his ears were nearly worn off by being cuffed so much, and it took a whole row of currant bushes to furnish whips to dust his jacket for one summer.

Emerson didn't know what fun was until Bob was eight years old. Then the boy began to launch out. He would bore gimlet-holes in the bottom of the water pail, put cartridges in the coal stove, unscrew the door-knobs, fill the kerosene can with water, and a good thrashing didn't burden his mind over five minutes. Sometimes his father would take him by the hair and yank him up to the sofa and sit down and ask:

"Robert Parathon Emerson, what in blazes ails ye?"

366

"It's the yaller jaunders, I guess," Bob would meekly reply.

"Robert, don't you want to be an angel?" the old man would continue.

"And have wings?"

"Yes, my son."

"And fly higher'n a kite?"

"Yes."

"And fight hawks?"

"Y-e-s, I guess so."

"Bet your beef I would—whoop! bully for the angels!"

"That's sacrilege, that is!" the old man would remark, and he would jerk Bob's hair some more and declare that the young rascal was bound for the gallows. After lying under the pear tree for six minutes Bob would recover from his sadness and go over to the barn and run the pitchfork through the straw-cutter, harness up the cow and stick pins into the family horse.

One night he brought home a wolf-trap and set it in the middle of the woodshed floor to catch a rat. He chuckled a good deal that evening at the thought of what would happen to the rats, and he fell asleep and dreamed that he was a hand-organ, and that some one stole the crank to him so that he couldn't be played on. Just before going

to bed old Emerson went out after a scuttle of coal, and he stepped his bootless foot into that trap. He made a mighty spring and uttered a mighty yell, and it took two men ten minutes to spring the trap off his leg.

THE OLD MAN'S ARGUMENTS.

"It's that boy's work!" he groaned as he nursed his foot, and he took up the bootjack, limped into the bedroom and gave Bob an awful clip, just as the child was dreaming of playing base ball with a mermaid.

"I'll pound ye to death if ye don't stop this fooling!" cried the old man, but he hadn't been out of the bedroom ten minutes before Bob was planning to stop up the chimney next day and smoke everybody out of the house. It wasn't many days before he fixed a darning needle in the cushion of his father's arm chair and bounced the old man three feet high, and his licking hadn't got over smarting before he exploded a fire-cracker in his mother's snuff box. That night the old man said to him as he took him by the ear:

"Robert Parathon Emerson, do you ever think of where you will go to?"

"Yes, sir," he answered, "I'll go to bed purty soon!"

Then he got another mauling and went to bed to dream that he was a three-tined pitchfork, and that a man was using him to load hay with.

Poor boy! Even three days before he died, and while on his death-bed, he managed to slip an eight-ounce tack into his father's left boot and get up another circus. If he's in Heaven now I truly believe he'll put up some job on the first angel that comes around him.

THE WOMAN WITH THE POETRY.

I WAS strolling around in Cleveland when I met "By." Brown, who flew the frisket and pulled the press when I first learned to ink the roller. We used to have "Sheep's-foot sling" together, suffered alike for the want of prompt pay, and I was glad to see him. He wanted to go down to the *Plain Dealer* office to see some of the boys, and I went along.

We reached the office soon after the editors had started out for dinner, and were overhauling the exchanges when a gaunt, sharp-nosed woman, looking red in the face from climbing the stairs, stood in the door and asked if she could see the editor.

"Come in, madam," said Brown, bowing with great gallantry—"I am the editor."

"Well, we've taken this paper for seventeen years," she continued as she sat down beside him, "and I want a little favor. We've lost our child—our little Ross, and I've written a few verses on him and would like to have 'em printed in the paper."

"With pleasure, madam," replied Brown, reaching out for the foolscap on which she had written twelve or fourteen verses.

"The neighbors say it's real poetry," she went on, "and though I don't purtend to be a poet I think there is something here to touch every mother's heart."

"Let's see?" mused Brown, as he glanced at the first verse; "it starts off good:

NOT A POET.

> We've lost our darling hoss,
> And we deeply mourn his loss."

"Hoss!" she exclaimed—there's no hoss in them verses!"

"H-o-ss, hoss—isn't that hoss?" he asked.

"*Ross*—our boy's name," she explained as she looked over his shoulder.

"Ah! I see, now. Well:

> He is with the angels now,
> With a garland on the cow."

"What!" she shrieked, snatching at the manuscript.

"With a garland on the cow, madam," he replied. "That's original and touching."

"It's a garland on his *brow*," she said, beginning to breathe hard.

"It may be—it may be," he continued in a dubious tone, "but I would advise you to leave it the other way. This poetry will be copied all over the world, and although I am no great judge of poetry, and the office is a little hard up for money just now, I should feel safe in offering you $1,000 for this poem just as it stands."

"Is that so!" she gasped, smiling clear back to her ears.

"I might even do better, but let's see the next verse:

> He was a joyous child,
> And he had a pie-bald eye."

"Pie—what—bald—bald what!" she screamed as she rose up again.

"Oh, I see now—'and his eye was blue and mild.'

Well, as a friend, as a disinterested friend, I would advise you to leave the line as I read it. Children are dying around us every day, madam, but it isn't once a year that a child with a pie-bald eye is followed to the grave. I tell you that this poem is certain to lift you from the pit of obscurity to the eminence of fame in just one day. But to go on:

"Is That So?"

> He was too pure to stay,
> And so he flew a dray."

"A what—a dray!"

"Yes, madam—he flew a dray. That expression alone is worth $500 to you, and I hope you won't alter it."

"And so he flew *away!*" she exclaimed as she put her finger on the line.

"I believe it is, but still I hope you won't change it. Those two verses are splendid, and now:

> We ne'er shall see him more,
> And it makes our heels so sore.

That's another five hundred dollar expression, madam, and if I were pinned——"

"Are you making fun of me?" she inquired as she rose up and laid a large-sized fist on the table and drew her mouth into a very serious shape.

"Could I have the heart to sport with your affliction, madam? By the beard of the Prophet, no! Let me finish:

> Our tears fall night and day,
> But we'll not forget to play.

That's good—excellent! Exercise is good for the health, madam, and——"

"Gimme them verses!" she demanded in a hoarse whisper.

"I will, madam, but I wouldn't make any corrections if I were you. Now hear the next:

> We miss his pattering feet—
> We miss his lamb-like bleat.

Now, madam, if one thousand dollars is any——"

She made a grab, secured the verses, and as she raised her umbrella over her shoulder she gasped out:

"Taken this—paper—seventeen—years!"

"Do not be agitated, madam—control your nerves. You see——"

"But I'll stop it—I'll stop it!" she screamed.

"Stay, madam. Let me argue with you—let me entreat——"

"I'll stop it—I'll stop it!" she screamed as she sailed down the hall.

"Madam, listen to me—a lone man—an orphan—a——"

"And I'll git all my neighbors to stop it!" she yelled back from the landing.

"Madam, would you ruin an orphan—crush down——"

"And I'll git up a club for the *Leader!*" she shrieked back, and—and——"

She was out of hearing.

SOMETHING ABOUT THE SELF-MADE MEN
OF DETROIT.

VERY city has a certain few citizens of whom it is proud, because of their long and victorious struggles against the frowns of Fortune. Detroit is no exception to the rule. As the modesty of the individuals here given would have prevented them from writing themselves up for any of the *Harpers'* publications, no matter what discount was allowed for geographical situation, the reader can congratulate himself that he would have never learned the histories of some of them but for the enterprise of your humble servant.

James McGee came to this city forty-nine years ago, with only seven cents in his pocket. By strict attention to business he has not only been enabled to increase his capital one-half, but is able to rent a house at fifteen dollars per month, where the landlord don't know who he is. At one time he was owing nearly six hundred dollars, such was his business energy; but at this writing he doesn't owe a cent—the debts having outlawed.

John Tweezer came here twenty-one years ago, having less than forty cents about him. He saw a fine opening here for a cotton factory, and he sees one yet. He believes he might have cleared five hundred thousand dollars by establishing a large factory of the kind, but he didn't start one. His habits of frugality, industry and perseverance

FRUGALITY.

at length attracted the attention of a gentleman connected with the House of Correction, and he "took him in" to assist in running the chair business. Although Mr. Tweezer didn't lose a cent, he came out of the partnership business after six months without a dollar. But he had a spirit which could not be put down, and prevailed upon a man to give him another start. He is now able to ride in a carriage— being coachman for a family in the western part of the city. He has never had the honor of having his wood cut appear in the *Phrenological Journal*, but the chief of police has on file a very nice photograph of him.

Henry Swipes took up his residence here nearly **fifteen** years ago, living for the first three months in the brown stone mansion on the corner of Beaubien and Clinton streets. He hadn't a cent in his pockets, no change of clothing, had to contribute from his earnings to the support of a mother and seven children, and any man of ordinary spirit would have been discouraged. Mr. Swipes was not of that metal. He saw that a boiler shop would pay a large profit, and so he—

DIDN'T GET DISCOURAGED.

tried to borrow ten dollars to start a saloon, but as no one could see where he was going to use so much money, he didn't get it. He then went to work as a laborer, and has moved in that sphere ever since, being able this spring to have the city assess seventy dollars on an alley sewer behind his landlord's house. He has never taken an office in his life, because he can't get one, and he looks upon political struggles with scorn and disdain.

J. H. R. N. Slags came here when Detroit was a town of a few thousand inhabitants, and he brought all his initials with him. After considerable discussion he decided that property would soon double, and would have purchased several blocks if holders could have been induced to do a credit business. He consequently didn't purchase, and has had to make his fortune in other ways. He decided never to tell the truth under any circumstances, and has stuck to his decision with remarkable pertinacity and force of character, and to this fact he owes most of his wealth—that is, the wealth his grandmother is going to leave him. He was in the habit of handling considerable money, but had to quit when the alarm-bell money drawer was invented, as it then became too risky.

Samuel Striker came here only ten years ago, and has already succeeded in outrunning three different policemen, and in keeping clear of seven or eight documents issued from various courts. Most any man would give up in despair and get across to Windsor, but Mr. Striker is bound to keep his residence in Detroit, and can't be persuaded that Jackson is any location for business.

John Quirk settled here fifteen years ago. He was as remarkable then as now for his great decision of character. He had been in Detroit but three hours before he decided to marry a brown stone house, and a half interest in a bank. Unfortunately, the young lady was endowed with the same great decision, and Mr. Quirk didn't marry. He is now driving team, patiently waiting his time.

Septimus Blank came here in indigent circumstances. He soon saw that there was a chance to speculate in real estate, and wrote to his uncle to lend him fifteen thousand

QUIRK'S VAIN LOVE.

dollars. His uncle replied that he hadn't even fifteen cents, and thus the speculation fell through. However, Mr. Blank could not be put back by such a trifle as fifteen thousand dollars, or even fifteen cents, and has worked his way against the tide until last year he was able to draw a check for thirty thousand dollars. He "drew it over" a country-man and got twenty-eight dollars on the strength of it, and is now spending a season in the Adirondacks, or somewhere else out of the reach of policemen.

Solomon Hope is the last on the list. He moved into Detroit on a hand-sled, and the first house he lived in was a stable. He has been many times heard to say that his sole food for the first year was nothing but corn meal and molasses. Our citizens all know where the post-office is? Well, Mr. Hope don't own that building, and never will. He started a small grocery store on Woodward avenue, and, by strict honesty and the utmost economy, succeeded in getting out of town one night with every cent he ever made and some which he didn't make. It is due, how-ever, to him to state that he shortly returned and com-promised the matter—by stealing a horse and getting where his creditors couldn't put up any job on him.

THE LATE ARTEMUS WARD'S WARM FRIENDS.

IN addition to being a good fellow, I think the late Artemus Ward had a large number of warm personal friends. I suppose that a great many of them have followed him " over the river," but I think there's enough left to quite cover an acre of ground. Among the letters received last week were the following:

"JERSEY CITY, August 20, 1875.

MR. QUAD—*Dear Sir*—I understand that you are going to publish a book. I hope you will make a success of it.

J. B. M.,
Warm friend of the late Artemus Ward."

And this:

"OVER THE RHINE, CINCINNATI, Aug. 18.

MR. QUAT—I haf understandt you will be going to make a vunny pook. Ish dot zo? Make zum goot bicture for her, und spheaks lots of shokes.

Very drooly,
HANS G.,
Der warm frent mit der late Ardemus Wart."

And this:

"PHILADELPHIA, August 16.

MR. QUAD—When is that book to be issued? Send me a copy C. O. D.

Yours,
B. F. L.,
Warm friend of the late Artemus Ward."

And this:

MR. McQUAD—I am a raspictable widdy woman, and I have to wash for a living. Dennis McCarthy was a sphaking to me uv that book uv yours, and I forward thray dollars by this mail to prhocure a copy. Send it airly.

Very raspictably,

B. McG.,

Warum frind of the late Artemus Ward."

And this:

M. Q.—*Dear Sir*—Is that book out yet? What is the price? Is it anything like a dictionary, and will it have red covers?

Yours ever,

V. L. S.,

Warm friend of the late Artemus Ward."

And this:

Dear Sir—I want to act as agent for your book. I think I can sell a large number of them, as everybody around here knows me as

S. T. F.,

Warm friend of the late Artemus Ward."

And this:

M. QUAD—I notice by the papers that you are going to get out a book. Is it a Sunday school book, and would it be safe to let my children read it?

Very truly,

L. A. M.,

Warm friend of the late Artemus Ward."

There were twenty-two other letters similarly signed, and more are coming in by every mail. It seems to me that a man as well provided with warm personal friends as Mr. Ward, should have died owing more borrowed money than he did.

THE BAD BOY.

CHAPTER I.—INTRODUCTORY.

HIS name was John Anderson Tompkins, and he was going on thirteen years old. He had freckles all over his nose, chewed plug tobacco, and loafed around select schools and put "tin ears" on boys smaller than himself. His father was killed by a Canada saw log, his only sister slept in the silent tomb, and his mother divided time between gossiping and canvassing for money for the heathen in Africa.

CHAPTER II.—THUSLY.

Thus it will be seen that there was no one to give John Anderson Tompkins any domestic attention beyond an occasional whack with a slipper, which made him the worse. He wasn't sent to school, never had to take a dose of castor oil, was allowed to go around with a letter in the post-office, and his pants supported by a magnificent belt of sheep twine, and if he wasn't home by ten o'clock at night his mother was sure he would dump down somewhere and be home in time for codfish and potatoes in the morning.

CHAPTER III.—SHAMEFUL NEGLECT.

John Anderson Tompkins' mother never took him on her knee and asked him if he knew where he'd go to if he grew up to be an awful liar and horse thief. She never told him about the children of Egypt, Moses in the bull-rushes, or Daniel in the lion's den, and it is no wonder that he grew up to be a bad boy. She never had sticking plasters ready when he got cut, and on Sunday mornings there was no one to rub him behind his ears, fill his eyes with soap water, and comb his hair the wrong way.

NOT IN SCHOOL.

CHAPTER IV.—HIS PECULIARITIES.

Everything that happened in the village was laid at John Anderson Tompkins' door: "It's some of that boy's work," whenever a bushel of plums, a watermelon, or a peck of peaches mysteriously disappeared. He was probably guilty of everything charged, as when he died they found where he had hidden seventeen stolen cow-bells, forty axes, ever so many saw-bucks, fifteen or twenty front gates, and I don't remember how many snow shovels.

CHAPTER V.—DOWN ON HIM.

In time, as the reader was informed in a previous chapter, the adult male population of the village got down on John Anderson Tompkins. Old maids jabbed at him with umbrellas, merchants flung pound weights at him, shoemakers dosed him with strap oil, and grocers always looked around for John Anderson Tompkins when they wanted to heave out bad eggs or spoiled fruit.

His Outside Friends.

CHAPTER VI.—HIS AMBITION.

You may think that they would have eventually succeeded in breaking the boy's spirit and dashing his hopes, but they couldn't do it. He had an ambition which nothing could check. He wanted to be a bold pirate and sail on the raging main, and he was patiently waiting for the time to come when he could wear No. 10 boots, and swear in a voice like the echoes of a bass-viol. He would be content to crawl into hen-roosts and to creep around horse barns for a few years, but then—but then——

CHAPTER VII.—EFFORTS TO REFORM.

Some of the most philanthropic citizens made strenuous efforts to reform the boy.   They locked him up in a smoke

EFFORTS AT REFORM.

house for a week; they clubbed him till he couldn't yell, and they held him under a pump until he was as limp as a rag, but as soon as they let him go, he went right back to his old habits again.

CHAPTER VIII.—NEARING HIS END.

John Anderson Tompkins had kept this thing up for eight or nine years when our story opens, and he was nearing his end.   Justice overtakes the guilty, sooner or later, and justice was lying low for this bad boy.   He had the cheek to believe that he would live to be a hundred years old, but he was to be taken down a peg or two, and his mother left an orphan.

CHAPTER IX.—THE END.

One day, while in the hey-day of his wickedness, John Anderson Tompkins came upon something new in the line of plunder.   It was a pile of little cans labeled " nitroglycerine—hands off—dangerous, etc.," but he couldn't read, and didn't care a copper.   He carried a can behind the meeting-house and sat down on a rock to open it.

There wasn't any guardian angel around to tell him that he'd " get busted " if he fooled with that can, and so he spit on both hands, and gave it a whack with a stone.

CHAPTER X.—OBITUARY.

The folks all ran out, and after a good deal of trouble,

they found and separated the pieces of boy, and got together enough of John Anderson to fill a cigar-box and answer as the basis of the funeral. They buried him in a quiet nook, and the grave-stone maker put a little lamb on the head-stone, to show that John Anderson Tompkins was meek and lovely.

THE GOOD BOY.

A SEQUEL TO THE BAD BOY.

CHAPTER I.—INTRODUCTION.

QUEERLY enough, once upon a time there was a very good boy living in the State of New Jersey. Some readers may think it singular that a good boy should live in New Jersey, but I am writing facts.

CHAPTER II.—HIS NAME.

The name of this very good boy was Charles Henry Worthington Adams, and he had white hair, a freckled face, an innocent look, and his highest aim was to please his father and mother. His father never had to tell him to take off his coat and come to the barn for a thrashing, and his mother never broke any of her fingers cuffing his ears.

CHAPTER III.—RETIRING DISPOSITION.

Charles Henry Worthington was of a very retiring disposition, always retiring to bed at early candle-light. He never made any fuss about going up stairs in the dark, as most boys do, and even if his parents had a strawberry festival in the house, or his father was reading a dime novel aloud, the little hero would promptly seek his couch at the usual hour without a murmur.

384

CHAPTER IV.—FORGIVING SPIRIT.

Charles Henry Worthington had a very meek, forgiving spirit, and he didn't hold a grudge as some boys do; he wasn't that kind. He didn't go around blowing how he'd fix the old man's ear, or that he'd make his mother mighty sorry, and he never threatened to run away to sea and become a bold pirate. He didn't know anything about prize-fights, duels or bowie knives; and if a boy went to put a head on him, Charles Henry Worthington always made a bolt for home.

His Love.

CHAPTER V.—HE LOVED HIS HOME.

Our good boy loved his home, and it was seldom that he wandered from it, unless his mother sent him to borrow Mrs. Bradly's quilt-frame or Mrs. Tyler's brass kettle. He never went out stealing water melons; never ran away to go in swimming; would never go with the boys to see a

dead horse or a sick cow, but he preferred to pick up chips, hoe in the garden or hunt out and kill the pesky potato-bugs. In the course of seven years this boy won four school medals, had the bilious colic twice, won a Sunday school prize, and had the honor of

Y

riding to a religious pic-nic with his legs over the end-board of the minister's one-horse wagon.

CHAPTER VI.—TAKEN SICK.

At last this boy was taken sick. You may have observed that all good boys generally die young, especially good New Jersey boys. His mother made him toast and catnip tea, soaked his feet and tied a towel around his head, but, alas! he grew worse. She gave him a pill in some pear sauce, made him some ginger tea, and promised him a bunch of fire crackers the next Fourth of July.

CHAPTER VII.—HE WAS DOOMED.

"Lemme See Your Tongue."

He grew worse, and the doctor was sent for. The doctor felt his pulse, looked into his mouth and made him run out his tongue; spit on the carpet, and said he guessed Charles Henry Worthington would soon get well. But

CHAPTER VIII—HE WAS SUCKED IN,

This doctor was. He wasn't used to doctoring good little boys, and within twenty-four hours after he left the house Charles Henry Worthington was a shining angel, and his father had to split his own kindlings and make his own fires. They buried him under a weeping willow, letting all the Sunday school children march around and have a sight of him, and it was two months before his mother could go to the sewing society and talk as freely as before.

CHAPTER IX—THE END.

There's nothing like being a good boy. I hope that all the little boys and girls who read this will try from this time forward to be a good boy, so that when they die they may have a marble lamb with a bushy tail on their tombstone.

CLEANING HOUSE.

E always begin cleaning house on the first of May. We have just commenced now, and I write these few lines on the bread-board, with a bureau drawer for a seat, while Long Primer is playing horse in the parlor with a bust of Andrew Jackson, and Small Pica is dipping lace curtains into a pail of whitewash.

We don't clean one room at a time, but go at it in a wholesale way and rake the old house from floor to roof. Three mornings ago when I started down town my wife said in her innocent, deceiving way, that she guessed she'd do a little house cleaning, and that we'd have a picked up dinner. When I returned home the bedsteads were circling around the back yard, the kitchen stove was buried under the straw beds, the curtains were down, windows out, carpets up, and four Africans were mildly drawing their whitewash brushes over the ceilings and having an animated discussion about cremation. My wife said she'd have it so clean that a fly would break its neck slipping down, and she was so enthusiastic about it that I cheerfully ate dinner off the mantel piece and made no remarks about it when I found the cork of the camphor bottle and the front door key stuffed into the spout of the coffee-pot. When I left the house Small Pica was hanging to the pegs of the hall-tree and singing "Mollie Darling," and Long Primer was trying to wipe the whitewash out of his left eye with a chromo of the Yosemite Valley, but my wife said I needn't stay on their account.

I came up at night believing that everything would be regulated, but the bedsteads in the back yard had increased in number, chromos were hanging to the clothes line, the clock was being dissected in the alley by a youth of great inventive genius, and carpets, stair-rods, looking-glasses, crockery, brackets and rolling-pins were so piled in together that my head swam.

THE BACK-YARD.

"I'm hurrying it up," said my wife in a joyful tone as she waved her hand at the painters, a scrub woman and a carpenter who had been added to the force.

I sat down on the teakettle and had supper served on the north end of a spring mattress, and when I broke a tooth on a glass agate concealed in a biscuit, and didn't say a word, Mrs. Quad threw her arms around me and said she might have married a man with a lightning temper.

I felt flattered and went in to encourage the white-

washers and painters.   They said if it didn't rain, or wasn't
too cold, or too hot, and they kept in good health, and
other jobs didn't distract their attention, they'd finish up
within a week or two, and one of them smashed a vase
and another punched out a three-dollar pane of glass by
way of emphasis.   I had blue paint on my coat tails, white
on my elbows and straw-color on my knees when I got
out, and a bad boy yelled:

"Here comes another of them variegated sunflowers!"

We didn't sleep much that night.   Somehow or other,
no matter how honest a man is, he can't rest very well on

"Now I Lay Me."

a straw bed on the floor, with stove covers gliding around
under his back, and teaspoons, potato-mashers and pint
basins feeling of his toes.   I dreamed that I was a panel
bedstead on castors, and I had a bet of five dollars with the
parlor stove that I could lick the front bedroom bureau in
just two minutes, but before the "mill" came off the
spice can rolled down into my ear and woke me up.

Next morning Small Pica, who was in bounding spirits,
essayed a lunch off of half a pound of putty which the

painters had left sticking to a bronze bust of Demosthenes, and Long Primer sat down on the butcher knife and got up howling; but my wife said that this was a world of trifling incident, and told me to go off feeling happy. Before I got down town I found the sugar spoon in my vest pocket and a towel hitched to my coat tail, but I went on. At noon there was an extra painter on hand, another scrubbing woman for the stairs, and an orphan boy about thirty-six years old had been hired to empty the straw beds on the front steps and tear out the pantry shelves. We haven't got through yet—in fact, this is chapter I. There are eleven more chapters to come, and to-night I am going

to sleep on the table, Small Pica in a six-gallon jar, and the rest of them on the window-sills, as the kitchen floor has just been painted and the paper-hangers don't want the other rooms mussed up until the paste dries and the paint sets.

DREAMING.

LATER—MIDNIGHT.—I fell asleep and dreamed that I was a silver-plated, six-bottle, revolving castor, and that the soup tureen called me a liar. I went to go for him, and awoke on the floor, with my elbow in a pan of flour and the meat broiler wildly clutching me by the throat. What the morrow will bring forth I don't know.

PATENT No. 249,826.

HIS patent is a device intended to reduce the mortality reports of the country by reducing the number of runaways. The "Fat Contributor" had a device by which a horse was lifted off his feet as he started to run, and Seymour, of the Milwaukee *News*, attempted to secure a patent on a device to draw a horse up into the buggy, but both were failures.

The device, as shown in the accompanying cut, is entirely of my own invention. As can be readily perceived, the horse is made to carry all the burden and the anxiety of

As an Ornament.

mind. The board can be painted a plain color, as blue or white or black, or striped off in red, white and blue. Some enterprising business men have already taken advantage of the occasion to adorn the board with an advertisement of their wares.

Any active and energetic carpenter can make one of these boards in three days, and each one will last a lifetime. After the horse is cured of his habit the board makes a handsome lawn ornament, when leaned gracefully against a peach tree. It can be sold for a black-board, used on the hay-mow for the boys to play euchre on, and there is no end to the uses to which it can be put.

A circular of instructions accompanies each board. The first engraving illustrates the manner of carrying the board. The side toward the carriage can be ornamented with engravings, patriotic mottoes, or otherwise rendered beautiful to the sight of the driver. The following cut illustrates the real value of the device. As soon as the horse passes from under control the ropes numbered *a* and *b* are pulled by the driver, and the board at once falls down in front of the flying animal, as shown. He has to bring right up, and his astonishment is only equaled by his admiration.

PUT TO USE.

The following are selected from the numerous testimonials received by the patentee:

"COURIER-JOURNAL OFFICE, June 18, 1875.

M. QUAD—*Dear Sir*—Just tried one of your patent Runaway Preventives. Never saw anything like it in Europe, Asia or Africa. If I owned the Erie canal I'd trade every rod of it for a Preventive, and then feel as if I owed you ten thousand dollars.

WATTERSON."

And gaze at this:

"BROOKLYN, N. Y., June 5, 1875.

M. QUAD—I snuffed at your Preventive when I first saw it, but the events of the last hour have convinced me that it is the biggest thing on earth. The life of my mother-in-law would have been sacrificed but for your genius.

Enclosed find $25, the paltry price of the Preventive, and ship me one with the motto 'Be kind to thy sister' on the back side.

Your grateful friend,

GEO. D. BAYARD."

And behold the following:

"MINING JOURNAL OFFICE,
MARQUETTE, July 1, '75.

HONORED SIR—Had a horse—habit running away—killed three wives—borrowed one of your Preventives—worked like a charm—stopped him like a bullet—felt so mean over it that he couldn't eat his rations for three days—bless you—send me sixteen by express at once.

Ever of thee,

SWINEFORD."

A voice from Ohio says:

"DAYTON, July 11, 1875.

DEAR SIR—I have been run away with 1,368 times, but the end has come. Your 'Preventive' is bound to produce a revolution in horse society. If you have not selected an agent for this State yet, please give me your best terms. It was only three weeks ago that twelve of my relatives, coming to spend the summer with me, were run away with and killed. Unless you have had twelve dear relatives mashed up at once you cannot imagine my feelings.

Very truly,

THE MAYOR."

Just one more—from Indiana:

"TIMES OFFICE, INDIANAPOLIS, July 4th.

Glorious day! whoop! Liberty and your 'Preventive' forever! Ninety-nine years ago to-day we whipped the British at Bunker Hill, and our glorious independence was forever secured! Have tried your patent; worked like a school ma'am sliding off a bench! Horse went right home and died of a broken heart. Send me two right away, and give me a State right if you can.

Hastily,   THE HEAD EDITOR."

PARTIALITY.

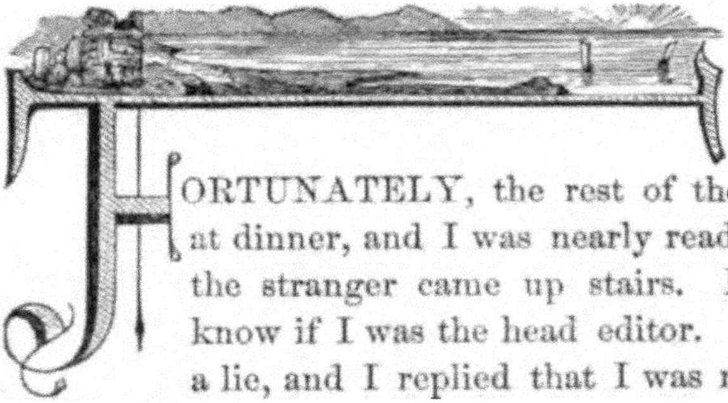

ORTUNATELY, the rest of the people were at dinner, and I was nearly ready to go, when the stranger came up stairs. He wanted to know if I was the head editor. I couldn't tell a lie, and I replied that I was not; explained to him that I was only a humble member of the editorial staff, having no particular routine work, but expected to write local, pick up marine, write obituary poetry, clip from agricultural papers and put heads on telegraph matter.

He was going away without further remark, but he turned as he reached the head of the stairs, came back, and in an indignant voice he said:

" I'm going to stop my paper !"

" No !"

" Yes, I am !"

" I wouldn't do it."

" I will, I will !" he exclaimed; " I've taken this paper for fifteen years, but I'm going to stop it now !"

" For why ?"

" For why ? Because you show partiality ! I don't claim to be better'n anybody else, but I'm just as good."

"Of course you are. Has this paper said that you weren't?"

"Not exactly—not in so many words."

"Well, now, we try to do right by everybody excepting politicians. If we have injured you in any manner state your case and we'll make it right. It isn't fair for you to come in here and stop your paper on the eve of a Presidential election, and just as we are recovering from a great panic."

"STOP 'ER!"

He hesitated for a moment, and then, opening a copy of the paper a week old, he pointed to a local article, and continued:

"You see that, don't you?"

"Yes, sir, I do; it is a local item how John Jones' boy got hooked by a cow."

"And there's fourteen lines of it!"

"One—three—seven—eleven—yes, sir, just fourteen."

"And you see this?" he inquired, as he laid the morning paper on the desk and pointed to a local item.

"Yes, sir; that is an item about how Thomas Thompson's boy got kicked by a mule."

"And there's only ten lines in it!"

"One—four—seven—ten—just ten."

"Well, sir, that was *my* boy, and I want to know if he isn't every bit and grain as good as Jones' boy! I want to know if Jones, who never took this paper in his life, is any better than I am! If that's the way you run your paper, I'm going to stop mine! My boy got hurt twice as hard as his boy, and yet you give his boy *four lines the most!*"

I tried to argue with him, but he was obstinate and ugly, and we lost his subscription.

THE OLD PIONEER.

YOU may not have encountered him, but every city or village over twenty-five years old has an "old pioneer." He is an aged man, walks with a cane, has a bent back and scant gray locks, and he is entitled to the unbounded respect of all citizens.

Many little privileges are accorded the "old pioneer." He can open the cheese-box in a grocery and help himself, hook apples, reach over for peanuts, have the head of the table when the firemen give a banquet, and if he crawls under the canvas on circus day none of the circus-men strike at him with a neck-yoke.

And if the "old pioneer" says that it's going to be a hard winter, a soft winter, a cool summer or a rainy fall, it would be like entering a den of lions for one to rise up and dispute him. He predicts political events, prophesies revolutions, remembers all about how the Free Masons killed John Morgan, and confidently expects a column notice in the local papers when he drops off.

I met one of the old fellows the other day on the cars. He assured me that riding on the cars was far more pleasant than making a journey on horseback, and he said that the country had improved some since he used to carry the mail between New York and Chicago. I was looking right at him, but he never blushed as he said that he used to make the round trip on horseback in five days. I was wondering how he could have done it when he went on to say that New York contained only eleven houses, and Chicago only four, at the time he acted as mail-carrier. I remarked that the mails must have been light in those early days, when he replied:

"Light! why bless you, my son, I never had less than fourteen full mail-bags, and sometimes as high as twenty!"

I expected to see him struck dead in his seat, but greatly to my surprise he continued to live right on, the same as if he had never told a lie.

"Ever have any fights with the Indians in those early days?" I finally inquired.

"Injun fights! Well, I should say I had a few—ha! ha! ha! I wish you could go home with me to old Che-mung county. I've got seven dry-goods boxes filled with Indian top-knots—seven boxes left, and I've been making horse-blankets and door-mats out of my pile for over forty years!"

"Is it possible!"

"Yes, it is. I don't say this to brag, but you asked me a plain question and I answered it. I suppose I killed 11,873 Indians during my early life, though I won't say that these are the exact figures. It might have been 11,874, or only 11,872—I am getting old and can't remember dates very well."

OLD PIONEER.

"Ever see George Washington?" I asked.

"See George Washington!" he echoed—"why, he boarded in my family over four years!"

"He did!"

"Yes, he did."

"When was that?"

"Let's see! Well, I don't remember just when it was, only I know it was quite a while ago. Yes, George boarded with me, and I've got a bill of forty dollars somewhere against him now. He was a little hard up for cash when he left us."

"Did you ever see William Penn?" I asked after awhile.

"Bill Penn! ha! ha! why, I wish I had as many dollars as the number of times Bill and I have slid down hill together! His father lived in part of our house for eight years, and Bill and I were like brothers. I could lick him, and he knew it, but we never even had a cross word between us. Poor Bill! When I read about his being blown up on a steamboat I said to myself that I'd rather have lost a brother."

I waited a good while and then inquired:

"Were you in the Revolutionary war?"

"The Revolutionary war! why, you must take me for a boy!" he replied. "Why, I was the first man to jine!

THE PATRIOT ARMY.

There was a week when the Patriots didn't have any army but me, and there was so much fighting and marching that I almost got discouraged."

"Then you must have met General Lafayette?"

"General Lafayette! Why, on the morning of the battle of Bunker Hill, Washington, Lafayette, Bill Penn and myself were playing a four-handed game of euchre in an old barn just outside of Boston. Lafayette was killed just as he was dealing the cards!"

"I thought he went back to France and died."

"No, sir."

"But history says so."

"I don't care a plum for history, young man! Didn't his blood scatter all over me, and weren't his last words addressed to me! I guess I know as much as any history."

"What were his last words?"

"Last words? Well, sir, he didn't have time to say much. A cannon ball struck him in the body, and all he said was 'Don't give up the ship!' Poor Laif! He was a little conceited, but when he borrowed a dollar of you it was certain to come back."

"You never saw Christopher Columbus, did you?" I finally asked, determined to wind him up.

He was staggered for a moment, but then recovered and answered:

"Christopher Co-lum-bus! Well, no, I never did. My brother used to talk a good deal about Chris, but I never happened to see him. They say he didn't amount to much, after all—used to get tight on election day, kept a fighting-dog and a race-horse, and was always blowing around what he could do. I was always careful of my character, and they can't say of me that I ever associated with low folks."

z

GETTING THE HAIR CUT.

LL of a sudden he said I had better have my hair cut, at the same time running his hand up and down my neck, over my ears and around the crown of my head. I said I guessed I wouldn't; I would come in next day; I was in a hurry.

"Pretty long," he continued, feeling of my head again.

I said I always wore my hair long, and he shut up for a minute or two while he lathered my face and strapped his razor. Then he drew a deep sigh and whispered:

"Guess you'd better have it cut."

I replied that I never had my hair cut—always wore it hanging down to my boots, but he looked so sad and disappointed that I felt ashamed of myself. He might be a man with a large family depending on him, and perhaps his very bread depending on my having my hair cut. Perhaps he had his house and lot mortgaged, and the last payment was due that day, and if I didn't get my hair cut his family would be turned out of doors. After a little time I meekly remarked that he might cut away.

The smile which covered his face was reward enough for a poor man like me. He drew an apron around me, dug his fingers down behind my collar, gave my head seven or eight preparatory knocks, and then commenced—snip! snip! comb! brush! snip!·

He ordered me to sit up a little straighter. Then he ordered me to hold my head to the left. Then he ran an old brass-pointed comb through my hair, plowing furrows in my scalp, and then he remarked that I had a good deal of dandruff in my hair.

"It's a base lie!" I exclaimed, for I knew he was getting around to ask about a shampoo.

He made no reply—that is, no direct reply—but as an indirect reply he snipped off a piece of my ear. He said he didn't mean to do it; and in another indirect way he complimented me with having more ears than hair.

He finally neared the end—not the end of the hair, but the end of his job. He cuffed my head to the right, ran his hand down my neck and his old shears over my ear, as the last finishing strokes, and then he paused. I knew what was coming. He ran his hand over my head, jumped back and shouted:

"Grashus!"

He thought I would be startled, but I knew his tricks. I sat perfectly still, and he said to himself:

"Dandruff—guess there is!"

I wasn't going to let him shampoo me, but there was something so sad and melancholy in his voice as he whispered that word "dandruff," that I felt my heart throb with pity.

I got down and told him to go ahead with his soapsuds, and he went. He bent me over the sink, dashed on water, rubbed on soap, twisted my hair up and down, filled my eyes and ears, enveloped my head in a crash towel, and then said:

"You look a thousand dollars better."

He knew my mouth was full of suds and my eyes full of soap bubbles, so that I couldn't reply, and he went on:

"There! I'll warrant you feel a million dollars better."

He mopped me off, drew that old brass comb over my tender scalp, rapped me with the brush, and softly whispered:

"You look like a new man—forty-five cents, if you please."

THE FAT MAN IN CHICAGO.

ERRILY whistling, he came into the ladies' sitting-room of the Chicago depot, as I waited there one night. He was a fat man, pretty well along in years, and one could see that he was good-hearted. He placed his traveling-bag on a bench, took a chain and padlock from his pocket, and, as he secured the bag to the seat, he smiled blandly and said:

"I don't know anything about traveling—oh, no! I have to sit right down and hang on to my baggage, to keep some one from stealing it, don't I?"

And he walked up and down the room, arms folded across his breast, and the self-satisfied look on his fat face was worth fifty thousand dollars in cash. When we had admired him he sat down beside an old lady who was en route for Cleveland, and inquired:

"Did you bring along any peppermint essence?"

She looked up at him with a smile in her eyes, and he continued:

"Old women are more affected by change of water than any one else, and are also apt to have colic while traveling. You should never have left home without a phial of peppermint essence."

405

She still refused to reply, and after a time he remarked:

"Well, I hope you'll behave yourself and keep out of bad company."

She grabbed up her parcels and crossed the room in a

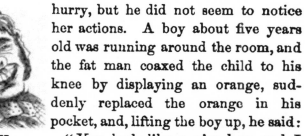

hurry, but he did not seem to notice her actions. A boy about five years old was running around the room, and the fat man coaxed the child to his knee by displaying an orange, suddenly replaced the orange in his pocket, and, lifting the boy up, he said:

No Essence.

"You look like a nice boy, and I hope you'll get through all right. Look out for pickpockets, my son—I've seen a dozen of the rascals around here since I got off the Quincy train."

The boy sought to release himself, and, as he dropped to the floor, the fat man continued:

"You are not as old as I am, and I want to give you a bit of advice: Never bet on another man's game; you're sure to lose if you do."

The boy ran back to his mother, and the fat man walked up to the ticket window and asked:

"What time does the train leave for Detroit?"

"Nine o'clock."

"That clock is right, isn't it?"

"Yes, sir."

"You are sure of it?"

"Yes, sir."

"And at nine o'clock by this clock the train starts?"

"Yes, sir."

"The Detroit train?"

"Yes, sir."

"Goes right through to Detroit?"

"Yes, sir."

"No change of cars?"

"No, sir."

"Some folks are always behind time, or take the wrong train, or worry themselves into a sweat," remarked the fat man, as he came over to me, "but I never have any trouble, and I'd like to see the ticket agent who dare sass me!"

"You are an old traveler, I see," I replied.

"Old traveler?—no, I never was away from home before—oh, no!"

And he pulled open his coat, showed me that his breast-pocket was tightly pinned up with a darning-needle, and then reached down behind his collar and fished up his rail-road ticket.

"I'm a country chicken!" he continued, smiling blandly, "and I ought to have a blind man along to take care of me!"

Catching sight of a man whose black clothes and white necktie proclaimed him a minister, the fat man crossed over and slapped him on the back, and said:

"Hello! my friend—going east?"

"I am!" exclaimed the startled stranger.

"Minister of the Gospel, I suppose?" queried the fat man.

"Yes."

"Well, that's a good trade, and I hope you'll do well, though just now money is tight and wages are low. I've probably traveled ten miles to your one, and my advice to you is not to have anything to do with bunko men. You may think yourself pretty sharp, but they'll beat you every time. Faro is a pretty square game, and poker has charms, but let 'em all alone!"

The minister had not recovered from his astonishment when the fat man slid over and sat down beside a young lady, whose satchels and bundles were piled up in front of her like a line of defense.

"All alone, I suppose?" he queried, as he pushed the bundles around with his foot.

" Y—yes," she gasped.

" I knew it the moment I set eyes on you; and, if I were a mind to, I could pick your pocket, steal your baggage, abduct you and carry you off to some unknown island in the ocean; but I'm not that kind of a man—no, sir!"

ALL ALONE.

She shrank away, a frightened look in her eyes, and he continued:

" You need have no fear of me. I came over here to drop you a word or so of advice. There's lots of three-card-monte men traveling on these roads, and you want to look out for 'em. It's amazing how they sling those cards around, and if you bet you are sure to lose. If I were you I wouldn't have anything to do with 'em—just cut 'em cold!"

He walked up and down again until he caught sight of a portly woman, and he dropped down beside her and remarked:

" Madam, I'm a stranger to you, but I want to give you a friendly word of warning. You are fat, madam—very fat, and, if you take my advice, you'll never jump off the cars while they are running at full speed!"

She was going to pour out her wrath on him, but he got away and went out doors, and I did not see him again until just as the passengers were boarding the train. Then

I heard his voice going in the midst of a crowd, and elbowed my way in to see him pointing to a great knife-

A WARNING.

wound over his breast-pocket, through which his wallet had been drawn. He likewise held up to view the traveling-bag which he had cutely chained to the seat. Some one had cut a hole in it and removed the contents.

As the whistle blew he lowered the satchel, turned around and humbly said:

"Gentlemen, stand clear and let that man with the stoga boots come forward and 'lift' this old traveler—lift him right on to the platform!"

TRUE LOVE.

I SAW them—they were going down from Saginaw on the boat, and as a swell rocked the old steamer the young lady screamed out and clawed around until she seized the young man's arm.

"Piller yer head right here, Susan!" he exclaimed, patting his heart with one hand and slipping the other around her waist. "When a feller loves a girl as I love you, he could take her on his back and swim eighteen miles in a bee-line, and then go home and hoe corn till sundown! Piller yer head right here, my love, and if she rains and hails and thunders blue blazes, don't you even squeal one squeal!"

"Are we safe?" she tremblingly inquired.

"Safe as a cow tied to a brick wall eighteen feet thick, my love! Just lean right over here, shet your pearly eyes, and feel as contented as if you sot on the top rail of the pastur' fence waitin' for a tin peddler to arrove in sight!"

She "pillered," and everybody remarked that he looked like a hero.

YE OLD SCHOOLMASTER.

'M sorry, now, that we boys used to vex and worry him, for he's been in his grave these many years, and perhaps our doings hastened his end.

I can remember his bald head, gray side-whiskers, wrinkled face and cat-like gait. I used to wish that I was "as big a man" as schoolmaster Ray, but now I can look back and see how dreary his life must have been, mixed up with obstinate scholars, log school-houses, one-horse geographies, primary arithmetics, and $11 per month.

One Way.

Many and many a time I looked over the top of my desk, doubled my fists, and vowed that I would maul him to a jelly the very moment I reached man's estate, and he secured satisfaction in advance by thinking up and administering some new punishment.

Schoolmaster Ray argued that pupils couldn't acquire an education without having a taste of the sprout now and then, and this theory of his kept all the boys' backs and the girls' ears sore. He didn't always whip, as that was a poor locality for sprouts, and some of us would burn his ferule as often as he made one. He had other ways of administering punishment, and they were original ways.

His favorite method, during the warm weather, was to throw open the stove door and oblige a boy to enter the yawning cavity, sometimes to be shut up there for hours. I've sat crooked up in that old stove and registered a bloody oath that I would borrow a shot gun and commit murder that evening, but when evening came I made up my mind to try old Ray once more—just once. When a pupil was too long to get into the stove his legs had to protrude over the hearth, and the old man would now and then bring his switch down on a calf in order to start a new current of thought.

Another plan of his was to sit a scholar on the floor and

turn the empty water pail over his head. If the lad didn't beg for mercy directly, all the spare books in school were piled on top of the pail.

I can't look back now and remember that we were such bad scholars. We used to whisper, take sly bites of dinner, skip paper-wads around and cut holes in the seats, but I do not remember that any of the boys

ANOTHER WAY.

were malicious. Schoolmaster Ray held that boys and girls should be men and women, and that it was a crime for a pupil to be absent-minded. One day he explained to the geography class what a peninsula was, told us the name of the longest river, highest mountain, etc., and also named over the presidents. Next day he suddenly asked Alf. Tyler:

"Which is the highest mountain in the world?"

"The gulf of Amazon!" promptly replied Alf.

"It is, eh?" sneered the old man as he slid around on his heel.

"Which is the longest river?

"Andrew Jackson!" called out Alf.

Tyler will always remember what followed. The old man placed two chairs, stretched Alf. across them, as shown in the cut, and piled weights on him until he broke the boy nearly in two.

THE HIGHEST MOUNTAIN.

The "big scholars" held a convention on the road home and resolved to waylay the schoolmaster and murder him in cold blood, but the trouble was to find the one who would do the killing.

I've got scars on me yet which old Ray inflicted because I couldn't tell him the difference between a bay and an isthmus, and if he were living I sometimes think I would hunt him out and spike him to a wall and draw hot curry-combs across him.

UGLY GREG.

HE best of prisons are gloomy, un-
lovely places, and the sunshine
which streams over the walls and
filters through the bars seems cold
and cheerless. The prisoners are
discouraged, and some of them desperate, feeling as if every man's
hand was against them, and the
keepers must be watchful, distant
and determined. Day comes, day goes, and sometimes
the rugged walls, paved floors and iron bars so change the
nature of a prisoner that his mind loses all good thoughts.
It used to be thus in all prisons, but there are exceptions
now. At the Detroit House of Correction, a year or so
ago, the high whitewashed walls of the corridors were
furnished with brackets and flower pots to relieve the
monotony and take away some of the gloom. One would
scarcely think that the rough looking, wicked men sent
there for robbery, burglary, arson and graver crimes, would
have cared for the change, yet they gladly welcomed it.
A rose, or geranium, or tulip, or pink, seemed to bring
liberty and sunshine a little nearer, and to drive the evil
out of their hearts, and it was a strange sight to see hardened criminals watering and nourishing the tender plants
and watching their daily growth.

Two or three months before the brackets were hung up a prisoner came from one of the Territories—an old, sullen-looking, bad tempered man, convicted of robbing the mails. They called him "Greg," as short for Gregory, and it wasn't long before they made it "Ugly Greg." He was ugly. He refused to work, cared nothing for rules and regulations, and twenty-eight days of his first month were spent in the "solitary" for bad behavior. He was expostulated with, threatened and punished, but he had a will as hard as iron. He hadn't a friend in the prison, and the knowledge of it seemed to make him more ugly and desperate. When the brackets were hung up there was one to spare, and it was placed near the door of Ugly Greg's cell until another spot could be found. No one had any hope that the old man's heart could be softened, and some said he would dash the flower pot to the floor.

When he came in from the shops his face expressed surprise at sight of the little green rose bush so close to the door of his cell. He scented it, carefully placed it back, and it was noticed that the hard lines melted out of his face for a time. No one said anything to him, but the next morning before he went to work he carefully watered the rose, and his eyes lost something of their sullen look. Would you believe that the little rose bush proved more powerful than all the arguments and threats of the keepers? It did, strangely enough. As the days went by the old man lost his obstinacy and his gloominess, and he obeyed orders as well and cheerfully as the best man in prison. His face took on a new look, his whole bearing changed, and the keepers looked at him and wondered if he could be the man Greg of four or five months before. He watched the rose as a mother would watch a child, and it came to be understood that it was his. While some of the other flowers died from want of care, the rose tree grew and thrived and made the old man proud. He carried it into his cell at night and replaced it in the morning, and sometimes he would talk to it as if it were a human being. Its presence opened his lonesome heart and planted good seed there, and from the day the bracket was hung up no keeper had the least trouble with Ugly Greg.

A few weeks ago he was taken sick, and when he went to the hospital the rose tree went with him, and was placed where the warm sun could give it the nourishment it needed. After a day or two it was hoped that the old man would get better, but he kept sinking and growing feebler. So long as his eyes were open he would watch the rose, and when he slept he seemed to dream of it. One day when the nurse found an opening bud he rejoiced as heartily as if his pardon papers had arrived. The bud was larger next day, and the rose could be seen bursting through. The flower pot was placed on the bed, near the old man's face, that he might watch the bud blossom into a rose, and he was so quiet that the nurse did not approach him again for hours. The warm spring sun glided in through the bars and kissed the opening bud, and then fell off in showers over the old man's pale face, erasing every line of guilt and ugliness which had ever been raised.

At noon the nurse saw that the rose had blossomed, and she went over and whispered in the old man's ear:

"Greg—Greg—the rose has blossomed—wake up."

He did not move. She felt his cheek, and it was cold. Ugly Greg was dead!

One hand rested under his gray locks, while the other clasped the flower pot, and the new-born rose bent down until it almost touched his cold face. His life had gone out just when his weeks of weary watching for a blossom were to be repaid; but the rose tree's mission was accomplished.

AA

OUR BOYS.

VEN to this day I sometimes fear to indulge in a hearty laugh, or to rip out my sentiments of surprise or disappointment, because my mother was continually pounding the idea into me that I was born for a preacher. I suppose that I would in due time have become a preacher, and had a scandal and a lawsuit, but for certain domestic accidents which changed the tenor of life all around.

But I was no exception. There was Jackson; he was continually pegging at his boy Tom, telling the lad that he was born for a judge, and there were years and years in which Tom did not dare to slide down a cellar door for fear that it would interfere with his becoming a judge. If he rolled under the currant bushes, climbed a tree or sat in the dust, his mother was on hand to call out:

"My sakes! Thomas Jackson, but you'll never be a judge if you act that way!"

They mauled that boy to make him look dignified, hurled such words as "retainer," "arraign," "*nolle prosequi*" and "champerty" at him, and his young days were made as dreary as life on a canal boat in January. At last they took him to a lawyer's office, found that he didn't know anything, and abused the Lord for not giving him the genius of a Patrick Henry. Thomas was driving a mule team on the plains when I met him last, and was yelling:

"Ho! there, Circuit Court, git up and hump yerself! Haw around there, Chancery—gee up, Exceptions—git around *thar*, old Decision in Admiralty!"

And the widow Logan commenced at her boy John as soon as he could creep. Some traveling swindler felt of his head, told the mother that the boy would be President of the United States, and she brought him up to believe it. He couldn't go out and tear his pants like other boys; was never allowed to fall into the river and be half drowned; had to have his hair combed and his feet washed, and the rest of us boys might have offered him $50 and offered in vain to get him to keel over on the hay-mow. He never

got to be President of the United States. The nearest he came to it was being elected foreman of a hose company, and he didn't hold that place over four weeks, as he was too fat to run. His mother cried when Filmore was nominated, saying that her son John had been overlooked from sheer jealousy, and I believe she grieved herself to death. John now does duty in a wholesale grocery

Never Keeled Over. house as porter, and his "cabinet" consists of the engineer and the man who 'tends the elevator. There are no foreign complications to vex his mind, no one threatens to assassinate him, and he can wear one shirt six weeks if he wants to.

And Mr. Wilkins was always telling his boy that he must save his pennies if he would be rich, and making him figure simple and compound interest, and warning him to pay out twelve cents for a shilling when he paid a debt, and to demand thirteen cents when it was paid him. That boy went through life without knowing the taste of peanuts, ginger beer, liquorice-root, lemonade, candy or figs. Once he was overcome by the sight of some spruce gum, and invested a cent, but the licking he received when he reached home made him forever sick of the sight of gum. He was afraid of wearing out his shoes, never sat down in the road, dared not sling his hat around, and we used to pity him.

"Save! save! save!" was the father's cry, and the boy grew up miserly mean, and was choked to death while trying to get a little more meat off a fish-bone.

I've got a boy or two around my house, and I say to them:

"Come, be doing something! Roll over in the road, wear out your shoes, tear your clothes, hook apples and have a good time, for by and by you've got to find out that life is a battle of kicks and cuffs, and you'll want pleasant memories to strengthen you."

PROFESSOR OF BOTANY.

WHEN we started out on the Powder River expedition, under Colonel Kidd, a long-haired, long-geared old chap, who had been hanging around Laramie for some time, got leave to go along.

He was a Professor of Botany, and had once been connected with some eastern college. He was, I believe, out west on his own account just then, and he was far more enthusiastic in his search for specimens than we were to hunt Indians, having had our fill of war down on the Potomac.

I forget the Professor's real name, but the boys called him "Old Bot." We saw that there was a heap of fun in him, and we were glad to have him along. He dressed in solemn black, wore a white cravat, spoke slowly and with great dignity, and it was " 'nuff to kill a feller" to see him cantering along with the column. He couldn't ride; it was simply hanging on. His horse was tall, shadowy, and as much of a curiosity as his master. His gallop was a sort of camel-motion, and when under full " go " the Professor held to the pommel of his saddle and pounded from side to side and up and down.

The old man did not know what fear was. The Indians hovered around us like bees over a sunflower, but, entirely

unarmed, he would ride almost upon them as his search
for specimens led him away from the column. One day
when one of the red-skins put a bullet through Old Bot's
hat, the Colonel said to him:

"These devils will get hold of you some day, unless you
are more careful."

"Is it possible that they want to get hold of *me?*"
inquired the Professor after deep thought. "What can be
their primary object?"

Half a dozen of us were detailed to scout ahead and kill
meat for the party, and one day the Professor brought
about a calamity. A score of red-skins had hovered
around us all the forenoon, the scouts being about two
miles in advance of the main party. At noon, as we halted
to rest our horses and bite a few hard-tack, Old Bot
mounted his horse and rode away after specimens, though

SPECIMENS.

warned again and again. He wasn't
half a mile away when a dozen reds
popped out of a grove of cottonwood
and gobbled him, retreating to the
grove again. As one man, we
charged the grove, believing that
the Indians numbered only twelve
or fourteen, and feeling ourselves able to whip the pile.

As we drew near they gave us a volley which emptied
three saddles, and the other three of us were prisoners
before the fight had hardly commenced. As I was being
tied I saw the Professor lying on the grass before me, arms
fastened behind his back. His face wore its usual profound
look, and he did not seem in the least frightened or
interested.

"I hope you're satisfied now!" I yelled at him. "We
shall all be burned at the stake, and all through your con-
founded ignorance and pig-headed obstinacy!"

"Is—that—you, cor-pu-rel?" he drawled, hardly looking up. "What special object have these gentlemen in view at this time!"

The Indians hurried us off as fast as they could, fearing a rescue. We were tied to our saddles, and when they were binding the Professor he said:

"I assure you, gentlemen, that this precaution on your part is entirely thrown away, as there is not the least danger of my falling off my horse!"

Just as we were ready to leave the grove his eye fell upon a new specimen, and pointing to it, Old Bot raised his voice and inquired:

"Will any of you people have the kindness to pluck that flower for me?"

One of the savages brandished his tomahawk in a threatening manner, and the Professor sank back in his saddle and sighed:

"There seems to be a total lack of courtesy out here in this country!"

It happened that I rode almost beside him as we left the grove, and when I had a chance I inquired:

"Well, Professor, this is a bad affair!"

He waited two or three minutes and then replied:

"I cannot speak advisedly at this time, but I assure you that I will take the matter into consideration and give you my opinion, perhaps this evening!"

I was provoked, and I said:

"You are a blamed old idiot, and if I'm roasted I hope it won't occur until after *you* catch it!"

"I—would—not—speak—rashly!" he drawled, after a long pause, and he returned to his work of looking over the prairie after new flowers.

After a ride of twenty miles we halted among the hills for the night. The Indians discovered that they had a

queer character in Old Bot, and they commenced to draw
him out as soon as we were unbound. He wore a plug
hat, sadly used by rain and sun, and one of them knocked
it "sky-high" with the handle of his tomahawk. The
Professor looked at him a long time, and then said:

"I have come among you in the interests of science, and
I sincerely hope that you will seek to restrain all further
desire to embarrass and annoy me!"

HAVING FUN.

The red-skins roared with laughter, and one of them
gave Old Bot a four-horse kick from behind. The old man
turned around, a look of amazement on his face, and
inquired:

"Will you explain the motive which actuated you in
that performance?"

Another Indian kicked him from the other side, and
turning to me Old Bot asked:

"Cor-pu-rel, is not this an unusual proceeding, consid-
ering all the circumstances?"

We had to laugh with the Indians, but as soon as they let him alone the old man began plucking flowers and naming them.

We were tied again as the savages made ready for sleep, and while securing us one of the Indians kicked the sacred plug hat yards high into the air.

"I cannot commend the spirit which induces such familiarity with total strangers!" drawled the Professor, reaching out for the hat.

Stretched out on the grass, his long hair was a temptation not to be resisted, and one of the Indians placed his foot on it.

"My dear sir," said Old Bot, "is it possible that you are not aware that I am a Professor of Botany—a regular graduate!"

We lay side by side, and in whispers I asked him:

"Professor, what will our fate be, do you think?"

"I have not yet given the subject the careful consideration which it deserves!" was his reply.

Soon after midnight we were rescued by a party of hunters, but the Professor took it as a matter of course, remarking:

"I had almost begun to fear that my researches in the interest of science were to be interrupted!"

THEIR SPELLING BEE.

ONE evening old Mr. and Mrs. Coffin sat in their cozy back parlor, he reading his paper and she knitting, while the family cat, stretched out under the stove, sighed and felt sorry for cats not so well fixed. It was a happy, contented household, and there was love in his heart as Mr. Coffin put down the newspaper and remarked:

"I see that the whole country is becoming excited about spelling schools."

"Well, it's good to know how to spell," replied the wife. "I didn't have the chance some girls had, but I pride myself that I can spell almost any word that comes along."

"I'll see about that," he laughed; "come, now, spell buggy."

"Humph! that's easy—b-u-g-g-y, buggy," she replied.

"Missed the first time—ha! ha!" he roared, slapping his leg.

"Not much—that was right."

"It was, eh? I'd like to see anybody get two g's in buggy, I would."

"But it is spelled with two g's, and any schoolboy will tell you so," she persisted.

"Well, I know a durn sight better than that!" he exclaimed, striking the table with his fist.

"I don't care what you know!" she squeaked; "I know there are two g's in buggy."

"Do you mean to tell me that I have forgotten how to spell?" he asked.

"It looks that way."

"It does, eh? Well, I want you and all your relations to understand that I know more about spelling than the whole caboodle of you strung on a wire!"

"And I want you to understand, Jonathan Coffin, that you are an ignorant old blockhead when you don't put two g's in the word buggy—yes, you are!"

"Don't you talk that way to me!" he warned.

"And don't shake your fist at me!" she replied.

"Who's shaking his fist?"

"You were!"

"That's a lie—an infernal lie!"

"Don't call me a liar, you old bazaar! I've put up with your meanness for forty years past; but don't call me a liar, and don't lay a hand on me!"

"Do you want a divorce?" he shouted, springing up; "you can go now, this minute!"

"Don't spit in my face—don't you dare do it, or I'll make a dead man of you!" she warned.

"I haven't spit in your old freckled visage yet, but I may if you provoke me further!"

NOT FRECKLED.

"Who's got a freckled face, you dilapidated old turkey-buzzard?"

That was a little too much. He made a motion as if he would strike, and she seized him by the necktie. Then he reached out and grabbed her right ear and tried to lift her off her feet, but she twisted up on the necktie till his tongue ran out.

"Let go of me, you old fiend!" she screamed.

"Git down on yer knees and beg my pardon, you old wildcat!" he replied.

They surged and swayed and struggled, and the peaceful cat was struck by the overturning table and had her back broken, while the clock fell down and the pictures danced around. The woman finally shut her husband's air off and flopped him, and as she bumped his head up and down on the floor and scattered his gray hairs, she shouted:

"You want to get up another spelling school with me, don't you?"

He was seen limping across the yard next day, with a stocking pinned around his throat, and she had court-plaster on her nose and one finger tied up. He wore the look of a martyr, while she had the bearing

One "g" in It.   of a victor, and from this time out "buggy" will be spelled with two g's in that house.

BARNABY'S BOY AND OLD JACK.

OU can never tell what a boy of ten or twelve is going to like or dislike, and you need not attempt to find a theory for any of his actions.

One day when a beggar knocked at Barnaby's door to ask for old clothes Barnaby's boy hit him in the ear with a potato and ran off in high glee. The very next day, when another beggar opened the gate the boy ran in and stole his father's Sunday boots and hurried the old alms-asker off with them before Mr. Barnaby could get to the door.

A week after that the Barnaby boy ran off with a hand-organ belonging to a crippled woman, and he and his companions turned the crank with such vigor that "Mollie Darling" and "I'm Sleepy Now" were worn down to soughs and sighs before the organ was restored. You wouldn't think the boy had any tenderness in his heart or any respect for the sorrows and misfortunes of old age and poverty. His father thrashed him for stealing fruit and being out nights, and his mother cuffed his ears for his coolness in appropriating the last piece of pie and for carrying pickled peaches in his pockets. And yet that boy developed a trait which more than made amends for all his young misdeeds.

One day as he was preparing to lasso a neighbor's dog, along came an old man, having a wooden leg, a blind eye,

429

and such ragged garments that it was a wonder how he kept the patches and tatters from falling off. The old man was weak and ill, and by and by he grasped the fence and sank down, unable to proceed another yard. Ordinarily, the Barnaby boy would have thrown fire crackers at the old man, or put on the penstock hose and "washed him out," but just then he was eccentric. Bending over the old man he asked:

"Uncle, are you sick?"

"I'm dreadfully taken, my lad," replied the old veteran, "and I fear I'm going to die!"

The Barnaby boy's heart opened like a book, and he knelt down and chafed the old man's hands, and smoothed the scant gray locks back from the damp and wrinkled brow.

"Haven't you any home?" he asked, tears in his eyes.

"No home—no money—not a friend on earth!" answered the old man.

"And you are sick?"

"I'm going to die, my lad! I'm old and broken down, and all the doctors in the State couldn't keep me alive a week!"

The boy could call the police, and the old man would be taken to the hospital or sent to the County House. He started around the corner, but turning back he asked:

"Can you walk down the alley? May I take care of you?"

Leaning on the boy's arm, and so blind that he could not see the walls and shade trees, the old man managed to drag himself down the alley to Barnaby's barn. There was no horse there, and the boy made a bed of hay and carefully laid the old man down. Then he went to the house after food and drink, and his guardianship of the dying man had commenced.

."God bless you, boy! That's the first mouthful of food I've tasted in two days!" said the old man as he ate his bread.

Any boy but the Barnaby boy would have straightway informed his parents, or at least the boys of the neighborhood, that a sick man was in the barn, but he was the Barnaby boy and he dropped no hint. The food and drink rallied the old man a little, but he felt that his end was at hand.

"I fought Mexicans," he said as the Barnaby boy wet his parched his lips, "and I fought Injuns, and this is my reward. Old, crippled, ready to die, I'm passing away as if I was a wolf instead of a man!"

The boy had faith that medicine would prolong life, and he went to the house and took an inventory of the family supply. A bottle of castor oil, another of liniment, and a box of pills were all that he could get hold of, and he hastened back to the old man. Dying as he was, old Jack smiled as the boy held up the things.

"May the Lord care for you always, my child!" he said, "but my hours are numbered. All you can do is to sit by me and give me a bit of drink now and then!"

When night came the Barnaby boy had to leave the old man and go in and go to bed, but the house was hardly still before he dropped from the window and returned to watch beside his patient through the long hours of night, darkness around him, death beside him. At midnight, when the voice of the solemn-sounding bells struck off the hour, old Jack roused, clasped the boy's hand with tighter grip, and whispered:

"I've been praying God to forgive me, and perhaps I'll go to Heaven! If I do, I'll tell the angels the first thing when I get there how kind you have been to me!"

The old man died hard. Day came, and passed, and the

shadows of evening gathered again. The boy hardly left him. No one came near the barn, and no one suspected his secret.

"My hour has come!" said old Jack as the sun went down. "I've nothing to leave you as a reward, but the angel will make a long mark for you in the recording book for this!"

The shadows gathered faster and closer, and by and by the boy had to bend over the white face to see it at all. His tears fell on the wrinkled cheek, and the old man reached out his hand, laid it on the boy's head, and whispered:

"Those are the first tears shed over me since I was a child and had a mother! I'm going now—I'm blind— God bless—— !"

The Barnaby boy laid the arms down beside the lifeless body, and went quietly to the house. Standing in the door he said:

"Old Jack is dead in the barn!"

And then he sat down, his courage gone at last, and he was the Barnaby boy no longer.

HIS ONLY ROMANCE.

A FEW GREAT MEN.

T is sad to reflect that Henry Clay is dead. He's missed a good many chances during the last few years of selling his vote to some steamship or mining company, and then swearing by the horn spoon that he couldn't remember how he came by that paltry check of $20,000.

Henry Clay was a great speaker, but when it came down to digging a woodchuck out of its hole he

CLAY IS DEAD

was a glaring failure. He never raffled for turkeys, attended spelling schools or husking bees, and he wouldn't believe any of the stories about Captain Kidd's buried treasure. The only romantic episode in his life was eating dinner on a saw-log with the handsomest girl in school. The girl is long since dead, and the saw-log is but a lonesome landmark of time's changes.

I sometimes wonder what he had to live for, and how he
lived as long as he did.

Oh, Henry Clay,
You have passed away—
We shall ever remember
The tenth of December.

Daniel Webster was a king bee in his time.   He could
get up at a moment's notice and speak on any topic, from
free trade to the best cure for poll-evil.   He understood

FIRST LEGAL PRINCIPLES.

all sorts of law, and even at that early day he held that it
was a lawyer's duty to get hold of every dollar which his
client could raise.   It was stated in a newspaper paragraph
last spring that Daniel once gave a boot-black a $1,000 bill
by mistake for a three-cent silver piece.   The boy indignantly denies the report.   He says that Daniel passed a
wildcat $2 bill on him, which looks entirely reasonable

and natural. Mr. Webster married, but she was not the woman of his choice. He had a fat girl selected for his life partner, but four weeks before he was to lead her to the altar she was carried to her grave by the bilious colic, caused by sitting on the horse-block and eating a rutabaga. His marriage was not a happy one, as his wife refused to build the fires, and whenever he wanted fried onions for dinner she was sure to have noodle-soup. Daniel Webster was the man who invented the method of telling a horse's age by looking into his mouth, and he discovered that a cow had a wrinkle on her horn for every year of her age.

EARLY TACTICS.

General Scott was a remarkable man. No cat could live in the neighborhood after he got so that he could aim a shot-gun. He early displayed those great military tactics which afterwards made him a famous general. For instance, when he was only nine years old he could skirmish down on an orchard as well as a grown man, and he could change his base like a streak of lightning when his father made for the boot-jack. During his young manhood he wrote several pieces of poetry, only one of which can I now recall to mind, viz:

"Mary had a little lamb,
Its fleece was white as snow,
And everywhere that Mary went
The lamb was sure to go."

His father intended to have him learn the trade of bologna sausage maker, but the boy took such an interest in military affairs that he piled up the sausages in the shape of a fort, bombarded them with beef bones, and the butcher raised the black flag on him. Scott was a very peculiar man. He would never sleep three in a bed, and he wouldn't hook an umbrella under any circumstances. The General never married. He once had all due preparations made, but being informed that his intended loved lager he backed out, gave her a mule and a one-horse wagon as compensation for her broken heart, and made a solemn vow never to love again. The only pet he ever had was a one-eyed yellow dog, and he would cashier a colonel as quick as dust for even winking at the brute. I had forgotten to say that General Scott was dead. I have subscribed for about one hundred and fifty different monuments for him, and he hasn't got one yet.

DANIEL BOONE'S BIRTH-PLACE.

Daniel Boone discovered Kentucky. He discovered Kentucky about the same time the Kentucky Indians discovered him. He was a man of great genius. He could load a shot gun faster than any other living man, and he didn't have to look twice to tell a coon track from a cat track. He was a very early riser. He sometimes got up at two o'clock in the morning and ran a mile or two through the woods, just for exercise—and to keep the Indians from being too familiar with him. Daniel's principal occupation was cutting his name on the beech trees of Ohio and Kentucky, and he prided himself on the fact that he could spell his name as correctly as any other man in America.

OUR FRENCH ENGRAVER.

ONE day when this book was in its childhood a stranger came to me and looked a sad look out of his eyes, and his nose, and his mouth—in truth, he was a sad-looking man. He spoke with a French accent, and the accent went to my heart when he said that he was in the middle of strangers, out of money, and hadn't tasted raisin cake for over four weeks.

There were tears in his eyes as he went on to say that he had heard of the proposed book, and while he couldn't think of begging for money, he would do some grand engraving for us at about half what Dore would ask.

When I see a man feeling sad it makes me feel sad with him, and it was arranged that the French designer should design and engrave a full-page cut, and I was to write a "Heaven piece" to match it. He went away and worked and toiled and had alternate fits of enthusiasm and despondency, and the engraving is before you. We accepted and paid for it because we felt a sympathy for the friendless man, and because he assured us that it was engraved after the latest French ideas in art. As for the "Heaven piece," I wrote the article found on page No. 225, entitled "In the Chimney Corner." Observe the cut and notice how the old man in the chair holds his hand. The idea occurred to me that he had a felon on it, and though the

438

Frenchman stood on his tip-toes and shouted "By gar! no!" I still held to my private opinion.

And the boy. Observe that head, and the hand which has fallen down. I insisted that his hand had been mashed in a corn-sheller, and that his head would take a No. 10 hat, but the Frenchman refused to believe it.

There's a roaring fire, as you will observe, and the smoke is piling into the room in a way to shame the big chimney of a locomotive works. It may be the smoke which makes the boy take on such a sickly expression around the mouth. Mosquitos couldn't live ten seconds in that room.

You see, the Frenchman's idea was to have the old man die in his chair. He died there, either overcome by indigestion or the smoke. He went to Heaven. If you don't believe it, look at him in the crowd of angels. There are two men-angels sailing around in the smoke, and you will observe that moustaches are allowed up there in the land beyond the skies. There are some angels with overcoats on, and some with sheets wrapped around them, and the old man who died stepped into his store clothes when he got above the fire-place. I suggested to the Frenchman to make at least one man-angel with top boots on, and a plug hat slanted over on his ear, but he called me an infidel.

As to the music, there is one angel playing on a banjo, and another looks around as if in search of a fiddle or a snare drum. I wanted a hand organ in there somewhere, but the Frenchman informed me that there was no such thing as a hand organ in Heaven.

I spoke to him about the enormous quantity of boards and timber used in the construction of the old man's chair, but he said there was no danger of exhausting the supply, and went down stairs growling about "wooden-heads."

The Frenchman still lives. He is a sensitive as well as

a sad man. I paid him for the cut, and it is mine, and I hope that the newspapers throughout the country will each have a "lick" at him. I shall show him each criticism, and smile maliciously, and poke him in the ribs, and dance up and down and yell at him that his new improved French method of engraving has been hoisted higher than Mr. Gilderoy's kite.

THE DARWIN THEORY.

HAVEN'T looked into the subject as one ought to, but Mr. Darwin's theory strikes me as very reasonable. It's all theory, of course, and it makes me feel sad when I reflect that it may always remain a theory.

My family traditions are few, owing to the fact that we can't get trace of our great great grandfather. Grandfather and great grandfather are all right; we can put our hands right on 'em, or rather on their records, but beyond them the trail is befogged and lost. But for Darwin's theory I shouldn't entertain the faintest hope of ever solving the genealogical mystery. There is hope now, every time I enter a circus tent, that I may run across one of my ancestors. I can't say who my great great grandfather was. He might have bled with Wallace, landed with the Pilgrim Fathers, or sailed with Columbus, but it's just as probable that he was a native of Africa, walked on four legs and made it lively for the cocoanuts growing on the top branches. If I should ever travel in Africa I should

PERHAPS.

441

look around in the expectation of seeing him out on a morning walk, or coming across him up to his elbows in business.

I do not know as any one need feel ashamed of the thought that some of his ancestors were gorillas. If a gorilla has stamina of character, is public spirited and pro-

gressive, he is entitled to respect. If I should come across the ancestor spoken of I should expect to find a genial hearted, liberal minded old chap, with no mania for buying lottery tickets, no desire for political office, and no care but to keep his character above reproach. It would be a crushing blow for me to find the old

MISSING LINK.

man in a menagerie, and have the man who explains the nature of each resident of a cage speak up and say:

"Ladies and gentlemen, that 'ere baboon over there is as mean as the man who sprinkled turpentine on the mince pie so that the children wouldn't injure their digestive organs. He's sly, malicious, deceitful and revengeful. He bit a boy's nose off in London, tore a man's eye out in Edinburg, and pulled the Mayor's whiskers in Cork. Beware of him! When you stand close to the cage keep a good ways off."

Neither Mr. Darwin or any one else could blame me, but I know I should feel like walking right out of the tent without stopping to see the sacred cow of India or the three-legged goose from Constantinople. I cannot say but that my ancestor is tearing around in Africa, cooking up a plot to dethrone the king of Dahomey, or getting up a "corner" on yams, but I flatly and positively refuse to be responsible for any of his bad actions. When the sad wind sobs and moans around the gables, and the rain-drops patter drearily, the mind will feel an anxiety to know if one's ancestor hasn't been turned into the street for non-payment of house rent; if his wood pile is low; if some of his children are not down with the croup, or if the plumbers haven't robbed and murdered him in payment for soldering up a pin-hole leak in the water pipe. It's annoying to live in America and have relatives in Africa to worry about, and it cuts one's pride to see leading members of the family content to be caged up, carried around the country, and have no ambition further than to catch the apple cores and "hunks" of gingerbread thrown by the town boys.

ON THE NIGHT BREEZE.

O one could say who owned that mule. Small boys had pelted him with liberal hand, and the police had made glorious but unsuccessful efforts to ensnare his wayward steps and turn him over to the pound-master.

A gray mule, well put together for an animal of the kind. The rotundity of form which distinguishes the well-fed mule was lacking. A bite of grass here and there, an occasional thistle-head, a nibble at a passing load of hay, may blunt the edge of hunger, but will not produce plumpness nor good nature.

He had wandered from home, this mule—started out with a desire, perhaps, of visiting strange towns, meeting with strange adventures, and seeing the world. His owner had been left one mule less, and mayhap he had diligently searched, and been patient and hopeful, trusting that the wheel of time would turn and return the mourned estray.

A WANDERER.

Down the street—around the corner—the gas-light playing for a moment on his faded coat—and the mule crowded close to the fence and peered over with hungry eyes at the juicy green grass. Thus have we raised the curtain of fact and introduced to orchestra, parquette, boxes and gallery, the leading character, playing not the role of the old man, but the role of the old mule.

In the parlor sat the lovers. She was beautiful—he was worth five hundred shares of Lake Shore stock, and was interested in a bridge contract where there was a chance for a splendid grab. He loved, and he trusted that she reciprocated. He had come prepared to announce his love, and she blushed as she read the fact in his eyes.

"My dear Isabella," he commenced, as he tenderly pressed her soft fingers, "I think you——"

"Gee-haw! gee-haw!" roared the wayward mule, rendered melancholy by the sight of the bountiful supper just beyond his nose.

The fair Isabella sprang up in alarm, and it was several minutes before the enthusiastic young man with Lake Shore stock could quiet her.

ONLY A MULE.

"It is nothing but a mule," he explained, as he looked from the open window; and he scowled darkly at the wanderer, and made threatening gestures. She sat down again, and the painful silence was at length broken by his grasping her hand and saying:

"I have to-day been analyzing my feelings toward you, and I find that——"

"O-h! hoo-haw, gee-haw—gee-haw!" announced the homeless, houseless mule, as he caught the scent of roses and tulips from the lawn. He saw things as a mule sees them—he hungered as mules hunger.

"It's that beast again!" whispered Lake Shore stock, as the fair Isabella uttered a little shriek of alarm.

He went to the window and ordered the gray-haired outcast to move on—to leave that locality without any unnecessary delay and secure standing room on the common.

They sat down again. He had something of interest to communicate, and she had a curiosity to know what it was. Minutes ticked away before he looked into her lustrous eyes again. He thought he saw the light of love shining brightly, and he stole his arm along the sofa and said:

"You must have seen—you must know, that I——"

"O-h-h! gee-gee-ah-ha! ah-ha!" came a voice from beneath the window. It was not the voice of a drifting sailor, going down to a dark, deep grave, after a gallant struggle for life. It was not the voice of a lost child crying out as it stumbled through the darkness, longing for the strong arm of a father to enfold it. It was the voice of the old gray mule, quavering strangely as hunger brought up recollections of corn cribs and timothy hay.

A smile flitted across her face. The human soul is so constructed that one may smile at a victorious, exultant champion, or at a downcast, discouraged mule.

Lake Shore stock approached the window again, and as he brandished his fist in the air he warned the intruder to dissolve in the dim distance, under penalty of being found dead with a severed jugular.

When a rubber ball is flattened it will spring back to its original shape as soon as the pressure is removed. When a lover's declaration has been thrice broken in upon, his thoughts are slow in gathering. They sat there and gazed at the opposite wall as if waiting for a railroad train, but she finally glanced up coyly and lovingly, and softly whispered :

" You were about to say something !"

" I was," he whispered in return, reaching out for her hand. " The public have acknowledged me as your—your favored suitor for months past, and this fact has emboldened me to——"

" Hip—hup—haw—ge-haw-ha!" came a voice on the night breeze—a voice which halted and gasped and hesita-

NOT A TROUBADOUR.

ted as if the owner had risen from beside the grave of a loved, lost friend. It was not the voice of a troubadour warbling notes of anguish set in rhyme. It was not the voice of a lone night bird calling for its lost mate. It was the voice of that same mule calling to the lilac bushes to come a little nearer—to come and get a bite.

" Is that an odious cow ?" she softly inquired.

" No ; it's a blasted mule !" he exclaimed.

" Such language, sir !" she said as she rose up.

" Such a mule, madam !" he replied, pointing to the window. " I'll kill the man—the mule—that has dared to come between us !" he shouted, and he rushed from the mansion.

He pelted that age-worn mule with lawn ornaments; he pelted it with stones picked from the street or found alongside the curbstone.

Halting under a lone tree on the dreary common—gazing through the deep shadows of night to discover why pursuit was abandoned, the old gray mule seemed to realize that, even as a mule, it was safe to have an accident insurance ticket in his pocket, and he sighed and gasped and tremulously soliloquized :

 "*Gee-haw—gee-ah—r-rr-raw—ge-haw !*"

And the shadows grew deeper, the night breeze sighed with renewed loneliness, the stars nestled behind the clouds to sleep, and he felt that he was a mule beloved by none.

THOSE CIRCUS BILLS.

RTLESS and innocent, she had one in her hand as she came up stairs, and she didn't say a word until after she had wiped her spectacles, placed them on her nose, unfolded the bill and read a few of the headlines.

She was quite old-fashioned in look. There were strings to her bonnet, she had no bustle, her gray hair was combed down smoothly, and there were only eleven yards in her black alpaca dress.

"Young man, don't you know that circuses are awful liars and humbugs?" she finally inquired.

The man at the table leaned back in his chair and refused to express an opinion.

"Well, I know it," she continued in a positive tone, "and I believe they git wuss every day. Now see here— listen to this: 'A gorgeous panorama of amazing wonders—a gigantic combination of astonishing acrobatic talent.' That's all right on the poster, but hev they got 'em? I'd like to see one o' them animals."

"You're laboring under a mistake, madam. It means a grand display of natural curiosities, and informs the public that the proprietor has secured many first class acrobats—the chaps who stand on their heads, turn head over heels, and cut up so many monkey-shines."

"It does, eh?" she mused; "waal, do you believe it takes a smart person to keel over?"

"Well, one has to have a good deal of training."

"They do, eh?" she remarked, as she put her umbrella in the corner and spat on her hands; "I'll show you that you are deceived! I'm an old woman, but if I can't——"

"Madam, hold on—don't do it!" exclaimed the man behind the table.

"I can flop right over there and never shake my bonnet!" she said as she rose up.

"It Does, Eh?"

"I know you can, madam, but don't. I am here alone, and I—I don't want you to. I'd rather you wouldn't. If you are determined on it I shall leave the room!"

"Well, you know I can do it, and that's enough. You may be right about what that means, but see here—hear this: 'The highways ablaze with resplendent chariots— the grandest pageant on earth.' I've bin to lots o' circuses, young man, and I never saw a pageant yet. If they had one the door of his cage wasn't open."

"You are also in error there. The bill refers to the fact that the great number of wagons, chariots, etc., make up a sight worth seeing as they pass along the street."

"Um-m-m," she muttered as she folded the bill over; "I don't see why they couldn't have said so, then. And now see here—read that: 'Sig. Govinoff, in his aerial flights.' Now, then, is that a boa constrictor or a cun-durango?"

"Just Once!"

"It is a man, madam—one of the performers. His real name is probably Jones, but that isn't grand enough, and so they put him down as 'Sig. Govinoff.' He is the man who jumps off a rope, turns over twice, and comes down all right."

"He is, eh? Well, if he's got an idea that he's the

smartest man alive I want to disappoint him. I never did try to turn over twice, but I'll do it right here and now or break my neck. Git the things off'n that table!"

"Stay, madam—don't. I wouldn't have you do it for fifty dollars."

"Just once!"

"For heaven's sake, madam, get down off'n this table—here—here's a dollar if you won't do it!"

"I don't want your money, and I won't try it if you are so scart, but I don't want no circus going around talking about aryal flights and deceiving the people!"

She sat down, the young man wiped the sweat off his brow, and presently she remarked:

"And here's another thing, right here: 'A sparkling asterisk, flashing across the field of the cloth of gold—Mons. Gomerique, in his great delineations of human character.' I'd like to know who she is."

"Madam, that is a man—a comic man who delineates character."

"How?"

"Why, he makes up faces—expresses mirth, sorrow, joy, and so forth."

"He does, eh? Well, what's that to blow about? Makes up faces—see here!"

And she shut her eyes, run her tongue out, and looked like the bottom of a brass kettle which had been kicked in by an army mule.

"They are humbugs, sir!" she said as she drew her tongue in, "and d'ye s'pose I'd pay fifty cents to go to one?"

"They are quite entertaining as a general thing."

"They are, eh? Entertaining, eh? Well, if I can't do more entertaining in five minutes than a circus can in all day I'll leave my bonnet up here! Here, hold on to this chair!"

"Madam, I earnestly hope you are not going to perform any tricks."

"I hain't, eh? You just hold on to the legs of this chair!"

"I can't madam—I wouldn't do it for all the diamond pins in Syracuse! Go away, madam—go home! I'm in an awful hurry!"

"Well, I won't, then, but when I say circuses are humbugs I can prove it. I don't keer two cents for their big words and their panoplies, pageants, asterisks, giraffes, aryals, gorgeouses and ourang-outangs—I can beat 'em all holler myself!"

"HOLD ON TO THIS CHAIR." And she took off her spectacles, lifted her umbrella, and went down stairs.

OLD SOL, OF COMPANY B.

AFTER the first year of the war a good many of us wanted to go home. We could get together and name three hundred and fifty thousand weighty reasons why we should return to the bosom of our families instead of longer biting hard-tack and dodging bullets, but we didn't get home. The only way to secure a discharge was to get a leg or an arm shot off, or to fall sick and hang around until the officers became worn out and bored to death.

The old dead-beats settled down on two favorite tricks. One was to eat Government soap until real sickness came, and the other to suddenly lose the voice. We had a man in company B, who one day made up his mind that he had saved the country enough, and he lost his voice. Suspecting that he was practicing deception, the captain kept Old Sol on duty as before, and every man in the company had a fling at him.

However, after two months had passed away and the old man had not been tripped up we began to believe that he was honest in his assertions. The officers used every artifice to expose him, but every attempt was a flat failure. He was challenged on the sentry line, suddenly roused from sleep, confronted with the colonel and savagely talked to, and yet he could not be betrayed into uttering a loud sound. He would have been discharged in another week if the captain had not discovered a new plan, and one that proved successful.

We were squatted before Yorktown then, two men to a tent, and old Sol's partner was out on the picket line one day, leaving the voiceless man alone in the tent. A mule wandering through the camp stopped near the tent and uttered a fearfully loud, long bray. Old Sol rushed out and drove the beast away, and the captain, who had seen the whole performance, at once struck a plan.

After a brief hunt he found among the teamsters a mule which was warranted to bray two hundred pounds to the square inch. A corporal was let into the plan, and when night came and old Sol had fallen asleep the mule was brought around and tied near his tent, having a lariat about twenty feet long. No sooner had the corporal skulked away than the beast cocked his ears, rolled up his eyes, and screamed out:

"O! yaw! yaw! yaw! yaw!"

Old Sol was out of bed in an instant, and though fire-wood was scarce he wasted several sticks on the mule, which sprang away the length of the lariat and was lost in the darkness. The voiceless man got into bed again, but in two minutes the mule walked up and pealed out:

"Yaw! ha! yaw! yaw! s-o-h! yaw!"

Old Sol threw more wood, the plaguey beast returned, and the soldier hadn't crawled under his blanket before the fearful bray shook his tent again. This was repeated five or six times, and finally as the mule started to improve on all previous brays the voiceless man leaped up and yelled out:

"Now dum my buttons if I'll take any more of *that!*

I want to go home and see Marier and the children mighty bad, but I'll kill that mule if I have to stay here and fight the whole durned Confederate army single-handed!"

Half the men in company B were on their hands and knees around the tent, and old Sol couldn't back water. He owned up that he'd been playing off, and after that no soldier in our division did his duty more cheerfully than the old man Sol.

A LONE HAND.

ONE day Mrs. Bliss found a euchre deck in her boy's pocket, and when she took him by the hair he calmly said:

"Hold, on mother—it isn't your play."

"I'll play you!" she hissed, tightening her grip. "How came you by these cards?"

"Mother, you shouldn't trump me this way!" he explained.

"Trumps! trumps! what do you know about trumps?"

"Why, mother, any fool knows that the right bower will take an ace every time."

"It will, eh?" she hissed as she walked him around.

"Of course it will. If diamonds are trumps, for instance, and I hold the ace and left bow——"

"Bowers! bowers! I'll bower you to death, young man!" she said as she walked him the other way.

"Or, suppose that spades were trumps, and you held the nine spot and king and turned up the ace, what would you do?" he earnestly inquired.

"Oh, I'll show you what I'd do!" she growled as she got in a left-hander on his ear. "I'll teach you a lesson you'll never forget!"

"That wouldn't be according to Hoyle, mother; you could pick up the ace and make a point every——"

"Point! point! Young man, I'll point you so that you'll stay sharpened for a hundred years if you don't drop such slang!" she screamed as she jumped him over a chair.

"But, mother, you shouldn't stack the cards on me this——"

She wouldn't wait to hear the rest, but drew him over her knee and played a lone hand.

MORAL COURAGE.

ORAL courage is a big thing. All the good papers advise everybody to have moral courage. All the almanacs wind up with a word about moral courage. The Rev. Murray and the Rev. Collier and the Rev. Spurgeon, and lots of other reverends tell their congregations to exhibit moral courage in daily life. Moral courage doesn't cost a cent; everybody can fill up with it until he can't eat half a dinner after going without breatfast.

"Have the moral courage to discharge a debt while you have the money in your pocket," is one of the "moral courage" paragraphs.

Mr. Mower read this once, and he determined to act upon it. One day his wife handed him five dollars, which she had been two years saving, and asked him to bring her up a parasol and a pair of gaiters. On the way down he met a creditor, and had the moral courage to pay him. Returning home, his wife called him 157,000 names, such as "fool," "idiot," etc., and then struck him four times in the pit of the stomach with a flat iron. After that he didn't have as much moral courage as would make a leaning post for a sick grasshopper, and his wife didn't forgive him for thirteen years.

"Have the courage to tell a man why you refuse to credit him," is another paragraph. That means if you

keep a store, and old Mr. Putty comes in and wants a
pound of tea charged, you must promptly respond:

" Mr. Putty, your credit at this store isn't worth the
powder to blow a mosquito over a tow-string. You are a
fraud of the first water, Mr. Putty, and I wouldn't trust
you for a herring's head if herrings were selling at a cent
a box."

Mr. Putty will never ask you for credit again, and you
will have the consciousness of having performed your
honest duty.

" In providing an entertainment for your friends, have
have the courage not to go beyond your means," is another
paragraph. If your daughter wants a party, and you are
short, don't be lavish. Borrow some chairs, make a bench
of a board and two pails, and set out some molasses and
watermelon, and tell the crowd to gather around the fest-
ive board and partake. They will appreciate your moral
courage, if not the banquet. -

" Have the courage to show your respect for honesty,"
is another. That is, if you hear of anybody who picked
up a five-dollar bill and restored it to its owner, take him
by the hand and say: " Mr. Rambo, let me compliment
you on being an honest man. I didn't think it of you,
and I am agreeably disappointed. I always believed you
were a liar, a rascal and a thief, and I am glad to find that
you are neither—shake."

" Have the courage to speak the truth," is a paragraph
always in use. I once knew a boy named Peter. One day
when he was loafing around he heard some men talking
about old Mr. Hangmoney. Their talk made a deep
impression on Peter, and he went to the old man and
spoke the truth. He said: " Mr. Hangmoney, when I was
up town to-day I heard Baker say you were a regular old
hedge-hog with a tin ear."

"What!" roared the old gent.

"And Clevis said that you were meaner than a dead dog rolled in tan-bark," continued the truthful lad.

"You imp—you villain!" roared the old man.

"And Kingston said that you were a bald-headed, cross-eyed, cheating, lying, stealing old skunk under the hen-coop!" added the boy.

Then old Mr. Hangmoney fell upon the truthful Peter, and he mopped the floor with him, knocked his heels against the wall, tore his collar off, and put his shoulder out of joint, all because that boy had the moral courage to tell the truth.

And there was young Towboy—it was the same with him. He had the moral courage to go over to an old maid and say:

"Miss Fallsair, father says he never saw such a withered up old Hubbard squash as you are around trying to trap a man!"

"He did, eh?" mused the old maid, rising up from her chair.

"Yes, and mother says it's a burning shame that you call yourself twenty-four when you are forty-seven, and she says that your hair-dye costs more than our wood!"

"She said that, did she?" murmured the female.

"Yes, and sister Jane says that if she had such a big mouth, such freckles, such big feet and such silly ways, she'd want the lightning to strike her."

And then the old maid picked up the rolling-pin and sought the house in which Towboy resided, and she knocked down and dragged out until it was a hospital. Then Towboy's father mauled him, his mother pounded him, and his sister denuded him of half his hair—all because he had moral courage in his daily life.

THE O'LONE INVENTION.

THE MOTIVE POWER.

THE public are herewith presented with a very faithful wood-cut illustration of a new patent just granted to Mrs. Bridget O'Lone, of Detroit—a patent in which I have a half-interest. No one but a woman would have invented this machine, and the entire credit of the invention must be given to a female whose opportunities of securing an education have been very limited.

Mrs. O'Lone is a married woman, having a husband but no children.

Mr. O'Lone was in the habit of putting on his hat after supper and remarking that he was going to step out for just a moment, and then she'd see no more of him for four hours. She argued, coaxed, clubbed and entreated, but though Mr. O'Lone is a kind-hearted man he loved to sit on the grocery steps and whittle a shingle better than he loved his own hearthstone.

462

After fourteen years of patient waiting and hoping Mrs. O'Lone fell upon this invention. The cut fully explains the invention up to the window. From that point is a coil of rope containing one hundred feet, one end attached to the wheel, the other having a stout hook. Mr. O'Lone gets up from the table and says he'd like to go down to the grocery and hear how the murder trial comes out. The hook is fastened to his clothing, the rope paid out, and Mrs. O'Leary looks at the clock and warns him to be home at nine. He promises, but after he gets seated on the head of a sugar barrel the interesting conversation kills time so rapidly that he does not hear the clock strike. He is arguing politics or talking about the crops, when Mrs. O'Leary steps to the wheel in the kitchen and begins to turn. The effect is wonderful, as the accom-

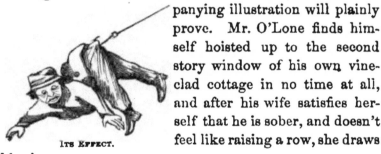

ITS EFFECT.

panying illustration will plainly prove. Mr. O'Lone finds himself hoisted up to the second story window of his own vine-clad cottage in no time at all, and after his wife satisfies herself that he is sober, and doesn't feel like raising a row, she draws him in.

I have seen this machine tried on twenty different occasions, and it worked successfully in every instance.

It is an invention which must revolutionize the country in a short time and bring about a different state of domestic discipline. Where one of these machines is set up in a house the husband will either remain at home altogether, or return five minutes ahead of time. He will desert his old haunts, glue the knobs on the bureau, get the kindlings for morning and draw the water for a big washing without a word of complaint.

It works just as well in the case of a boy fourteen or fifteen years old. It will bring him home when a police-man couldn't stir him a foot.

He won't come over the alley fence and through the wood-shed window, but he'll trot right along by the shortest route, and won't stop to lay any plans for the next night.

Three of these machines are in use in Euclid avenue, Cleveland; two on Fort street, Detroit; one in Cincinnati, and four in Chicago, and money couldn't purchase

OLD HAUNTS.

them of the owners. There is no more hanging around corner groceries where these machines are in operation— no stepping around to Johnson's—no going to the lodge. The husband and sons are in bed at nine o'clock, and wives and mothers haven't been so happy in seven years.

JOHN JONES, SICK MAN.

E was "grunting around" for two or three days before he would give up. Mrs. Jones advised him to take pills or quinine, but he said he guessed he'd be all right as soon as the weather changed again. On the third morning he had a high fever and couldn't stand up.

Mrs. Jones seemed delighted. He hadn't been sick before for thirteen years, and she had a splendid stock of herbs and powders and liquids in the pantry.

"Now, just give right up, John Washington," she replied, as he groaned and sighed, and declared that he'd get up and go down town as usual if it killed him. "There, let me turn your pillow over, hang your clothes in the closet, and then I'll run in and make you some toast."

He had to submit. She darkened the bedroom, put a clean spread on the bed, and a grand smile covered her face as she sailed into the kitchen.

"Sarah Jane, you go and fan your father with a newspaper and keep the flies off'n him while I get the poor man something to eat. Your father is a very sick man, Sarah Jane, and I can't say that you won't be fatherless next week at this time."

Sarah went in, and Mrs. Jones rushed from the stove to the pantry. She toasted four large slices of bread, broke

three eggs into hot water, got down a pint glass of jelly,
sent for half a pound of crackers, and in about half an
hour had the sick man's breakfast ready.

"I don't care what all the doctors in the land say," she
remarked, as she drew three chairs within his reach and
loaded them down with the provisions. "I know that
people can't be sick without something on their stomach."

He tasted the toast, sipped at the tea, groaned, growled
and sighed, and she pleaded:

"Now, John, do try and eat something. I know just
how you feel, and I know you haven't any appetite, but
do try."

"O thunder!" he groaned, as his stomach rebelled
against the food.

"Poor man! poor, dear man!" she sighed, as she placed
her hand on his head. "John Washington, if you should
die this would be a sad house. I don't believe I could
stand up under the blow three weeks, and I know the
children would give right up!"

"Hadn't we better have a doctor?" he inquired, becoming frightened.

"Not now, John—not until we see that *I* can't do you
any good. I know those doctors to a T. They'd come
here and dose and dose and make a great bill, and you'd
probably die just the same."

She carried out the food, put on a kettle of water, got
out a clean towel, and as she entered the bedroom with a
dish of warm water in her hand, she said:

"Now, then, I must wash your feet and cut your toe-
nails."

She sat beside the bed, took his foot in her lap, and that
sweet smile on her face proved that his illness would be a
gain to her of a pound of flesh per day.

"My soul! but I'm glad I thought to wash your feet,"

she exclaimed, as she rubbed them with a wet towel. "I wouldn't have had any of the neighbors come in and see those feet for all we are worth."

She wanted to scrape the sole with an old case-knife, but he wouldn't permit it. She, however, got out the shears, and had a good time cutting his toe-nails and digging under them. She worked industriously for half an hour, and then held the last foot off and looked at it admiringly, and said:

"There! I'll take my dying oath you've got the cleanest feet in this town."

She took a second look, gave the foot an admiring pat, and continued:

"If this fit of sickness should carry you off, I could always look back with pleasure to the fact that your feet were bran span clean and as good as new."

He half admitted that he felt better, and, greatly encouraged, she sent Sarah Jane out to pull some horse-radish leaves. These were trimmed, laid on the stove, rolled in her hand, and she went back to Mr. Jones and said:

"Now, then, we'll put on the drafts."

She put a leaf on the sole of each foot, tied clean cloths over them, hunted up clean socks, worried them on over the cloths, and, as she tucked the spread down, she asked:

"Now, John Washington, don't you feel better—a little better?"

"Oh, I dunno!" he groaned, turning over.

"You poor man! How providential for you that you have got a wife who knows all about herbs and sickness."

She turned over his pillow, put a damp cloth on his forehead, counted his pulse, and whispered:

"See if you can't catch a little sleep while I go and wash the dishes."

When she went out Sarah Jane had her brother William harnessed to a chair, and was driving him round the kitchen for her horse.

"What! didn't I tell you that your father was dangerously ill?" exclaimed the mother, as she boxed their ears. "It would be a pretty story to go out that you children were playing horse when your father lay dying!"

The children subsided, and as the mother piled the dishes together and carefully scraped the crumbs from each plate on to a platter, she couldn't help but wonder how she would look in crapes. Her husband was well known, belonged to the Odd Fellows and a debating society, and of course everybody would turn out to the funeral. She would have lots of sympathy, and the head man of the Odd Fellows would see that the funeral passed off all right. She wouldn't never marry again, of course, though it would be hard for her to bring up two small children and settle up her husband's business and earn her own support. She would be the "Widow Jones," and if she smiled at all it must be a faint smile, and if she talked she must have a handkerchief ready to wipe the tears from her eyes.

As the last dish was wiped, her revery was broken by a howl from William, who had fallen over a log in the back yard.

"What! howling like that when your dear father is dying!" she exclaimed, as she shook him right and left.

He subsided, and she sent Sarah Jane down to the market after some lean mutton to make the invalid a broth.

"The poor man!" she sighed, as she started for the bedroom. She reached it to find him out of bed and dressed and ready to go down town. The horse-radish drafts were hanging on the bedstead, the pillow was on the floor, and the spread—her best—was in a heap under the bed.

"Why, John Washington!" she exclaimed, raising her hands.

"I'm going down town," he replied, in a determined voice.

"And hain't you going to have a fit of sickness?"

"No, hanged if I will!"

And the poor woman sat down and cried. All those herbs and powders and liquids must remain on the shelves, and she might not have a chance to cut his toe-nails again for a whole year.

M'GRADY'S BASE TRICK.

WE hadn't much amusemont in "Buttermilk Diggings," and days when the weather was bad and silver mining couldn't be pursued, the man who owned a novel could lend it at a big price per hour. One night a fire consumed several of the shanties, and burned every pack of cards, dice-box and scrap of reading in the place. The next week nearly finished half the men, and when a man riding a small brown mule hove in sight over the ridge one afternoon, the pair were greeted with a powerful yell of welcome. He was the first stranger who had come our way for four months, and the boys took to him at once.

The man was a quiet sort of fellow named McGrady, and the mule had a listless, dreamy look, and a slouchy gait. He was a curiosity to some of the men, and attention was about equally divided between mule and master.

Within two hours after reaching the Diggings McGrady was taken ill of fever, and for a week we gave him the best we had, and took prime care of the mule. The beast was as whist as a mouse, never braying a note during the whole week, and "Buttermilk Diggings" passed him a vote of thanks for his natural modesty and retiring disposition.

470

When the man got on his legs again he was very grateful, and gathering the men around him one noon, he let out something to astonish us. He called the mule up, and all the mules which ever played tricks in circuses couldn't hold a candle to the tricks of that mule. He would rear up, lie down, roll over, stand on a barrel, kick up, strike, jump, nod his head or shake it, and he acted as if he had human brains. When we had recovered from our astonishment, McGrady confessed that he had come to clean out the Diggings with the mule's tricks, but gratitude had caused him to forego his designs.

It wasn't five minutes before we had put up a job on our neighbors in the bend of Duck creek, four miles away. They had heaps of silver up there, and the fifty miners were puffed up over their luck and wore their hats over their left ears. We had been aching for a long while to get even with them, and we saw that the chance had come. They were a betting set, and they'd go their pile against McGrady's mule.

In about a week we were ready. We got up a grand wolf-dinner for Sunday, and invited the whole crowd over. They had only caught sight of the mule when they began to poke fun at him, calling him the president of Buttermilk Diggings and all that, but we bided our time. After dinner we began to throw out hints about the mule's cuteness, and he was brought out and made to perform a few of the least important tricks.

The Duck Creek fellows sneered and snickered, declaring that they had a tame wolf which could beat anything like that, and by and by they seized hold of the mule, threw him over, and rolled him down hill. McGrady then began to brag about what his mule could do, and he laid out a programme, and we offered to back him. The Duck Creek men came to time like a tornado, and offered to bet us even that the mule couldn't perform even one of the dozen tricks on the programme.

Here was our chance, and every dollar which Buttermilk Diggings could turn out was put up. It took a good half hour to get the preliminaries settled, and finally we had $1,565 up against an equal sum laid down by the Duck Creek men. We went around grinning and nudging each other, and we felt a bit of pity for the greenhorns from the Creek.

The mule was finally called up. He'd been browsing around while we fixed the bets, and he came forward looking as innocent and unconcerned as a mule could look.

"As I understand it, Duck Creek bets that this mule can't be made to pick up a barrel with his teeth, carry it to the door of the fourth shanty, and take my hat off the bench and bring it here," said McGrady.

"That's her—that's the bet," cried the fellows.

We'd seen the mule go through that performance thirty times, and we grinned some more.

McGrady whispered in the beast's ear, and then pointed to the barrel and at the shanty. The mule seized the barrel, gave it a toss to one side, and started up the creek as fast as he could go, and was out of sight in five minutes.

The Duck Creek fellows yelled until they were hoarse, and after they had departed with the money we found McGrady had gone with them. It wasn't long before we discovered that the Duck Creek chaps had sent him to put up the whole thing on us. He had trained the mule to go through the tricks or to run away, as occasion demanded, and his sickness was all a sham.

If wolf meat hadn't been unusually plenty that spring, Buttermilk Diggings would have been wiped out by starvation.

Some of our folks cleaned up their revolvers and hung

around the Duck Creek camp for the best part of the next week, hoping to get a shot at McGrady and to ventilate the mule, but the pair slipped away between two days, and "Buttermilk" held a mass meeting and

"*Resolved*, That we be carm and bear up."

AS THE PIGEON FLIES.

-Z-Z-Z-Z-Z! A monster of iron, steel and brass, standing on the slim iron rails which shoot away from the station for half a mile and then lose themselves in the green forest.

Puff-puff! The driving-wheels slowly turn—the monster breathes great clouds of steam and seems anxious for the race.

A grizzly-haired engineer looks down from the cab-window, while his fireman pulls back the iron door and heaves in more wood—more breath and muscle for the grim giant of the track.

The fire roars and crackles—the steam hisses and growls—every breath is drawn as fiercely as if the giant was burning to revenge an insult.

Up—up—up! The pointer on the steam-gauge moves faster than the minute-hand on a clock. The breathing becomes louder—the hiss rises to a scream—the iron rails tremble and quiver.

" Climb up!"

It is going to be a race against time and the telegraph.

" S-s-s-sh!"

The engineer rose up, looked ahead, glanced at the dial, and as his fingers clasped the throttle he asked the station-agent :

" Are you sure that the track is clear?"

" All clear!" was the answer.

The throttle feels the pull, the giant utters a fierce scream, and we are off, I on the fireman's seat, the fireman on the wood. The rails slide under us slowly—faster, and the giant screams again and dashes into the forest.

This isn't fast. The telegraph poles dance past as if not over thirty feet apart, and the board fence seems to rise from the ground, but it's only thirty-five miles an hour.

" Wood!"

The engineer takes his eyes off the track and turns just long enough to speak the word to his fireman. The iron door swings back, and there is an awful rush and roar of flame. The fire-box appears full, but stick after stick is dropped into the roaring pit until a quarter of a cord has disappeared.

" This is forty miles an hour!" shouts the fireman in my ear as he rubs the moisture from his heated face.

Yes, this is faster. The fence-posts seem to leap from the ground as we dash along, and the telegraph poles bend and nod to us. A house—a field—a farm—we get but one glance. A dozen houses—a hundred faces—that was a station. We heard a yell from the crowd, but it had scarcely reached us before it was drowned in the great roar.

Nine miles in fourteen minutes—we've lost time! The engineer takes his eyes from the rail, makes a motion to his fireman, and the sticks drop into the roaring flames again, to make new flames.

Seven miles of clear track now, and the engineer smiles
a grim smile as he lets more steam into the giant's lungs.

Ah! Not a mile a minute yet, but how we shake from
side to side—how the tender leaps and bounds! Is there
a fence skirting the track? There is a dark line keeping
pace with us—it may be a fence. Where are the telegraph
poles? Were all those trees falling toward the track as
we dashed through the bit of forest?

A yell—houses—faces—that was another station. Word
has gone down the line that a "wild" locomotive is rushing a journalist across the country to catch the lightning
express on another Road, and the people gather to see us
dash past. Seven miles in eight and a half minutes—that's
better, but we must run faster!

The finger on the dial creeps slowly up—we want a
reserve of steam for the last twelve of road—the best track
of all.

The noise is deafening—the swaying and bumping is
terrible. I hang fast to the seat—clutch, cling, and yet it
seems as if I must be shaken to the floor.

Every moment there is a scream from the whistle—every
two or three minutes the engineer makes a gesture which
calls for the iron door to be opened and the roaring, leaping flames to be fed anew.

Houses—faces—a yell! That was another station. We
made the last five miles in six minutes. Did you ever ride
a mile in one minute and twelve seconds? But we were
to beat it.

Like a bird—like an arrow—like a bullet almost, we
speed forward. Half a dozen men beside the track—sec-
tion-men with their hand-car. They lift their hats and
yell, but their voices do not reach us. We pass them as
lightning flashes through the heavens. That was a farm-
house. We saw nothing but a white object—a green

spot—two or three apple trees where there was a large orchard.

Scream !

Hiss !

Roar !

Shake—quiver—bound !

We are going to stop—going to halt for an instant at a station to see if the track is clear for the rush—for a mile a minute, and faster !

Scream ! Scream !

The station is a mile ahead—it is beside us ! The fireman leaps down with his oil-can—the engineer enters the telegraph office. Both are back in fifteen seconds.

Twelve and a half miles to go—twelve minutes in which to make it.

"We can do it !" said the engineer. "Hold fast now ! We have been running—we are going to fly !"

Scream !

"Good-bye !"

As a mad horse runs—as an arrow is sent—as the carrier-pigeon flies ! Yes, this is a mile a minute ! Fences ? No—only a black line, hardly larger than my pencil ! Trees ? No—only one tree—all merged into one single tree, which was out of sight in a flash. Fields ? Yes—one broad field, broken for an instant by a highway—a gray thread lying on the ground !

It is terrible ! If we should leave the rails ! If—but don't think of it ! Hold fast !

Eight miles in eight minutes, not a second more or less ! The lightning travels faster—so does a locomotive ! Four and a half miles to go—four minutes to make it ! We must run a mile every fifty-three seconds.

Scream !

Sway !

Tremble!

We are making time, but great heavens it is awful—this **roar**, this oscillation!

One mile!

Two miles!

I dare not open my eyes! I would not look ahead on the track for all the gold ever mined!

Three miles!

Can I ever hear again? Will I ever get this deafening roar out of my ears? Will the seconds ever go by?

Scream!

The engineer shuts off steam—the fireman hurrahs—I open my eyes—we are at the station! The lightning express is not two seconds away!

"I told you!" says the engineer, "and didn't I do it!"

He did, but he carried three lives in the palm of the hand that grasped the throttle.

SOME SAD THOUGHTS.

HOWEVER the reader may feel, the man who wrote this book cannot resist a feeling of sadness as he sits down to this last article.

There are many sad things connected with writing and publishing a book. For instance, the newspapers now and then get after a man and sprinkle his January weather with August breezes. The book may be a failure in a financial point of view, leaving the author to carry a night-mare burden on his back during the rest of his natural life. He sees a good many paragraphs, and some whole articles, which he knows he could better, but the printer won't let him try.

The author has written this book " between times "— sandwiched the work between writing for a dozen publications. It has been the means of keeping him home nights, and of preventing him from joining Fenian raids, expeditions to the Black Hills, or running for office. But for this work he could have secured seven or eight hours sleep each night, grown fat, preserved a placid expression of countenance, and been in a position to criticise the book of another.

Hereafter, the book being in the hands of the public, the writer will sadly sit and nibble at his pencil, and think and ponder and think, and unless he can secure a job on a Congressional report or a dictionary, life's charms will slip from him as the boy and his shingle glide down the steep to the level.

If a perusal of the volume saves any family fifteen per cent in fuel, ten per cent in clothes, and re-moulds pirates, brigands and highway robbers into toil-hardened agriculturists, then its chief object has been accomplished, and the writer will stub along through life with a heart full of joyfulness.

THE END.

Milton Keynes UK
Ingram Content Group UK Ltd.
UKHW042305160224
437951UK00004B/290